The Strange Disappearance of Kitty Fox

Lisa Hall is the #1 bestselling author of six psychological thrillers, including *Between You and Me*, *The Perfect Couple* and *The Woman in the Woods*. Lisa lives in a small village in Kent, surrounded by her towering TBR pile, a rather large brood of children, dogs, chickens and ponies, and her long-suffering husband.

Also by Lisa Hall

The Hotel Hollywood Mysteries

The Mysterious Double Death of Honey Black
The Case of the Singer and the Showgirl
The Strange Disappearance of Kitty Fox

LISA HALL
THE STRANGE DISAPPEARANCE OF KITTY FOX

hera

First published in the United Kingdom in 2025 by

Hera Books, an imprint of
Canelo Digital Publishing Limited,
20 Vauxhall Bridge Road,
London SW1V 2SA
United Kingdom

A Penguin Random House Company
The authorised representative in the EEA is Dorling Kindersley Verlag GmbH.
Arnulfstr. 124, 80636 Munich, Germany

Copyright © Lisa Hall 2025

The moral right of Lisa Hall to be identified as the creator of this work has been asserted in accordance with the Copyright, Designs and Patents Act, 1988.
All rights reserved. No part of this publication may be reproduced or transmitted in any form or by any means, electronic or mechanical, including photocopy, recording, or any information storage and retrieval system, without permission in writing from the publisher.
No part of this book may be used or reproduced in any manner for the purpose of training artificial intelligence technologies or systems. In accordance with Article 4(3) of the DSM Directive 2019/790, Canelo expressly reserves this work from the text and data mining exception.

A CIP catalogue record for this book is available from the British Library.

Print ISBN 978 1 83598 165 8
Ebook ISBN 978 1 83598 164 1

This book is a work of fiction. Names, characters, businesses, organizations, places and events are either the product of the author's imagination or are used fictitiously. Any resemblance to actual persons, living or dead, events or locales is entirely coincidental.

Printed and bound in Great Britain by Clays Ltd, Elcograf S.p.A.

Look for more great books at
www.herabooks.com | www.dk.com

For Lisa

Chapter One

A gasp flutters between her lips – a weightless breath that seems to hang in the air – before his hand circles her throat, squeezing tightly. She makes an odd noise, half gargle, half sob, as his fingers tighten, cutting off her air supply.

She tries to speak – *please, please stop* – but the words won't come, can't form against the pressure on her windpipe. Her eyes widen, her cheeks flushing an ugly red as her hand comes up and grasps feebly at his wrists, trying to tug him away, desperate for air. It's pointless. He's too strong, too determined, his eyes focused on her face as she struggles against the heft of him. He pushes harder and she stumbles, overturning the chair behind her, the furniture clattering to the floor with a crash.

'Anddd... cut!' Leonard Langford, esteemed Hollywood director, calls the scene, his voice ringing out clear in the heavy silence, and I finally draw in a breath of my own, my pulse pounding in my ears as the actors scatter back towards their trailers. 'Take a breath – especially you, Kitty – grab some lunch and we're back in twenty.'

I still can't believe I – Lily Jones, displaced Brit – am here in 1950s Hollywood, after a bump to the head in the twenty-first century somehow catapulted me back seventy years in the past. I still can't quite wrap my head around going from a pretty lonely existence, juggling two jobs as a chambermaid at the Beverly Hills Hotel and a waitress at a chophouse on Sunset, to a life with my dream job working for one of the greatest movie directors in the industry, and Louis and Tilda – two of the best friends I've ever had. After finding myself in Honey Black's Beverly Hills Hotel suite in 1949, with the knowledge that Honey would be murdered in two weeks' time, it was Louis – who was working in the Polo Lounge at the time – and Tilda who came to my aid as I tried to stop it from happening. And when I found myself back in Hollywood in 1951 it was Louis and Tilda who joined my desperate race against time to save Louis's ex-girlfriend, Evelyn, from a terrible fate, solving a murder in the process. Now I resist the urge to pinch myself, the sheer joy of still being here sending shivers down my spine, despite the ever-present feeling of never quite belonging.

'Wasn't that wonderful?' The short blonde girl beside me turns to look at me with a grin, her curls bouncing around her head. 'Kitty is just *incredible*.'

'Incredible,' I agree, swallowing down the slight distaste at the back of my throat. It's only my second day on set as Leonard's assistant and I know this is a movie, I know Kitty Fox wasn't really being strangled, but even so, it was a difficult scene to watch.

'You're Lily, right? Jean's replacement?' Blondie reaches out and grabs my hand, pumping it in a quick shake. 'Bunny Truman.'

'Nice to meet you, Bunny.' Her hand has left my palm feeling sticky and damp and I surreptitiously swipe it over my skirt. 'Have you been in the movie business for long?'

'Just getting started.' Bunny grins at me, her freckled nose wrinkling. 'I want to be a director one day.'

'Wow.' I like her already. Ambitious, confident. She kind of reminds me of myself, if I hadn't been born forty-four years after this movie was filmed.

'I started in the catering truck,' Bunny goes on as she gestures towards the canteen trailer, following me as I hurry towards Leonard's office to pick up his messages. 'Serving up sloppy joes and macaroni and cheese, but now look at me. The best runner on the set.' She pauses and turns, casting a critical eye over me. 'Maybe you can put in a good word for me? You're friends with Leonard. He put you on the movie, after all.'

'Oh, well, I don't know about *friends…*' I begin as I reach my tiny desk in the corridor outside Leonard's office just as Leonard steps out, dropping me a wink.

'Hey, kiddo. Don't worry about fetching me lunch, I'm going to grab something myself from the truck.'

'Uh, OK.' I give Leonard a smile as he hurries out, trying to hide the fact that I hadn't realised I was supposed to fetch him lunch. 'You've got…' I hold up the sheaf of messages that I took for him this morning before I headed to the set, but he's already gone.

Bunny smirks. 'Maybe later. Did anyone give you the proper tour yet?' I shake my head. I spent most of yesterday trying to familiarise myself with the telephone system, and wading through a backlog of letters Jean had left on the desk. Despite my best efforts there is still a healthy pile of correspondence to respond to, as well as a stack of scripts to read through and analyse. 'Let me show you around real quick before we pick up shooting again.' She gestures back towards the studio. 'That's our set, obviously. The inside of Kitty's house. Most of the interior shots of the movie are going to be filmed there.' The movie is a thriller about a woman who finds herself betrayed by the man she loves... who turns out not to be the person she thought he was at all. 'Follow me.'

Bunny leads me through the lot, to an outdoor set at the back of the studio. It's the façade of an Old South house, propped up from behind by thick wooden struts. At the front there are three steps leading up to a porch, a rocking chair at one end. The windows are tall, and the front door is ornate and intricately carved. It's gorgeous, and even though I know it's just a set, half of me is expecting Scarlett O'Hara to fly out the front door in a temper at any moment.

'Wow,' I breathe. 'This is incredible. Even better than I imagined.'

'And also fake,' Bunny laughs. 'This is the exterior of Kitty's house, and we're filming here later. There's a paddock further out as well – we'll be filming some scenes there too.'

I read through the script again last night in an attempt to familiarise myself completely with the film, but now I've seen the set the story feels more alive than it ever did on the page.

'Who's that?' I incline my head discreetly towards a man in a suit, his face set and stern as he marches across the backlot, a younger man scurrying behind him, his hands gesturing in a way that seems to be attempting to placate him.

Bunny turns, her face dropping. 'That's Oskar Goldstein. He's a studio exec, and we do not want to make him mad. He's in charge of... everything, basically.'

The name is familiar, and I glance down at the messages in my hand, Oskar Goldstein's name screaming out at me from the top page. 'I should probably get these to Leonard.'

I follow Bunny as she hurries across the lot towards the catering truck, quickly shoving me inside. 'If you wanna eat you should grab something now. Leonard won't stop shooting this afternoon for anything or anyone.'

'I'm good.' I know Leonard's style, having worked on a movie with him and Honey Black back in 1949.

I glance around the bustling food trailer. Leonard sits at a table, shovelling a sandwich into his mouth, as a stout man wearing a straw boater leans over him, murmuring in his ear. It doesn't seem as though Leonard is listening and I stifle a smile, before heading over and handing Leonard his messages.

'There's one from Oskar Goldstein,' I say, as Leonard nods distractedly and waves me away. On the other side of the trailer, a blond man, his hair neatly slicked back from his forehead, leans back in his chair, lacing his hands behind his head as he stretches out his long legs. He doesn't take his eyes off me, watching carefully as he brings a hand down to dip in and out of the paper bag in front of him, and he munches on pick-and-mix candy.

'If you're not gonna eat, let me give you a quick tour of the rest of the set,' Bunny is saying as I drag my gaze away and follow her back out into the warm California sunshine. 'This here is the prop store.' She gestures to a small room at the back of the set, filled with various random items that would look more at home at a car boot sale. The paint-peeled flamingo, for one.

Bunny hurries through the studio as I follow along behind her, taking in as much as I can. There is an odd sense of déjà vu as I pass the wardrobe department, the make-up trailer, all of it reminiscent of the last movie set I worked on. *And I'm still here, in 1950s Hollywood. Seventy years out of my own time.* A ripple runs down my spine as Bunny jabbers on about make-up and how William Tuttle was supposed be the make-up artist on this picture, only now he's working on some Gene Kelly movie about dancing in the rain.

'*Singin' in the Rain*,' I say distractedly, remembering my mum singing along to that movie before she died. My stomach lurches, the way it always does when I think about going home, back to the twenty-first century.

After what went down in Las Vegas just a short while ago – facing down the Mob with the help of my friends Louis and Tilda, in order to try and save Louis's ex-girlfriend from a horrible fate – I was sure I would be pinged back to my own time, and when it didn't happen immediately I made the conscious decision to stay in 1951, with the offer of this job from Leonard, and the friends I've made, but I can't help but wonder… why am I *really* still here? There is a part of me that remains clenched tight, a fist of anxiety and uncertainty, wondering whether I really am here for good or if there's something else lurking around the corner, another impossible situation that I'm going to have to fight my way through to save someone.

'Lily?' Bunny has stopped and I've walked into the back of her, the toes of my Converse trainers snagging on the heel of her court shoe. 'Were you even listening?'

'Of course.' I turn on a smile and smooth down my pencil skirt, swiping away the wrinkles at my hips. 'You just said these are the actors' trailers.'

'Right.' Bunny nods. 'I don't really go in there, but I guess you probably will. Jean used to. You know, to help out with stuff. Take script pages in, make sure the leads have water… or Martinis.'

I let out a laugh at that. 'It sounds like you won't stay a runner for long,' I say, as the door to the nearest trailer creaks open and Bunny lets out a gasp, straightening her spine. A woman steps out, and I recognise her as the actress who less than half an hour ago had a man's hands around her throat. She smiles as she steps down onto the dusty ground and Bunny grins fit to burst.

'Hello, Miss Fox.' The words bubble out of Bunny like a soda fountain. 'I was just... we were... I mean...'

'Hi.' I step forward and offer my hand. 'I'm Lily Jones, Leonard's new assistant. He's a bit tied up at the moment so couldn't make the introductions.' I leave out the part about him shovelling in a sandwich. 'So, Bunny here was just showing me around the set. I'm sorry if we disturbed you.'

'Not at all.' The woman shakes my hand firmly. 'Kitty Fox.' Her voice is warm and low, as though she's smoked a hundred cigarettes before leaving her trailer, and washed them down with whisky. Not in a bad way. She's petite, maybe five foot three or four, with gleaming blonde hair pulled away from her face in neat victory rolls and eyes a startling shade of green, emphasised by the porcelain white of her skin.

'Kitty is the star of this picture!' Bunny bursts out, as Kitty shakes her head.

'Bunny, you are too kind,' Kitty says. 'But there is more than one lead on this movie.' She smiles again but it doesn't quite reach her eyes. *She looks tired*, I think as I run my eyes over her face, my gaze catching at the base of her throat where there is the faintest hint of fingermarks against the pale ivory of her skin. A combination, I suppose, of long hours on set, and being throttled by your co-star just before lunch. 'It's lovely to meet you, Lily,' Kitty says, 'I'm sure we'll be seeing a lot of each other during shooting. Jean always took very good care of me.'

'Of course. Oh! Can I get you anything from the canteen? A sandwich? It smelled like meat loaf was on the menu. I could bring you a plate?'

Kitty pauses for a moment and then shakes her head. 'That's very kind of you, Lily, but perhaps just an iced tea?'

'I'll go!' Bunny shoots off across the lot towards the canteen trailer, her heels kicking up dust as she goes.

'She's very sweet,' Kitty says fondly as she watches Bunny head off. 'She's desperate to be a director, you know. Who knows? Maybe one day. After all, Ida did it.'

'Ida?'

'Lupino.' Kitty gives me a puzzled look. 'Our first female director, if you like. How wonderful it must be, to have that control.' Kitty looks oddly wistful. 'Anyway, Lily, you must tell me how you and Leonard—'

'Lily? You *are* Lily Jones?' The door to the slightly smaller trailer next door flies open and a redhead tumbles out, her hair a mass of neat curls around her head. Her red lipstick clashes horribly with her hair, and she almost shoves Kitty to one side in her haste to get to me. 'Leonard's Lily? Darling, I am so thrilled to meet you.' She grips my hand, firmly squashing it against her ample bosom as I can barely catch my breath. 'I'm—'

'Camilla Rey,' I finish for her, finally extracting my hand. I recognise her from a hundred old black-and-white movies. 'You're Camilla Rey.'

'Yes. Yes, I am.' Camilla beams at me, as Kitty narrows her eyes.

'Camilla,' Kitty says, with a hint of acidity to her sweet tone. 'Lily and I were just having a conversation. Perhaps you'd like to come back later?'

'Oh, I don't think so,' Camilla says sharply as she turns to me. 'Lily, darling, I've heard so much about you from Leonard. I hear you and he are *great* friends.'

I'm not sure where all these people are hearing that Leonard and I are besties. Sure, I do love Leonard and I have enjoyed working with him before, but he's my boss. I don't go to his house for dinner. I haven't met his parents. And his wife, Jean, tolerates me because it's easier than fighting with me, I think. We are most definitely not *friends*.

'Camilla—' Kitty tries again, but to no avail.

'We should all go to Musso and Frank,' Camilla exclaims. 'You, me, Jean, Leonard, maybe Art too. I have a few things that I want to run by Leonard and I just know that having you onside will help *so* much—'

'I really don't thi—'

'And then perhaps you and I could do a little shopping? Let me take you to Saks,' Camilla forges on, ignoring the dark look that crosses Kitty's face. 'There are always so many events in this old town, and I never have anything to wear. It's so important to be *seen*, Lily.'

'Camilla.' Kitty's cigarette-and-whisky voice cuts through Camilla's babble, icy-cold and sharp enough to skin a cat. 'How *dare* you? Lily and I were having a conversation and you've just rudely interrupted. Don't you have *any* manners at all? You may think you're the star of this picture,' Kitty leans in close, her green eyes stormy, 'but it's *my* name above yours on the title card, and you'd do well to remember that.'

Camilla stops mid-flow, pressing her bright red lips together, just as Bunny arrives back with Kitty's iced tea. I'm not sure how it happens, but as Bunny moves to hand the iced tea to Kitty, I am almost one hundred per cent certain that Camilla's elbow flies out, nudging Bunny forward and causing iced tea to slop all over the front of Kitty's blouse.

'Oh!' Kitty yelps, pulling the wet fabric away from her skin as Bunny's hands fly to her mouth and the iced tea falls to the floor, splashing tiny droplets of dark liquid all over my shoes. 'Oh my gosh! My blouse. It's *ruined*.'

'Miss Fox, I am so sorry.' Bunny begins to apologise as Camilla makes no move at all to suppress the smile tugging at her mouth. 'Let me...' She begins to dab ineffectually at Kitty's blouse with a handkerchief she pulls out of her sleeve. It doesn't look entirely fresh.

'Leave it,' Kitty hisses, as there is the crackle of a loud-hailer, and then a booming voice instructs everyone to get to their places, *please*. 'Just, leave it.'

'Kitty, darling,' Camilla drawls. 'Chop-chop. We're needed back on set. You absolutely can't be late, Leonard will go crackers. You know he's a stickler for punctuality.'

'Shut up, Camilla,' Kitty says in a low voice. 'Don't think I don't know that was your fault.'

'Oh, please.' Camilla gives a hoot of laughter as she begins to sashay back towards the set, where Leonard is glowering in the direction of the trailers. 'You can't blame me for Bunny's butterfingers.'

Kitty gives Camilla one more steaming stare before she turns on her heel, leaving a teary-eyed Bunny and me on the trailer steps.

'It was an accident,' Bunny whispers as we turn and follow in Camilla's footsteps. 'I never meant to spill it.'

'I know,' I soothe, guiding her by the elbow to hurry her along towards the ranch house façade on the backlot for this afternoon's exterior shoot. Picking up the clipboards containing the new script pages, I hand one to

Bunny as we stand to one side to watch Camilla shoot her scene. I'm certain Camilla's elbow jogged Bunny into spilling the iced tea; in fact, I'd put money on it.

Camilla isn't what I was expecting. My mum loved her movies, and I recognised her the moment I stepped on set earlier that day. While Kitty was being throttled by her leading man, Camilla had been standing in the wings, watching with what I read as admiration on her face. I thought that Camilla was impressed by Kitty's acting skills, but now I wonder if she was just enjoying watching Kitty being strangled.

'There's some tension between them, isn't there?' I whisper as Kitty finally arrives on set, in a fresh version of the white blouse she was wearing earlier.

Bunny glances up at me, her blonde curls seeming decidedly less bouncy than they did earlier in the day. Her eyes are a little pink and she gives a delicate sniff. 'Who? Kitty and Camilla?'

I nod. I rack my brains to try and remember if I've ever read anything about a rivalry between the two actresses, but I'm coming up with nothing. I am familiar with Camilla, thanks to my mum's obsession with old movies, but I barely know anything about Kitty at all. I get that ripple down my spine again, a cold finger of dread. 'They don't seem as if they get along too well. And I'm pretty sure Camilla nudged you so that tea would spill all over Kitty deliberately.'

Bunny turns her gaze back to the set, where Camilla is comforting Kitty – her on-screen best friend – following the revelation of her husband's cheating.

'Don't get along?' Bunny snorts. 'That's an understatement. You know the feud between Bette and Joan? Well, that's got nothing on these two, and it's only a matter of time before it all boils over.'

Chapter Two

'Where the hell is Art?' Leonard is almost blue in the face he's yelling so loudly. 'I said *back in twenty*. Lily' – he jabs a finger in my direction – 'go and find him.'

I turn, not even really sure who it is I'm looking for, as Oskar Goldstein appears at the edge of the set, a disdainful look on his face as he glances over at Leonard, who is flicking through pages and yelling directives to the closest camera operator. Before I can scurry away to search for the elusive Art, there is a murmur from the rear of the backlot, and then a voice says, 'Now, now, Len, what's all the yelling for? Sure you weren't yelling for me, were you?'

A man saunters around the edge of the house façade, and for a moment it feels as though my heart stutters in my chest, my breath catching at the back of my throat. I've met some handsome men in my time here in 1950s LA, but this man is *fine*. Tall, broad-shouldered, with dark hair that flops over his forehead, he just oozes star quality. He gives a charming smile to Leonard, who ceases his yelling and instead tosses his clipboard to the ground.

'Art Calloway,' Bunny breathes, her hand fluttering to the base of her throat to toy with the scarf she's tied jauntily around her neck. 'Now there's a man I wouldn't mind getting under.'

A stream of laughter rips out of my mouth as I step forward to pick up Leonard's clipboard, but the sound is drowned out by Camilla's squeal.

'Art! You naughty thing, you're so late! You can't honestly think we'll wait around all day for you?' Camilla crosses the set, her arms stretched wide in welcome and for a moment I think Art is going to drop a kiss on the cheek Camilla has lifted towards him in anticipation, but he strides past her without a second glance.

'Kitty, darling.' Art reaches Kitty, who stands off to one side, pulling her into his arms and dashing a swoon-worthy kiss on her lips, and Camilla's face changes. Her lips move into a pout, and her eyes darken as her arms drop to her sides. 'I've missed you.'

'It's been half an hour, Art.' Kitty pulls away, her cheeks a fierce, hot pink. From this angle, with Art looming over Kitty, I recognise him as her co-star. The man whose hands were wrapped tightly around her throat less than an hour ago. 'And you *are* late.' She looks to Leonard, who still wears a thunderous look, and then pats Art on the chest. 'Quickly, let's get back to it.'

'Marks, people,' Leonard yells, a small muscle twitching at the corner of his eye as he glances towards the edge of the set, where Oskar Goldstein still lurks.

Kitty pushes Art away and moves to her mark on the front porch, her face settling into what can only be described as a blank page, as Art shrugs off his jacket and allows his make-up girl to dab at his face with powder. Glancing over in Camilla's direction, I frown. She is watching Kitty, that mutinous expression still written all over her face, and I feel it again, that tickle of unease. *Maybe I am still here for a reason*, I think, my throat suddenly dry. *Maybe there's something big about to blow up between these two women, because there's no doubt about it, they can't stand each other.* Camilla isn't the only person watching Kitty – from the side of the set, another man watches as Kitty looks to Leonard for her cue, her face lighting up as she begins to speak. It's the blond man from the canteen, and I keep my eyes on him as he watches Kitty, his lips moving in sync with hers. He must be another actor, a smaller part, perhaps? Or maybe a stagehand? Either way, he seems to know the movie inside out.

'You'll never take him from me. *Never!*' Kitty cries, as she finds out that Camilla is the woman her husband has been cheating with, their roles on set reversed from their earlier scene. 'Even if it kills me!'

Bunny and I watch, rapt, as the scene unfolds. There is something about Kitty, the way she captures the camera completely, that makes her a joy to watch. Camilla is just as talented, her emotion raw and unbridled. Until:

'You're the first person… oh, shoot.' Camilla gives Leonard a rueful grin. 'Sorry, Leonard, darling, can we go again?'

Leonard, unlit cigar clamped between his teeth, gives a brisk nod.

'I'm telling you, I'm the last person… oh, *dang* it.' Camilla stamps her foot. 'I'm sorry, folks. I don't know what it is about this scene…'

'You could try learning your lines?' Kitty says, her face the picture of innocence.

'You hush your mouth,' Camilla hisses, but her tone lacks conviction.

'For Pete's sake,' Leonard snaps, glaring first at Camilla, then Kitty. 'Can the two of you stop? We need to get this scene in the can before the light goes… unless you two gals are prepared to stump up the cash the studio loses every time you drag your heels and wreck my scenes?' He pauses. 'I didn't think so.'

'Perhaps you should have taken my suggestion on board?' Oskar says briskly from the sidelines. 'As studio exec, I did try to warn you that you didn't have the budget for both of these ladies.' He gives Camilla an appraising look as she shifts on the balls of her feet, looking anywhere other than at him. 'An unknown would have been cheaper. And maybe more talented.'

Leonard's jaw works briefly, before he squares his shoulders and turns to face Oskar. 'And as I told *you*, the movie only works with Kitty *and* Camilla. Now, if you'll excuse me, time is money.'

Oskar looks down his nose at Leonard, Leonard returning his stare until finally Oskar turns on his heels and stalks away, and the entire crew feel as if they can breathe again.

Art steps forward, one hand raised, and Leonard turns his glare on him. 'Not you, either, Calloway. You might be a big shot, but this is *my* movie so let's get to it. Camilla, do you know your line?'

'Yes, sir.' Camilla's voice is meek now.

'Yes, sir,' Art parrots, and just like that the scene is back on.

Camilla hits her mark, her face twisting as she stares Kitty up and down. 'You're the last person on earth he would want to be with.' Her lips twitch in a quirk of triumph that could just as easily be down to remembering her line as her character's satisfaction.

Last year, when I found myself on a movie with Honey Black, I was enchanted by her work – by the way she became Sofia Budd, the Goodtime Gal, so completely – but with Camilla and Kitty, they really are the talent. As I watch them film their scene, spotlessly this time, I am so caught up in it I could almost believe the two of them hate each other. And then it hits me. They *do* hate each other, and now I'm not sure how much of what I'm witnessing is acting or real life.

With a brief instruction from Leonard, we move to the next scene, the air growing thicker and hotter under the lights with every minute that ticks by. Art's make-up girl is called out more than once to dab at the sheen on Art's forehead, as Camilla fans herself every time the camera cuts away from her. The scene is almost done, Kitty giving her last big monologue when she pauses, her throat working as she tries to swallow. Her face is pale, prickled with sweat, and her eyes meet mine in a panicked glance before they roll back in her head and she slumps to the floor.

—

'Kitty! Oh, for... *Cut!*' Leonard shouts, his hands going to his head to clutch at his hair as I hurry to where Kitty lies on the dusty floor.

'She fainted, that's all,' Camilla is saying, as I crouch over a still-unconscious Kitty, tucking my cardigan under her head as a pillow. Bunny hovers nearby, a glass of cold water in her hand.

'Kitty? Kitty, are you all right?' The blond man has pushed his way across the set to get close to Kitty, but Art blocks his way, one large hand pushing him firmly back.

'Kitty?' I say quietly, as her eyelashes flutter and then moments later her eyes open. She pushes herself up on her elbows, wincing as she presses one hand to the back of her head. 'Are you OK? Just stay there a moment. You fainted. Bunny, pass me that water.'

'Here. Give her this.' Leonard hands me a glass bottle of Pepsi. 'She needs the sugar.'

Kitty lets Art help her into a sitting position and takes a delicate sip from the glass bottle. 'I'm OK, Art. Really. You can let go of me.'

Art reluctantly takes a step back, his arm still reaching out for Kitty's shoulders.

'Maybe give her a little space,' I say, watching as Kitty closes her eyes, pressing her palms into the floor. 'Kitty, let me get you something to eat. You didn't eat lunch, did you? Maybe if you have some cake, a chocolate bar, that might make you feel better?'

Bunny tugs at my sleeve and shakes her head. 'Kitty can't have chocolate, but I can get her an apple from the canteen?'

I nod. Chocolate would be a better way to get her blood sugar back to normal, but if Kitty can't eat it then an apple will have to do. The last thing I need to do is make things worse by giving Kitty an allergic reaction to something.

The man in the straw boater that I saw in the canteen with Leonard bustles through the crowd surrounding Kitty, and gently nudges me to one side. 'Step aside, please. Kitty, how are you feeling?'

'Much better, thank you, Doctor Astor.' Kitty practises a wan smile, as Camilla rolls her eyes behind her.

'Here.' The studio doctor hands Kitty a small pill. 'Take this. It'll make you feel your old self again.'

I want to ask what the doctor is giving her, but before I can speak Kitty has washed the pill down on a wave of lukewarm Pepsi and is allowing Art to help her to her feet. The colour is back in her cheeks as she gratefully accepts the apple Bunny holds out to her and takes a dainty bite.

'I'm sorry, everyone,' Kitty says. 'I don't know what came over me. Leonard, shall we roll?'

'Everybody, marks, please.' Leonard claps his hands together, and it's with my heart in my throat that I tug gently at his sleeve.

'Leonard… Kitty just fainted. It's almost five o'clock, maybe we—'

'Lily, with all due respect, who's the director on this picture? It's not too late for me to get another replacement for Jean.' His tone is acid, and even Camilla drops her gaze as my cheeks burn. If this doesn't persuade people that Leonard and I aren't best friends then I don't know what will.

'The girl has a point.' The blond man from the canteen steps forward. 'I know you're under pressure to finish the movie, Leonard, but pushing on today, when the light is going anyway, could mean Kitty faints again tomorrow if you push her too hard. Right, Doctor Astor?'

The doctor nods, although he doesn't seem a hundred per cent confident on going against Leonard. 'I agree with Mr Knox. It might be best for Kitty to rest for today. Come back fresh tomorrow.'

Leonard sighs, his face set. 'Fine, we'll leave it for today. But I want everyone back on set early tomorrow morning and prepared for a long day. Tomorrow, I don't care who faints – none of you are leaving until this scene is in the can. Lily, wait a moment.'

Murmurs ripple through the set, and people begin to drift away. I look for the blond man who showed such concern for Kitty, but there is no sign of him.

Once Leonard and I are alone, he sighs. 'Lily… I know it's only your second day…'

Oh, here it comes. Forty-eight hours and Leonard is going to fire me. This must be some kind of record. 'Leonard, I swear I didn't mean to piss you off. I'll keep my thoughts to myself in future—'

Leonard holds up a hand. 'Shush. Please. Let me speak.'

I press my lips together and wait.

'You saw Oskar Goldstein on set? He's the studio executive on this movie, and I have had to fight him tooth and nail to get what I want.'

'Oh. Like Francis Ford Coppola on *The Godfather*?'

Leonard frowns. 'What? Listen, Lily, I know you're supposed to be my assistant, but you see what I'm dealing with here, with Kitty and Camilla? This can't happen. I don't have the time or the budget for these women to keep holding things up with their petty squabbles. I don't give a damn about messages and letters and script coverage. I need you to keep Kitty in line.'

'Keep her in line? But—'

'Keep her in line,' Leonard says firmly. 'I need this movie to come in on time and on budget, and Kitty needs to be managed. Showing up late, fainting all over the place... it can't happen. I want your focus on Kitty, you hear?'

'Uh... sure.' I nod.

Leonard reaches out and squeezes my arm. 'Attagirl, Lil.'

-

Collecting up the script pages that drifted to the floor when I dropped my clipboard as Kitty fainted, I say goodbye to Bunny as she pulls on her jacket and then move to say goodbye to Kitty.

'…just for ten minutes, it won't take long at all,' Art is saying as Kitty shakes her head.

'No, Art. I don't want to. You can though, I'm not stopping you.'

'Everything OK?' I smile widely at Art, whose arm is now draped around Kitty's shoulders again.

'Fine,' he says, with a grin that threatens to stop my heart. 'I was just telling Kitty here that we need to head out to the gates and sign some autographs. Folks have been waiting out there all day for us to finish on set.'

'Art, please,' Kitty says, weakly. 'I don't feel so good right now. I just want to go back to my hotel and lie down.'

'I know, sweetie,' Art says, 'but these folks… they'd give their right arm for a moment of your time. I feel bad if we let them down. You have to leave out of those gates anyway.'

'Mr Calloway, sir?' I say, quickly.

'Art. Mr Calloway is my father,' Art replies with a rich, deep laugh that oozes charm like honey from a comb.

'With all due respect, Kitty did just faint, and Doctor Astor did recommend that she rest. I think perhaps the best thing for her to do this evening is go back to her hotel, get something to eat and lie down for a while.'

'And we have a premiere later this evening, remember?' Kitty reminds him. 'You wouldn't want me to miss that.'

Camilla sashays over, clearly having listened to our entire conversation. She rests a hand on Art's forearm and shakes her hair away from her face. I can't help but notice that while Kitty was lying on the floor, Camilla took the time to refresh her lipstick. 'Art, darling,' she coos, 'Lily is right, Kitty did just faint. Perhaps she should go home. I'll go and sign autographs with you.'

Art hesitates as Kitty ducks out from under his arm. 'Camilla—'

'This is a *great* idea,' I say. 'Art, people will love to see you sign autographs with Camilla. There might even be a photographer out there, can you imagine? That would be a front-page photo for sure.'

Camilla squeals and claps her hands together. 'Give me five minutes to change my shoes,' she says, whirling away back to her trailer and completely missing the way Art's eyes narrow and his lips press together. Behind Art's back, Kitty mouths a thank you in my direction.

'Lily Jones, is that you?' A familiar voice comes from behind me, and I turn to see Jean Langford, Leonard's wife, approaching from the set entrance, Leonard following behind. Jean leans in to kiss me on my cheek. 'How were your first couple of days?'

'Eventful,' I say with a laugh. When I first arrived in Hollywood Jean wasn't too taken with me at all, and I thought there was a chance she might hate me forever, but it turns out the old girl isn't too bad after all. When she married Leonard and made the decision to quit working as his assistant, mine was the only name she would consider as her replacement. 'You look wonderful,' I say. 'Glowing. Married life must agree with you.'

Jean gives a coy smile in Leonard's direction, as she clutches her handbag against her midriff. 'Well, yes. And it'll only be the two of us for just a few more months.'

My eyes drift down to her Hermès Dépêches bag – to be renamed the Hermès Kelly in the 1970s – hiding her belly. 'You're...?'

'Yes!' Jean beams, and I throw my arms around her in a hug. 'Due in just under six months. Redfern if it's a boy, Gail if it's a girl.'

'Oh, Jean, that's wonderful news. I am thrilled for you.' Mental calculations reveal that Jean must have been unknowingly pregnant at her wedding to Leonard only a few weeks previously, but I don't mention that, of course. 'Leonard, you must be—'

My words are cut dead by a spine-chilling shriek coming from one of the trailers, and seconds later Camilla erupts through the open door, wailing like a banshee. She hurtles across the set waving something in her hand, before launching it in Kitty's direction. Kitty ducks, cowering behind Art, who steps forward and grabs Camilla by her slender wrists.

'You *bitch*!' Camilla shrieks, wildly grasping at the air behind Art as she tries to get to Kitty. 'I know you did this!'

'I didn't do anything,' Kitty yells back, but there is something on her face that looks suspiciously like satisfaction. 'You're crazy! Running out here, yelling and throwing things!'

'Camilla, stop,' Art pleads, as Camilla continues to fight against him like a wildcat. 'Kitty, enough. You're not helping matters.'

Leonard gives Jean a glance and sighs. 'Like I said, Lily. Keep Kitty in line.' He walks across the set, stooping to pick up the object Camilla hurled at Kitty. It's a pump. A cute one too, or at least it would be if it still had a heel.

'You're wicked.' Camilla is crying now, her bare feet dusty and dirty. 'A wicked, wicked woman. What kind of maniac snaps the heels off of someone's shoes? And not just one pair, all of them!'

'And *you're* crazy,' Kitty responds with a smirk. 'I had nothing to do with your cheap heels.'

Camilla pauses just long enough for Art to relax fractionally, enough so that she can get free. She nips past him and reaches out, snagging a lock of Kitty's blonde hair between her fingers and yanking hard. 'I'll kill you,' she shrieks, 'I'll *kill* you, I swear!'

Chapter Three

After disentangling her golden locks from Camilla's fingers, I hurry an angry Kitty out of reach as Art soothes a furious Camilla.

'You can't go out there like this,' he says as Camilla's chest heaves in fury. 'Take a breath, calm down.'

Camilla nods, drawing in a deep breath as she presses her hand to her bosom.

'Come on, old girl,' Art soothes. 'Our public is waiting – we should go out there, sign some autographs and put all of this behind us. It's a silly misunderstanding, right, Kitty?'

Kitty doesn't reply.

'OK, well then, I'll see you at the Chateau in a couple of hours? I'll pick you up for the premiere.' Art gives Kitty a beseeching look, before gripping Camilla by the elbow and leading her out to her waiting fans.

Kitty reluctantly nods and turns away, marching towards the other side of the lot where there is an alternative exit that the autograph hunters haven't discovered yet. I scurry after her, scooping up the handbag she's left behind, my mind working overtime. Kitty doesn't seem like the sort to snap the heels off another woman's shoes in spite, but she *was* smirking, and she did take a long time to come back on set after Bunny spilled the tea on her. *Longer than it would take just to change a blouse?* Quite possibly.

I wonder why I've never heard anything about this rift between the actresses before. Everyone knows about Bette Davis and Joan Crawford, and how they allegedly couldn't stand one another, but Kitty and Camilla... I've never heard about a feud between them.

'Good night, Miss Jones.' Bobby, the security guard on duty, doffs his cap at me with a grin, his thick New York accent cutting the air like a knife. 'You lookin' for Miss Fox? She just hurried through here. I'm still waiting for her to get me that signed photo, you know.'

'Good night, Bobby.' I flash him a thumbs up, and call out to Kitty as she ducks into her waiting car. 'Kitty! Wait!' She leaves the door open and, as I reach the car, panting, holding her bag aloft, she pats the seat beside her impatiently.

'Come on,' she tuts. 'Get in.'

Pausing for just a second, I slide into the back seat of the car beside Kitty. Jean had warned me that Kitty could sometimes be a little needy, but I hadn't realised it extended to accompanying her back to her hotel.

'So...' I say after ten minutes of silence, in which Kitty stares blankly out of the window as Melrose Avenue passes us by, her eyes on the billboards above us advertising soap and ale. 'Are you feeling better?'

'Probably better than Camilla right now,' Kitty says, turning to me with a twinkle in her eye. 'I know she made Bunny spill that tea deliberately. It's not the first time she's done something like that.'

'Really?'

Kitty snorts. 'You don't know the half of it, but I'm not going to waste my time talking about that bitch.' She turns to me. 'Sorry, that sounded awful, didn't it? Camilla is just difficult to work with, that's all. Sometimes I think she means every word her awful character says.'

'I'm sure she doesn't,' I lie, thinking over what I saw on set today. There is definitely no love lost between the two women. 'It must be wonderful working with Mr Calloway... Art. I'm a big fan of his work.'

Kitty gives me a sideways glance. 'Most of the girls are,' she says dryly. 'Art is... Ah, we're here.'

Whatever she was going to say about Art is cut short as the car arrives at Chateau Marmont, the infamous Hollywood hotel where the stars of Leonard's current movie are staying. Hidden from the street by a low wall topped with hedges, a discreet sign is the only evidence from the street that the hotel even exists. That old Hollywood adage slips into my mind.

'If you want to be seen, go to the Beverly Hills Hotel. If you don't want to be seen, go to Chateau Marmont.'

'What?' Kitty frowns at me quizzically, and I realise I have spoken aloud.

'Nothing. Sorry.'

The car winds its way up the short driveway towards the garage and I have to catch my breath a little. While the Beverly Hills Hotel will always have my heart (perhaps more so now, after meeting Louis Jardine, my sort of boyfriend there – less so in 2020, when I spent my days there as a housekeeper), there is something about the Chateau that marks it out as special. This is the place where Jean Harlow lived while married to Harold Rosson, all the while allegedly carrying on an affair with Clark Gable (after seeing Clark in the flesh at Honey Black's birthday party in 1949, who could blame her?). The place where John Belushi died after a fatal heroin overdose. Where James Dean jumped out of a window in order to impress director Nicholas Ray, and where Bette Davis fell asleep in her bungalow with a lit cigarette and caused the entire hotel to be evacuated. Twice. Of course, some of these things haven't happened yet, but even so, there is already a rich catalogue of stories about Chateau Marmont.

'Lily?' Kitty pulls me from my thoughts about the Chateau past and present. 'Are you coming up?'

I look down at her hand on my arm, at the way her wrist bones protrude and how her rings slip on her fingers. 'Of course. I'll be up in a moment. I just need to run across the street to Schwab's.' I slide out of the car, handing Kitty her bag, and wait until she walks into the lobby before I head across the street to the drugstore.

Kitty is so thin it's almost painful, and I know she didn't eat lunch today, so I wait in line for a turkey sandwich at Schwab's Pharmacy to take back to the hotel for her. Leonard told me to keep her in line, and if I don't want her to hit the headlines in the morning for fainting on the red carpet at tonight's premiere, I need to get some food in her before she leaves.

Ten minutes later, turkey sandwich in hand, I hurry out of the drugstore back towards Chateau Marmont. There is a flicker of excitement in my veins as I scurry up the driveway. I've never been to the Chateau before, not in my own time or now, and there's something thrilling about stepping inside a piece of Hollywood history. The entrance is quaint-looking, the arched doorway giving the impression of an old French castle as I step inside the lobby, and I have to resist the urge to stop and gawp. Even the windows are arched, and the lighting is dim and cosy.

Pausing at the reception desk, I say, 'Kitty Fox's room, please? I have a delivery for her.' I hold the turkey sandwich aloft.

'Room seven.' The woman on reception pauses for a moment, before reaching under the desk. 'Someone left these for Miss Fox. Would you mind taking them to her?'

'No problem.' I take the box of chocolates she holds out – a creamy-yellow box with *Whitman's Sampler* emblazoned across it, that I recognise from an advert starring Esther Williams (no Hershey's Kisses here, with their faint aftertaste of vomit) – and an already chilled bottle of champagne, a note tied tightly to the neck. 'I'll see she gets them.'

Hurrying up the twisting staircase, my thighs aching, I pause on the landing, glad once more that I am still stubbornly clinging on to wearing my 2020 Converse sneakers. When I first arrived here, Jean especially was horrified at the sight of my sneakers, and had more than a little to say about them, but I stuck to my guns. Thankfully now – aside from the odd glance here and there – people seemed to have accepted my choice of footwear. The champagne bottle sweats condensation all over my fingers, and I juggle the box of chocolates and the turkey sandwich in the other hand as I peer down the corridor, spotting room seven on the left.

'Kitty?' As I approach, the suite door stands open, but Kitty is nowhere in sight.

'In here.' Her voice comes from the bedroom, at the far end of the suite. Stepping inside, I shift the chocolate box under one arm and take in my first glimpse of a Chateau hotel room. While it's not as glamorous as the suites at the Beverly Hills Hotel, there is something charming and quaint about it, just like the lobby downstairs. There is a small living room, a kitchen with delicious mint-green tiles on the wall and a separate bathroom off the hallway, with a claw-footed bathtub and a big square sink. Outside there is a small balcony with a tiny table and two chairs looking out over Sunset Boulevard, the sky awash with deep pinks, oranges and lilacs as the sun begins to set.

Kitty is in her bedroom, tugging her large gold teardrop earrings from her ears and throwing them onto the nightstand. She's already slipped her heels off.

'Here.' I lay the chocolates down on the bed, and hold the champagne aloft. 'These were left downstairs for you. I also brought you a sandwich. I know you didn't get a chance to eat lunch, and you should probably have something before the premiere tonight.' Now she's taken off her sweater, I can see the way her collarbones stick out, and the xylophone of her ribs beneath her thin silk shirt. She's tiny. I mean, really tiny, even by twenty-first century standards.

Kitty sniffs at the sandwich bag before laying it down without even taking the food out. 'Thanks, Lily. That's very thoughtful of you.' She glances at the champagne and then at the chocolates, a look I can't read passing over her face. My stomach turns over, and I suddenly feel my mouth go dry. *Should I not have brought the gifts up to her?* I have a dizzying flashback to Honey Black's suite, to the brownies that were gifted to her by someone who wished her harm.

'I can take those away. In fact, maybe I should just...' I reach out, remembering the way Bunny said, 'Kitty can't have chocolate,' but Kitty has already slipped the box open and is reading the note inside.

'They're from Art,' she sighs. 'Just leave them, Lily. If I throw them out, there'll only be another box delivered tomorrow. Best to keep them here until the maid disposes of them in the morning.'

'Art?'

'He insists on sending them, even though I never eat them.'

How romantic, I think. Although, if someone was sending me chocolates every day there's every chance I'd eat the entire box. 'But won't they… won't you get sick?' I don't know just how allergic Kitty might be to chocolate – what if she breaks out in hives and her tongue swells up just from the smell?

'Sick?' Kitty frowns and, before I can stop her, lifts a raspberry cream from the tray and brings it to her nose, inhaling deeply.

'Bunny said you can't eat chocolate… I don't know how bad your allergy is, but maybe I should—'

'Allergy?' Kitty lets out a hoot of laughter. 'Oh, Lily, it would be so much easier if I were allergic, but I'm not. The studio, however, would have a fit if I ate something so fattening as chocolate, despite Art sending box after box.'

My cheeks burn a hot, feisty red as I realise my mistake. Of course Kitty isn't allergic, I'm just an idiot. 'I'm sorry, I just assumed—'

'Never assume,' Kitty says briskly. 'Now, I'd like to rest before the premiere tonight if you don't mind, Lily. Shut the door on your way out.'

—

Dismissed, and with my cheeks still blazing, I hurry out of the Chateau, past the flowering shrubs and bushes that bring a little bit of exotica to Sunset Boulevard, and onto the street. *Allergies, Lily? You absolute dolt.* I really, really hope that Kitty doesn't tell Art, or even Camilla – I'll feel even more of a fool. I feel the prickle of eyes on me as I reach the sidewalk, and I turn back towards the Chateau, wondering if Kitty has changed her mind about my leaving. Instead, a man loiters at the entrance to the hotel, his collar pulled up as if he doesn't want to be seen, and I glance in the direction of the valet, about to call his attention when the man turns to enter the lobby and I recognise him as the blond man from the set earlier today. *How odd*. Maybe he's staying here. Maybe he was just having a cigarette. Maybe he wasn't watching me leave at all, although I imagine I can still feel his eyes on me.

With one last glance back at the now empty hotel entrance, I turn right and walk along Sunset Boulevard, headed to Villa Nova, a charming Italian restaurant and bar where I know my friends Louis and Tilda will be waiting for me. They'd promised to meet me for a stiff drink and something carb-heavy after my first day on set with Leonard, and boy do I need it. The walk takes me around half an hour, and as I stroll I can't help but compare the Sunset Boulevard I walk along now to the Sunset Boulevard I walked down every day in 2020. I pass Ciro's – a boxy building painted black, well known as a nightclub frequented by celebrities in the 1950s, but The Comedy Store in my own time – followed by The Melody Lounge, previously The Last Call nightclub, aka The Viper Room in the twenty-first century, a nightclub where I once wrote my name on the toilet wall. I pass a Bank of America building, more familiar to me as the Whisky a Go Go bar, until finally I reach Villa Nova. The restaurant sits on the site where the Rainbow Bar and Grill is in 2020 – a place my room-mate Eric and I used to go to all the time – so to see the familiar faces of Louis and Tilda sitting at a table waiting for me stops my head from spinning momentarily, as I try to keep my timelines straight in my head.

'Lily! We thought you weren't coming after all.' Louis gets to his feet and my heart flips in my chest as he leans in to kiss me on the cheek. While every man I've ever met – even Art Calloway – pales in comparison to Louis, and while I know he would be with me in a heartbeat, I still can't quite get a handle on what we are to each other. The fact that he doesn't know I shouldn't be here – doesn't know that not only am I actually seventy years younger than him, but that I won't even be born until 1995 – is probably part of the problem.

'Long day?' Tilda, Louis's sister and my best friend, asks. She looks cute with her bright auburn hair in a high ponytail, a red blouse and full white skirt, a red and white chequered scarf at her neck.

'Weird day,' I say, sliding into the booth beside her and gratefully accepting the Tom Collins Louis hands me. It's strange how I so often feel out of place and out of time here, except when I am with Louis and Tilda.

'Weird how?' Louis asks, fixing his green eyes on me. I feel a blush creep up my neck.

'Well, there was a spilled glass of iced tea, a screaming match, a vandalised pair of shoes and a fainting fit for starters,' I say, 'although maybe that's just a regular day in Hollywood.' I smile up at the waitress who takes our food order – spaghetti and meatballs for Louis, minestrone for Tilda and a bowl of linguini alla vongole for me, all for the princely sum of $2.75 each.

'Fainting fit?' Tilda asks, her fingers inching towards the notepad she carries in her purse. Halfway through college and studying journalism, Tilda always has a pencil and paper on her person – even more so since she started being the eyes and ears of infamous newspaper gossip columnist Louella Parsons, working with her informally after a chance meeting in a ladies' bathroom.

'Tilda...' I give her a warning glance. 'What's said at the table stays at the table.'

'Of course,' she says, sliding her hand back into her lap. 'Who was it though?'

I glance over my shoulder to check we won't be overheard. 'Kitty Fox.'

'Was she OK?' Louis asks.

I nod, sipping at my drink again. 'She was fine, although... I think it's because she didn't eat enough. I mean, I don't think she ate all day, and then I wanted to give her a piece of chocolate but I thought she was allergic, but it turns out...' I flap a hand, oddly emotional.

'She fainted because she didn't eat?' Tilda says, with a shrug. 'They all do it, you don't get a tiny little waist like that from eating burgers every night.'

I stare at her, not entirely sure she's serious. 'But... it's not healthy. I bought her a sandwich and she promised she'd eat it before tonight, but I have a feeling she just said that to get rid of me.' I made peace with the size of my thighs a long time ago, and I'm not sure now whether I feel furious or sad that Kitty – or the studio – clearly doesn't like the way she looks.

Tilda shrugs again, and I find myself feeling irritated by her blasé attitude. 'No biggie, Lil. All actresses want to be skinny, and that's the fastest way to achieve it. She probably pops diet pills too.'

I think of the pill Doctor Astor gave Kitty, of the way she washed it down without even asking what it was. I know in my own time actresses and real housewives and other celebrities fast, and take diet drugs, and have Botox and surgeries, but there's something that feels grubby about seeing it with my own eyes. Of course I've heard about Judy Garland and the way she was treated by the studio – forced to stick to a strict diet, sleep deprived and hand-fed a range of different pills to keep her going – and I scrub my hands over my skirt, as if I can wipe away the ugly taint of it all. Nausea burns the back of my throat as the waitress puts a plate of steaming linguine in front of me, the thought of eating when Kitty might be starving herself feeling wrong somehow.

'I guess,' I say, as both Tilda and Louis dive into their own meals.

'Do you want to go get a milkshake after this?' Louis asks, as he dabs his mouth with a napkin. 'We could go for a walk, dip our feet in the pool at the Beverly Hills?'

There is nothing I would love more than to stroll hand in hand with Louis through the darkened streets of West Hollywood, the promise of a kiss in the air, but I shake my head. 'I can't. I have to head back to Chateau Marmont to help Kitty get ready for a film premiere.'

'Oooh, at Grauman's?' Tilda says, wriggling in her seat. 'I'm headed there on Louella's behalf this evening.' Grauman's Chinese Theatre is *the* place for premieres, and I'll never get bored of seeing the hand- and footprints of the stars pressed into the concrete outside.

'I'll see you there,' I say, 'as long as I can get Kitty ready without Camilla Rey taking a chunk out of her. There's some real tension between them and I don't think Art Calloway is helping.'

Tilda drops her spoon. '*Some* tension? Lily, that is World War Three on the cards right there. Tell me you know about the history between those three?'

I shake my head. All I know is that I have a strong sense of foreboding about the two women, and I am pretty sure something bad is going to go down before this movie is finished shooting. Tilda leans in close, her eyes going to the restaurant door as it creaks open behind us. I turn to follow her gaze, only to see Leonard, Jean and Camilla Rey entering with a man I don't recognise, Leonard gesturing wildly as Camilla trills a laugh. I sink into the booth out of sight.

'Well,' Tilda says, 'rumour has it Art and Camilla were a thing years ago. She thought they were going to get married, have kids, the works, and then Kitty Fox burst onto the scene. There was some low-level rivalry for years, apparently, but it all came to a head when Camilla was up for a part in a movie that was going to make her a star, but Kitty snaffled it from under her nose and also got Art into the bargain. Camilla was furious – they've been feuding publicly ever since. Apparently Camilla divorced her last husband right around the Academy Awards last year, purely to take attention away from the fact that Kitty was nominated.' Tilda pushes her soup bowl away. 'Kitty didn't win, but it didn't matter. Before the movie came out starring her and Art, Art had had some harsh reviews but once people saw him with Kitty, they fell in love with him again. There's something magical about the two of them together. You can imagine how Camilla Rey feels about *that*.'

I knew it, I think. I knew there was something about Kitty, something that I should have remembered but couldn't. That sinking feeling in my stomach that I got on set earlier today when she and Camilla had their altercation repeats on me now, and I press a hand against my belly. *Something bad is going to happen, and Kitty is involved.*

'Here.' Tilda digs in her bag and pulls out a copy of *Life* magazine, Kitty's smiling face staring back at me from the cover. 'There's an article in here about Kitty and Art, full of speculation about when he's going to propose, because God forbid a woman should make her own way—'

'Don't start on that again, Til,' Louis sighs. Since Tilda jilted her long-term boyfriend, Reg, before he could even get her to agree to a wedding date, she's been a thoroughly modern Millie, moving out of her parents' house to share an apartment with me in West Hollywood (not something Louis approves of, entirely), going to college and writing titbits for Louella Parsons's gossip column, and tossing her red ponytail at any fella who even thinks about asking her on a date.

'Tilda's a modern girl, Lou.' I grin at him, pulling the magazine towards me. As my fingers brush the cool, glossy cover, my smile drops, my pulse spiking. Pressing my hand flat against Kitty's face, I remember. 'I know what's going to happen to her,' I say, raising my eyes to look at a shocked Tilda and an unsmiling Louis, as the restaurant hubbub seems to die in my ears. 'Kitty Fox. And it's not good.'

Chapter Four

'She's going to disappear.' The words seem to ring out, loud and ugly over the restaurant chatter, but no one turns to look.

'What do you mean, *disappear*?' Louis asks, as Tilda leans in on her elbows, her gossip antennae twitching.

'I mean, *disappear*,' I hiss back, quickly raising my eyes to check Leonard and co. haven't spotted us. 'Vanish. Wander off into the ether never to be seen again.'

'Well, what happens to her?' Tilda's eyes are wide.

I let out a breath, my stomach knotted. I can feel my pulse beating in the hollow of my neck, faster than is comfortable. 'That's just it. No one knows.' I lay a hand on Kitty's face on the cover of the magazine, the memory of where I've seen that picture before sharp in my mind. It was a documentary I streamed late one night – one of those on Prime, with the title written in bright red slasher font – about Hollywood mysteries. It was mostly murders and robberies, but Kitty stood out in my mind – for a time at least – because she had literally just vanished into thin air.

'And you got that from the magazine cover?' Louis's voice is somewhat sceptical. I don't think he's ever really bought my explanation that I have a psychic ability – a way to read the future from placing my hand on a newspaper article, or letter, or photo – but there is no way in hell

I could ever tell him the truth about how I know what I could not possibly know in 1950. That I time-travelled my way here from 2020 after a nasty bump to the head in the bathroom of the Paul Williams suite in the Beverly Hills Hotel.

'Yes,' I say, my mouth puckered with the sour taste of lies.

'What else?' Tilda nudges Louis to shut up. She is far more ready to believe I have a psychic ability, and right now I could kiss her for it, as the memory of the documentary swims into my mind.

'No one knows what happens to her,' I say, slowly, pulling the pieces together. 'She's meant to show up on set and she doesn't. Rumours will fly around for years about what happened to Kitty Fox, before she fades into oblivion, forgotten by almost everyone.' I pause, a horrible vision from the documentary clear in my mind. 'There'll be a suicide attempt. It'll happen a few weeks before she vanishes, and she will survive, but it'll be enough that when she does disappear there is speculation that she tried again and was successful.'

'But if she vanishes, surely there's no body?' Louis says with a frown.

'That's right. There's no body. People will speculate that she went off into the desert and harmed herself, and coyotes dragged her body away.' I swallow, the nausea back again. All three of us have spent time out in the desert and we know it can be unforgiving. 'They'll also wonder if she was having an affair and things got out of hand, they'll say she was difficult to work with and suggest that someone at the studio got rid of her.' At that, I think of Leonard's fury at losing the light, of Doctor Astor handing Kitty a pill, of Oskar's glowering face as he commented on a cheaper, potentially more talented unknown, of Camilla's rage over her shoes, and my stomach clenches. 'People will even wonder if she was involved with something infinitely darker and murkier than acting, and she came to a sticky end that way.'

'Wow.' Tilda sits back in the booth, her face pale, and sips at her Martini as if fortifying herself. 'This is…'

'A nightmare,' Louis interjects. 'I mean, it's awful for Kitty, but really it isn't anything to do with us.'

Tilda and I both turn to stare at him. 'Louis,' I say, 'I'm working with Kitty. I *know* her. I don't think I can just brush this under the carpet.' *Maybe this is really why I'm here?* The thought is like a lightbulb going off over my head. While a part of me hopes that the reason I didn't ping back to my own time after we arrived back from Las Vegas was the universe conspiring to keep me with Louis and Tilda, now I wonder if Kitty could be the reason I'm still here. If saving Kitty is something I *have* to do. 'How can I go to the studio every day knowing something dreadful is going to happen to Kitty and not try and do something about it? Imagine if I'd never tried to help Honey.'

Tilda already has her notepad and pencil to hand and is jotting down notes. 'So, Camilla hates Kitty, obviously. What about anyone else? Anyone on the set who she seems to have an issue with?'

'You guys have *got* to be kidding me!' Louis says, in a frantic whisper. 'After everything we've all been through? We are *not* doing this.'

'Oh hush,' Tilda says. 'Go back to Mom and Dad's and eat meat loaf and listen to the wireless if your heart can take it, you old man.'

'Louis,' I place a hand on his arm, 'I can't not do anything.'

'Yes, you can!' He turns to me, his fingers wrapping around mine and squeezing them tightly. 'Why can't we just live our lives? Go to work, make dinner, go dancing on the weekend? Why do we have to always get involved in things that could cost you your life?' He pauses, pressing my fingers to his lips and making my stomach somersault. 'I'm putting my foot down.'

'You're... what?' I say with an incredulous huff of laughter, tugging my fingers away as Tilda presses her lips tightly together.

'I'm saying no to any of us getting involved. Lily, you're important to me. If we're going to be together, you should be listening to what I say. I don't want you to get involved in something that could be dangerous. I'm ready for us to settle down together, start thinking about, I don't know... the rest of our lives, having a family.'

Oh, good Lord. I press my feet against the tiled floor beneath the table, suddenly sure the world is about to tilt and I'll fall off. Maybe, in another life, that's where Louis and I would be. If we were both in 2020, perhaps we would be starting to think about moving in together in my crappy apartment in WeHo, or maybe finding a less shitty apartment of our own, but not here. Not now. The realisation hits me that before too long I'm going to have to make some very important decisions when it comes to my relationship with Louis.

'That's not how it works,' I say gently. 'Louis, I appreciate you're worried about us getting involved in something... complicated, but I have to do this, and you don't get to tell me what I can and can't do.'

Tilda lets out a squeak at that.

'I just don't want something awful—'

'I get it, I do,' I say, 'but I'm an adult and whatever this is between us,' I flap a hand in the empty space between my seat and his, 'I'm my own person, and I make my own decisions. I can't not do anything, knowing what I know.'

'Amen to that!' Tilda claps her hands together, ignoring the scowl Louis throws her way.

'What if it isn't dangerous?' I say to Louis, never taking my eyes from his face. 'What if it's simply that Kitty is miserable, and she does try and take her own life? I couldn't live with myself if I knew someone felt that dreadful and I didn't do anything to try and help.'

Louis is silent for a moment. 'And what if it's not? What if Kitty is involved in something nefarious and it's the Mob who take her out?' He places a finger under my chin and lifts my face so I have no choice but to look at him. 'Lily, I guess I can't stop you, but all I ask is that you're careful. You know how I feel about you. I lo—'

'Lily!' Jean's voice interrupts Louis's, cutting short something I wasn't sure I was ready to hear, as she passes by our booth. 'Hope you enjoyed your dinner – see you at the premiere?'

I nod, as Tilda's eagle eyes take in the handbag still clutched to Jean's belly.

'Something Jean wants to tell us?' Tilda asks, with a sparkle in her eye.

'Redfern for a boy, Gail for a girl,' I say with a grin. 'But you didn't hear it from me.'

'Awesome news. Evelyn will be next.' Tilda tips me a wink.

'Oh, gossip girl,' I say, relieved to have the subject changed for a moment. I was pretty sure that Louis was about to tell me he loved me, and seeing as neither of us has actually mentioned that word before, panic was about to set light to my veins. 'You're not writing your column now.'

'No,' she says, 'but I did see Evelyn with Paulie Brooker, sporting a huge engagement ring, so do with that what you will.'

I suppress a smile at this news, although I'm not surprised. Louis had dated Evelyn since high school until recently, and it's never been a secret that all Evelyn ever wanted in life was to get married and have babies.

'I should go,' I say, regretfully. All I'd really love to do now is take Louis up on his offer of a milkshake and a walk, if anything just to reassure him that while I won't be told what to do, it doesn't mean I don't think he's someone special. 'I have to help Kitty get ready for the premiere, before Art arrives to pick her up.' *And maybe I'll get the chance to start poking around, to see if I can figure out how Kitty will disappear.*

'I'll walk you back to the Chateau.' Louis stands, already reaching for his jacket, but I shake my head.

'Don't be daft,' I say, 'I'll be getting a ride to the premiere from someone at the studio, even if it isn't with Kitty. You don't want to walk all that way and back again. Escort your sister instead and make sure she gets there safely. I'll see you at Grauman's in an hour or so.' I lift my face and he presses his lips to mine, with a kiss that makes my knees turn to jelly, not caring that the other diners might see us.

'Be careful.' Tilda follows me to the restaurant door as Louis calls to settle the bill. 'It's getting dark out already.'

'I'll be fine, I've walked this way a hundred times.' And felt far more unsafe in 2020 than I do here, in 1950s Hollywood.

'Yes, but the police found a body last night,' Tilda says. 'Down one of the side streets off Sunset. So, just... you know, keep your wits about you. Actually, maybe you should get a cab.'

'Til, I'll be fine. See you in a little while.' Hugging her close, I wave through the window to Louis and step out onto Sunset Boulevard.

A chill has set in, and I pull my jacket tighter around my body as I hurry along the street towards Chateau Marmont. Maybe it's Tilda's words about the police finding a body last night, or maybe it's Louis's insistence that I need protecting, but I feel uneasy as darkness brings a different vibe to the town. It's still fairly well lit as I walk but the streets seem oddly empty. Maybe the crowds are hanging out further up on Hollywood Boulevard, outside Grauman's Chinese Theatre, waiting for the stars to arrive for the premiere.

Hurrying past closed stores and bars that are yet to get going, I keep my head down, only raising my eyes when I reach a pedestrian crossing. As I pause, I think I hear footsteps behind me, and when no one comes to stand beside me, my skin begins to prickle. I cross the street, aware of every side road and alley that I pass, Tilda's words reverberating around my mind as I strain my ears to listen.

Tap, tap, tap. My pulse ratchets and my breath sticks in my throat as fear squeezes my chest in a vice-like grip. *There's someone behind me. Following me?* Maybe I'm being overdramatic, Tilda's tales of bodies in alleyways making me oversensitive, and I slow down. Whoever it is must be in a hurry: if I slow down they can overtake me and I'll realise that I'm just being a drama queen. Slowing to a halt on one side of the pavement, I stoop to fiddle with my shoelace, although I thread the key to my apartment through my fingers just in case. No one passes me. A man hurries past a soda shop on the other side of the street, paying me no mind, and as I risk a cautious glance over my shoulder I am relieved to see the street behind me is empty, apart from a young woman stepping into a cab a few blocks back.

You're an idiot, Lil, I chide myself as I slip my keys back in my pocket and start walking towards the Chateau. Maybe I'm the one who should have taken up acting and dramatics, not Kitty. The smile dies on my lips seconds later as I hear it again. The tap, tap, tap of footsteps behind me, just slightly out of sync with mine. I speed up, horror spreading like ice through my veins as the tapping on the pavement behind me also speeds up, the sound a brisk clip that jars against the low thud of my sneakers. The streets are deserted, in a way they never usually are, and a sob threatens to strangle me as I thread my keys back through my fingers. The sign for Chateau Marmont is just a block away and I fix my gaze on it, the hairs on the back of my neck standing to attention, as the tap of the footsteps seem closer with every minute, and then I throw caution to the wind and sprint, as fast as I can, towards the safety of Chateau Marmont.

Chapter Five

Ignoring the curious stare of the valet, I tuck myself behind the hedge and peer out in hopes of spotting whoever was following me, but the path crossing the hotel entrance is empty. There is no one else there. Emboldened, I move to the middle of the driveway and look left and right along Sunset Boulevard. There are people around, more than I first realised, but no one is behaving suspiciously, creeping around like they want to bash my brains in. *Maybe I was imagining it after all?*

A shout from above gets my attention as a five-dollar bill floats past my nose, followed by another, and another.

'Will this make her happy? I don't think so!' a voice yells from above, and as the valet scrambles to pick up the money seemingly raining down from the sky, a dark head appears on the balcony of a second-floor window, shaking out a briefcase full of cash. 'Take it, folks, take it all!'

A second head appears in the window, this one with bright red curls surrounding a familiar face, as the first figure is yanked back out of sight, and the high-pitched sound of a woman cursing and yelling fills the air.

'Is that…?' I say, as the valet snatches up the bills that have fallen by my feet, valiantly trying to stop the ones he's already collected from bursting out of his fist and blowing away again.

'Yes,' he says wearily. 'Miss Ball and Mr Arnaz appear to have had yet *another* falling-out. With a bit of luck they'll run out of steam before he tosses all their money away.'

Yikes. I'd heard the stories of Desi Arnaz running around on Lucille Ball, but it seems as though this time things are really fired up. 'Here.' I hand him another dollar bill as Desi yells back at Lucy and more money floats down over our heads.

The valet takes the bill with a grimace. 'If I were you, I'd head inside before Miss Ball tries to leave and they take things out into the lobby.'

Letting out a long breath, I smooth down my dark, unruly curls and walk on shaky legs up the drive to the hotel, passing through the empty, dimly lit lobby when I hear my name.

'Lily? You're as white as a sheet.' Camilla Rey appears from the other side of the staircase, where there is a door leading out into the gardens, her cheeks flushed and her breathing slightly uneven. 'Are you all right?'

'Fine,' I manage, peering past her into the darkness outside. 'Although I don't think the same can be said for Desi Arnaz.'

'I heard the yelling,' Camilla says, pressing a hand to her chest. 'He didn't yell at you, did he? You look as if someone's given you a fright.'

'I'm fine, honestly. Just heading up to meet Kitty.'

'Oh. She is attending the premiere then?' Camilla smiles, but there is a tinge of disappointment to her voice. 'I guess I should let you get on. After all, she needs all the help she can get with her hair and make-up.'

She sweeps past me into the lobby and I pause for a moment, watching her go, before I turn my attention back to the doors at the rear of the hotel. Cracking them open, I peep out into the softly lit gardens, at the pathway snaking down to the bungalows, and rake my eyes over the shadows cast by the trees that keep the hotel guests' privacy intact. *Camilla could have followed me*, I think, a frown creasing my brow. She was at Villa Nova, and she could have sneaked in through the back entrance as I was running for my life (at least, I thought I was). *Why, though? It's Kitty she hates, not me.*

I turn and take the stairs as quickly as my wobbly knees will allow me up to Kitty's suite, almost stumbling as a man pushes past me in the hallway outside her room.

'Sorry, ma'am,' he mutters as he hurries for the stairs, the wall lights casting a golden glow over his blond hair as he descends.

Shaken, I watch him go for a moment, frowning as I try to place him, and then I tap on Kitty's door, unnerved when it swings open under my touch.

'Kitty? Are you here?' I step into the narrow hallway, following the sounds of clinking glasses to Kitty's bedroom. 'Woah. What happened in here?'

Kitty turns to me with a slightly sloppy smile and I note the Martini glass in her hand. The room is full – and I mean *full* – of bouquets of pink roses, littering every available surface. 'Jeremy came to visit.'

'Jeremy? The guy I just passed on the stairs?' The blond man from the set – that's where I recognised him from. What was he doing visiting Kitty alone in her hotel room? Something tells me Art might not be too pleased about this.

'That's the one,' Kitty sighs. 'Jeremy Knox. Always there when you need him.' Sarcasm laces her words.

'Did he…?' I gesture to the bouquets.

'Oh no, this was all Art, after I failed to acknowledge the chocolates he sent earlier today. And the ones he sent yesterday, and the day before.' Kitty smiles now, but it doesn't quite reach her eyes. 'He means well, of course, dear Art, but it can be… a *lot*, sometimes.' She claps her hands together briskly and changes the subject. 'Don't you know Jeremy? You must have seen him on set. He's in the movie – playing Camilla's brother-in-law or something, this time.'

'This time? You've worked together before?' My ears prick up at this new information.

'Many, many times,' Kitty says, draining the last of her Martini. 'He stopped by this evening to see if I was still planning to attend the premiere tonight… and to remind me of our anniversary, although I had no idea it was *any* kind of anniversary.'

Something dark turns in my stomach. It really *was* him lurking outside the lobby as I left earlier. Was he waiting to make sure Kitty was alone? 'Anniversary? That sounds… official.'

Kitty smirks, the light catching her eyes and making her breathtakingly beautiful. 'We go way back, Jeremy and I. Apparently tonight is the anniversary of the first night he ever laid eyes on me, although I had no idea. We dated, you know. Years and years and years ago.'

'I… didn't know that,' I say. It seems kind of intense on Jeremy's part to stop by for an anniversary that Kitty didn't even realise existed until Jeremy flagged it. 'That's nice of him, I guess.' It's not nice. It's weird. But I feel as though I should be polite.

'It's a bit much, isn't it?' Kitty presses her lips together. 'But it's always been this way, between me and Jeremy.'

'What way?' I follow as Kitty weaves her way down the short hall to the kitchen area and starts fixing herself another Martini. She lifts an empty glass in my direction and I shake my head, noting the other dirty glass beside her, a large smudged fingerprint on the rim.

'Wherever I go, Jeremy will follow.' She closes her eyes as she takes a large sip of her fresh drink. Kitty is still in the clothes she wore on set, her feet bare, and her face has been scrubbed of make-up. 'He's very attentive. Every movie I've been on Jeremy has found some way to be involved. He usually manages to snag at least a small part, although once or twice he's played my opposite number. He was even a carpenter on set once, way back in the beginning, when he didn't get the part he auditioned for.' Kitty smirks. 'Jeremy is utterly useless at woodwork.'

Shock makes my legs feel even more wobbly than before. 'Kitty, aren't you worried? That seems really excessive.' In 2020 I would have called the cops if someone turned up at every place I worked. 'It's *stalking*.'

Kitty lets out a burst of laughter. 'Oh, Lily, don't be so dramatic. Jeremy is just… a little intense, that's all, and if I tell him to stop he'll just double his efforts. I mean, I do wish he'd rein it in a little, but it keeps Art on his toes.' Her smile drops as she glances at the clock on the wall. 'I should probably get ready for the premiere. Art did offer to send his make-up artist but I can't bear to make small talk, not this evening.'

'I could help you,' I say. If I help Kitty get ready there's a chance she won't be so late that she misses the premiere altogether. 'When I worked with Honey Black I would often help her with hair and make-up. And we don't have to talk at all if you don't want to.'

'You did?' Kitty perks up at this. 'Honey always looks like an absolute doll. You think you can make me look half as good as her?'

'Better.' I grin, relief washing over me as Kitty sets down her drink and moves towards the bedroom.

Fifteen minutes later she's showered and I am helping her into a girdle that squeezes her waist to a tiny twenty-four inches.

'Oof,' she huffs, as she adjusts her bosoms, and then steps into the red silk dress I hold out to her. 'How do I look?'

'Gorgeous.' I'm not lying. Kitty is stunning, the red of the fabric setting off the pale creaminess of her skin, making her green eyes almost luminous. 'Sit down and I'll do your make-up.'

Kitty closes her eyes and lets out a sigh as I pull out her make-up bag and open her powder compact, brushing lightly over her skin. I'm getting to be a dab hand at cosmetics in the 1950s – it's rather refreshing to not have to deal with the layers of primer, bronzer, foundation and highlighter that I would have used in my own time.

'I'd rather stay here this evening,' Kitty says after a few minutes of silence. 'Imagine an evening spent lying in a hot bath, with no lines to learn, a good book and clean sheets on the bed. No one to talk to, no one to smile at. Heaven.'

'You did have kind of a rough day.' I open her mascara cake, and dot the wand in the glass of water beside her bed. I don't have it in me to spit on it – I'm not sure I ever will. 'Fainting and all.' After darkening her lashes, I dab two tiny dots of rouge on her cheeks, to give her flawless complexion a hint of colour. No one would be able to tell she'd fainted earlier.

Kitty flaps a hand as if that's all in a day's work. 'Flannel pyjamas,' she goes on, 'you know the kind you'd wear as a kid when it got really cold? I grew up in New York and winters are hard there, let me tell you. A steaming bowl of mac and cheese and Nat King Cole on the wireless.' She sighs again. 'Maybe in another lifetime.' She opens her eyes and blinks, her lashes heavy with black mascara, and reaches for a lipstick in a shade of red matching her dress.

'Kitty? Honey?' The door is thrown open and Art bursts in, looking hellishly handsome in a fitted black suit and a skinny red tie. 'Are you ready to go?'

Kitty sighs and reaches for the gold cigarette case on the table. She expertly flicks out a cigarette and lights it, breathing out a long stream of smoke. 'Don't I look ready?'

Art grins and leans in to kiss her cheek. 'Darling, I'm sure you were born ready.' He glances around the room, beaming as he catches sight of the vast bouquets that fill the space. 'Flowers, huh? Someone's popular. Who are they from?' He moves to one of the bouquets, lifting a sprig of greenery out of the way with an ear-splitting grin.

'Just a fan.' Kitty flaps a hand, playing along, smoke curling in a wreath around her head as she puts her cigarette in the ashtray and picks up a necklace from the glinting pile in her jewellery box. 'Nobody important.'

'Ha. I think you mean the love of your life.' Art drops the greenery and flashes me a quick smile, one that makes my mouth go dry. 'Here, let me.' He gently lifts Kitty's hair from the nape of her neck and secures the clasp on the necklace, a beautiful square-cut ruby pendant on a heavy gold chain. 'Well, sweetie, let's hit the road. If we get there too late there'll be no one to welcome us.'

Stubbing out her cigarette, Kitty avoids Art's gaze as she speaks. 'Would it be so terrible if we just… skipped it?' she says, quietly. 'We could have an evening here, together. Just you and me.'

Something I can't read flashes across Art's face. *Irritation, maybe?* Surely not. He is smiling at Kitty now as he steps across the room and pulls her into his arms, no trace of anything except love on his features.

'Kitty, honey, I know you've had a rough day. Believe me, there is nothing I'd love more than to spend the evening curled up here with you, but,' Art pulls back to look at her, 'Leonard would have our guts for garters if we skipped this premiere. The picture is made by the same studio – don't you think there would be plenty to say about us not showing up? Oskar would certainly have something to say.'

I press myself against the wall, the urge to flee almost overwhelming. This is a private moment between two people, and I've never felt more uncomfortable in my life.

'Let me get you a drink, help you get into the party mood.' Art steps to one side, passing me on his way to the kitchen as Kitty follows, and I slip into the corridor. Peering into the kitchen I see Art throw a shot of vermouth into a shaker, followed by two shots of vodka, and he shakes enthusiastically.

'Lily!' Art calls with a grin. 'Can I make you a Martini?'

'Uhh, no thanks, Mr… Art.' I can think of no worse drink in the world. 'I should probably…' I point towards the door as Kitty gives a tiny shake of her head. 'Or, I can wait until you folks are ready to go.'

Kitty gives me a quick smile, and turns to the mirror in the hallway to reapply her lipstick. I watch as she rings her mouth carefully with her trademark red, turning back to the kitchen just as Art's hand hovers over Kitty's drink, before slipping it into his pocket. My stomach flips and I push a smile onto my face as Kitty accepts the Martini Art offers, and takes a huge gulp, draining half the glass in one.

'I just need to powder my nose,' she says with a slight hiccup, 'and then, of course, we must leave, Art.' She totters off towards the en suite bathroom, glass still in hand. Art hums under his breath as he does something I wasn't expecting, and begins to hand-wash the cocktail shaker and glasses in the small sink, pushing his sleeves up out of the way of the warm water. There is something oddly domesticated about it, and I don't even register the silence between us until Kitty comes back along the hall, heels on and a clutch bag under her arm. She seems much more upbeat, positively sparkling as she smiles at us both and urges Art to dry his hands.

'No time for all that,' she says with a wicked laugh, her eyes twinkling. 'We'll miss the party! Lily, we'll see you there.' And she sweeps out of the suite into the corridor.

Once the door clicks shut behind her I turn to Art, my heart hammering fit to burst as he wrestles with a cufflink. Suspicion burns like lava in my belly.

'Art... Mr Calloway.' I run my tongue over my lips, my throat dry. 'Did you... did you put something in Kitty's drink?'

'What?' Art pauses in his fiddling, before raising his eyes to meet mine. 'Are you accusing me of drugging Kitty? My heart, my love? Is that what I'm hearing?' His gaze narrows and I take a step back.

'No, no, of course not. She just seems... I thought I saw your hand over her drink, is all, before it went back in your pocket. I jumped to conclusions. I apologise. I didn't mean to offend you. Kitty is… I guess I feel as though she's my responsibility, that's all, seeing as I've taken over from Jean.'

Art stares me down until I feel the prickle of sweat under my collar. 'I appreciate you looking out for Kitty, but you can rest assured she is one hundred per cent safe with me.' His tone softens, but I can't relax as he takes a step towards me until he's so close I can smell his cologne. 'You really want to see what I have in my pocket?'

Coming from a movie star like Magnus Michel, the sleazeball actor I wrestled with when I was trying to save Honey Black – or, indeed, anyone else – this would be enough for me to knee him in the balls, but I am concerned about Kitty so I give the tiniest nod. Art reaches into his pocket and then opens his fist.

'Oh. Oh, wow.' I look up at Art's grinning face. 'I'm sorry. Really sorry.'

Art shrugs as he holds up the ruby earrings he's pulled from his pocket. 'I was taking another peek at these. You think Kitty will like them? I wanted to give them to her before we left, but I guess in the car will do.'

'She'll love them,' I manage. 'They match her dress and that gorgeous necklace she's wearing perfectly. You should probably go, Kitty will be waiting for you.'

Art gives me that crinkly-eyed grin again, and then hurries out to the staircase, leaving me drained and exhausted, leaning against the wall of Kitty's suite. *Earrings, Lily, you fool*, I think as I let out a long breath. *That's all it was.* Even so, I think of the way Kitty's eyes sparkled as she came out of the bathroom, of the way Art whipped his hand back in his pocket, and realise that while I believe Art, something still feels off. Turning to leave, I take one last look around the room, at the bouquets of roses that Kitty said Art had sent. Jeremy came by just to see if Kitty was still going to the premiere… and to remind her of an anniversary she didn't even know existed. *Kitty, Art and Jeremy*. Could I be looking at some sort of love triangle? Is Jeremy the one I should be keeping an eye on? Shuddering, I pull the door closed on the bouquets and make my way downstairs to the lobby, unable to shake the feeling that something isn't quite right.

Chapter Six

Sharing a car with Bunny Truman isn't quite the experience I thought it would be, as she chatters in my ear all the way to Grauman's theatre about everything and nothing. By the time I make it out to the sidewalk, Art and Kitty have left, thankfully, the prickle of sweat still drying under my collar. Bunny, however, has waited for me, lounging against a beat-up but gleaming, clean Ford.

'Hop in,' she says, as the last of Desi Arnaz's dollar bills flutter to the ground around us. 'I figured you'd need a ride.'

There begins a waterfall of one-sided conversation in which I learn that the car belongs to Bunny's father but he lets her drive it, that she bought her dress in Saks and it cost more than she could ever confess to her mother, and when I finally tumble out of the car a little way along from the theatre, my ears are ringing and I haven't had a chance to mull over the interaction with Kitty and Art at all.

'Oh, who's that cutie?' Bunny nudges me as we step out of the car and into the thronging mass of people on the pavement outside the theatre, all desperate for a glimpse of the stars. 'You know him?'

Louis lounges against a street light, the orange glow lighting his features as he smiles warmly at me, lifting one hand in a wave.

'Thanks for the ride. Shall I meet you inside?' I say to Bunny, hoping I might be able to shake her off for a few minutes, just long enough to talk to Louis about Kitty and Art.

'Uh, sure.' Bunny gives Louis another curious glance. 'Is that your boyfriend?'

'It's complicated.'

'Oh, I see.' Bunny nods sagely. 'Well, I guess I'll leave you to it. See you in there.' With one last look at Louis she walks towards the edge of the red carpet, as if not wanting to be noticed, but also aware that she *is* being noticed, just by walking this side of the barrier. I shake my head with a wry smile. She's something else, is Bunny.

'Hey, Lil.' Louis leans in and kisses my cheek as my stomach free-falls. He smells like sandalwood and limes, with an undertone of beer.

I return the kiss, on the lips this time, and wish not for the first time that the two of us were connected in the twenty-first century instead of the stuffy 1950s. I'm pretty sure that if we did live in 2020 Louis would have seen me naked more than once by now, but as it is, we are in 1951 and Louis is the perfect gentleman. Almost *too* much of a gentleman at times, if you ask me.

'Hey, yourself.' I peer over his shoulder at the crowds that line the red carpet, at the newspapermen that jostle against each other, all fighting for the scoop of the evening. 'Did Tilda make it?'

'She's over there.' Louis points to the entrance to the theatre, where Tilda appears deep in conversation with Louella Parsons, although I know both of them will have one eye on the red carpet. Hedda Hopper, Louella's biggest rival in the world of gossip columns, scowls at the pair of them from the other side of the rope barrier.

'Hedda keeps calling and asking if Tilda will consider working with her instead. I'm pretty sure Louella has found out about it.'

Yikes. That explains the glares. It doesn't explain the prickle on the back of my neck though, as if eyes are on me. I turn, whipping my head around, but while the streets are crowded, there is no one specifically looking my way. A shiver runs down my spine as I think about the footsteps behind me as I walked to Chateau Marmont earlier.

'Lily? Are you OK? You seem kinda…' Louis peers at me with concern, resting his hand under my elbow as he guides me towards the red carpet.

'I thought…' I drag my gaze away and turn back to face Louis. 'It's nothing. I'm just being silly.'

'How was Kitty when you got back to the hotel?' Louis pauses for a moment, one hand rubbing over the slight stubble on his chin. 'Did you… find anything?'

I shake my head. 'No. But I do feel kind of weird about things. Kitty seemed a little off, I suppose. She didn't want to come out at all this evening, even going so far as to try and persuade Art to stay home, but then it was like a switch was flipped and she couldn't wait to leave.'

'Maybe she just gave herself a stern talking-to,' Louis says with a shrug.

'Maybe.' Doubt clouds my voice. 'And I made a complete arse of myself with Art. I accused him of spiking her drink, when all he did was slip some earrings into his pocket, so now he probably thinks I'm crazy.' I sigh. 'Maybe I am. Maybe all of this is just bonkers.'

Louis reaches out and clasps my hands in his. 'Don't say that, Lily. I've spoken to Tilda on the way over here and she told me I was being a fathead. You're right. If you think something is going to happen to Kitty then we absolutely do need to try and prevent it.'

Relief floods my veins, but I don't have time to enjoy it as cheers go up from the crowds and Louis tugs me towards the entrance to the red carpet, where Bunny stands waiting for us.

'What's going on?' I peer past someone I vaguely recognise from the set, as the cheers grow louder and flashbulbs pop left, right and centre.

'It's Camilla Rey,' Louis says, as we reach Bunny. 'She's on the red carpet.'

'It's not *just* Camilla Rey,' Bunny breathes. 'She's on the red carpet with Daniel O'Hara. As in her *ex-husband* Daniel O'Hara.'

'Wow.' I recognise the man on the carpet beside Camilla as the man at Villa Nova with her earlier, and can only imagine the smoke pouring out of Tilda's pencil at this; after all, she was the one who told me Camilla timed her divorce to spite Kitty.

'I overheard her saying that she was going to make a splash this evening, and boy has she done that!' Bunny claps her hands together like a little kid.

Camilla and Daniel make their way into the theatre, Camilla smiling and waving graciously at her adoring fans as Daniel tries to fend off questions about a reconciliation from the journos. More stars trip their way along the carpet, and I glance around for Kitty but there's no sign of her.

Leonard appears, Jean on one side of him clutching tightly to his arm and Oskar Goldstein on the other. Leonard seems to want to rush his way along the carpet, barely pausing to speak to the cinephiles that line the walkway to the theatre, but Oskar calls him back time and again, waving and smiling even as Leonard grits his teeth, and for a moment I think I'll choke on the tension between the two of them. The moment he can, Leonard peels away, speed walking towards the theatre entrance as Jean hurries to keep up, leaving Oskar to grin and charm his way along the red carpet alone.

We watch as Michael Rennie and Patricia Neal walk the carpet together, Patricia stunning in a ruffled, strapless gown in the lightest silvery blue, and I am about to suggest to Louis that I should leave him here and head inside myself, thinking that Kitty and Art must have already taken their seats, when I catch sight of Kitty's blonde hair and red gown.

She glides onto the carpet, alone, and I wonder where Art is, as Bunny nudges me. 'Isn't she beautiful?' she sighs. 'I heard they wanted Kitty for this movie but she refused to do it because it's science fiction, so they got Patricia instead.'

'I guess Kitty knows—' Whatever Louis is about to say is cut off, as a tall figure barges through the rope barrier and onto the red carpet, snatching up Kitty's arm in a vice-like grip.

Kitty shrieks, a high-pitched, desperate sound, as she fights to pull her arm away, stumbling over the hem of her dress in her heels. 'Let me go!' she sobs, as the figure leans in, pressing his face close to hers. He wears a long trench coat and a hat pulled down over his face, meaning it's difficult to make out his features.

'Hey!' Louis is already pushing his way past the scrum of journalists who are desperately popping flash after flash in a bid to get the scoop, not one of them stepping forward to help.

I glance around, searching the crowd for Art, for Leonard, for anyone who can help, before shoving my way towards the carpet after Louis.

'Kitty! Kitty!' The cry comes from somewhere behind me and hands press into the small of my back, pushing me to one side as a figure blurs past me. 'Get your hands off her!'

It's Jeremy Knox, tall, blond and utterly furious as he shoves Kitty's assailant to one side. The man stumbles and Jeremy steps in again, raising his fists and laying one right on the guy's nose before turning back to Kitty, who sags against him. Jeremy pulls her close, muttering into her hair.

Fighting my way onto the carpet, I reach Louis, Jeremy and Kitty, just as Louis staggers back and Kitty's assailant disappears into the crowd.

'Kitty, are you all right?' I hurry towards her, as she nods weakly. She's crying, one hand gripping her elbow, and in the artificial lights I can already see a deep purple bruise forming in the shape of fingerprints. 'Who the hell was that guy?'

'I have no idea, but he'd better not show his face around here again.' Jeremy's voice is richer and deeper than I imagined, and he tightens his arms around Kitty. 'It's OK, honey,' he soothes. 'He's gone. He hotfooted it out of here, and I won't let anyone get near you now.'

'I think we should get you inside,' I say, as the crowds begin to close in again, the buzz of gossip on their tongues. 'You'll be safe in there.'

Jeremy guides Kitty along the red carpet, her head down, with Louis flanking her other side, shielding her from the gawping mob. Flashbulbs still pop here and there, but an odd hush descends over the crowd, and I catch

Tilda's eye as we reach the doors to the theatre, discreetly signalling for her to follow us inside.

Oskar and Leonard are already at the doors as we enter, Leonard peering over my shoulder at the flashbulbs still popping outside.

'What in Sam Hill is going on out there?' Leonard frowns. 'Lily, what's the commotion about?'

'Someone tried to grab Kitty on the red carpet,' I say, adrenaline making the words wobble as they leave my mouth. 'The newspapermen captured it all.'

Leonard scrubs a hand over his face as Oskar turns a beaming grin on me. 'This is marvellous,' he says, clapping his hands together.

'Marvellous?' Leonard snaps. 'How is this marvellous? I don't call one of my stars being terrified on the carpet *marvellous*.'

'Think of the publicity,' Oskar crows. 'We'll be front-page news tomorrow morning – even people who don't like the movies will hear about it, and they'll all want to see the picture that caused such a commotion. Think of the opening numbers at the box office!'

Leonard can barely hide his disgust towards Oskar as he turns back to Kitty and runs his eyes over her. 'Kitty, are you all right?'

'Here, sit down for a moment.' Louis and Jeremy help Kitty onto a stool, and seconds later Tilda appears with a drink in one hand.

'Drink this.' Tilda hands it to Kitty. 'It's a Brandy Alexander. I figured it's got brandy and sugar in it, so it's perfect for the shock.'

Kitty takes the tumbler from Tilda, her cheeks whiter than chalk. She has just raised the glass to her mouth when a shout comes from the theatre entrance.

'Where is she?' Panic laces every word. 'Where's my girl?' Art storms into the lobby, pausing as his eyes alight on Kitty. 'Kitty, sweetie! Are you all right?' He glares at Jeremy as Kitty hops off the stool and steps towards Art.

'Oh, Art, it was awful.' A sob erupts from Kitty's throat. 'He just… grabbed me, I was terrified. I thought he was going to kill me, right there in front of everyone.'

Ice trickles down my back at her words, as Louis widens his eyes at me over Kitty's head.

Art pats Kitty's shoulder sympathetically. 'Aww no, sugar. He wouldn't have done that, not in front of all those people. You're OK, don't cry.' He pulls a handkerchief out of his top pocket and Kitty dabs gently at her eyes. 'Where is the fella now?'

'He's gone, disappeared into the crowd. We should call the police,' I say.

'Surely no need for that,' Oskar says hastily.

'No,' Kitty says softly in agreement, as she hands Tilda her empty glass with a shaking hand. 'It'll cause even more of a scene if the police show up. It'll derail the premiere, and then all the reporters will want to talk to me.'

Art shakes his head too. 'He'll be long gone now, thank God.' His arm tightens around Kitty's shoulders as Jeremy shifts from one foot to the other.

'Where were *you*?' Jeremy demands. 'Why weren't you looking after her?'

Art's head snaps up and he glowers at Jeremy. 'Excuse me?'

'Where were you?' Jeremy says again. 'You're supposed to be Kitty's date. You should have been beside her – this wouldn't have happened if you'd been on the carpet next to her.'

Art scoffs, looking Jeremy up and down as if he's a bug Art is just itching to squash. 'It's none of your damn business where I am or what I'm doing. Just like Kitty isn't any of your damn business either. Go back to learning the few lines you've been given, bit-part boy.' Kitty gasps at this, but Art just clutches her tighter to him.

'OK, I think that's enough,' Leonard says sternly. 'No real harm done, and we don't need any more of a scene in here. Jean, come on.' Without waiting for a response, Leonard turns towards the interior theatre doors.

'Fantastic publicity,' Oskar says again, with a friendly tap on Art's arm before he follows Leonard into the theatre, and I have to physically swallow down the sharp retort that scratches at my throat.

'Sweetie, let's go and sit down. The movie is about to start, and Leonard's right, we don't want to draw any more attention to what happened out there,' Art says, with one more venomous glance in Jeremy's direction.

I glance at Louis, who frowns sharply as Tilda steps forward. 'With all due respect, Mr Calloway,' Tilda says, 'do you think it's wise for Kitty to stay out? I mean, she's had a dreadful shock.'

Art narrows his eyes. 'You. You're the gossip column girl, aren't you? I'd better not catch any of this in your grubby little rag tomorrow.'

Tilda opens her mouth to respond but I jump in before she can speak. I can already tell the words about to spill out of her mouth aren't going to be kind to Art Calloway. 'Art, Tilda is a good friend of mine. I promise she won't write anything about Kitty and what happened this evening, but perhaps we should consider taking Kitty back to the hotel, if that's what she wants.'

Kitty's eyes fill with tears. 'I do feel shaken up, Art.'

Art pauses for a moment, his eyes flicking towards the theatre door, where an usher stands waiting. The boom of the 20th Century Fox drum roll signalling the start of the movie echoes from behind the doors.

'I'll take her home.' Jeremy Knox steps forward and holds out an arm to Kitty. 'I'm not worried about seeing the movie, and to be honest, Kitty darling, you look like you could do with a night at home, with a hot chocolate and the wireless on.'

An eerie sense of déjà vu creeps over me. *That's almost exactly what Kitty wished she could do earlier.*

Art steps in front of Kitty so quickly I almost get whiplash watching him. 'I don't think so,' Art says, looking Jeremy up and down again as if finding him lacking, which is kind of rude in itself as Jeremy looks very dapper in a light grey suit and two-tone brogues. 'Kitty stays with me.'

'I really don't mind, Art,' Jeremy says, insistent. 'If Kitty would rather leave I'll certainly make sure she gets home safely. I wouldn't leave her side.'

'I'm sure you wouldn't, Jeremy, but you aren't needed.' Art takes off his jacket and wraps it around Kitty's shoulders. 'Let's go, sweetie, of course we don't have to stay. You've had a horrible experience.' With one last look at the closed theatre doors, Art guides Kitty towards the doors out onto the street.

'You coming, Lily?' Kitty turns back to look at me, her eyes huge in her pale face.

'Uh, sure. One second.' I turn to Tilda and Louis. 'I guess I should probably make sure Kitty is OK.'

Tilda nods. 'Let me make my excuses to Louella and I'll come with you, I'm sure she'll understand.' She watches Kitty exit the theatre. 'I really hope tonight isn't an omen for what's to come.'

'Me too.' Louis reaches out and grabs my hand. 'I'll come back to the Chateau with you too, Lily. No arguments this time.'

Louis won't get any protest from me, not after the clip of footsteps I heard on the path behind me earlier, and we hurry out into the cool Los Angeles evening. As we hit the pavement I turn back, to see Jeremy watching us leave. I think I can feel the press of his gaze even as the studio car pulls up, leaving me feeling oddly off-kilter, so much so that I don't notice Kitty scrambling onto the back seat beside me until she presses her hand into mine.

'Are you all right?' I whisper in a hushed tone as her fingers wrap tightly around mine.

'Lily, I'm so afraid,' Kitty whispers. 'What if he comes back? What if he tries to hurt me again?'

'That guy?' My heart wants to break for her as Kitty peers behind us out of the rear window, a gasp escaping her lips as she turns back to face me, her eyes bright with fear.

'We're being followed,' she says. 'That car behind us... it's followed us all the way along Sunset Boulevard.' She reaches forward to tap Art on the shoulder where he sits up front with the driver.

Twisting in my seat, I am relieved to see the familiar shape of Louis's beloved Cadillac, Christine. 'It's OK,' I say in a soothing tone. 'That's my friends in the car behind. And you don't need to worry about that guy coming back for you. I won't let him. I'll speak to Bobby on the gate tomorrow, and make sure the studio knows what happened. He won't be able to get within a mile radius of you. The guy is probably just some random, trying his luck at getting close to an actual movie star, that's all.'

Kitty stops, shaking her head as her eyes fill with tears again. 'No, Lily. That I could handle – I've had my fair share of disgusting fan letters over the years. This guy was different. As he grabbed me, he leaned in and said, *you're next.*'

Chapter Seven

'Do you remember what he looked like at all?' Tilda licks the end of her pencil and prepares to jot down Kitty's words.

We are back at Kitty's suite at Chateau Marmont, the five of us all sequestered in her bedroom. Kitty sits up in bed, wrapped in a cosy robe, Art perched on the bed beside her, holding her hand tightly.

'I don't think so,' Kitty says quietly, shaking her head. 'I just remember he smelled like liquorice or aniseed. Strongly, as if he'd just eaten some.'

'So you don't think you'd recognise him if you saw him again?' Tilda asks, as I press down on her foot with my own. 'What? It's a valid question.'

'It is,' I agree, 'but I think it's one that Kitty probably doesn't want to think about right now.' Kitty still looks terribly pale, and her hands shake as she moves to push her hair out of her eyes.

'It's fine, Lily,' she says. 'I should probably try and remember while it's fresh in my mind. Like I said, he smelled like aniseed or liquorice, and I think he had dark hair, although it was difficult to tell under his hat. His fingernails were sharp.' She shudders. 'I could feel them digging into my skin when he snatched my arm. And I think he wore a gold ring on his pinky finger.'

'This is all great,' Tilda says, her pencil scratching at nineteen to the dozen as she jots everything down. 'We should probably pass this information on to the police. I'm sure they'll have questions.'

'Police?' Art shakes his head firmly. 'Didn't you hear Oskar? There won't be any police coming to speak to Kitty. If they do get involved the studio will deal with it. It's bad enough that this happened at the premiere, without Kitty being questioned by the police. Let the higher-ups at the studio deal with things so we can all get back to normal.'

'It's what I would prefer,' Kitty says, her voice barely above a whisper. 'This isn't the first time something like this has happened, Lily. I get crazy fan letters all the time, and the studio works overtime to make sure I'm safe. Although...' She trails off.

'Although?' Louis prompts, forcing a frown from Art.

Kitty sighs. 'I'm probably just feeling jittery after what happened tonight, but...' She glances at Art, who squeezes her hand as if encouraging her to go on. 'I have felt once or twice as though someone might be following me.'

'Following you?' Something sharp spikes in my chest, a rush of adrenaline filling my veins. 'Did you see them? Or just sense something?' The echo of footsteps behind me rings in my ears.

'I didn't see anyone, I just... felt them, I guess. I was walking back from Schwab's, across the street, a few nights ago. I only went to get a salad, but it was late, so I covered my hair and didn't wear any make-up, trying to stay a little incognito, you know? As I crossed the street on my way back I thought I heard footsteps behind me, but there was no one there.'

I swallow, suddenly cold. Schwab's Pharmacy is feet away from the hotel, and is where all the guests head out to, to grab a bite or a drink, since the Chateau doesn't have a restaurant. 'What did you do?'

'Well, I ran.' Kitty laughs, somewhat hollowly. 'And then I felt ridiculous for the rest of the evening, because there was no one behind me that I could see. I couldn't even eat my salad in the end. And then a few days later I was on set early, before anyone else arrived, and I felt it again. As though someone was watching me. But there was no one there.' She sighs. 'I feel like I might be going a little crazy.'

'Honey, no one is watching you,' Art says, pressing a kiss to her forehead. 'And even if they were... it doesn't mean that they mean you any harm. You know how many gals follow me out of the lot some evenings?' He booms a laugh that fills the room, squeezing the air out it. 'Tens of 'em. All calling my name, asking me to sign things. Heck, I even had one of them break into my room one time. That was a surprise when I turned on the light, let me tell you.'

'Seriously, Art?' Tilda raises an eyebrow.

'What?' He holds up his hands in surrender. 'All I'm trying to say is, first of all, that guy tonight was a one-off. I was there, I would never have let him hurt you. And second of all, it's part of the job, Kitty. People see us on the screen and they want what we have, they want to *be* us. So if they see you out in public, at the store or grabbing a salad, of course they're going to watch you, maybe even follow you down the street. It's a normal reaction for them.'

'Well, it shouldn't be.' Kitty's voice is pitchy and shrill. 'It shouldn't be normal for people to *follow* me. I became an actress because I wanted to do what Judy Garland was doing – I wanted to *be* Judy. That doesn't mean I followed her home or grabbed her arm on the red carpet.' Kitty pauses, her chest hitching as her voice grows thick with tears. 'I just want to act, to do my job. I never wanted all these other things that go with it. The camera flashes, and the constant scrutiny.'

'Oh, hon.' Art presses Kitty's hand to his lips, kissing her wrist. 'You just have to smile and learn to accept it. You can't have one without the other. You can't be up there on the silver screen and go unrecognised. If that's what you wanted, you should have stuck to the stage.'

I wince at Art's delivery – I know he's trying to reassure Kitty, but by gosh he's clunky with it – but I am inclined to agree with him. Thank goodness Kitty isn't a twenty-first century gal – she'd never cope with TikTok videos made by fans as she shops for groceries, with the paparazzi camping outside her hotel, her every movement recorded and broadcast to the public. 'Maybe we should just keep an extra-close eye on you, for the next few days,' I say, as Louis nods in agreement. 'Just until you feel a little more like your old self.' *And that way, maybe we can figure exactly how you're going to disappear into thin air.*

The knock that comes at the door makes all of us jump, and Art slides off the bed with a sheepish grin, opening the door to a portly man in a straw boater.

'Doctor Astor! Come on in.' Art stands to one side and the studio doctor enters, his medical bag in one hand and a cup in the other.

'Kitty, dear. How are you feeling? I heard about the dreadful scene at the theatre this evening.' Doctor Astor hands Kitty the cup. 'Hot chocolate, from Schwab's. Art asked me to bring it to you, he knows it's your favourite.'

Kitty takes the cup and inhales the sweet steam rising from it. 'Thank you. I'm a little shaken up, but he really didn't hurt me.'

'I'll stay here with you tonight,' Art says authoritatively. 'You shouldn't be alone.'

Kitty shakes her head and sighs. 'No, Art, there's no need. I doubt I'll sleep much, and you have to be on set early. I'll be fine. I'll put the chain across the door.'

'You need your sleep too, darling,' Art says gently. 'If I stay, you know you're safe.'

'Honestly, Art, I'd rather be alone.' Kitty stiffens slightly, pulling herself out of Art's cloying embrace.

'Well, won't you at least let the good doctor give you a little something?' Art nods at Doctor Astor, who begins to rummage in his bag, pulling out a small brown pill bottle.

'Here, this should do it.' Doctor Astor drops two yellow pills into Kitty's hand and she raises them to her mouth.

'Wait!' I say, reaching out to stay Kitty's hand. 'What are you giving her?'

'Just a sleeping pill.' Doctor Astor stares at me over the top of his glasses.

'Just a sleeping pill, Lily,' Kitty repeats. 'It's no big deal, everybody takes them once in a while.'

'Do you really need it?' I can't explain why I feel so on edge about Kitty taking pills. Maybe I'm overreacting. Louis and Tilda don't seem fazed, and Art is looking at me like I'm crazy, but then I did accuse him of drugging her himself just a few hours ago.

'I need to get some sleep and right now, every time I close my eyes, I feel that man's hand grab at me,' Kitty says, with the hint of a sob in her voice.

'It's for the best,' Astor says firmly, adjusting his boater more securely on his head. 'Kitty has to be on set early, and she's had a horrible shock.'

'Sorry,' I say, forcing a smile onto my face. 'I suppose I'm a little shaken up by all of this too.'

'I'm happy to give you something to help you sleep, Lily, if you think it would help?' The doctor smiles back at me sympathetically.

'No, no. All good. I guess we should let you rest, Kitty. See you on set tomorrow.'

—

Tilda, Louis and I head out onto Sunset Boulevard, sidestepping the last couple of Desi Arnaz's dollar bills clinging to the hedge and sticking to the mouth of the drain on the kerb.

'So, what do we actually think?' Louis is the first to break the silence, and I force myself to stop listening for footsteps behind us.

'I think that fella was probably a one-off, someone crazy who took a chance when he saw it,' Tilda says. 'Although, knowing what we know about what's going to happen to Kitty, I don't think we can write it off just yet.'

'Lily?' Louis looks to me when I don't respond.

'I think we do need to take it seriously,' I say, fear lurching in my belly. 'I think it might be related to Kitty's disappearance, and that we need to keep our eyes open all the time.'

Tilda frowns. 'What are you not telling us? I know there's something. You get this... *tone* to your voice when you're hiding something, so whatever it is just spit it out.'

Knowing Louis is going to be pissed at me for not telling him when it happened, I take a deep breath. 'I think someone probably is following Kitty, because I think they might have followed me too.'

'What?' Tilda's voice is a vixen-like screech.

Louis stops, grabbing me by the elbow. 'Lily, when did this happen?'

'And were you ever going to tell us?'

'I'm telling you now,' I say, my cheeks burning. 'When I walked back to the Chateau after we had dinner, I thought I could hear footsteps behind me. I didn't see anyone, but I'm pretty sure someone was following me.'

'Jeez, Lil. I said I'd walk you back.' Louis snakes his fingers through mine. 'You didn't see anyone at all, no one passed by?'

I pause. There was one person, besides the valet. 'The only person I saw was Camilla Rey.'

'Camilla?' Tilda frowns. 'Why would Camilla follow you?'

'Exactly. That doesn't make any sense, but she's the only person I saw. No one passed by the end of the driveway, and the only person I saw in the lobby who could have come in through the back is Camilla.' I pause. 'She seemed flustered... almost out of breath. As if she'd been hurrying.' *Or maybe it was sheer adrenaline at shadowing me all the way back to the hotel.*

'So do we think Kitty really is in danger?' Tilda asks. 'Or is she just paranoid? She said herself she's had odd fan letters before.'

I explain to Tilda and Louis what Kitty revealed to me, that the man told her she was next, biting my lip as horror spreads across their faces.

'Next for what?' Louis asks. 'Gosh, Lil. Maybe it isn't a good idea for us—'

'No!' Tilda snaps. 'If Kitty is going to disappear, we need to help her. The thing that worries me…' – she looks me over critically – 'is did the person who was following Lily think he was following Kitty? From the back you two are very similar. I mean, your legs are a little chunkier, Lil—'

'Gee, thanks, Tilda.'

'No, I don't mean it like that, but you have to admit, from behind you're the same height, and with your hair in a bun like that, you could easily be mistaken for Kitty in the dark, if someone was expecting to see her popping out to Schwab's. Don't you think?'

Before I can answer, a hand lands on my shoulder from behind and I can't stop the ear-splitting shriek that erupts from my throat.

'Sorry! Oh God, I'm sorry.' Jeremy Knox stands behind me, one hand pressed against his chest.

Bending double, I wheeze, trying to catch my breath as Louis rounds on Jeremy, a fury I've never seen before darkening his features. 'What the hell are you doing? You scared Lily half to death!'

'I'm so, so sorry,' Jeremy says again in that rich chocolate-brown voice of his. 'I never meant to frighten you, Lily, I just didn't think.'

Straightening up, I stare at him, not sure if I fully believe him. 'You thought coming at me from behind was the best way to approach me? Jesus. You're lucky I didn't have a Taser.'

'A…?' Jeremy looks confused, and Tilda shrugs when he catches her eye.

'She says things like this sometimes,' Tilda says. 'Just go with it. But first, explain why you jumped out at us like that.'

Jeremy runs his hands through his thick blond hair, a tiny muscle twitching beneath his eye. 'Kitty. Is she all right? I wanted to go to her suite but I knew Art would be there and he wouldn't let me see her. I saw you leave, and I was waiting for the right moment...'

'She's fine,' Louis says curtly. 'Like you said, Art is with her. She doesn't need you hanging around.'

'I was looking out for her,' Jeremy says sharply. 'Lord only knows what would have happened to her if I wasn't on the carpet tonight.'

I step forward, raising one hand. 'Jeremy, I think what Louis means is that Kitty is safe with Art tonight, so you should probably just go on back to wherever you're staying. We all have to be on set early tomorrow, so maybe you should get some sleep.'

Jeremy looks as though he wants to say more, but he catches Louis's eye and finally gives a slow nod. 'OK. I'll be keeping an eye on Kitty though. None of you can stop me from looking out for her.'

Tilda waits until Jeremy has turned on his heel and is walking back towards Chateau Marmont before she speaks. 'Ugh,' she says. 'Is it me or is there something creepy about him? He really has a thing for Kitty.'

'They used to date,' I say, and proceed to tell Louis and Tilda how Jeremy has seemed to follow Kitty from job to job, studio to studio, always finding a way to be involved somehow with whatever movie she's working on.

'We should definitely keep an eye on him,' Louis says, gesturing for Tilda to add his name into her notebook.

Tilda, however, is looking thoughtful, one hand stroking her chin.

'That kind of explains one thing,' she says, after a moment's pause. 'Did you see Jeremy's date for the premiere this evening? She looked exactly like Kitty.'

Chapter Eight

'Morning, Miss Lily.' Bobby grins at me from his post at the gate as I arrive, his jaw working on a wad of gum.

'Morning, Bobby.' I pause as I scrawl my name in the log. 'I'm sure you're aware but Miss Fox had a… well, a bit of an incident last night.'

'I don't think there's anybody in the state of California who isn't aware that Miss Fox had an incident last night,' Bobby says, reaching under the counter and pulling out this morning's copy of the *Los Angeles Times*. Kitty's face stares back at me, pouting and glamorous in a studio headshot, and then a smaller picture below shows Jeremy shoving the unknown assailant to the floor. Scanning the article I see it hails Jeremy as a hero for coming to Kitty's rescue, and my heart sinks.

'Maybe don't show this to anyone else,' I say, handing the newspaper back. While Oskar might be thrilled with the publicity, I'm not sure how Leonard will react, and I know Art won't be happy with Jeremy being named hero of the hour. 'Can you be super vigilant today? Make sure no one tries to come in who shouldn't be here? Let me know if there's anything unusual. I don't want anyone near Kitty who I haven't approved.'

'Why, of course, Miss Lily.' Bobby grins, showing stained teeth, and a gust of cinnamon-scented breath wafts from his mouth. 'You know, Miss Fox is my favourite actress – after Miss Rey, that is. I'm still waiting for that signed photo, by the way.' He gestures to the wall of the booth behind him, where signed photos of Ingrid Bergman, Claudette Colbert and our own Camilla Rey grin back at me, each of them slightly grubby as if they've been manhandled more than once. Camilla's even has a greasy red lipstick print on it. *Ew.*

The chaos that greets me as I arrive on set isn't entirely unexpected, but my heart rate still triples as a sharp wail cuts the air.

'What is it?' I say, grabbing Bunny as she hurries past me. 'What's happened? Please don't tell me there's been another breach of Kitty's security?' My mind races with visions of the faceless assailant from the previous evening waiting for Kitty in her trailer, hidden in the shadows and ready to pounce. Something unsettling turns like a worm in my stomach, as I remember what Tilda said last night about Jeremy's date looking just like Kitty.

'No, no,' Bunny replies, hastily. 'Nothing like that.' She glances over to the other side of the set, where Leonard is trying to placate a red-faced Kitty. 'Maybe you could go and speak to Kitty, calm her down a little? We're already losing time.'

Dodging over the actors' marks on the set floor, and flashing a grin at my favourite camera operator as he slides out of my way, I approach Kitty and Leonard.

'...isn't the time,' Leonard is saying, his hands on Kitty's shoulders. 'We can't afford to—' He stops as he sees me. 'Lily, glad you're here.'

'Is everything OK?'

'No,' Kitty says sharply, her cheeks stained with tears. 'Absolutely nothing is OK.'

Leonard sighs, pushing his hands through his hair. 'Talk some sense into her, would ya, Lily? I don't have time for this. If we lose any more shooting time the studio is going to have my guts. These two scenes need to be shot today and no one leaves until we're done.' He glares at me. 'Let's hope Oskar is too busy reading the newspapers to notice we're running behind schedule.'

Oh, yikes. I should have known Leonard would have seen the papers already. I nod briskly, even though I'm not sure whether this is about the article or something more serious, and wait until Leonard has marched over to Bunny before I turn back to Kitty. 'Is this about what happened last night? I know you're shaken up, but Leonard is right. He really needs to get today's scenes in the can before the light goes... but I can talk to him if you need to take some time.'

Kitty stares at me incredulously. 'Last night? No, it's not about last night, it's about this morning.' She jabs a finger at her face. 'This is the problem, Lily.'

'Your... *face*? Your face is the problem? Sorry, Kitty, I'm not following. You look fine.'

Kitty snorts. 'I do *not* look fine, Lily. Take another look.'

I peer in closer, running my eyes over her perfectly made-up face, but I can't see anything wrong. I shake my head.

'Look at my eyeliner!' Kitty wails. 'It's not right! And the powder on my cheeks... I look... *dry*.' She sniffs, her eyes welling up. 'I got to my trailer this morning and my make-up artist wasn't there. You know I only like Veronica to do my face. It was some other girl who is utterly *useless* and I know that... that *bitch* is behind it.'

'Bitch?' I know she can only mean one person. One woman who hasn't shown up on set yet. 'You think Camilla did this?'

'I know she did.' Kitty slams her hand down on the table that holds her script. 'I asked that new girl where Veronica was, and she told me outright, "She's with Miss Rey". Apparently Veronica said I left her a note saying I didn't want to use her anymore, when I did no such thing! Camilla *poached* her from me, Lily, knowing that I would have to come to set looking like this.'

Kitty really doesn't look any different than usual, but I don't say that. 'Maybe there was a misunderstanding? Maybe Camilla didn't realise that Veronica was supposed—'

'Oh, please. Of course Camilla knew what she was doing. Everyone knows that Veronica does my face. It's utter disrespect, that's what it is. That woman has no manners. She does these things to spite me.' Kitty presses her hand to her mouth, a black smudge of marker pen marring her pinky finger.

'We can get this all smoothed out,' I say, gently. 'I'll have Bunny get Veronica to your trailer when we break, and I'll have a word with Camilla about it, just as soon as she shows up.'

'Oh, you mean she's not on set yet?' I think I see the hint of a smirk on Kitty's face but it's fleeting. 'Leonard really will be furious. Like you said, we're already late to start shooting.' She shakes her hair away from her face, and flicks her fingers in the direction of a waiting make-up artist, seemingly not bothered now that it's not Veronica. 'You. See if you can't make me look less dry. Then let's get to work.'

Moments later Kitty is on her mark, but there is still no sign of Camilla and I feel a flicker of concern run through me. Leonard is pacing, his temper rising, and I know it's only a matter of time before he explodes. My eyes go to the closed door of the set, imagining Camilla's trailer beyond, and I wonder if I should perhaps knock, see if she's OK, when the door opens and Camilla spills onto the set, hurrying the best she can in her ridiculously high heels and tapered pencil skirt. I can't help noticing that her make-up is immaculate.

'Leonard, I'm ready when you are,' she trills, finding her mark on the floor, with no hint of an apology.

'Nice of you to join us. We've all been ready for hours,' Kitty lies, the words dripping with a lemon-sharp acidity.

Camilla shoots her a look full of white-hot fury. 'I would have been on set on time, only *someone* had been in my trailer. My script was missing, and when I eventually found it, *someone* had blacked out my lines in marker pen. I had to find another copy.'

Wincing internally, I think about the black smudge of pen on Kitty's pinky finger. I think it's going to be a very long day.

–

Crack. The slap that lands on Camilla's cheek resounds through the quiet set, the only other noise the involuntary gasp that slips between Bunny's lips.

'Oh my,' she whispers, as Leonard calls cut.

'Fantastic work, ladies,' he says. 'One scene down, one to go. Let's take a break and be back in fifteen minutes.'

Camilla presses a hand to her cheek, Kitty's fingerprints etched in vivid scarlet onto her white skin. 'You weren't supposed to make contact,' she hisses at Kitty.

'Oh, honestly, Camilla,' Kitty says with a smile, 'I had to do what was best for the picture. It's not my fault you simply can't react properly when I *don't* make contact. I had no choice, and anyway, Leonard was pleased with it.'

'Perhaps if you knew how to *act out* slapping someone, you wouldn't have to actually do it,' Camilla retorts, her other cheek flushing to match the slapped one.

'Kitty, here. Take one of these.' I step in with a tray of muffins Bunny fetched earlier, hoping to defuse the situation. 'None of us are at our best when we're hungry. Maybe we'll all feel a little better once we've had a snack.'

Leonard pauses as he stalks past, doubling back as he sees the muffins in my hand. 'Lily, what are those?'

'Um, muffins?'

'Are you kidding me?' Leonard snatches the tray out of my hands and throws it down. 'What am I supposed to tell Oskar when the wardrobe department has to let out all of their clothes?' He gestures to Kitty and Camilla, and I am horrified to find tears pricking my eyes.

'It's one muffin... I don't think...'

'No, you don't think,' Leonard snaps, the stress of the morning etched all over his face. 'Salad. Grilled chicken. That's it until we wrap, you hear?'

I nod meekly, my cheeks burning as I stare at the ground until Leonard has stormed off completely. 'I'm sorry,' I say to the actresses. 'I didn't think one muffin would be a problem. Let me get you something else.'

'I don't want anything,' Kitty says, even as her stomach growls in protest. 'Although...' She gives Camilla a sideways glance. 'Get Bunny to fetch me a Pepsi from the machine. And bring Veronica over to freshen me up.'

'Of course.' I hurry out towards the catering truck where Bunny is picking up coffee, leaving Kitty and

Camilla glaring at each other, my eyes still smarting from Leonard's harsh dressing-down.

Bunny is hovering outside the catering truck, a sheaf of studio-headed papers clutched tightly in her fist. Her face lights up as I approach.

'Lily! Oh, Lily, it's so exciting!' She reaches out and squeezes my arm with one hand.

I'm not sure I can take any more excitement today, but even so I force a smile and take the clipped papers she holds out to me. 'What is it?'

'Look!' She flips to the second page. 'You probably already know all about this, seeing as the studio have been told, but Oscar nominations are out! And we're cleaning up!'

I haven't been told anything – and I'm not even sure if Leonard has been made aware, given that we've been working on a closed set all morning. 'Really?' Sparks of excitement fizz through my veins. Of course this is exciting – actors, producers, directors, hell, the *studios* wait all year for the Academy Award nominations to come out. Following Bunny's finger, I run my eyes over the nominations.

Best Actress – Camilla Rey, Vivien Leigh,
Gloria Swanson, Kitty Fox

Best Actor – Art Calloway, William Holden,
Spencer Tracy, Jeremy Knox

Blimey. I'm not sure if this is a good or a bad thing.

By the time I get back on set with a Pepsi for Kitty, word has already got out about the Oscar nominations.

Camilla speaks loudly as she has her hair re-pinned, tendrils of auburn floating around her face after her tussle with Kitty in the last scene. 'Best Actress!' she cries. 'I mean, I knew it was going to happen, everyone raved about my performance in *Shotgun Charley*. Lily,' she calls out to me, 'you'll help me find a dress for the big night, won't you?'

Beside me, all ready to shoot her next scene, Kitty rolls her eyes. 'She's already agreed to help me,' she says briskly. 'You'll have to find your own assistant, Camilla. It's bad enough that you stole my make-up artist.'

Oh, man. Kitty absolutely *hasn't* asked me to help her yet, but I can hardly say that now. Camilla narrows her eyes and I suppress a sigh. I'm not doing a very good job at keeping Kitty in check so far – and there's no way I'm going to be able to stop her from disappearing if she keeps this up, because Camilla will be first on the list to bump her off.

'I'm sure we can figure something out.' I try to placate the feuding pair. I don't say that actually, I work for Leonard, rather than either of them. I could really do with Tilda and her negotiating skills on this movie set.

Leonard calls for everyone to take their places for the next scene and immediately the smile drops from Kitty's face. Before I can ask her what the problem is, she steps forward to hit her mark and straightens her shoulders. Jeremy steps out of the shadows from the edge of the set, taking his place beside her, and as I rifle through the pages of the script I see what has Kitty's smile disappearing. It's a love scene. With Jeremy. *Oh, boy*.

Bunny and I stand together as Kitty and Jeremy begin to film. It's a scene in which Jeremy confesses his undying love for Kitty, the wife of his best friend. All the time Kitty's husband has been cheating on her with Camilla, Jeremy has been waiting in the wings, ready to scoop her into his arms and into another, better life. Shifting on my feet, I force myself to watch, even though it all feels a little too close to home. Thank goodness we're not filming the scene in which Art shoots Jeremy with the prop gun today.

'This is *electric*,' Bunny whispers in my ear as she fans herself, and she's right. The way Jeremy looks at Kitty, brushing her hair tenderly away from her face, is enough to make any girl's knicker elastic twang. But then I remember that Jeremy is a creep… although that doesn't stop me from wishing that Louis wasn't such a gentleman.

The atmosphere on set is crackling with sexual tension, and it's not just Bunny who wipes away a bead of sweat as Jeremy leans in to kiss Kitty. The chemistry between the two of them is incredible, and Leonard claps as he calls to wrap the scene. There's no doubt about it – as handsome and charming as Art is, Jeremy is a far superior actor and he and Kitty together are dynamite.

'Amazing,' Leonard yells as applause erupts all over the set. 'This is exactly what I'm looking for – see the way he gazes at her, like she's everything? That's what I want from you.' He jabs a finger at Art.

'Maybe it's easier for Jeremy because he doesn't have to act,' Camilla says, loud enough to be overheard by Art.

Leonard goes on, 'If I can get this from you, Art, then this movie is going to be a box office smash hit. But you need to up your game, be more like Jeremy. Feel it, with your heart and soul.' He claps his hands together. 'Well done, everybody. Party in the Chateau gardens tonight to celebrate the Oscar nominations.'

Art raises his chin, his jaw twitching as if biting back something he knows he shouldn't say, waiting until Leonard has reached the door out on to the lot before he approaches Kitty. 'What was all that?'

Kitty frowns, her fists clenching by her sides. 'What do you mean, *what was all that*? I was just doing my job, Art.'

'Hey.' Jeremy taps Art on the shoulder. 'It was nothing, just a scene. Don't forget Kitty and I have been acting together for years. Everyone knows she's your girl.'

'Yeah, they do,' Art snaps. 'That's not what I meant. Kitty, I'm a better actor than this guy. It should be me and you getting the high praise from Leonard, not this...' He waves a hand in Jeremy's direction, his mouth twisting like he just bit into an unripe lime.

'Yikes,' Bunny whispers in my ear. 'I wouldn't be surprised if these two come to blows over Kitty – I mean, it's not impossible. If I were a man I'd fight for her.'

'If you were a man, you'd be manufacturing tractors in Buttcrack, Alabama,' Camilla retorts. 'We all know you got the job because you're pretty and your daddy went to college with Leonard.'

Bunny blinks, her eyes filling, and I squeeze her hand. 'You're great at your job, Bunny.' I turn a harsh gaze on Camilla. 'And *that* was uncalled for.'

'Oh, cry me a river.' Camilla turns her attention back to Kitty, Art and Jeremy, who are still in the centre of the set. Jeremy throws his hands up and stalks away, and to my relief Camilla scurries after him.

I send Bunny out to fetch me a cup of tea, and make a show of collecting up the scripts from today's shoot, skirting the edge of the set where Art and Kitty are still talking.

'Do you prefer working with him, is that what it is?' Art's voice rings out, and I pause, script pages in hand as Bunny steps back onto the set, her eyes wide. 'We're a dream team, Kitty. We're up for Oscars! Best Actor and Actress! We have everything at our feet, and Leonard is pulling me up on my performance?' He lets out a huff of disgust.

'Art, it was just one scene. You know how temperamental Leonard is,' Kitty soothes, but her voice catches, thick with a hint of tears. 'Like Jeremy said, we've known each other a long time, we know how to get the best out of each other. You know I much prefer my scenes with you.'

'It's just frustrating,' Art says, his hand running through his hair. 'Of all the people to be compared to, Jeremy is…'

'Hey, Art,' I interrupt. 'You were great today. Leonard just gets enthusiastic when he does a take in one go, you know?' Kitty takes this opportunity to skirt past Art and head to her trailer, and I keep my eyes on him, giving her time to leave. 'But you're brilliant – an Oscar nomination! Only a handful of people get to say that every year.'

Art pauses, the sour look dropping from his face as his shoulders straighten. 'Absolutely right, Lily. I'm sorry for getting all het up there. I know it's not Kitty's fault. I just want to be the *best*, understand?'

'Of course, isn't that what all of us want? To do the best we can? Say, why don't you let Bunny escort you out to your car and I'll check on Kitty before she leaves.' I pause, pretending to think. 'You know, following the announcement of the Oscar nominations I reckon there'll be a big old crowd waiting for you to sign autographs out there this evening.'

Art nods, his eyes lighting up at the prospect of his adoring fans waiting at the gate for him, and Bunny walks him out to the parking lot, as I make my way to Kitty's trailer. The door is closed, and I am about to walk up and knock when the door opens, and Doctor Astor steps out.

He tips his hat at Kitty as she appears in the doorway, and I recognise the gleam in her eye.

'Kitty, are you OK?' I follow her into the trailer, as she sighs and sinks into a chair, her pupils slightly dilated.

'Just peachy,' she says, reaching for her cigarettes. She pauses as she lights one, blowing a plume of blue-grey smoke into the air. 'You ever wonder if it's all worth it, Lily?'

'What?'

'This.' She wafts a hand. 'You always wanted to work in the movies?'

'Ever since I was a little girl.'

Kitty gives a wry smile. 'Just like all the others. I guess we're the lucky ones, huh? Even when we don't always feel that way.' I want to ask what she means, but she draws deeply on her cigarette and carries on. 'Ignore me,' she says with a huff of laughter. 'It's been one of those days.'

'Can I get you anything before I leave?'

'What? Like a muffin?' Kitty shakes her head and I slink out of the trailer, feeling the sting of her words at my back as I wonder just what exactly she was trying to say.

At the rear of the lot, Camilla leans into the security booth, flicking her hair back and smiling as Bobby grins and blushes, presumably feeling as though all his Christmases have come at once, while Art stands on the inside of the gates, smiling and chatting as people – mostly young girls – thrust autograph books through the gaps at him, swooning and clutching them to their chests as he returns them. I stifle a smile, glad to see Art in his element again – he's usually so upbeat, it felt odd to see his confidence slip

– and slide out onto the street, weaving my way through the throng to the pavement.

The sun is warm overhead despite the fact that evening will soon start to draw in, and I let out a long sigh, my feet aching despite my comfy Converse sneakers. My blouse sticks to me, and while I'm all about the 1950s fashions, my full skirt complete with petticoat – purchased on Tilda's say-so – wouldn't be my choice if I were back in my own time. A pair of those casual shorts from Hollister, maybe, the soft cotton ones that are perfect for the beach. Or a worn pair of Levi's, washed down to the right shade of blue. It's odd, the things you miss when you're out of place and time. Maybe I'll see if I can find a pair of the figure-hugging, high-waisted jeans that Marilyn Monroe is going to wear in *Clash by Night* in 1952. If they're good enough for Marilyn, they're good enough for me. I'm so deep in my own thoughts, I don't hear my name at first.

'Hey! Lily!' Tilda's voice cuts into my thoughts and I turn to see her running towards me, her red ponytail flying. 'Did you go deaf, or are you just ignoring me?'

'Sorry.' I grin, pleased to see her. 'I was thinking about beach shorts from Hollister.'

'Whatever.' Tilda holds out a newspaper. 'I've been waiting for you to get done on set for what feels like hours. There's something in here that I think you're going to want to see.'

Chapter Nine

'If it's about the Oscar nominations, Bunny is way ahead of you. And I've already seen Jeremy's heroics plastered all over the *LA Times* this morning.'

'It's not about either of those.' Tilda pushes the paper into my hands and jabs at the headline on page five. 'See?'

FOX ABOUT TO LEAVE HER STUDIO? Actress's job in jeopardy due to her difficult behaviour, is the headline that jumps out at me. Quickly I scan the article, my heart rising in my chest until it's halfway up my throat. 'Who wrote this?'

Tilda shrugs. 'Someone I've never heard of, and when I asked Louella, she didn't know them either.'

The article is scathing about Kitty, calling her unprofessional and difficult to work with, saying she regularly needs prompting for her lines and rarely – if ever – turns up on set on time. It insinuates that Kitty regularly has to be pulled up on her performance and that the head of the studio has already been in talks with the production company about having her replaced. Leonard is going to be utterly furious when he sees this, and I don't dare think about how Oskar might react. While he might have classed Kitty's assault as 'good' publicity, the news that progress on this movie might be stuttering due to Kitty's behaviour will surely incense him.

'This is utter nonsense,' I say, my blood rising. 'In fact, this couldn't be more inaccurate if it tried – just this afternoon Leonard was singing her praises after her scene with Jeremy...' Narrowing my eyes, I pause before turning back to the article and rereading it. 'None of this sounds like Kitty. It sounds more like Camilla than Kitty.'

'Camilla?'

'Yes. She's never on time for set and she isn't the greatest at learning her lines – we were held up this morning because she couldn't find a clean script. Hers had been vandalised.' I peek over my shoulder to check no one is within earshot. 'I think Kitty might have been the one to vandalise it, to be honest.'

'Oh yikes,' Tilda sighs. 'So there isn't any truth to Kitty's job being on the line? I did wonder if that might have some relevance to... you know... the *disappearance*.' She hisses the last word.

'Not that I know of. Leonard was thrilled with her work today.' A thought strikes me. 'Camilla wasn't though. She was absolutely vile to Bunny, and it seems as though she was taking her annoyance at Kitty out on poor Bunny instead. I know this can't be about anything that happened on set today, but do you think Camilla could be behind this article?'

Tilda raises her eyebrows so high they almost disappear under her bangs. 'You think? I mean, it's possible. She might have a contact at the paper and if they knew she was the source they would definitely run it.'

We're almost at Googie's, the diner on Sunset, and as we approach I nod in the direction of the entrance.

'Heck, yes.' Tilda moves past me, shoving the door open, and we slide into a booth and order milkshakes. Both of us try and fail not to stare at Montgomery Clift as he pays his bill at the counter, and I feel unbearably sad as he tips me a wink on his way. I know that there are only another five or so years until Elizabeth Taylor will save his life after his car comes off the road on the way home from a dinner party, leaving him with terrible injuries.

Once the waitress has served up a chocolate malt for me and a Coke float for Tilda, we turn back to the newspaper.

'It makes sense if this has come from inside the studio,' I say, ink staining my fingers. 'All of it is true, but it relates more to Camilla than Kitty. What if Camilla is trying to ruin Kitty's career? We know neither of them gets along.'

'It wouldn't surprise me,' Tilda says. She pauses, thinking. 'What if Camilla is trying to destroy Kitty, and when it doesn't work, she goes a step further and gets rid of Kitty herself? She could be behind the disappearance.'

The thought makes me go cold. Could she be that underhand? Does she really hate Kitty that much?

'There's something else,' Tilda says, flicking over the page to a smaller article buried between adverts for laundry detergent and cigarettes. 'They found another body.'

'Another one?' Fear prickles along my spine. 'Where?'

'One of the streets off Sunset, down an alley.' Tilda's face is set, her lipsticked mouth pressed into a thin line. 'She was found in the very early hours of the morning, and one of the newspapermen who covered the premiere must have still been around for it to already be in the paper this morning.'

I pull the paper round so I can read the article properly. There is barely any information, just a brief description of the girl – five foot four, slim with blonde hair – naming her as Doris Gray. The article says the police believe she was strangled, and a red silk scarf was found in her hand.

A grainy photograph accompanies the wording and I peer at it closely. She looks strangely familiar, but I can't place her.

'This is awful, Tilda. Why isn't this front-page news?'

Tilda shrugs. 'No one is interested. These girls aren't anybody important. I just wanted to make you aware, because you often walk home along Sunset, and I really don't think you should be walking alone. Maybe this is unrelated to the other body they found, but two in a week feels...' She trails off, her face pale. 'Just keep Louis around to walk you home. Don't be gallivanting around after dark.'

'I won't,' I swear, my eyes going back to the poor-quality photograph. 'Speaking of being out after dark, I have to meet Louis at the Chateau – he's my date tonight.'

'Leonard's nominations party? Louella already got an invite.' Tilda gives me a grimace. 'Well, I guess I should scoot too, seeing as I'm your friendly neighbourhood reporter. Although Louella doesn't trust me to cover it on my own, I'm only tagging along with the photographer.'

Pushing the newspaper to one side, we slide out of the booth and hurry back to the apartment to change for Leonard's party. I can only hope that no one else has seen the article about Kitty's alleged behaviour yet.

—

Tilda cranks up the wireless as we jostle for position in the tiny bathroom of our apartment, getting ready for Leonard's Oscar nominations party. Despite the article about Kitty, and the shocking news about another body being found, I can't help the fizz of excitement that sparks in my belly. Back in my own time I missed out on parties and nights out as my mum was so poorly, and most of my time was spent looking after her. Then, when she died and left me the money to move out to Hollywood, I had to work two jobs just to pay my bills and there was never really a lot of time for girlfriends.

'Lil? A little help?' Tilda gestures to the rollers tangled in her hair as she finishes brushing her lashes with mascara.

I reach over, dodging the pairs of pantyhose drying over the side of the bath and the spilled make-up that lines the shelf above the sink. 'Jeez, Til, you're going to need a heap of hairspray.' I remove the rollers and she turns to let me brush her new curls smooth, blasting them with Revlon Satin-Set until we both cough. 'There. Perfect.'

Tilda preens in the mirror, as Hank Williams croons about his 'Lovesick Blues', and I search for my favourite lipstick, only realising that Tilda is wearing it after I upend powder compacts, a tub of rouge and the rest of Tilda's rollers into the sink.

'Tilda.'

'What?' She is a wide-eyed picture of innocence.

'My lipstick. I know you've sneaked it into your purse.' I grin, holding out one hand.

'I can't help it if it suits me best.' Tilda winks as I quickly run it over my mouth and start to clear the mess I've made in the bathroom. 'Oh, Lil, leave that. We're going to be late!'

With one last look at the mess of cosmetics in the sink and Tilda's skirt and sweater on the floor beside the laundry basket, the scent of Dior's Diorama in the air, I snatch up my purse and hurry out of the apartment after her. Sharing a place with Tilda might be chaotic, but there are some things about living in 1951 that I would never change. Let's just hope tonight's party doesn't go off with too much of a bang.

—

The garden at Chateau Marmont glitters with fairy lights and the low hum of conversation when I arrive on Louis's arm, Tilda following behind us. Louis has scrubbed up very nicely in a suit that I swear I've seen on Clark Gable before, while Tilda and I both wear sleeveless cocktail dresses, nipped at the waist and full in the skirt. Mine is black, to complement Louis's suit, and Tilda's is a delicious shade of teal which sets off her red hair perfectly.

'Lily! And Louis, of course.' Jean is on hand, welcoming Leonard's guests with an air kiss in the general vicinity of their cheeks, her voice rising over the sound of the string quartet playing vaguely recognisable classical music on the edge of the gardens. 'Lovely of you to come.'

'We wouldn't miss it, Jean,' Louis says warmly, making her blush. 'You remember my sister, Tilda?'

'Of course.' Jean casts her eye over Tilda, lingering on her purse and no doubt the pencil that is sure to be inside. 'Nothing too salacious in the column tomorrow, please.' With that, she moves on as Tilda fails to hide her grin.

'Same old Jean,' she says, with a laugh, before moving into the crowd already intent on mining as much information and gossip as she can this evening.

Leonard catches my eye and crooks a finger in my direction. 'One second,' I whisper to Louis, and walk over to the edge of the garden on leaden feet to where Leonard stands.

'Lily.' His voice is stern and my stomach does a full somersault. 'You know what I'm going to ask you about.'

'The newspapers?' My voice comes out meeker than I would have liked and I lift my chin, meeting Leonard's gaze head on.

'The *LA Times* I can live with,' Leonard says with a sigh, 'and of course Oskar was thrilled with the article, but the one in that rag, the *Hollywood Post*.' He leans in, lowering his voice. 'Do you understand how much damage that article could do? If film fans find the main star of the picture unlikeable, do you honestly think they'll come to watch her in a movie?'

'No... I—'

'I *told* you to keep Kitty in line!' Leonard's voice rises, and I see one or two guests glance our way. 'Get her to set on time, make sure you smooth out the issues she has with Camilla, and promise me that nothing like this is printed again.' He presses his lips together tightly. 'This must have come from someone on set...' He pauses, his eyes roaming the garden before they fix on Tilda. 'Or someone close to the crew.'

Does he suspect me? I am surprised by how much this idea hurts. 'Leonard, with all due respect the behaviours described in the article sound more like Camilla than Kitty. I wondered...'

'What?'

'I wondered if perhaps Camilla was behind the article. She's really not a fan of Kitty and it would benefit her...'

'Lily.' Leonard fixes his eyes on me now. 'I couldn't give a flying fig who it came from, but I am telling you now this can't happen again. *Don't let this ruin my picture.*'

'Yes, sir,' I say quietly, as Leonard raises a hand to Billy Wilder and moves off leaving me slightly breathless and battling tears. I have no idea how Leonard thinks I am going to be able to stop leaks from the set... cut every telephone cord? Ground Kitty and Camilla, confining them to their trailers? Threaten the rest of the crew? I give myself ten seconds – long enough to blink back the tears and pull in a deep breath before I fix a smile on my face and head back to Louis.

Although it is still early the garden is already full of guests, holding saucers of fizzing champagne but definitely not holding their tongues. The air is alive with conversation, and I scan the crowd looking for Kitty. William Holden is leaning in, whispering in Vivien Leigh's ear, her mouth curving up in a cat-like grin. Over by a station holding oysters, which waiters are serving up with a sprinkle of vinegar and shallots, is Gloria Swanson, looking devastating in a red gown, and I have to stifle the sensation of being star-struck. *Sunset Boulevard* was one of my mum's favourite movies, and before she died we must have watched it a thousand times.

I catch sight of Doctor Astor, smart in a navy suit, the boater on his head now sporting a matching navy band, and spy Bunny, hovering by a waiter holding more champagne, her eyes flicking towards Spencer Tracy and Katharine Hepburn as Jean greets them at the garden entrance.

'If you go over I'm sure they'll say hi,' I say, as Bunny jumps at the sound of my voice.

'Oh! Lily, it's just you. Isn't he divine? For an older man, I mean. I wonder what it would be like to be married to him?' Bunny glances at Spencer Tracy again.

'I'm not sure who you'd ask,' I say dryly. 'He hasn't lived with Louise for years, and he and Katharine will never… *have* never married. And anyway, Bunny, he's old enough to be your father.'

'He's a friend of my father, actually,' she says dreamily.

'Have you seen Kitty?'

Bunny refocuses her gaze on my face, smoothing her blonde curls away from her forehead. She's wearing a lilac dress, with puffy sleeves and a belt, that is more suited to a woman ten years older than her.

'She's over there.' Bunny gestures to where Leonard is talking to a small group, Doctor Astor hovering on the fringes. 'She and Art arrived separately – Art didn't get here until about thirty minutes after Kitty. To be honest, I think they might have had an argument. They've barely spoken to each other.'

'Oh.' I turn to Louis. 'Do you think you could fetch me a drink? I want to go and check in on Kitty, and I'm not sure she'll be very chatty with you around.'

'Sure.' Louis brushes his lips against my forehead before turning towards the bar.

Leaving Bunny to gaze at Spencer Tracy from afar, I make my way over to Kitty. Her eyes are a little too bright as she smiles and nods, constantly scanning the garden, the smile on her face a little too wobbly to be real.

'Kitty. Are you OK?' What I mean is, *Have you taken something?* But I could never ask that question out loud.

'Yes. Fine.' Kitty sounds fine, but her fingers knot together, and I watch as her eyes go to Art, standing on the other side of the garden, a little too close to Camilla. Camilla's head is thrown back as she laughs, her hand reaching out to tug at the sleeve of Art's jacket. 'Absolutely fine. Never better. I'm at a party, Lily, why wouldn't I be OK?'

'Really?' I look pointedly in Art and Camilla's direction, just as Camilla looks up at Art from beneath her lashes in the most nauseatingly flirtatious way. *Ugh.*

'Yes, really,' Kitty insists, her wired smile glued to her face. 'There's plenty of champagne, and I have an Oscar nomination! Everything is just peachy. Oh for… This is the last thing I need.'

I turn to see Jeremy bearing down on us in a cloud of Acqua di Parma cologne, his hair slicked away from his face.

'Lily.' Jeremy gives me the briefest of nods before turning to Kitty. 'Kitty, you look exquisite this evening.' Kitty does look gorgeous in a fitted silver gown, the silk fabric draping elegantly over her body as if she was born to wear it, but even so, Jeremy comes off as over-complimentary, almost to the point of being slimy. 'I wondered if you'd like to dance?'

'Oh, Jeremy, this is hardly music to dance to,' Kitty says, her voice weary as she casts another brief glance in Art's direction. 'It's background music, not a ball.'

'Don't be like that,' Jeremy says, concern crossing his brow. 'The Kitty I've always known loves to dance. Come on, it'll cheer you up after your row with Art.'

'My row…?' Kitty gives Jeremy a sharp look. 'How did you know I had a row with Art?'

Jeremy can't contain the flush that creeps up his neck as he looks away, to where Camilla is still flirting her socks off with Art. 'I didn't *know*, I just… assumed. You looked so sad, and I thought there can only be one thing making Kitty feel unhappy on the night she's been nominated for an Academy Award.'

Immediately something twinges low in my gut and I frown. Kitty hardly looks sad – if anything, she's been overly cheerful while I've been talking to her. So why would he think she is unhappy?

'Everything is fine.' Kitty gives Jeremy one last look before turning on her heel and disappearing into the crowd, skirting her way past Art and Camilla without stopping.

'Why did you say that about Kitty and Art having an argument?' I demand, once Kitty is out of earshot. 'Have you been speaking to Bunny?'

Jeremy looks confused. 'No. I haven't seen Bunny all evening, what does she have to do with things? I simply wanted to cheer Kitty up, that's all.'

He looks so sad, I almost forget that I am supposed to be suspicious of his potential involvement in Kitty's disappearance, and then I remember him loitering outside the hotel the other night, and the sound of footsteps on the pavement behind me. 'Have you been following Kitty?'

'What?' Jeremy's tone is indignant but something shifty flits across his face.

'I saw you the other night, outside the hotel. And then you were leaving Kitty's room as I arrived back there.' I pause. 'She said she thought someone was following her… was it you?'

'There's nothing wrong with visiting an old friend. I look out for Kitty,' Jeremy says icily. 'Someone has to in this godforsaken town, but to be accused of following her is taking things a little far, don't you think, Lily?' He leans in close, so close I can smell a hint of cinnamon on his breath. 'I'm not quite sure who you think you are, because the last time I checked you were nothing more than a lowly assistant on this movie. And furthermore, might I remind you that you've known Kitty for all of five minutes… I've known her for years. If anyone has the right to be concerned about Kitty Fox, it's me.'

Aware of the fact that we are in a public place, and this probably isn't the best time to challenge him further, I back down, my heart galloping in my chest. 'Just give her some space, perhaps,' I say eventually, a little more shakily than I'd like, before turning on my heel and leaving Jeremy alone.

As I walk through the party, hoping to see Louis and grab that drink before tracking Kitty down, something makes me pause at the oyster station. *Eyes, on me.* It's that insistent prickle that I've felt before, the sensation of being watched. Pausing as if pondering my oyster choices, I whip my head round, only to find Leonard standing behind me.

'Ah, shit,' I say, without thinking. My cheeks start to heat up, and I am half expecting Leonard to bawl me out again, but instead he just laughs.

'Lily, just the gal. I wanted to introduce you to an old friend.' He stands to one side, the woman beside him holding out a hand for me to shake. 'This is Katharine.'

Katharine. Hepburn. For a moment I feel light-headed as I plaster on the most ridiculous grin. 'So, so honoured to meet you,' I can't help gushing. Just when I thought I'd got over feeling star-struck, Leonard puts my hand in *Katharine Hepburn's*.

As Katharine makes small talk about her latest movie, Leonard moves away and calls for speeches, Jean tapping a fork on the side of her glass to get everyone's attention. Leonard smiles as a hush descends, and he begins to speak. It's only as he starts praising the nominees – Art raising a hand in a regal wave and William Holden lifting his glass as Leonard gestures to them – that I realise it's been a really long time since I've seen Kitty. Excusing myself regretfully, I leave Katharine and begin to circle the guests, eyes searching for Kitty's distinctive silver gown.

Tilda stops me as I reach the edge of the garden, her eyes wide. 'Did I just see you shaking hands with Katharine Hepburn a moment ago?'

'Yep. Leonard is the gift that keeps on giving. I may never wash this hand again. Have you seen Kitty anywhere?'

'Not for a while.' Tilda frowns, as Louis notices us from where he stands at the edge of the crowd, before sneaking over to us. 'Have you seen Kitty, Lou?'

'Nope. Sorry.' He shakes his head.

'Shit.' I scan over the crowd, my heart sinking when I realise that not only can I not see Kitty, but I also can't see Jeremy's blond head towering over the crowds either. 'Jeremy's gone too.' Panic beats a frantic tattoo in my chest.

'Let's split up.' Tilda jumps straight into action. 'Lily, you go and check her room – maybe she just went upstairs. Lou, you check out front of the hotel, and I'll check the garden. Meet back here in ten minutes if there's no joy.'

'OK.' Without another thought, I push my way through the crowd, noting that there is also no sign of Camilla. As I reach the makeshift bar before the lobby entrance, I spy Art sinking a Martini in one gulp.

'Art? Have you seen Kitty?'

Art raises his eyes to mine, his lids heavy with booze. 'No. She's not talking to me, but I'm sure she'll be fine by tomorrow. At least, I hope she will. We're shooting a love scene and I have to show Leonard I'm better than Jeremy. There's no reason why I can't – Kitty and I are in love, after all.' He looks lost and lonely, stood there by himself. 'Can I get you a drink?'

'No, thanks.' I hurry inside, up the curved staircase to Kitty's suite, where I knock twice before trying the door. A huge bouquet of roses sits outside, and I almost trip over them as I push my way inside, only to find there is no sign of Kitty.

'Bloody hell, Kitty. Where are you?' I mutter to myself as I pull the door closed behind me, dodge the huge bouquet again, and jump down the stairs two at a time in a fashion that would give Jean a heart attack if she saw.

The lobby is empty, the dim lighting and curved archways giving the area a faintly Gothic air, and I try to squash down the unsettling dread that cloaks my shoulders. Kitty can't have vanished into thin air, not yet. Not before I've had a chance to figure out what the deal is here. The thought of Camilla and Jeremy both missing as well does nothing to stop my breath coming sharp in my throat as I call Kitty's name again. The third time I call, I think I hear something and I pause, my pulse pounding loud enough in my ears to make me think I imagined it.

'Kitty? Are you here?' It comes again, a rattling noise, followed by a knocking. I follow it to a tiny water closet hidden away under the stairs. 'Kitty? It's me, Lily.'

'Lily?' Her voice is muffled by the door, but it is most definitely Kitty in the loo. 'Help me, please. I'm locked in.'

Rattling the door handle, I find Kitty is right, and I thank my lucky stars that one thing I've learnt back in the past is how to pick a lock. Sliding a bobby pin out of my hair, I jiggle it in the lock until it clicks and the door swings open, a tear-stained Kitty tumbling out into my arms.

'Oh my gosh, Kitty, are you OK? What happened? Did the lock break when you locked the door?'

Kitty heaves a great sob, her chest hitching as tears spill over her cheeks. 'I never locked the door, Lily. I just went in there to wash my face and touch up my make-up, and then I couldn't get out. I was stuck there in the pitch-dark for I don't know how long.' Her face is pale, chalky with terror as I peer past her and see the bathroom is indeed in thick, inky darkness.

'You didn't lock the door?' My eyes go first to the lock, and the absence of a key, and then to the wall beside the door, where the light switch sits in the off position.

'No.' Kitty leans against me as she sobs. 'Someone locked me in there and turned out the light. They trapped me and left me in the dark deliberately.'

Chapter Ten

'Here, let me fix you up.' I gently manoeuvre Kitty back towards the tiny bathroom, but she clutches my arm tightly and shakes her head, her eyes squeezed tight shut.

'No! No, Lily, please don't make me go back in there. I can't go back into that pitch-dark room.'

Choosing not to wrestle with a movie star in the lobby of Chateau Marmont, I step back and give her a moment, my mind whirring as I reach out and snap the light on. 'Kitty, are you... afraid of the dark?'

Kitty's eyes are huge, ringed with traces of black mascara, her deep coral lipstick smudged at the corners of her mouth as she looks up at me and nods. 'Terrified. I got locked in a basement as a child and I don't think I'll ever get over it.'

'I promise I won't force you to go back in there, but we have to do something about your face. There'll be all kinds of questions raised if you go back out to the party with mascara streaming down your cheeks.' I hold out a hand. 'Come on. I'll come inside with you and,' I reach into the water closet and pull out the hand towel, 'I'll stuff this between the door and the jamb and then the door won't be able to close on us. There's no one in the lobby now, so if we fix you up real quick we can be back out there before anyone notices anything's wrong.'

Kitty hesitates for just a moment, long enough for laughter from the garden to come floating in through the rear doors, before she nods and we step into the water closet. It's tiny, with just a toilet and a mirror hanging over the porcelain sink. Pulling open a tiny cupboard under the sink, I find a clean washcloth and pass it to Kitty, who begins to wash her face. Thankfully, Kitty had the foresight to put her mascara cake and lipstick in her purse, and within a few moments she's back to looking much more like the Kitty I am used to.

'Lily?' My name filters through the gap between the door and the frame and Kitty pauses, her lipstick halfway to her mouth.

'It's OK,' I say, 'it's my friends. They were helping me look for you.' I peep out into the lobby to see Tilda and Louis. 'Guys, over here.'

'We were wondering what happened when you didn't meet us back in the garden. Did you find Kitty?' Louis runs his eyes over me, checking to see if I am still in one piece, a long, lingering look that makes my stomach flip.

'She's here.' I stand to one side and Kitty offers up a tentative smile. 'She was locked in the bathroom.'

'Yikes,' Tilda says. 'Good job Lily came looking for you, you could have been in there for hours!'

I wince as Kitty's lower lip wobbles, and shoot Tilda a harsh look. 'All's well that ends—'

'Is this a private party, or can anyone join in?' Doctor Astor's booming voice, laced with a jovial tone that doesn't match the expression on his face, fills the lobby.

'Oh, Doctor!' Kitty simpers, tucking her lipstick into her purse. 'We were just… I was just…'

'I was helping Kitty freshen up, that's all. She has to look her best out there!'

'Quite,' the doctor agrees, holding up a large Martini glass. 'Art's had me looking all over for you, Kitty. Here, take this. Leonard's been making a speech and he wants you up on stage to join him. I think he wants you to say a few words.'

'Of course.' With a practised smile, and no hint of the weeping, puddled mess of a woman who'd stood in front of me mere minutes ago, Kitty takes the drink Doctor Astor holds out and he watches carefully as she raises the glass to her mouth, taking a large sip. 'Here, Doctor, won't you escort me back out to the garden?'

It's like a lightbulb has been switched on as Kitty sweeps out of the lobby on Doctor Astor's arm, smiling graciously and nodding to the folks who mill about by the garden entrance. No one would ever know that ten minutes ago Kitty was a shaking, snivelling state.

'She really deserves that Oscar nomination,' I say as we follow them into the garden, watching as Kitty takes the stage beside Leonard with a radiant smile. 'I was half expecting her to refuse to go back out there.'

'What happened?' Tilda whispers. 'You were gone for ages.'

'Someone locked Kitty in the dark in the water closet,' I hiss back, goosebumps rippling along my arms at the memory of the terror etched on her face.

'That's horrible,' Louis says. 'Who would do something so mean? Are we sure it wasn't an accident?'

I shrug. 'I don't know. If it wasn't then whoever did it must have known Kitty is terrified of the dark. She was out of her mind with fright, poor thing.'

'I know how she feels.' Louis's breath is warm as he whispers in my ear. 'I was frantic when you didn't come back, I didn't know what had happened to you.' Shivers run down my spine as he strokes one hand over the bare skin on my shoulder, and I am trying to get a handle on the sensations running through my nerve endings when I see Camilla approaching.

'Kitty hogging the limelight again?' Camilla tuts with a roll of her eyes.

'Hardly,' I say. 'Leonard didn't ask you to say a few words? You've been nominated too.'

Camilla shakes her head. 'He wanted me to, but obviously I said no. This isn't a party for me, it's a party for everyone who was nominated. It looks as though Kitty was the only person to take Len up on his offer to speak. Gloria didn't want to, and Vivien left already, I think.' Camilla pauses, cocking her head on one side as she considers Kitty, who is still making her speech, her hands gesturing. 'Has she been crying?'

I look to Kitty, now joined by Art, who pulls her into a bear hug to whoops and cheers from the crowd. Art is right – people do love to see the two of them together. 'Why would you ask that?' From this distance, and in the soft glow of the garden lighting, there's no way to tell Kitty has been crying.

Camilla shrugs. 'She gets that sallow look when she's turned on the waterworks.'

Kitty hardly looks sallow from where I'm standing. If anything, she's glowing as she beams up at Art, planting a bright, lipsticky kiss on his cheek. A kernel of suspicion takes root in my stomach.

'It was you, wasn't it?'

'Me, what?' Camilla bites her lower lip but it doesn't stop the smirk that spreads across her face.

'You locked Kitty in the bathroom! You knew she was terrified of the dark, and you thought once she got let out she'd go straight to her room.' Fury makes my hands shake, and I ball them into fists at my sides. 'Leonard never even asked you to make a speech, did he? Did you think if you locked Kitty away he'd ask you to step in? That's horrible, awful, mean-girl behaviour, Camilla.'

'It was a prank,' Camilla hisses. 'It was funny – much funnier than having your face slapped in front of an entire movie crew. She's lucky I didn't complain to Leonard about that.' She gives me a haughty look. 'And I don't entirely like your tone, Lily. I hope I don't have to speak to Leonard about your behaviour too.'

'Lily.' Louis's voice is low and steady and pulls me back to myself, stopping me from saying something that would very likely get me fired.

I swallow back the words I want to say, that I don't blame Kitty one bit for slapping Camilla's face, and instead I offer, 'I apologise for my tone, Camilla.' The words taste toxic on my tongue. 'But Kitty was very distressed when I found her. Perhaps you might think your *pranks* through a little more carefully in future.'

Before Camilla can respond, Kitty waves at the crowd and I move towards her, turning my back on Camilla as Louis and Tilda follow.

'What a nasty old shrew,' Tilda murmurs in my ear. 'You think she knew about Kitty's fear of the dark?'

'I wouldn't put it past her,' I hiss back. 'Make a note of it, Til, you never know, she might have something to do with Kitty's disappearance. Kitty! You were wonderful.'

Kitty beams at me, as she leans against Art's shoulder. 'Was I? I felt dreadfully nervous, Lord knows why.'

'Because you're a star, honey, and all eyes were on you.' Art kisses the top of her head. 'I couldn't be prouder. Just imagine, those two beautiful golden statues sitting on our mantelpiece in our home, us telling our kids about the year Mommy and Daddy both won an Oscar.'

'It's certainly something to dream about,' Kitty says, her eyes shining. 'Oh, there's darling William, and he's leaving! I've barely had a chance to speak to anybody all night.'

'It's been a busy evening, for sure,' I say. Kitty's eyes are glassy, and her cheeks are flushed while the rest of her face is pale. While you can't tell she's been crying, she is beginning to look exhausted. 'The party is certainly winding down now. How about I see you to your room, Kitty? If that's OK with you, Art?'

Art looks across the garden, to where Leonard and Jean are beginning to say goodbye to the party guests, although it's only a little after midnight. 'Kitty, honey, you go and get some sleep. I'm going to say good night to Leonard and Jean, and then I'll come up to you.' He leans in and whispers in her ear, and Kitty swats him playfully on the arm.

'No, Art! Goodness, what would people think?' She flashes her eyes in my direction. 'I have an early call, so I'll see you tomorrow, OK?' She reaches up and kisses him, before turning to me.

'Keep an eye on Camilla,' I whisper to Louis, as Tilda moves off to circulate, hoping to catch the last dregs of party gossip. 'And see if you can spot Jeremy. He seems to have disappeared, I haven't seen him for hours.'

Back at Kitty's room, I stoop to pick up the bouquet that still sits wilting outside her door, but Kitty waves a hand tiredly, gesturing for me to leave it there. The moment we left Art downstairs, Kitty seems to have flagged. Whatever she might have taken – along with the adrenaline of being locked alone in the dark – has worn off, leaving her looking washed out and drained.

'Would you stay?' she asks, as we enter the suite. 'Just while I get ready for bed? I don't really feel like being alone yet.'

'If you'd like me to.'

'I would.' Kitty raises a tired smile. 'Just until I get into bed, that's all. Thank you, Lily.'

Kitty heads into the bathroom, her robe under one arm, and moments later I hear the splash of running water. Feeling at a bit of a loose end, I do what Tilda would expect me to do – I start to snoop. There has to be something here, somewhere, that can give me some sort of idea of how Kitty is going to disappear.

Moving first to the wardrobe, I gently – silently – push the hangers along the rail, dipping into pockets of skirts and coats, only to come up empty-handed. The bottom of the wardrobe is a bust too, the shoes neatly stacked next to each other sadly not stuffed full of clues to Kitty's vanishing. I slide my hands under pillows and between the mattress and bed, but Kitty doesn't seem to have anything dodgy to hide that could get her in trouble further down the line. Lifting her perfume to my nose, I inhale her familiar lilac scent, before recapping it and setting it back where it was.

The dressing table drawers are the only thing left to search, when the water turns off and I hear Kitty humming through the bathroom door. My heart rate jumping, I know I only have a few minutes left until she's back in the bedroom, and I slide open the drawer, expecting to find only make-up.

'Oh,' I breathe, as a jumble of photographs fills the bottom drawer. Snatching up a handful, I flick through them. A sepia-toned photo of a young couple; the woman has Kitty's bouncy blonde curls and the man her twinkly eyes, which shows me they must be her parents. A scar runs the length of her mother's face, from her eyebrow to just above her chin, marring her perfect features. Another photo shows the same woman bouncing a chubby baby on her knee – a baby that can only be Kitty. There are more, one of a black and white dog; a headshot from early on in Kitty's career; a picture of Kitty on the beach, a bathing suit covering her from neck to mid-thigh. The photograph at the bottom of the pile is the one that makes me pause. It's a shot taken from the back of a theatre, showing the cast of a show on the stage, and the first few rows of the audience in the foreground. Flicking it over, written on the back in a hand I don't recognise is the caption:

Kitty in Beverly Hills, Fulton Theatre, Broadway, 1940

I pick out Kitty in the middle of the front row of the cast, in a skimpy dress and high heels, her face overly made-up. At the far end of the row is a man I recognise as a young Jeremy Knox, and my breath catches. In the picture, everyone else's gaze is facing forward – presumably the cast are about to take their final bow – but Jeremy's head is turned in Kitty's direction. It isn't that, though that pulls at my gut. There is something else that is off about the picture; I just can't work out what it is.

The snapping of the latch on the bathroom door makes me jump, and without thinking I slide the photograph into the tiny purse I've been carting around all evening, finally glad it's come to some use, and slip the rest of the photos back into the drawer.

'That's much better.' Kitty is bare-faced, her robe buttoned up to her neck, and she smells like cold cream as she lays on the bed. 'Stay for a while? I'm not quite tired yet. How about another drink? Would you close the curtains while I pour us a brandy?'

'Sure.' I move to the window, peering out on to the street below before I tug the curtains closed. Kitty's window looks out over the street that runs behind the hotel, a dark, poorly lit backstreet that offers more privacy than the rooms that look out on to the boulevard. A figure loiters on the sidewalk, leaning against the lamp post directly across from Kitty's window and my heart stutters in my chest as they appear to look up in my direction. *How long have they been out there? Did they see me rifling through Kitty's things?* Pulse pounding, I whip the curtains closed, before opening them a fraction and peering out again. *Were they watching me, or hoping to catch a glimpse of Kitty?* The street is empty now and I tug the curtains tightly shut, wondering as I do where Jeremy Knox sloped off to this evening. *Was it him loitering outside? Was it the man who grabbed Kitty on the red carpet? Or is my imagination working overtime and whoever it was wanted nothing to do with Kitty at all?*

I perch on the end of the bed, aware of the photograph hidden in my purse, as Kitty pours us both a hefty shot of brandy. I don't think I'll ever get used to the amount of booze consumed in the 1950s.

'Tell me about Jeremy,' I say. 'You said you two dated? You must have known him for a while.'

'Oh, gosh. Years and years.' Kitty smiles faintly. 'We went to school together in New York, and then we both discovered a love of acting. We went to the same stage school, and even ended up on Broadway together for a brief stint.'

That explains Art's comment about Kitty sticking to the stage if she didn't want fame, I think as Kitty rattles on.

'We broke up when I moved to Hollywood, but soon after, Jeremy moved out here too, so it seems he's always been around, ever since I can remember.'

'Did you always want to be in the movies?'

Kitty sighs. 'Yes and no. I mean, I thought I did. I had no idea how exhausting it would be… what a toll it would take on me to be so *on* all the time, to be so controlled by everyone else around me. It can be lonely, you know? Even when I'm surrounded by people all day long. It's a far cry from how I imagined it would be as a teenager.' She gives a wistful smile. 'I loved Judy Garland, and she was my inspiration, but in all honesty, the movies were more my mother's dream. She was an actress herself, until she had a car accident that left her injured.' *The scar that ran the length of her face.* 'She couldn't get work anymore so she pushed her ambitions on to me. Maybe if it really had been my *own* dream, then I might have found the difficult parts a little easier to bear. I've never told anyone, but I always wanted to be a nurse before that.' She gives a little huff of laughter. 'I probably would have been dreadful at it. Art always says I have the bedside manner of a rock.' She yawns, not bothering to cover her mouth with her hand.

'I think you'd have been wonderful,' I say, 'but you should probably get some rest now. You look exhausted.'

'It's been a tough few days, Lily,' Kitty says, wearily. 'I keep having the sensation that someone is watching me, and then for that man to *grab* me, and now tonight...'

'Let me take care of things,' I reply, frantically thinking how best to put it. *If someone is trying to kill you* is probably not the most tactful approach. 'If someone is bothering you, I'll do whatever it takes to keep you safe.'

Kitty nods, just as a knock comes from the door. 'If that's Art, tell him I'm already sleeping,' she says, slipping under the blankets.

When I open the door, Jeremy stands outside, his eyebrow raising as he looks at me. 'You again. Is Kitty here?'

'She's in bed.' I pull the suite door closed behind me. 'What are you doing here?' As I run my eyes over him I realise he could have been the shadowy figure lurking outside. He's the right height and build, and I grip the door handle tightly, trying not to show that my fingers are shaking.

'Someone told me Kitty was upset earlier,' Jeremy says, trying to peer past me to the tiny crack between the door and the frame. 'I came to check on her, seeing as Art is still swanning about in the garden, playing the big movie star.'

'He'll be up in a minute,' I say, half hoping he appears at the top of the staircase. 'Were you outside just now?'

Jeremy sighs, and I can smell the Fireball candy he loves so much on his breath. 'Just let me in, Lily. Let me know she's OK.'

'I told you, she's *fine*,' I hiss. 'It was you, wasn't it? Loitering in the street, watching her through the window. It's not right, Jeremy. It's *stalking*. There are laws for this kind of thing.' *Only there aren't*, I realise as Jeremy lets out a snort of laughter that brushes my face, *not yet*. My foot knocks against the bouquet that still sits by the door. 'And these? Did you send these too?'

'Lily—'

'Just stop, Jeremy,' I say, my voice deadly quiet. 'Stop following Kitty, stop harassing her. She loves Art, not you. Please. Before… you do something you regret.' Heart thundering in my chest, I whirl around and slam the door in his face, resting my forehead against it as I wait for my breathing to return to normal. *Have I just made a huge mistake?* No. Whether Jeremy is responsible for Kitty's disappearance or not, it's weird for him to hang around Kitty so much, spying on her day and night. The more I think about it, the more convinced I am that it was him watching Kitty's window from the street.

There is a tap at the door, right next to where I am leaning my head against it, and I gasp, my knees wobbling. Yanking the door open I grit my teeth, ready to confront Jeremy again, but it isn't Jeremy who stands there.

It's Doctor Astor, with the hideous bouquet in his hands, and there is no sign of Jeremy. 'Lily. Put these in water, would you? Kitty, it's just me.'

Willing my pulse to slow to a regular beat, I follow the doctor into Kitty's room and raise the bouquet so Kitty can see it. 'Did you want these? There's a note attached.' I pull it off and slide it from the tiny envelope. It's unsigned, but the message makes my mouth go dry.

'Who are they from?'

'No one,' I say, my eyes scanning the message. It simply reads:

Not long until we are together forever.

Innocent enough, if I didn't know Kitty was going to vanish into thin air. 'It's unsigned.'

'How lovely,' Doctor Astor says. 'You must get so many gifts from fans. Art asked me to check in on you, Kitty, before he heads home. Are you feeling OK? I'd like to check your blood pressure quickly, if I may?'

'She's fine, just tired.' I open the door, an invitation for the doctor to leave, but he just glances at Kitty.

'It's OK, Lily. I have low blood pressure, it's best I get it checked,' Kitty says. 'You can go now, Lily. I'll see you in the morning.'

'Definitely. Bright and early.'

Still feeling unsettled, I close the door behind me and slip my hand into my purse to pull out the photograph. I still can't see what is bothering me about this picture, but I know that something isn't right.

Louis is waiting for me in the lobby and I breathe a sigh of relief. The thought of walking back to the apartment alone is a horrible one, given the murdered girl found in the alley, and I am more than happy to link hands with Louis as we walk along the street.

'Quite the evening,' Louis says, as we turn onto the boulevard. 'Is Kitty all right?'

'She's fine,' I say, 'but I'm still no closer to figuring out what's going to happen to her.'

'Maybe you need some time away from it for a bit? You know when you think about something too much and you can't see the wood for the trees.' Louis knows I am about to argue and he holds up a hand before I can speak. 'All I mean is, how about a date? Let me take you out somewhere, without my sister for once.'

It sounds like a perfect antidote to the last few days, even though my stomach flips. The thought of spending time alone with Louis is dreamy, but I know I have to put the brakes on our relationship sooner rather than later. As we approach the apartment I share with Tilda, I stop outside the front door and lift my face to his. He leans down, his mouth covering mine, and shivers run down my spine as his hand snakes its way into my hair, pulling me closer to him. I've kissed a lot of frogs in my time, but this time I know I've found my prince. If only we had been born in the same decade.

We kiss until my knees are weak and I feel as though I have no breath in my body. 'Are you coming in?' I manage to gasp, as we come up for air. *Please, come in*, I want to say, even though I know kissing is as far as Louis will take things, because he 'respects' me so much. Sometimes, this out-of-place twenty-first century girl wants to be *disrespected*, although I could never tell him that.

'Lily,' Louis groans, pressing his face into my now unruly curls. 'You know I can't. It wouldn't be... proper.' He shifts, and I can feel him pressing against my thigh. *Yikes.*

'You're right,' I say, regret immediately washing over me as he pulls himself away. 'But a date with you sounds wonderful.'

'I meant what I said the other day, you know.' Louis looks down at his feet, his cheeks flushing a violent shade of pink.

My mouth goes dry. 'What you... said?'

'About us. Settling down.'

Oh no. A lump rises in my throat and, try as I might, I can't swallow it down. I've spent night after night tossing and turning in bed, thinking about my relationship with

Louis. If we were in the twenty-first century, it would be a no-brainer; I'd let him snap me up as soon as look at me. Hell, even if I'd been born in *his* decade, I would have let him put a ring on it. But we're not, and I'm not, and as much as this is going to break my heart just as much as it is his, at some point really, really soon I have to have the conversation I've been putting off ever since I got back here.

'I mean it, Lily,' he says when I don't speak. 'I want us to be together properly. Get a little house in Santa Monica after the wedding...'

'Wedding?'

'Well, I mean... one day, soon.' Louis takes my hand and I gently tug it free.

'I can't.' I gulp the words out, tears making my throat thicken. 'I'm sorry, Louis, but I can't. I'm not who you think I am.'

'Lily—'

'It won't work, Louis. It can't.' I can't say any more, the cracking of my heart making it difficult to speak. 'The two of us... we can only ever be friends.'

Louis is silent, his eyes searching my face as I refuse to blink, refuse to allow the tears burning behind my eyes to cascade down my face. 'You mean it.' It's a statement, not a question.

I nod. 'If there was any way things could be different between us, I swear to you they would but... that's all we can ever be, Louis. I'm sorry. It's not you—' I catch myself before the world's worst cliché can tumble out of my mouth. 'Please, maybe one day I can explain it, but for now, please, just believe me. You mean the world to me, but we can't ever be together. Not like that.'

'But you won't tell me why? I know we're a little different, Lily, but if everyone was the same the world would be a boring place.'

'It's... complicated,' I sigh. 'I wish I could put it into words but... we're worlds apart, Louis. I'll never properly fit, not the way you want me to.' A tear slides over one cheek now, and I sniff. 'I shouldn't have let you kiss me, I shouldn't have let you take me on dates, not when I knew it could never be anything more than friendship.'

Louis gives me one more searching look, and tears run down my cheeks at the hurt in his eyes. 'OK.' He nods reluctantly, but makes no move to wipe away my tears. 'I mean, it's not OK. It's not what I want at all, and I wish you'd just been honest with me from the start.'

There's nothing I wish more too, but let's be *really* honest – if I told him why I really couldn't be with him, he'd have me committed.

'If being friends means I still get to be with you, be part of your life, then I have to respect that. Maybe one day things will be different.'

'I'm sorry,' I whisper, as he shoves his hands in his pockets and gives a brisk nod, before turning and hurrying back down the stairs from our second-floor apartment and out to the street. Hoping I haven't made a mistake that I'll regret for the rest of my life – *oh, who am I kidding? I'll always regret this, despite knowing it's an impossibility* – I turn to enter the apartment. Pushing the front door open, I pause. There is an unfamiliar scent on the air and immediately the hairs on the back of my neck rise.

'Tilda? Til?' Stepping inside, I let my purse slide to the floor and wait for her to answer, but there is no response. The sitting room looks just as we left it, a jumble of dresses thrown over the back of the sofa where we tried them on before we left, Tilda's hairbrush abandoned on the floor. Her bedroom door is tight shut, and when I peep inside, the bedroom is empty. Glancing along the small hallway, I freeze. My bedroom door is open. Wide open, when I know I closed it before I left. My heart hammering in my chest so hard it's painful, I snatch up an umbrella from Tilda's room, wielding it like a sword, and creep along the passage to my room.

'Hello?' My voice rings out, clearer and stronger than I imagined it would. 'Is someone there?' The silence that echoes back at me is thick and heavy. Maybe I didn't close the door. Maybe I'm imagining the scent of sandalwood and something spicy on the air, an aftershave I don't recognise. Stepping into my room, I know immediately that I'm not. There is a dent on the end of my bed, as if someone has sat there, and the diary I keep on the nightstand is on the floor beside the bed. The top drawer of the small chest in the corner of the room is slightly open, and I know the bottle of cologne on top of it had the lid on, whereas now it sits beside it. *Someone has been in here*. I take a deep breath, eyes scanning the room one more time. We left the apartment in a rush this evening – maybe I'm wrong? *But I would never leave my door open. And I know the diary was on the nightstand*. Below me, a door slams, and my heart leaps into my throat.

'Lily? You home?' Tilda's footsteps thud along the passageway. 'You'll never believe who I got a ride with—'

'Have you been back here tonight?' I cut her off, as she stops dead in the doorway to my bedroom, eyes going to the umbrella in my hand.

'Huh? No. I've been at the party all night, you know that. Lily? What is it?'

'Someone's been here,' I say, through lips that feel numb. The fingers wrapped around the umbrella feel cold, and I drop it to the floor. 'Someone has been in our apartment while we were at the party – in my bedroom, yours hasn't been touched. I don't know what they're looking for, but they've definitely been searching for something.'

Chapter Eleven

Tilda casts her eyes about the room. 'Are you sure? Because everything looks kinda… normal in here.'

'I *know* someone has been here. Things have been moved.' I gesture to the diary, to the half-open drawer.

'What do you think they were looking for?' Tilda picks up a pencil and pokes at the underwear spilling from the open drawer. 'Do we think it was something random? A burglar you might have disturbed? Maybe we should call the police.'

The thought of it makes my mouth fill with saliva, but I shake my head. 'No. Surely a random burglar would have trashed the whole apartment, and there's no point in calling the cops, I don't think anything has been taken. They didn't step foot in your room, just in here.'

'You think this is related to Kitty's disappearance,' Tilda says, dropping the pencil and straightening up to look me in the eye. 'It has to be, right?'

I shrug, but deep down I do think the two things might be connected. I've been protective of Kitty on set, and I've not been shy about it. I've tried to not be rude, but anyone working with us can tell that I'm doing my best to keep a close eye on Kitty. 'Maybe it's a warning.'

Tilda's eyes widen and she plops down on the edge of the bed with a thump. 'That's exactly what it is,' she says. 'By breaking in and only moving things around in your room, someone is sending you a message.' She pauses, her brow crinkling the way it does when she's trying to put puzzle pieces together. 'They were looking for something, perhaps?'

I glance around the bedroom again, noticing more tiny disruptions in the orderly space I've made for myself. The sheet, slightly untucked at the end of the bed as if the mattress has been lifted. The curtains, pulled back as far as they will go to expose every inch of the window ledge. The two pairs of heels I own, tumbled onto their sides as if turned upside down and shaken.

'They were looking for something,' I repeat, slowly. 'But what?'

'Something that could discredit me? Get me thrown off the movie? If someone does mean Kitty harm and they want me out of the way, if they could find some dirt on me that would give Leonard no choice but to sack me, surely this is the best place to look.'

'Like... *drugs?*' Tilda whispers, her eyes wide. 'I know you would never, Lily, but if someone thought you smoked *marijuana*...'

'I don't know.' And I really don't. I can't think of anything anyone could find that would get me booted off of the movie – I'm not even sure a fat blunt would be enough, given the pills that fly around on set – but the thought that someone might want to get me out of the way to get to Kitty makes my blood run cold.

'Any idea who it might have been?' Tilda gets to her feet and takes my hand, leading me out into the sitting room, where it's a little warmer. 'Here. Let's get you on the couch – you look exhausted and frozen to the bone.'

I shake my head, sinking onto the couch and letting Tilda tuck a blanket over me. I feel dog-tired after confronting Jeremy, telling Louis I can't be with him the way he wants and now finding someone has broken into our apartment, but I don't want to sleep in that room tonight, with the invisible fingerprints of an intruder staining my things. 'No idea. I have no clue who would want to break into our apartment.' But Jeremy Knox's is the last face I see before I eventually drop into a fitful doze. *Where did he go when he left the party earlier? Did he hang around outside Kitty's window... or could he have snuck away to my apartment, in the hopes of finding something that will put me out of the picture?*

—

The next morning, I am stiff and achy from a night on our second-hand couch (kindly donated by Tilda and Louis's parents, despite Andy, Tilda's father, not entirely approving of Tilda's moving out), but when I go to my room to dress, everything has been tidied and put back as it was. Tilda's work, no doubt. She is still sleeping, so I leave her a note thanking her and then head out.

Schwab's is busy, but I agreed to pick up the breakfast sandwiches and coffee for this morning's meeting before shooting starts on set. The line takes forever, and when I finally pick up our order I am already late.

'Thanks.' I pick up the bag of food from the young guy behind the counter. 'Oh wait, you didn't give me creamer for the coffee.'

'Sorry.' He hands me packets of creamer and I peer past him, looking for the girl who usually serves me. She knows our order inside out and would never have forgotten the creamer. 'First day.'

'Where's the other girl? She's usually here in the mornings.'

The boy shrugs. 'I don't know. Didn't turn up, I guess.'

Thanking him again, I hurry across the street, swearing lightly under my breath as I see Leonard, Jeremy and Camilla are already sat at the table in the garden for our meeting. Camilla sips daintily at a glass of water, while Jeremy pops a Fireball candy into his mouth, making my stomach roll.

'Sorry!' I yelp, as hot coffee slops onto my hand. 'The line in Schwab's was out of the door.'

'You didn't miss anything,' Leonard snaps, reaching for a breakfast sandwich, cheese oozing out of the side. 'It's not like Kitty and Art have turned up on time. Bunny has gone upstairs to wake them up.'

Oh. Art must have gone to Kitty's room after I left, after all. Before I can answer, Bunny appears at the edge of the garden, her blonde hair pulled back neatly with a green Alice band that matches not only her dress, but her pumps too.

'Oh, Mr Langford!' she calls, her hands fluttering to her mouth as she buzzes towards our table. 'I knocked and knocked and there's no answer. I don't think Kitty is even in her room.'

'Are you sure?' I get to my feet, my chair scraping across in the patio as I hastily shove it back. A curling sense of unease unfurls in my stomach, and I swallow as Bunny nods.

'What?' Leonard barks. 'Of course Kitty is in her room. She knows she has an early meeting this morning, and I saw her socking away the drinks last night. She's overslept, that's all. Get back up there and *knock louder*.'

'Little Miss Perfect isn't so perfect, after all,' Camilla drawls as she reaches for a coffee, pushing aside the packets of creamer with her red fingernails.

'I'll go up and check her room myself, Leonard.' Kitty has to be there – she knew we had a meeting this morning, and she wouldn't miss it deliberately, knowing how furious Leonard would be. I go cold at the thought of finding an empty room, of Kitty disappearing before I've had time to find any clues at all. 'Bunny, ask at the desk for the key to room seven, just in case she still doesn't answer.' Bunny scurries away and I turn back to Leonard, plastering on a feeble smile that I know doesn't reach my eyes. 'I'm sure there's a reasonable explanation. I'll get her down here as soon as possible.'

After knocking three times hard on Kitty's door, there is still no answer, and that panicky sense of unease whips up my insides, making me feel nauseous. When Bunny arrives at the top of the stairs, panting a little, I take the key and hurriedly push the door open.

'Kitty? Are you in here? Time to get up.' Bunny is hot on my heels as I peep into Kitty's bedroom, the bed empty and the covers pushed back. 'She might be in the bathroom,' I say, hope flaring in my chest. 'Maybe you woke her and she realised she was late.'

It's only as I reach the closed bathroom door that I realise I can't hear the shower running. Pressing my ear to the door, I can just make out the soft plink of dripping water, and a twisting vine of fear raises the hairs on the back of my neck, instinct telling me that something is very wrong.

'Bunny,' I say, trying to keep my voice level. 'Go and get Leonard.' I try the bathroom door but it's locked, so I step back, take a deep breath and shoulder-barge the flimsy door as hard as I can. It takes three goes before the door cracks out of the frame and I stumble into the bathroom, my shoulder throbbing.

'Oh my God. Oh—' Bunny is still behind me, her voice a rising shriek.

'I told you to get Leonard! Go, now! *Fuck.*'

Kitty lies naked in the bathtub, the ends of her blonde hair damp, her eyes closed and her cheeks waxy and pale. An empty whisky tumbler sits on the edge of the bath, and on the floor by my feet is a brown pill bottle, three tiny white pills scattered by the toilet. Kitty doesn't stir as I shout her name, begging her to wake up, adrenaline firing through my veins as I reach for her, wanting to pull her higher up the enamel to keep her face from hitting the water. As my hands reach for her, I realise the water is cold, and I have to blink to keep my focus as dark spots dapple my vision. *This is it, Lil*, my brain screams, *this is the suicide attempt you read about.* Yanking out the plug, the chilly water begins to drain away as I reach for her robe hanging on the back of the bathroom door and tuck it around her damp body, shielding her from view. As I pull the fabric up and tuck it over her shoulders, the sharp edges of her collarbone press against my fingers, and I am aware that I can see every rib as I cover the rest of her body. She almost looks like a child, she's so tiny and frail.

'Jesus Christ!' Leonard's voice is a welcome break into my thoughts, and I press my fingers to Kitty's neck, feeling the faintest thud of a pulse before Leonard pushes me to one side. 'We need to get her out of here.'

'We need to call a doctor,' I say, the words wobbling their way out of my mouth. 'She's alive. I felt a pulse.'

Leonard has his head to Kitty's mouth and he nods. 'She's breathing… just.'

'Kitty? What's happened? Where is she?' Bunny is shoved aside, her hand still pressed to her mouth as Jeremy forces his way into the bathroom, a shocked Camilla trailing behind him.

'Let me see her.'

'Please, Jeremy,' I beg. 'Let Leonard help her. She needs to see a doctor. We need to get her to a hospital.'

Leonard glances up from where he tucks Kitty's robe more securely around her. 'No hospital.'

'What? Leonard, you can't be serious. She's...' I gulp back the words. 'She needs to go to hospital, she needs help.'

Leonard's face is grave as he slides one hand beneath Kitty's hair and the other beneath her knees in preparation to lift her out of the tub. 'Lily, I can't send her to hospital.' His voice is hoarse, as he looks down at Kitty's pale face. 'The studio... can you imagine the backlash from this? The studio can't hear about this. They could cancel the picture. It would be over for all of us.'

I can barely believe what I'm hearing. Leonard would really rather risk Kitty's life than let the studio suffer a bit of scandalous publicity?

Leonard turns to a trembling Bunny. 'Go back down to the lobby and get them to call Doctor Astor's room.'

'*No.*' Jeremy steps back, barring Bunny's escape. 'She doesn't need to see him. Don't call Doctor Astor, Bunny.'

'She needs a doctor, Jeremy!' I cry. 'She's breathing, but not well. If she doesn't get help, she could die.'

'Lily's right, Jer,' Camilla says, her voice cracking as she catches a glimpse of Kitty's still, silent body. 'Kitty needs to see a doctor.'

'Not Doctor Astor,' Jeremy insists. 'I'll take her to the hospital myself.' His hands shake as he pushes them through his hair, never taking his eyes from Kitty.

'No, son,' Leonard says, gently. 'Studio aside, do you really want to put Kitty through a media circus?' He lifts Kitty swiftly from the tub as if she weighs nothing at all, cold water dripping all over his legs and feet.

Camilla steps forward, her voice calm and measured despite the panic that still laces the air. 'Leonard, with all due respect, I think the studio can go hang in this instance. Look at her.' She gestures to Kitty's pale, thin frame. 'She needs a hospital, and if you don't get her there you'll have far worse things to explain than this. I'm sure you'll find a way to keep this from the studio.'

Leonard sighs, the internal battle between doing the right thing and saving his picture waging over his face. 'OK. But I'll take her to the hospital. You're in no fit state to drive, Jeremy.'

Kitty's robe slips as Leonard moves towards the bathroom door, and I tuck it around her motionless body to protect her modesty. There is a thunder of feet on the stairs in the corridor outside, and then Art appears, wild-eyed and sweaty.

'Is she dead?' he asks, his hand going to his throat. 'Kitty? Is she dead?'

I reach out, gripping him by the upper arms as he tries to enter the bathroom. 'She's alive,' I say, 'but you need to give Leonard some space, he's taking her to the hospital.'

Art stands to one side, watching dumbly as Leonard hurries out with Kitty in his arms, Bunny following behind. Jeremy is standing on the other side of the bathroom, his head low, as Camilla wraps her arms around him. Positioning myself in Art's eyeline, masking Jeremy's presence so as not to rile him, I gently steer him out into the hallway, to the entrance to Kitty's bedroom.

'You should probably follow on in your car,' I say, as Art nods, blankly.

'How did this happen?' he asks, his voice hollow. 'Is she going to live?'

I swallow, a lump the size of a golf ball in my throat. 'I don't know. I hope so. She was still breathing and there was a faint pulse, and she's going to be in the best place really soon. I am worried about her though, Art, if she does pull through.'

Art looks at me, his brow crumpling. His eyes are bloodshot, and he doesn't look as if he's slept well. 'Why?'

'She told me she doesn't know if she wants to do this anymore. This whole movie star thing.' I think of the whisky tumbler, the pills, everything lined up and pointing to Kitty doing this to herself.

Art's eyes widen, and he shakes his head. 'No. No, Kitty would never have said that and meant it. Acting is her life – it's all she's known since she was a child. I know sometimes she makes a fuss about giving autographs and having her photo taken, but she would wither and die without fame. I know her, Lily, better than you do. Better than she knows herself. Being a movie star, being with *me*... that's Kitty's destiny, Lily.' He reaches out and squeezes my hand. 'Thank you. For finding her. I have to go, I have to get to the hospital.'

I nod, not sure what else I can say to him, and he is gone in three loping strides, leaving me alone in Kitty's bedroom.

'Lily? Are you all right? It must have been a terrible shock, finding Kitty like that.' Camilla's voice is soft, as she appears in the hall, Jeremy behind me.

'Yes, I'm fine. Honestly. You two should probably...' I glance at Jeremy, who is still white-faced and grim. 'You should probably get a Bloody Mary into him. I don't think we'll be on set today, somehow.'

Camilla nods and takes Jeremy's hand, the two of them disappearing out into the hallway. It seems odd to see spiky Camilla being so gentle, so soft, and I wonder if I got her all wrong, before remembering the fear on Kitty's face when I let her out of the bathroom the previous evening. Finally alone, I move towards the bathroom, when something catches my eye. On the nightstand, beside Kitty's pillow, is a sheet of paper.

I'm sorry, Kitty's scrawled handwriting says, in violet ink that matches the pen beside the note. *I can't...* That's it. Is that enough to count as a suicide note? Something in my chest cracks, and I feel unbearably sad for Kitty. Folding the paper, I slip it into my pocket, not knowing if Leonard will want to see it, and head into the bathroom. *I can understand why Leonard was initially reluctant to take Kitty to the hospital – even if I don't agree with his thinking at all – but why was Jeremy so adamant that he didn't want Doctor Astor called? Was it because he knew Kitty wouldn't want the doctor to see her like that? Or some other reason?* Icy fingers march their way down my spine as I picture Kitty's still, white face, and for a moment I think I might throw up. Turning to leave, my foot makes contact with the pill bottle on the floor and I stoop to pick it up, tucking the remaining three pills inside and capping the lid. Kitty's name is stamped in black typewritten font on the front, and I give the bottle an experimental shake. I can't read the name of the pills – the label has peeled away where it would be – and I wrap my fingers tightly around the bottle and put it in my pocket next to the letter. My eyes light on the empty tumbler, and I pick it up and give it a sniff. *Definitely whisky*.

With one last look at the bathroom, I head out into the hallway, intent on getting a ride to the hospital to see Kitty. All I can picture is her tucking herself into the blankets as I left last night, tired and emotional, but not suicidal. Not that I could tell. *Did Kitty really do this to herself?*

Chapter Twelve

In the lobby of the Chateau there is no indication that anything amiss has happened on the floor above, and I put through a call to Louis at the Polo Lounge, my chest tight as the operator tells me she's connecting me. I am half expecting him to decline to take my call after our conversation the previous evening, and when I hear his voice on the other end of the line a wave of relief washes over me.

'Lily? Are you all right?' Confusion clouds his words. I've never called him at work before.

'Louis, I...' I swallow, suddenly overwhelmed by the vision of Kitty's still, pale face and the sharp angles of her dreadfully thin body. 'Something terrible has happened.'

Twenty minutes later, Louis's familiar Cadillac draws up outside the Chateau and I slide into the passenger seat beside him.

'Let's get you to the hospital. You OK? You're white as a sheet.' Louis squeezes my hand. 'Do you want to talk about it?'

Settling back against the seat, I sigh. I'm so grateful to him for not making things weird, for not making my plea for help into something about us. 'It was awful, Lou, to see Kitty lying there like that. I honestly thought she was dead at first, until I found that faint pulse.'

'Do you think...' Louis swallows, glancing at me for a second before turning his eyes back to the road. 'Do you think this is the suicide attempt you told us about?'

'I hope so. It sounds dreadful, but I honestly don't think my heart could take it if there was more than one.'

'How did Art take things? I'm assuming he was there.'

'Dreadfully. He's so shaken, I just hope he was OK to drive himself to the hospital. Maybe I should have offered to drive him?'

Louis suppresses a smile. 'I think it's probably safer if he drove himself. No offence, Lil.'

I raise an eyebrow and try to smile. 'This is a big car, Louis. All big cars are hard to drive – it's not my skills that are at fault.' Louis laughs and I manage a smile, just being in his presence lifting my spirits, even though I feel guilty about it. Maybe, even though I called time on anything romantic between us, we can still enjoy each other's company. 'Jeremy seemed more distraught than Art, if I'm honest. And he was weird... he didn't want me to call for a doctor.'

'Really?' Louis's tone is sharp. 'Surely that's the first thing you'd do?'

'You'd think. I mean, Leonard was very reluctant to let Kitty go to hospital, but I know it's because he's worried about the press – and therefore the studio – getting wind of what happened. I'm going to try to speak to Kitty once she's awake, and ask her if she has any idea why Jeremy might react that way. Kitty certainly didn't seem suicidal when I left her last night.' My fingers slide into my pocket and curl around the pill bottle, rubbing at the worn label.

Louis drives the rest of the journey in silence, as if sensing that I don't want to talk. There is one thing I do need to speak to him about though, and my stomach churns at the thought of bringing it up.

'Louis?'

'Hmmm?' He doesn't take his eyes off the road, and for that I'm relieved. He's not going to like what I'm about to say.

'Last night, after I got home.' I swallow, nerves making my mouth dry. 'When I went into the apartment... someone had been in there.'

'What do you mean? After we... spoke on the doorstep?' Louis flicks on his indicator and we pull into the parking lot of the hospital. 'Who?'

I look down at my hands, not wanting to meet his gaze. He'll be furious that I didn't call him up to the apartment once I realised someone had broken in. 'That's just it, I don't know. I thought maybe Tilda had come home before me, but the apartment was empty. Someone had been in my bedroom and things were disturbed, as if they had been looking for something.'

'And you're only just telling me this now? Why on earth didn't you call me back? I...' He pauses, his cheeks flushing. 'I know things... *changed* between us last night, but heck, it doesn't mean... You should have yelled out the window. Jeez, Lil.'

'It was fine, whoever was in there was long gone, but they were definitely focused on me.'

'Maybe it's time you call it a day with this whole Kitty thing.' Louis's gaze is set as he stares out of the windscreen. 'Maybe she really doesn't want to be here... or maybe she is actually in danger and you're going to get yourself killed.'

'I already told you,' I say softly. 'You don't get to tell me what to do. I have to help Kitty. I think they were just looking for something to try and get me thrown off the set, to keep me away from Kitty. But they won't find anything.'

Louis turns his green eyes on me and I resist the urge to squirm under his gaze. 'Lily,' he says, 'after everything we've been through together, after losing you for months and then everything we went through in Vegas, I'm not going to risk losing you again.' He holds up a hand as I open my mouth to argue. 'I still care about you, even if you're not my girlfriend. I know there are things you haven't told me, things you've held back, but if something like this happens again, you need to tell me. If I can't stop you from getting involved with Kitty, then at least let me help you. I won't let you do this on your own.'

—

As I approach Kitty's hospital room, in the same quiet wing of the hospital where I visited Honey Black in 1949, the sense of déjà vu is overwhelming. That is until I hear Art's less than dulcet tones, and turn the corner to see him pacing outside her room.

'Art? What's happened?' Dread slows my footsteps as I near Kitty's room. Surely, if she was OK, Art would be sitting beside her? 'Kitty... is she...?'

'I wouldn't know,' Art says bitterly, as he continues his pacing, the soles of his shoes squeaking on the hospital lino. 'They won't let me in her room. Leonard says she needs to rest, but I need to see her.'

'Art. Please, stop pacing, you're making me dizzy.'

Art shoves his hands through his hair, his lips pressing into a tight line as he walks past me again. 'Why won't they let me see her? How could Kitty do this? Doesn't she know how much I love her?' He looks up at me, seeming to have aged five years in the time he's been at the hospital.

'She's going to be OK,' I say, crossing my fingers behind my back and saying a tiny, silent prayer. 'I know you're worried, but why don't you sit down? Kitty is going to need you when she wakes up, and you'll be exhausted at this rate.'

'I can't just sit and wait. I want to see for myself that she's all right. I want to be the first person she sees, the first person she speaks to when she wakes up.' He pauses, pressing a hand to his mouth. 'Kitty is the love of my life, Lily.'

An ache forms deep in my chest at his words and I fumble to find the right thing to say.

'What if this ruins everything?' Art's voice is barely above a whisper now as he begins to pace again.

'Ruins…? Art, you're not making any sense.'

'Lily.' Art stops pacing and grips me by my upper arms, forcing me to listen to him, his fingers digging into my biceps until I am sure they're going to leave a mark. 'What if… what if Kitty doesn't love me anymore? Kitty and I… we're a golden couple. We have *expectations* put on us by our public. What are people going to say about this? About Kitty? What if Kitty is fired from the studio? I need to see her, I need to know how she…' He breaks off, his voice cracking.

'Calm down, Art, of course Kitty still loves you. She'll need you more than ever now. And the nurses will never let her see you while you're like this. Leonard will only be repeating what they've told him, so maybe he's right. Kitty is probably exhausted. And you've had a terrible shock too. Here.' I pull a crumpled dollar bill from my purse. 'Why don't you head down to the canteen and fetch yourself a coffee, and I'll see if they'll let me peek in on Kitty. I might be able to persuade them to let you say hi.'

Art looks down at the bill in my hand, his nose crinkling slightly. 'I can buy my own coffee, Lily. And I don't know what makes you think they'll let *you* see her any more than me.'

The fact that I'm not pacing around like a caged tiger with a face like a beetroot will probably do it, I think to myself. 'I don't know that they will, but right now I'm probably your best hope.'

With a reluctant nod, Art moves away to the elevator and I tap lightly on Kitty's door, before popping my head round the door frame.

Kitty is sitting propped up by pillows, her blonde hair spread around her head as if the cameras are about to roll. Her cheeks are still pale, but she is breathing and she beckons me inside with a crook of her finger, much to my relief. The nurse finishes fussing with Kitty's blanket and then scoots away, leaving us alone.

'Is he gone?' Kitty asks, her eyes going to the door behind me. Her voice is raspy, as if she has a terrible cold.

'Who? Art?' I turn, checking the door is tightly closed. 'I sent him down to grab a coffee. Do you want to see him?'

Kitty pauses for a second, then shakes her head. 'Not yet. I'm not ready.'

'That's OK. You can take things at your own pace. He is terribly worried about you though.' I lower myself into the seat beside the bed. The room smells of antiseptic and I suppress a shudder, the scent making goosebumps ripple over my body. I've never been good with hospitals. They remind me of the hours spent with my mum, as cancer slowly ravaged her from the inside out. 'How are you feeling?'

'Sore.' Kitty attempts a smile. 'My throat hurts and my stomach is tender where they pumped it. Embarrassed. I'm sorry you had to see me like that.' A tear spills over one cheek and Kitty lifts a hand to dash it away.

'You have nothing to feel embarrassed about, Kitty.' I reach out and take her hand; her fingers are icy-cold. 'Do you remember much about last night?'

Kitty turns her gaze to the pristine white ceiling, her brow furrowing. 'The dark,' she says eventually. 'I got locked in that little bathroom?' She looks to me for confirmation.

'Camilla's idea of a prank.'

'Right.' Kitty blinks, another tear sliding over her bottom lashes. 'You and I went back to my room… but after that I don't remember anything.'

'You don't remember Doctor Astor coming to your room?'

Kitty frowns harder, then pushes herself up the pillows so she's upright. 'Yes. Yes, I think I do remember that. I think he was worried about my blood pressure after the bathroom incident.'

'That's right. I left just after,' I say. 'Did Jeremy come back to your room?'

'Jeremy? No. At least, I don't remember him coming to my room.'

'What about Art? I thought he was going to come up after he'd finished at the party downstairs.' I remember Leonard at the breakfast meeting telling Bunny that Art and Kitty had overslept, and I assumed he had gone to her after all.

Kitty shakes her head, hesitant. 'I know I was thinking about him...' She closes her eyes, resting her head back against the pillows. 'Leonard. Leonard was here when I woke up... does he know what happened?'

I nod. 'He was the one who brought you to hospital.'

'Oh no.' Kitty's eyes fill with tears. 'He'll be furious with me. I'm holding up filming again... and Oskar Goldstein... I saw the newspaper article saying the studio are thinking of replacing me. I'll be blamed for the delays after this.'

I hadn't realised Kitty had seen the article. 'It's just a silly rumour, Kitty, that's all.'

'Maybe it won't be once this gets out,' she says, her face blank. 'And the newspapers... imagine what they'll all be saying about me. If Oskar isn't furious already he soon will be. I'm sure he'll find it cheaper to replace me than put up with all this circus.'

'Kitty,' I say, gently. 'How are you really feeling? Inside, not just your sore throat and stomach.'

'Inside?'

'Are you... do you...' *Oh blimey, I don't know how to say it.* 'Why did you do this to yourself? Are you really so unhappy that you'd want to kill yourself?'

'*Kill* myself?' Kitty's eyes shoot open and her hand clutches the blanket in a death grip. 'Lily, what are you talking about? I didn't try to kill myself!'

I had been worried that Kitty would be deep in the depths of denial, and now it looks as though I might be right. 'Kitty, you were found in the bathtub, an empty whisky tumbler on the side, and there was a pill bottle. They didn't pump your stomach for fun.'

'There's nothing illegal about taking a glass of whisky into the bath. I do it all the time to relax after a hard day on set. It doesn't mean I want to kill myself.'

'Everybody struggles,' I soothe, still trying to figure out how best to play things. 'There's nothing to be ashamed of – honestly, where I come from, mental health is talked about widely, and it helps so many people to...'

'I am *not* mentally ill, Lily,' Kitty snaps, with a hint of her usual feistiness. 'And I never tried to kill myself.' Her voice thickens. 'I don't remember drinking whisky last night, but I probably did. And as for taking pills, I never took anything last night.'

Reaching into my pocket, I pull out the pill bottle I found on the bathroom floor. 'This is yours, and I found it beside the bathtub. Look, it has your name on it.'

Kitty takes the bottle, turning it over in her hands. 'This isn't mine, Lily, I swear. I know I sometimes take a little something to get me through the day, but this bottle isn't mine. I've never seen it before in my life.' She shakes the remaining pills into her hand and inspects them closely. 'These are... *Mother's Little Helpers*, Lily. My own mother takes this brand, has done as long as I can remember after the accident left her so scarred. I don't take these. I wouldn't, I've seen how they leave her... lifeless and bland, without a spark of joy in her.'

'But...' Kitty's words have turned everything I thought I knew on its head. 'There's this too.' I pull the note from my purse and smooth it out so she can read it. 'It reads like a suicide note, Kitty. *I'm sorry... I can't*. It reads as if you can't go on anymore.'

Kitty drops the pill bottle onto the blanket and takes the note, holding it up to the light. 'It's my writing,' she says quietly. 'You're right, Lily, this is my handwriting. I wrote this note but...'

I say nothing, just wait for her to gather her thoughts.

'It's not a suicide note,' Kitty says firmly, tossing it down to join the pill bottle. 'I know that, deep in my heart. Lily, I might be miserable sometimes, but I do love my life. I do.' She sounds more like she's convincing herself than me. 'I complain about the fame, and yes, there is a part of me that sometimes wishes I could run away from it all, but don't we all feel a little like that sometimes?'

I think of my old life, back in twenty-first century Hollywood. Of the apartment I lived in with the mould that constantly grew on the bathroom wall no matter how much bleach I sprayed on it; of scrubbing the toilets at the Beverly Hills Hotel until my knuckles were cracked and bleeding. Of the hours on my feet waitressing at the Saddle Ranch Chop House. I had run away from everything I had there, including my best friend Eric, to be here, in 1950s Hollywood, with Louis and Tilda. *Yes*, I think, *we all feel a little like that sometimes*.

'Sometimes, when I'm up in front of those cameras, those lights, that's the only time I feel truly myself,' Kitty goes on, 'and I know it won't always feel that way. More and more I feel as if there is something more out there for me, away from movies and lines and someone directing every minute of my life from sun-up until sundown, but I don't want to *die* to escape it. I'm excited to know that one day there might be a different path for me.' She pauses, biting down on her lower lip. 'Can I trust you, Lily?'

'Of course.'

'I know the public have expectations around me and Art, that they see us as a golden couple. The new Douglas and Mary, the *New York Times* said, and look what happened to them. What if I don't want that? What if I want to be alone?'

'Oh, Kitty. My mum used to say, today's news, tomorrow's fish and chip paper. And anyway, you and Art are nothing like Douglas Fairbanks and Mary Pickford. Art loves the bones of you, but maybe you need some space from him, cool things off for a while just until you feel yourself again. He loves you, I'm sure he'll understand.' I get to my feet and scoop up the note and pill bottle from the blanket. 'I believe you, Kitty. You're too strong to let your life trickle down the plughole with booze and pills. You should get some rest. I'll tell Art you're sleeping, shall I?'

With a weary shake of her head, Kitty settles herself back against the pillows. 'Let him in. He's been patient enough.'

I keep the smile on my face until my back is turned and I reach the door. I do believe Kitty when she says she had no intention of ending her own life, but if Kitty didn't do this herself, *then someone did it to her.* Someone left her unconscious in the bathtub, full of whisky and pills, knowing there was a chance that she might never wake up. This is confirmation that at least one of the rumours surrounding Kitty's disappearance isn't true. She never killed herself. Which means now I have to find who did try to kill her before she vanishes into thin air.

Chapter Thirteen

Art is outside the door when I step into the corridor, and he whips around to look at me. 'Is Kitty awake?'

'She's awake and she's asking for you.' I move to one side and Art hurries to Kitty's bedside, perching on the edge of the bed as he smooths her hair away from her face and drops kisses onto her cheeks. 'I should go.'

'Oh no, Lily, stay,' Art says, turning to me with a beaming smile. 'Kitty wouldn't be here if it weren't for you.' He turns his attention back to Kitty. 'Darling, how are you feeling?'

'I've been better,' Kitty says dryly, seeming more her old self now Art is here. 'I'm sorry for worrying you.'

Art kisses her forehead and gazes at her as if she might break – or disappear. 'My love, it was worth all the worry just to know you're all right now.' He pauses, concern flitting across his features. 'You are all right, aren't you, darling? You feel OK?'

'I feel fine,' Kitty reassures him, letting Art link his fingers through hers. 'I'm sure I'll be out of here in no time.'

'I had Bunny go to your room and fetch a few things,' Art says, and I feel a burst of something warm and fuzzy at his thoughtfulness. 'Just the essentials – your favourite cardigan, your hairbrush and your rouge. I know you'll want to look your best. She should be here any moment, but if there's anything else you want...'

Kitty smiles, fatigue around her eyes. 'I'm fine, Art. I don't need anything.'

There is a light tapping at the door. 'That'll be Bunny, I expect,' I say, moving swiftly to let her in so Art can stay by Kitty's side. But it isn't Bunny.

'Am I interrupting?' Doctor Astor asks quietly, as he peers past me into Kitty's room. He holds up a huge bouquet of roses and a sheaf of magazines, a gold ring on his pinky finger glinting as it catches the light.

'Doctor!' Kitty smiles from her bed. 'Come in.'

Doctor Astor enters, and hands me the flowers to put on the nightstand, before laying the magazines on the bed beside Kitty.

'Roses! How lovely.' Kitty beckons to me to bring the flowers closer so she can smell the blooms.

'I know they're your favourite,' the doctor says with a quick glance at Art. 'And rest assured I went through these magazines with a fine toothcomb to make sure there's nothing upsetting in there for you. I've spoken to the doctors here, and they seem to think you should be able to go home later today. You'll be back on set before you know it.'

'Wonderful news!' Art beams as Kitty gives a smile that doesn't quite reach her eyes. 'Isn't that wonderful news, Lily?'

'The best,' I say. 'Listen, it seems like you have things all under control here, Art, so I'd better leave you to it.' I lean over the bed and kiss Kitty on the cheek, as Art stands to clap Doctor Astor on the back, thanking him for the flowers. 'Are you really OK?' I whisper in her ear.

'Of course,' she whispers back. 'You heard the doctor – I'll be back on set before I know it.'

Stepping out into the corridor, I pause, taking a deep breath. I hate hospitals, but I'm still glad I came, able to see for myself that Kitty is going to be all right.

'Lily? How is she?' Louis stands against the wall of the corridor, the familiar scent of his aftershave tickling my nose, and I smile, pleased he waited for me.

'Tired, but she's going to make a full recovery,' I say. 'She's got Art taking care of her – I'm not sure he'll want to let her out of his sight for the next few days. Can you take me back to the Chateau? I think I want to see Kitty's room again.' There's something nagging at me, something that doesn't feel right, but it's like that feeling when you're searching for a word on the tip of your tongue. I just can't reach out and grab it, and every time I try and put my finger on it, the feeling disperses like mist.

'Wait!' I yelp, as Louis slams on the brakes on the corner of Sunset and N Sierra Bonita. 'Isn't that Tilda?'

There is a flash of distinctive red hair, and Louis lets out a groan. 'And a police officer.' He pulls over, parking neatly on the side of the road. Tilda stands on the pavement, at the entrance to a dingy alley that leads behind the buildings on Sunset, her notebook in her hand as the police officer shakes his head and makes a shooing gesture. Tilda argues sweetly back, tilting her head coyly to one side as she smiles, clutching her notepad to her chest. The police officer shoos her again, and Tilda finally takes a step back as he disappears down the alley.

'Tilda?' Louis hurries over to her and I scramble out of the car, craning my neck to see why the LAPD are loitering down an alley off Sunset at lunchtime. 'What's going on? What are you doing here? I thought you had classes this morning.'

'Oh, I do,' she says, 'but then something much more exciting came along.'

'What's happened?' The alley behind us is dark and foreboding, stinking of damp and old urine, and despite the warm sunshine overhead I shiver, rubbing my hands over my upper arms.

'They found another girl,' Tilda says, her voice low. The police officer has disappeared at the other end of the alley now, and all that remains to say that anything was there at all is a mishmash of footprints. 'I think it might be the same attacker as before… and if it is, it means he's becoming more prolific. The first girl was a couple of weeks ago but now this is two girls in as many days.' She peers down the alley, her brows knitting together.

'It could be a serial killer,' I say, something churning in my gut at the thought of a murderer rampaging through Los Angeles. I mean, I know there are supposed to be hundreds of active serial killers in the United States at any one time, but this is the closest I've ever potentially been to one.

'A what now?' Tilda rolls her eyes.

'A… someone who's killed more than one person.' It seems the phrase 'serial killer' hasn't been coined yet. 'Like, more than three people, I think? So if this is all the work of the same guy, then he's killed at least three girls.'

'Wait, wait. Hold up a second.' Louis raises a hand, shushing both of us, as the police car moves off down the street several feet before pulling to the kerb outside a soda store. The fat cop slides out and disappears inside, one hand on the gun on his belt. 'Tilda, how did you know all of this was going down? And don't even try to tell me you were "just passing", because you know that's not going to fly.'

'Well, no,' Tilda says. 'I didn't just stumble across it, a friend told me.'

'A friend? Who? The only friends you have are me and Lily.'

'And Louella,' I add.

'That is *not true*,' Tilda huffs. 'Evelyn says she's my friend. Although... I don't know if I actually want her to be. Anyway, I met a guy when I was out at a party that Louella sent me to a couple of weeks ago. His sister is something to do with the studio, so he was a plus-one. We got chatting and it turns out he has a very interesting job.'

'What?' Louis demands.

'Ty is a police dispatcher,' Tilda says, a smile tugging at her lips. 'Which is proving to come in very handy. Plus, he's cute.'

'Tilda!' Louis has only just got over Tilda dumping her fiancé, Reg, before they could even set a wedding date.

'He is! He's got blond hair and he sings like a dream.' Tilda looks starry-eyed for a moment. 'Anyway, he got the call to say a body had been found down this alley, and he tipped me off.' She sobers now, her eyes going to the alley entrance. 'I arrived just as they were taking her away. *Oh*. Oh no.'

While Tilda has been waxing lyrical about Ty the singing police dispatcher, the cop has bought his coffee and doughnut and pulls up alongside us now, his beefy face red and his drooping moustache glittering with crystals of doughnut glaze.

'I thought I told you to get outta here.' He glares at Tilda, before turning his eyes on me. They rake over me, from my unruly curls down to my sneakered feet, and I feel Louis shift beside me. 'All of you. Scram. Goddamn vultures.'

'Please, sir,' Tilda says, just as he is about to roll up his window. 'I work for the *Los Angeles Times*.' This isn't strictly a lie, seeing as Louella's column is published in that newspaper. 'I know you told me to leave, but this poor girl... Could I just get a word or two on it for my editor?' She widens her eyes. 'I'm desperate! I need to fill my inches and if I go back to him with nothing, then gosh... I don't know what I'll do.' Tilda blinks, and a tear slides over one cheek. I swear, journalism is the wrong profession for her – she should be up in front of the cameras with Kitty.

'Hardly worth writing about,' the cop huffs.

'Sir, a girl is dead.' I can't stop myself, even as Louis presses his foot on top of mine. How can this police officer – someone supposed to protect and serve – say she's hardly worth writing about?

'Miss,' the police officer says, peering at me through the crack in his window. 'Do you know how many crimes are committed in this city every day? Hundreds. If we were to solve every single one we'd have to enlist every household in the state to help. This girl today... she was nobody. A runaway, no doubt. Another one who came to town thinking the streets were paved with gold, when everybody here knows that's a lie. She probably drank too much, or sassed a john, and that's how she ended up in that alley. So if I were you,' he looks to Louis, 'I'd get these ladies home before they cause any more trouble for you.' With that he gives Louis a brisk nod, and pulls away.

'That's…' Tilda blinks, and this time her eyes are filled with genuine tears. 'That's an awful thing for him to say. Even if she was a runaway maybe somewhere she has a family that'll be looking for her.'

'Hey.' Louis puts an arm around her and pulls her close. 'Come on. You have to get used to this kind of thing if you want to be a reporter, Til. I know it's hard. How about we get you a drink? You're freezing, and seeing the police removing her body… well, that's gotta be tough.'

Tilda nods, and slides into the back seat of Louis's Cadillac, still clutching her notepad to her chest. Moments later we pull up outside Villa Nova, where inside the atmosphere is warm and inviting, the scent of tomato sauce, wine and garlic on the air. Vincente Minnelli is in a booth at the back of the restaurant, and I can't help but peep to see if Judy Garland is sitting beside him. Sometimes I still can't believe I am here, mixing with people I've admired from my own sitting room for years. Villa Nova still exists in my time, only it's called the Rainbow Bar and Grill and, while it's still a popular hangout, it's a little dingy and lacks the charm of this version of it.

The three of us slip into a booth a little further along from Vincente, and none of us speaks until two Martinis and a Tom Collins arrive at the table.

'What a day,' Tilda sighs, 'and it's barely past lunchtime. Wait a minute.' She narrows her eyes at us. 'It's lunchtime. On a Friday. Where the heck have you two been? Lily, shouldn't you be on set right now?'

'Things didn't go quite according to plan today.' I tell Tilda how Kitty didn't show for the breakfast meeting, and how I found her in the tub, unconscious.

'She tried to... *Oh.*' Tilda's hand flies to her mouth. 'Did she...? Is she...?'

'She's OK, but that's the thing,' I say, my stomach churning at the memory of Kitty's adamant denials. 'She says she never tried to harm herself. She remembers Doctor Astor and me coming to her room, but after that everything is a blank.'

'You think someone did this to her?' Louis leans in, his voice low.

'There was a whisky tumbler on the side of the bath, and a bottle of pills on the floor,' I say slowly, grasping for that one thing that doesn't feel right, finally managing to hook it on the corner of my brain. 'I knew it. I knew Kitty was telling the truth.'

'What? What is it?' Tilda asks, as the three of us huddle over our drinks like witches over a cauldron.

'Kitty was already in bed when I left. Doctor Astor was going to take her blood pressure, and then she was going to sleep – she was utterly exhausted after the trauma of being locked in the bathroom in the dark.' I swallow, nausea leaving a foul taste in my mouth. 'I found her in the bath.'

'And?' Louis's brow furrows as he takes a mouthful of Martini.

'If she was already in bed, ready to go to sleep, why would she suddenly decide to take a bath? Maybe if she'd still been wired I could understand it, but she wasn't. I don't think Kitty took a bath herself at all.' Fear makes my mouth go dry and I sip my own drink, screwing my nose up at the tangy taste of the gin. 'I think someone put her in there. Kitty didn't try to kill herself, the whole thing was staged.'

'But... why?' Tilda's eyes are wide, and not even the potent Martini has done very much to bring any colour to her cheeks.

'More importantly, *who*?' Louis says. 'Who had access to Kitty's room last night?'

I shrug. 'Me. Doctor Astor. Kitty was fine when I left, she was just sleepy, like I said.'

'Doctor Astor?' Tilda raises an eyebrow. 'He has access to pills... if he was there when you left it would have been easy for him to give Kitty something and then lift her into the tub.'

I frown, remembering what Kitty said about taking something to get her through the day. Tilda is right, the doctor would have access to pills, and I'm sure he would give Kitty something if she asked him, only she said the 'Mother's Little Helpers' weren't hers. 'Why, though? He's a doctor. Surely it would go against everything he stands for. And not only that, he's the studio doctor – if he did something like this and the studio found out, he'd lose his job.' I think about the way the doctor spoke so gently to Kitty when he visited, the gifts he brought her.

'I'm putting him on the list anyway,' Tilda says.

'What about Art?' Louis chimes in. 'Did he go to visit her after she went to bed?'

'Nope.' I shake my head. 'Kitty told him not to, and when I asked her, she said she didn't remember Art coming to her room at all. And anyway, Kitty had the key. He wouldn't have been able to get in unless she'd let him in.'

Tilda sits back, tapping her nails on the table as she thinks. Louis and I wait in silence – this is how Tilda does her best thinking, and both of us know not to disturb her.

'Jeremy,' she says eventually, her mouth twisting. 'Where was Jeremy?'

'He left the party early,' I say, not sure where she's going with this. 'He turned up at Kitty's door when I took her back to her room. I thought I saw him... outside, peering up at her window, before he knocked.'

'What did he want?' Tilda asks, her brow crumpling. 'Did you let him in?'

'No.' I shake my head. 'He said he wanted to check on Kitty after she was locked in the bathroom, but I'm not sure he was even still at the party when that happened.'

'We all agree that Jeremy seems to be obsessed with Kitty, right?' Tilda says, her mouth twisting.

'He does seem to always be around. I confronted him about it last night. I basically called him a stalker and he just shook it off like it was nothing.'

Louis places a hand over Tilda's notepad, pausing her scribbling. 'What about the other guy, talking about people who might be obsessed with Kitty? The guy from the movie premiere who attacked her?'

'He's in the wind. Maybe if the studio had called the police after all there might have been a chance of them catching him, but as it is he's out there, scot-free. All those newspapermen and not a single one managed to get a photograph of his face.' Tilda shifts in her seat, as if she's got ants in her pants, and she reaches out and necks the rest of her drink.

'Steady on, Til.' Louis pulls her glass away, as she pulls a face at him.

'I'm sorry,' she says. 'I know figuring out what happened to Kitty is important but I can't stop thinking about the girl. The one they just found in the alley. I *saw* her as they took her away. She looked so... still.' Tilda blinks, pressing her lips together as if trying not to cry. 'It was strange, she was wearing a dress that had seen better days, but she wore the most beautiful earrings. Emeralds, I think. She was young – younger than us, Lily. She had blonde hair, and... I think I recognised her.'

'Jeez, Til. Did you mention that to the cop?'

Tilda shakes her head. 'I didn't realise at the time, not until we sat down. I'm not sure, but I think it might have been the girl Jeremy brought to the premiere the other night. The girl who I thought looked like Kitty?'

I feel as if I have been sucker-punched. 'Do you still have that article you showed me the other day? Of the other girl they found?'

Tilda nods and pulls the article out of her purse. The ink is smudged now, the paper soft and worn from being carried around with God only knows what else is in Tilda's purse. Pulling it towards me, I smooth it out and run my eyes over the article, lingering on the blurry photograph in the bottom corner.

'I recognise her too,' I say quietly, my stomach churning as something finally clicks. 'She worked in Schwab's behind the counter. She knows... knew our breakfast order off by heart. She wasn't there this morning, the boy working said she didn't turn up. Look at her, guys.' I shove the article towards them. 'She has blonde curly hair, like Kitty. She was slim and pretty, like Kitty.'

Tilda breathes out a long, low sigh, pulling her ponytail tighter on her head. 'What are you saying, Lily?'

'These girls, these poor girls who are being treated like nobodies by the police... they all bear more than a passing resemblance to Kitty. What if there's a connection to whoever is killing these girls and Kitty?'

Chapter Fourteen

The idea of the murdered girls somehow being connected to Kitty haunts my dreams that night. My sleep is filled with nightmares – thick, dark, shadowy images of chasing Kitty down dimly lit alleys in an attempt to rescue her, but every time she disappears just as I reach for her. I wake up with my nerves jangling, the idea of a day on set and keeping an eye on Kitty feeling daunting as I seem to see danger everywhere. I don't even know if my hunch is correct – there are lots of women in town who look like Kitty, after all. She wears her hair in a style that women all over America have copied, dresses in the latest fashions. Could it all just be a coincidence? Either way, Kitty is still going to disappear, and I need to figure out how and why before it happens.

'I heard she almost died,' Bobby whispers as I sign in to the lot. 'That's what Camilla told me.'

'Camilla?' I look up sharply, dropping the pen on the desk. 'The two of you are on first-name terms?'

Bobby shifts on the balls of his feet and blushes slightly. 'She's nice to me, is all. She said I could call her Camilla. And she gave me a photo.' He points to the wall behind. 'I'm still waiting on Miss Fox. I guess she thinks she's too good for my wall.'

My eyes go the photos behind him. Specifically to the one of Camilla, that she has signed *Love, Camilla x* beside her lipstick mark. 'You're friends, huh?'

Bobby nods. 'Uh-huh. Good friends. She even remembered my birthday.'

'That's really great, Bobby, but I have to get to work.' I wink at him and slip inside. *Well, how about that. Camilla does have one friend.*

—

Kitty is subdued when I enter her trailer, her face pale, a plate of uneaten watermelon beside her.

'Good morning, Kitty. Are you ready to get back on set?' I hate to ask her, but Leonard will be waiting and I don't want there to be any reason for anyone to yell at her this morning.

'As I'll ever be,' she says, shaking back her hair and getting to her feet. 'Just think, if I'd been a nurse, there wouldn't be all this fuss. Maybe it's not too late for me to abandon the studio for the operating room.' I don't quite know how to respond, and then Kitty rolls her eyes and laughs. 'I'm kidding. Of course.' Although her tone is not as light as I would have expected, if she really was joking.

'You don't want to eat something before we go?' I point to the watermelon, my own mouth watering at the sight of it.

Kitty shakes her head. 'Doctor Astor gave me my breakfast this morning, Lily. I couldn't eat a thing if I tried.'

Her words cause a tightening sensation in my gut and I follow her out towards the closed set. Does she mean that Doctor Astor has given her something to get her through her first day back on set? Somehow I don't think she means tea and toast. Before I can think it through any more, we step onto the set and there is a sudden hush. People turn to watch as Kitty makes her way towards Bunny, who holds the script pages for today, and I get the feeling that Kitty might have been the hot topic of conversation before we arrived.

'Kitty!' Leonard booms with a welcoming smile, as if by being jovial enough he can erase the events of the past couple of days. 'Good to see you back. Are we ready? Art, Jeremy – you're up.'

Art and Jeremy take their marks, and Kitty steps into the shadows on the side of the set, waiting until she hears her cue. Doctor Astor is also on the sidelines, along with Oskar Goldstein, and a weight sits on my shoulders. Neither of them is paying particularly close attention to the scene playing out in front of them where Art is threatening Jeremy, his rival, with a prop gun that looks a little too realistic for my liking. Instead, both the doctor and the studio exec keep their eyes on Kitty, as if half expecting her to expire before their eyes. As I scan the set, it seems that almost everyone else is doing the same – casting furtive glances in Kitty's direction instead of watching the scene that's being filmed.

When Leonard finally calls cut, Doctor Astor hurries after Kitty as she heads to her trailer and the low hum of gossip begins to buzz in my ear so loudly that I am almost relieved when Oskar Goldstein grabs my arm.

'Lily? Come with me, please.'

I cast a panicked glance at Leonard, who nods at me, and then follows me and Oskar to a small meeting room inside the lot. Oskar sits and holds out a hand towards a chair, gesturing for me to do the same.

'I heard what happened with Kitty,' Oskar says, steepling his fingers under his chin. 'As I'm sure you can imagine, Lily, this is somewhat of a problem.'

'I understand,' I say, although I don't. Where is the concern? Where is the worry that Kitty might be struggling? As far as anyone else knows Kitty did this to herself, and I wonder who might have told Oskar. Leonard was very clear that he didn't want the studio to get wind of it.

'Do you?' Leonard asks. His eyes are ringed with dark circles, and he seems to have more wrinkles around his mouth than he had before. 'Lily, this has to stay under wraps at all costs.'

'There's already talk,' Oskar says abruptly. 'My men have had to leak rumours of Desi cheating on Lucy again to Hedda Hopper in exchange for her keeping this under wraps. It's not as if it's not true, but even so.' He leans in, so close that I can smell the sausage he ate for breakfast on his breath. 'I want…'

'Yes, we know,' Leonard interrupts. 'We know. It's all—'

Oskar turns a blazingly furious gaze on Leonard, his voice rising to a dull roar. 'Don't *yes* me. Don't agree until you know what I'm asking for.' He turns to me now, and I feel my legs turn to jelly. For someone who doesn't look dissimilar to Elmer Fudd, he exudes a terrifying aura in this mood. 'I want you to leak good news about this movie. Tell them Camilla is going to win Best Actress at the Academy Awards. Tell them Art has adopted a puppy from a shelter. I don't care how you do it, just stir up news ahead of the ceremony this week. This thing with Kitty… it *doesn't leave the studio*. Do you understand? No one on the outside can find out what happened with Kitty. There have been enough rumours already about this ridiculous feud between Kitty and Camilla – and this picture is our biggest chance at next year's Oscars.' He sits back, surveying the pair of us, and I am heartened to see that Leonard's face still carries a spark of anger. 'I want the rest of this picture to go off without a hitch, you hear me? Not one word about Kitty's... medical issue is to hit the stands. Otherwise you're all out of a job.'

—

'Lily? Are you even listening to me?' Kitty pouts, a few days later as she sits in the make-up chair, and I have to confess I'm not. I have been wholly focused on making sure that any rumours about Kitty's hospital stay are squashed before they are leaked from the studio. Now the day's filming is done, there's barely been a peep of gossip about Kitty today, and the air is thick with heightened excitement. It's Oscars night, the biggest night of the year and quite possibly the night when my nerves explode and I expire completely.

'Um, yes?'

Kitty sighs. 'I know you weren't, you were miles away.'

'Sorry. I was just thinking about... tonight. The awards. Are you sure you're all right to go? It was only a little while ago you were... feeling poorly.'

Kitty's cheeks flush slightly at the mention of her 'suicide attempt' and she brushes away the hands that dab at her face, patting eyeshadow onto her lids. 'Honestly, Lily, that was just a little hiccup. Of course I'll be fine to go tonight. It's not as if there's really any other option. You'd be mad to miss it.'

'Even after the premiere? You know, that guy grabbing you?' Worry makes my stomach churn, a thick, heavy knot forming in my gut. 'Has the studio arranged any extra security? Maybe I should speak to Leonard.'

'No, Lily.' Kitty's voice is firm. 'There's no need. I don't want any fuss – that chap was probably drunk or high, and he didn't actually do me any real harm. Can you imagine Camilla if I turned up with extra security? She'd have a heart attack.' Kitty gives a hoot of laughter as I struggle to raise a smile in return. She flicks her fingers, gesturing at the make-up girl to continue.

'I suppose she would have plenty to say.'

'There'll be enough people with eyes on me,' Kitty says, as she meets my gaze in the mirror, the spotlights surrounding it giving her skin an ethereal glow. 'Not going is simply not an option.' She pauses as the make-up girl brushes her lips a vivid red before declaring Kitty's face done. 'Not an option at all. It will be fine, Lily. I've sat through this ceremony before, and tonight will be no different to any other night.' She gets to her feet, wrapping her robe more tightly around her body. 'Excuse me, Lily. I'm going to get dressed.' She casts her eyes over my plain grey pencil skirt and pink blouse. 'And I suggest you and Bunny go and raid the wardrobe department. I'm not letting you go to the Academy Awards in *that* outfit.'

Bunny and I spend a delightful hour rummaging through the wardrobe department, trying on different dresses, hats and accessories. Bunny makes me curl up laughing when she appears in a dress more suited to lounging on the set of *Gone With the Wind* (complete with an enormous bonnet tied under her chin), and when I step out in a strapless dress that I think Rita Hayworth might have once worn, a cigarette holder between my fingers, Bunny sends me straight back inside to change with a spluttered laugh, telling me I look like I might have murdered my first husband.

Eventually I settle on a Givenchy floral dress with a high neckline, full skirt and belted at the waist, in a deliciously rich shade of cream, while Bunny goes for a ruffled gown in a shade of green that highlights her eyes and her pale skin tone, both of us feeling like actual movie stars.

While Bunny fusses with her hair in the mirror of the dressing room we are sharing, I am thinking about Louis, about how I need to tell him to keep his eyes peeled tonight – this isn't a date, him coming to the Oscars as my plus-one, this is *surveillance*. Tilda has spent the last few days trying to dig up information on the missing girls, but she's hitting dead end after dead end. When the cop said no one was bothered about the deaths of these girls, he was right, and something cracks inside me every time I think of them, splintering my heart. I'm so deep in thought that when the earth-shattering scream splits the air, I drop the powder compact I'm holding, pale dust showering the hem of my borrowed gown.

'Kitty?' On shaking legs I run to Kitty's dressing room, throwing the door open and certain I'm about to see her being viciously attacked. *I told Bobby not to sign anyone in.* 'Kitty? Are you OK?'

Kitty stands in the middle of the room, alone, a swathe of silk in her hands. 'Look at this, Lily.' She thrusts the fabric towards me, the silk slipping through my fingers as I reach for it.

Her dress – the one it took almost two weeks to settle on, the dress she's had planned since before the nominations were even announced – is ruined. Completely shredded. The silk is in tatters, and I am speechless, not knowing what to say to make this better.

'That... that *bitch*.' Kitty's fists are balled at her sides, her mouth set in a grim line as she pushes past me, the ties of her robe fluttering behind her as she strides towards Camilla's dressing room. Dropping the ruined dress to the floor, I run after her, my heart in my mouth.

'Open up!' Kitty hammers on Camilla's room before turning the handle and throwing it open. Camilla stands in the middle of her dressing room in her underwear, her mouth open in a gaping O of shock.

'What the hell? Get out of here, Kitty, I'm trying to dress.' An exquisite black gown hangs on the rail at one end of the room, fitted to the knee and then flaring out in an elegant froth of cream tulle, framed by scalloped black velvet. A matching pair of elbow-length gloves sits on the table beside the rack.

'*You're* trying to dress?' Kitty screeches. 'What about me? What in the name of God am I supposed to wear now that you've *destroyed* my gown?'

Bunny skids to a halt as she enters the dressing room, her face rosy and her eyes wide. 'What's happened?' she hisses to me in an urgent whisper.

'Kitty's dress is ruined,' I hiss back, as Camilla's face changes, the fury mixed with the tiniest hint of a smirk.

'Me? I haven't touched your gown. Please, Kitty. Don't you think you're being paranoid?'

'Paranoid? Yards of shredded silk tells me otherwise. I know it was you, Camilla, you're nasty and jealous and...'

Camilla snorts, reaching for the rail that holds her dress. 'Jealous? Oh please, Kitty, give me a break. I have no need to be jealous of you! And I certainly don't need to stoop to ridiculous tactics like ruining your dress for tonight. I'm going to win, Kitty. Word is I'm a shoo-in. Look.' She gestures to a vast bouquet of dahlias and lilies as I inwardly cringe. Leonard must have gone with Camilla's 'win' as news to take the heat off Kitty. 'Even darling Vivien has sent me flowers. *She* knows how to lose graciously.'

'*You absolute f—*' Kitty lunges across the room, intent on grabbing Camilla by the hair as Bunny reaches out and executes an almost perfect rugby tackle, grabbing Kitty before she can do something she'll regret.

'Temper, temper, Kitty.' Camilla's smirk and catty tone is enough to make my blood begin to boil.

'Enough, Camilla.' I stoop down to where Kitty sits on the floor, her blonde curls mussed. 'Kitty, let's get out of here. It doesn't matter about the dress, I can fix things. Let's just get you back to your dressing room.'

With a harsh stare in Camilla's direction, Kitty gets to her feet and then slowly, deliberately, steps towards her. Before I can stop her, she reaches out and slides her hand down Camilla's face, smearing her eyeshadow, dusky pencil liner and lipstick down to her chin.

'There,' Kitty says softly. 'That's better.'

Camilla stares Kitty right in the eye, without flinching. 'One of these days,' she says, 'I am going to kill you.'

—

'Sorted!' I call out half an hour later, hurrying back into Kitty's dressing room, where she is still muttering about Camilla under her breath as she sips on a Martini. 'I called Charles at Fox – he dressed Honey Black when I worked with her before. He's sending a gown right now. In fact, Bunny, could you go out to meet the courier?'

Kitty's hair has been tamed, and as the make-up girl had already left I touched up her make-up myself. When

Bunny hurries back into the room carrying a huge dress bag, I feel my shoulders lower themselves from around my ears somewhere towards their usual position.

'Here.' Bunny unzips the bag and holds up a dress that makes Kitty gasp. 'Try this on.'

'Lily! It's gorgeous!' Kitty's sullen pout disappears as she wriggles out of her robe. 'You really are a miracle worker.'

As Kitty lets Bunny zip her into the dress, my breath catches in my throat. It's a gown I recognise. Black, off-the-shoulder, with a cinched-in waist before fountains of black netting fall to her feet, studded with what look like tiny stars. Kitty is wearing the dress Marilyn Monroe is supposed to wear tonight. Suddenly dizzy, I place a hand against the wall to steady myself. Kitty is a nominee tonight, and Marilyn is merely a presenter, so of course Charles LeMaire – head of wardrobe at Fox – is going to prioritise Kitty, but even so I feel breathless with the thought that I might have tweaked history somehow. There is a tap at the door as Kitty slides her feet into black pumps, and then Art pokes his head inside.

'Kit? Darling? Oh, you look exquisite.' Art slides into the dressing room, and the same could be said for him. He wears a regular black tux, his hair combed neatly with a side parting, and to be honest, on anyone else it would simply look like a tux. On Art, however, he seems to elevate the outfit, just by being Art Calloway.

'You both do,' I blurt out, cursing myself as heat rises in my cheeks.

'As do you, Lily.' Art sweeps his eyes over me. 'What a lucky man I am, to ride to the Academy Awards with two such gorgeous women.'

A giggle bubbles out of me, and Bunny widens her eyes. *What the hell? Lily Jones doesn't giggle, for Pete's sake.* I clear my throat. 'Thank you, Art. Although I'm still not sure Kitty attending is a good idea, after everything that's happened recently.'

'Don't be absurd!' Art snorts. 'Of course Kitty has to attend. This is the event of the year, right, Kit?'

Kitty catches my eye and there is the tiniest pause before she nods. 'Yes. That's what I've been telling her, Art.'

'There's no argument about it. Hold still, both of you.' Art pulls out a camera, a boxy black thing that looks old-fashioned to me, but clearly not to Kitty.

'Art! A *camera*? When did you get that?' Kitty presses her hands to her mouth in glee. 'They're so expensive! Let me see.' She reaches out and turns the camera over in her hands. 'I always wanted my own camera,' she says, 'but we could never afford one. Art, take my picture.'

Art takes the camera and Kitty stands in front of the mirror, the spotlights haloing her hair around her head. She strikes a pose, one hand behind her head as she smiles, her teeth white and straight. Art snaps a photo, and then Kitty holds out a hand to me.

'Lily, come on. I want a picture with you.'

'Oh, no.' I shake my head. 'I'm not very photogenic.' *And I'm not sure it's a good idea to have my photograph taken forty-odd years before I was even born.*

'Don't be silly,' Art says, as Kitty tugs me towards her and even Bunny steps into the frame. Kitty squeezes me tightly, her arm wrapped around my waist, and as Art snaps the picture, I move my head to look at Bunny, hoping I've blurred my features enough to hide my face.

'Kitty? Shall we go? The car is waiting.' Art holds out an arm for her to take, but now Kitty has turned her back, staring into the mirror somewhere far away from the dressing room. 'Kitty?'

'Oh yes, of course.' Shaking her head, Kitty downs the rest of her drink, slaps on a smile and they sweep out of the dressing room.

—

There is a crowd outside RKO Pantages Theatre, where the awards ceremony is being held, and as we step out of the car flashbulbs pop and the cheers are loud enough to hurt my ears. Louis is waiting on the sidewalk, and his eyes widen as he spots me.

'Wow, Lily! That is some dress,' he breathes in my ear as he leans in to kiss my cheek, and my stomach flips.

'It's not mine,' I say with a laugh. 'Remember, we need to focus tonight. This is *work*. Any sign that anything is off, give me the signal.' Louis raises his hand in a Vulcan salute, which was the only hand signal I could come up with off the top of my head, and I nod approvingly.

William Holden and Gloria Swanson leisurely stroll up the red carpet ahead of us, waving and smiling as the crowds go wild. Shaking away the sense of déjà vu that washes over me at the memory of Kitty on the red carpet at the premiere, I fuss with the bottom of her dress, making sure it sits perfectly as the cameras pop, readying Kitty for her own walk along the carpet.

Behind me I hear Louis greet Jeremy and Camilla, and there is a strained moment of awkwardness as they reach us.

'Camilla,' Kitty says with a wicked smile, running her eyes over Camilla's face and her perfectly patched-up make-up. 'Don't you look gorgeous?'

Camilla looks Kitty up and down from head to toe, and I catch a whiff of alcohol on her breath as she speaks. 'As do you. Although,' she leans in, her words slipping slightly as she cuts her eyes to the left where Marilyn Monroe is stepping out of a car in a white dress that flows to mid-calf, 'I do believe that dress is more suited to someone a little curvier.'

'Kitty, you need to get on the carpet,' I interject hastily, manoeuvring Kitty so she stands between Art and Jeremy, hoping I am the only one who spots the hard stare Jeremy gives Art.

The plan is for Art, Kitty, Jeremy and Camilla to walk the carpet together, seeing as they are shooting a movie together and all four of them are nominees. Now I'm wishing I'd pushed back at the studio's suggestion as the tension is so palpable you could cut the air with a knife. Art takes Kitty's hand and they begin to walk, the pair of them looking elegant and other-worldly, stars that shine brighter than the rest of us mere mortals. The crowd screams Kitty's name and I watch as she falters for a second, turning back to look at me. Louis nods, I give her a thumbs up, and then Jeremy and Camilla are on the carpet too, Camilla leading Jeremy over to one side to sign autographs.

It happens so quickly. One minute, Camilla is smiling at her fans, nudging Jeremy towards the crowds for a photograph and to sign the autograph books waved in their direction, and the next minute she is sprawled out on the carpet.

Jeremy gasps, and then stoops down to hold out a hand to help Camilla to her feet. Flashbulbs pop left, right and centre, and at the far end of the carpet I see both Louella Parsons and Hedda Hopper, their eyes on Camilla, one hand pressed to Hedda's mouth as if hiding a smile. Camilla gets to her feet, her cheeks blazing, and it's only when I see Kitty turn back at the entrance to the theatre, amusement dancing in her eyes as she watches Camilla hobble towards her on Jeremy's arm, that I realise I didn't imagine it. I most definitely did see Kitty's foot fly out and trip Camilla into a sprawling mess in front of the whole world.

Chapter Fifteen

Inside, Kitty and Art are sat with Camilla and Jeremy, with Bunny and I seated on the other side of them, and Camilla shoots Kitty the darkest of looks as she takes her place. Part of me wants to cheer Kitty, especially if Camilla was responsible for ruining her gown, but the other part of me feels terribly sorry for Camilla. Even if she wins tonight, the newspapers will be full of her trip on the red carpet, instead of her success at snagging an Oscar.

'You tripped me,' Camilla hisses as Kitty shifts in her seat, rearranging her gown around her.

Kitty turns to face her with a cutting smile. 'Honestly, Camilla. What a ridiculous thing to say.' She glances at the glass of wine in Camilla's hand. 'I think we all know guzzling wine in your dressing room can sometimes lead to carpet malfunctions.'

Camilla narrows her eyes. 'I guess you can take the girl out of the gutter, but you can't take the gutter out of the girl. Where was it you grew up, Kitty? The Bronx?'

Thankfully, before Kitty can respond, Fred Astaire takes the stage and begins a witty speech, before introducing the presenter of the first award. We sit through awards for film editing, art direction, cinematography and costume design, the drinks flowing effortlessly the entire evening, as I realise that while I may have thought I was a diehard fan of the Oscars in 2020, I've never actually had to sit through the entire show before. Usually, Eric and I would take turns to make drinks and snacks, missing entire chunks of the early awards as we spiralled down TikTok rabbit holes and gossiped about people we knew. There is a pang deep in my chest, as I wonder what he's doing. There's lots of things about LA in 2020 that I don't miss, but Eric isn't one of them.

Camilla whoops, clapping loudly as George Sanders collects his Oscar for Actor in a Supporting Role. 'I kissed him at a party once,' she says with glassy eyes, rather more loudly than intended, as Leonard turns to glare at the waiter who leans in to top up Camilla's wine.

'Maybe you've had enough,' Jeremy says quietly, reaching for her glass, but Camilla slaps at his hand.

'Don't be a party pooper, Jer,' Camilla slurs, taking another gulp of wine. 'It's a *celebration*. And I'm going to have plenty to celebrate in a minute. Poor old Kitty, I hope she's been practising her gracious loser face.'

Kitty reaches into the tiny clutch she carries, rummaging until she pulls out something small and pops it into her mouth as Helen Hayes takes the stage to announce the winner of the Best Actor award.

'Hey,' I hiss. 'Are you all right?' Kitty looks pale, although I'm not sure if it's just the dim lighting. I'm hoping it was gum she popped into her mouth, but judging by the way she swigs at her drink, it wasn't. 'What was that?' I gesture to her bag.

'Just a vitamin, Lily,' she snaps, and I see a faint sheen of sweat over her upper lip. 'I'm a little nervous, is all.'

'You really want to win, don't you?' All the things Kitty has said about giving up fame and fortune seem irrelevant now, as I realise that perhaps she only meant it in the heat of the moment. This moment, tonight, means more than anything to her.

'Of course I do.' Kitty twists in her seat to face me, so the others can't read her lips. On the other side of her, Camilla is running an acerbic commentary to Jeremy on why Judy Holliday should have presented the next award instead of Helen, at a volume that could be deemed offensive. 'And more importantly, I want to beat Camilla. I know I'm better than her.'

Helen Hayes picks open the envelope on stage, the spotlight beating down on her. 'And the winner of the Best Actor award is…' She lets the silence stretch out, as Art grins down at Kitty before adjusting his bow tie and getting ready to get to his feet. '…Jeremy Knox for *The Last Station*!'

Jeremy's shock is evident as he presses a hand to his mouth and then stands to make his way to the stage, smiling and waving. The cheering and clapping becomes a wild roar, and I realise that whatever Jeremy's persona is off screen, on screen he is adored.

'Woo! Jeremy!' Camilla yells with a hiccup, holding her wine glass aloft, barely noticing when it slops over one hand, staining her gloves.

Sneaking a peek at Art, my heart stutters in my chest. His face is dark with rage, his jaw clenched, but as all eyes turn towards him it melts away and his trademark wide smile is back, as he claps heartily.

Beside him Kitty also claps, as she looks up at Jeremy on stage, pride rippling over her features. Clearly, despite the way she claims to feel about Jeremy now, she does still care for him – I guess it would be hard not to after knowing someone since childhood. As I watch them, Art leans down to Kitty's ear and her smile drops.

'He doesn't deserve it,' Art says through gritted teeth, even as he claps and smiles. 'He must have bought someone off. Everyone knows I'm the one who should be up there.'

Kitty gives a tiny nod and drops her hands into her lap as Jeremy begins to give his acceptance speech. He thanks the studio, Leonard, his parents and then Kitty.

'I wouldn't be here without the one woman who spurred me on. Kitty Fox. Everything I've done is because of you. You have no idea how important you are to me. Thank you.'

'Anyone would think you were his girlfriend.' Art's voice is terse, as Kitty reaches out and takes his hand.

'Oh, Art, don't be silly. Everyone knows I've known Jeremy for years.'

Camilla sniggers on the other side of Art. 'Art darling, don't worry. I'll thank you in my speech in a moment.' She side-eyes Kitty, who presses her lips together and stares resolutely ahead as Broderick Crawford appears on stage to present Best Actress.

'Ladies and gentlemen, I am honoured this evening to present this award. The nominees are...' As Crawford reels off the list of impressive names, Kitty's hand sneaks into mine and she squeezes tightly. I squeeze back as I glance at Camilla. She doesn't seem nervous at all, in stark contrast to Kitty, but I don't know if it's the effects of all the wine she's drunk or Leonard's leak to the press that she's going to win. She rolls her eyes as Kitty's name is read out, and then smiles graciously when hers is mentioned, offering up a little wave to Vivien Leigh at her mention. I almost feel as if Camilla must know something we don't – maybe Leonard really did get a sneak peek at the winners' envelopes – so when Kitty's name is announced as the winner, I think I must have misheard.

'Kitty Fox, for *The Last Station*!' Broderick Crawford looks out over the crowd, eyes searching for Kitty.

'That's me,' she whispers, her eyes wide as she turns to look at me. 'That's my name. Lily, I won.'

'That's you!' I laugh, gently nudging her to her feet. 'Go and get your Oscar!' Kitty leans down and kisses Art full on the lips and then makes her way onto the stage, thanking her award presenter and clasping the golden figure to her chest.

'I don't know what to say,' she gasps, tears making her voice thicken.

'This is absurd.' Camilla gets to her feet, wobbly and unsteady thanks to the wine she's been sinking, her voice rising above Kitty's even without a microphone. 'It's a sham, that's what it is! This whole thing is fixed!' People around us begin to murmur, as Art tries to tell Camilla to sit down. 'Oh, go boil your head, Art. You're a loser as well.' Camilla hitches up her dress and storms out of the theatre, seemingly unaware of the eyes on her as she wobbles her way to the rear doors.

On stage, Kitty swallows and tries again, her eyes on the back of the room watching Camilla's exit. 'Sorry. Sorry about that. I was saying… erm… thank you. Thank you to the studio, Leonard Langford, my co-stars and everybody who has supported my career. I never went into this game with a view to being rich and famous – all I wanted was to be someone else for a little while. You never know in the movies, how long your success is going to last. This might be my only award – the last time I ever get up here and thank you all. This time next year I might be on a farm, milking goats.' There is a ripple of laughter, overexaggerated for the poor quality of the joke.

As I glance around the room everyone has their eyes on Kitty. She is holding the movie business in the palm of her hand. Even Art is laughing at Kitty's crappy joke, his eyes lighting up as he watches her on stage. While he may be terribly disappointed at his own loss, he is doing a good job of masking it and letting Kitty have her moment to shine. The only person who doesn't seem to be enthralled by Kitty is Jeremy. If anything he looks troubled, his brow creased as he watches her end her speech and wave as she prepares to step aside for the next presenter. *Was it her comment about this being her last award? Is he concerned that if Kitty does drop out of the limelight he won't be able to get as close to her all the time?* Something tickles the back of my neck, the scratching, unsettling instinct that something isn't right, and then it happens.

Shots ring out.

Chapter Sixteen

'Down! Get down!' Louis grabs my arm and yanks me off my chair, onto the theatre floor.

Bunny scrambles down beside me, her eyes wide, face frozen in terror. Around us pandemonium breaks out as screams fill the auditorium, and people begin to run towards the exits, shoving and stumbling over one another. You can almost taste the panic on the air, but my only thought is for Kitty. *I knew this was going to happen.* The thought that hits is bright and bold, almost technicolour. I *did* know that there was a shooting at an Oscars ceremony, but I didn't know it was this one – *Kitty's* one. I thought it happened a few years down the line. I don't have time to follow the thought process now and, shaking off Louis's hand, I raise my head, trying to peer between the crowd towards the stage.

'Lily! What are you doing? Stay down!' Louis reaches for me again, but I shrug him off.

'Where's Tilda? I can't see her!'

Louis tugs at the back of my gown, and I fall back down to floor level. 'She left already. She was only here to grab a few lines from the actors – Louella is covering the event.' Shouts rise and my stomach turns over.

'Kitty!' I say, horror coursing through my veins at the idea that somehow maybe something I've done has already changed the course of history, and this is the end for Kitty.

'She's up there on the stage, in full view of the shooter! We have to get her away.'

Louis wraps his fingers around my wrist so tightly it hurts. 'There are other people closer to her, Lily. They'll get Kitty to safety. Look, Art is already making his way to the stage and so is Jeremy. You need to stay here.'

Shouting comes from the back of the room, hysterical and wild, and louder than the frantic yells of panic that fill the theatre.

'She should *never* have won,' shrieks a voice I recognise, and I peep up cautiously to see Camilla, waving something around in one hand. 'It was *my* part in *my* movie and she stole it from me!'

Camilla. Camilla has the gun. I think I can talk her down. Shaking Louis off and ignoring Bunny's call for me to *please, be careful*, I raise my hands in a gesture of surrender and walk slowly towards Camilla. She is dishevelled, her make-up sliding down her face for the second time this evening as she sobs. She blinks, her gaze not quite focused as the hand holding the gun shakes unsteadily, and I swallow down the urge to follow Louis's advice and get the hell out of here.

'Camilla.' I keep my hands up and my voice steady, even though my heart is beating fit to burst out of my chest. 'Camilla, put the gun down. You don't need to do this.'

'*You*,' she sneers, tears streaming down her face. 'I should have known you'd jump to her rescue. Do you know what she's really like, Lily?'

'Why don't you put the gun down and then we can talk about it. I don't really feel—'

'I don't care how you feel!' Camilla points the gun at my chest and I stop walking. 'Did anyone care about how

I felt? Of course they didn't. Kitty stole that part from me – my agent told me it was mine and then two days later I got a call to say I'd been replaced.' Her chest heaves, and behind her I see the doors creak open and two police officers enter. 'I don't know what she did, who she slept with, but Kitty Fox stole my part and she stole my award!'

'Listen, how about you put the gun down and we get a drink? I'm sure all of this can be sorted out if we just—'

Camilla snorts, shaking her head wildly. 'The only way this can be sorted is if Kitty Fox is gone for good. I'm sick of her ruining my life. She needs to be dealt with.' Camilla raises the gun again and points it towards the stage.

My feet move seemingly of their own accord, placing my body between the gun and the stage as Camilla's finger slowly squeezes the trigger. Closing my eyes, a tear slides down one cheek as I brace myself for the bullet to hit me. *I'm sorry, Louis. I'm sorry, Tilda.* If I die, I hope they can save Kitty themselves.

Time seems to slow down, and it's almost as if I am dreaming, as the screams and panic around me fade out. I see my mum, holding out a hand as she smiles at me from her hospital bed, her face grey and washed out, but her eyes still full of love. I see myself, on a plane to LAX alone, my stomach like a washing machine on spin as I leave London and everything familiar behind to start my new life, a life that doesn't include my mum anymore. I see Eric, clinking a beer bottle against mine the first night we went out together after work, can feel my stomach muscles aching from laughter. And then the bathtub in the Paul Williams suite of the Beverly Hills Hotel, right before I slipped and fell, hitting my head and waking up in 1949 for the first time. *Is this it? Am I going to die?* How would that even work? Can I die forty years before I've been born?

There is a pop and then the sound of shattering glass, but nothing hits me. Cautiously opening one eye, I see Camilla being wrestled away by the police, smashed champagne saucers littering the carpet as Leonard stoops to pick up the gun. A second later, I am almost bowled over by two sets of arms wrapping themselves around me.

'Lily, you were so brave.' Bunny beams up at me with eyes ringed by melted mascara, her arms around my waist.

'What in the name of God did you think you were doing?' Louis's arm wraps around my shoulder, pulling me close to him, his shoulders almost vibrating with fear and rage. 'You could have been killed!'

'I knew she wouldn't shoot,' I lie, offering up a shaky grin that Louis doesn't return.

Leonard approaches, the gun dangling from one finger, followed by Kitty and Art. Kitty is almost translucent she's so pale, and Art couldn't be closer if he was stitched to her side. 'It's a prop,' Leonard says. 'The gun. Camilla must have taken it from the set.'

Of course, it's the gun Art and Jeremy were using for their scene earlier. 'See?' I say to Louis. 'I wouldn't have been hurt.'

Before he can reply, Kitty wraps me in a hug that smells strongly of perfume and face powder, and Art also leans in. 'You were magnificent, Lily,' Kitty breathes. 'No one has ever put themselves on the line like that for me before.'

'But also silly,' Art says sternly, and I feel as if I am being scolded by my father, if I'd ever known him. 'Maybe you need to take some time off? Rest and recover? I think perhaps all this, along with Kitty's... *hospital stay* might have been a bit much for you.'

'Just doing my job,' I say, the words falling flatter than the perky tone I'd hoped for. Tears sting my eyes and Louis reaches for me, pulling me close to him.

'I think I'll take Lily home now, if that's OK.'

I allow Louis to lead me through what remains of the crowd out onto the street outside. The newspapermen are all still loitering on the streets and they call out to us as we leave, clamouring for information, aware of the shots fired inside. I feel desperately cold all of a sudden, longing for the warmth of my bed in my apartment with Tilda, the flannel nightgown under my pillow and maybe a strong tot of brandy.

'Maybe we need to rethink the hand signal,' I say, with a weary smile.

—

Camilla is hollow-eyed as she arrives on set the next day, her face drawn and tired, although she still looks better than I expected after spending the best part of the night in a jail cell. A studio lawyer had been sent over to bail her out, and half the studio execs seem to be holding crisis PR meetings this morning. The rest of us are on tenterhooks as Camilla slides into her trailer without making eye contact, and even Kitty doesn't have a biting word to say. An hour later Leonard strides out of Camilla's trailer, his face set, gesturing for all of us to gather round.

'What happened last night,' he begins, shoving a hand through his thick salt-and-pepper hair, 'was unacceptable. To be frank with you all, the studio would be more than happy for me to fire Camilla and reshoot her scenes with a new actress, particularly if we can't employ some kind of damage control with the press. There's a girl I have my eye on who's about to start shooting the new Henry Hathaway movie. She's very beautiful, very talented, and should Camilla be fired, she would be perfect for this role.'

Racking my brains, I try to think who it could be. *Surely not?* 'Grace Kelly?'

Leonard looks at me with surprise. 'Yes, Lily. Grace Kelly. Her test reel for Henry was outstanding.'

'That would be a mistake.' Art straightens his shoulders as he looks Leonard dead in the eye. 'Camilla is fragile enough at the moment. To fire her could break her, and besides, she's excellent as Maud in this movie. The friction between her and Kitty translates so well on screen. The picture shouldn't suffer simply because Camilla let things get on top of her.'

I frown, surprised that Art seems to be defending Camilla given the way Kitty feels about her, and even Leonard looks taken aback. 'Art, with all due respect, I am the director of this movie. I know exactly how well things do and don't translate.'

'I think the real question here is can Kitty continue to work with Camilla?' Jeremy says, Art turning a harsh glare on him as Kitty shifts awkwardly on the balls of her feet. I'm realising that for someone who is on the silver screen, Kitty hates to be the centre of attention off screen. 'Camilla tried to shoot her, for Pete's sake, surely Kitty's safety must come first?' He eyes Art closely. 'I would have thought Kitty's safety would have been your first concern too.'

Bunny raises a hand. 'Actually, Camilla tried to shoot Lily first.'

Art rolls his eyes, causing Bunny to flush a roasting fiery red. 'I'm sure you'll agree Lily put herself in the firing line.'

'It could have been so much worse,' I say. 'Kitty could have been shot. It could have been someone else entering the theatre with a real gun, instead of Camilla with a prop.'

'The fact remains, Kitty is the one who was in danger. Kitty, can you work with Camilla after this?' Jeremy asks.

'The costs of replacing her will be astronomical,' Leonard says. 'With the delays in production… there's a chance we'll miss the Oscar nominations for next year for this movie.' He rubs at his forehead as if he has a tension headache, and I note the tightness in his shoulders. I have no doubt that Oskar Goldstein has already had Leonard in his office this morning, reading him the riot act over the headlines that will have appeared by dawn, all focused on Camilla's behaviour last night.

Kitty purses her lips, and I can almost see her inner struggle. The idea of getting Camilla off the movie for good versus the chance to win another Oscar next year… 'I want a full apology,' she says eventually. 'No more of her petty bitchiness either. And she has to understand that I won fair and square.'

'Excellent.' Leonard claps his hands together, relief flooding his features and his shoulders lowering by a good two inches. 'The two of you will do a short interview with the press this morning before shooting starts, just to clear things up. Lily, I've notes for you to give the girls so they know what to say. Do *not* deviate from them.'

The idea of a press conference, however small, makes me shudder. It was ridiculously easy for Camilla to smuggle the prop gun into the theatre last night – it could be just as easy for someone to smuggle a real gun into a press conference. Of course, only I know that Kitty is going to disappear. I know she's in danger, but no one else does.

'Is that a good idea?' I say tentatively. 'It's just... I don't feel comfortable putting Kitty on the front line again so soon after this has happened. Someone else could—'

'Damage control, Lily,' Leonard says, his tone sharp. 'I'm trying to save this picture.'

'I'll be there the entire time,' Jeremy says. 'I'll keep an eye on both of the women. Kitty will be safe with me there.'

That's just it, I think to myself. Given the way Jeremy has been sneaking around Kitty's room, spying on her and following her, I'm not sure that Kitty is safe with him around.

That evening, Louis picks me up and we drive over to Musso and Frank for drinks with Tilda and her police dispatcher. Louis is clearly not enamoured with the idea of hanging out with Tilda and a man who isn't Reg, but I am looking forward to it after the last twenty-four hours, especially now I know that Kitty is at dinner with Leonard and Jean at their house, safe from gun-wielding actresses and dark, dingy alleyways.

'Guys, this is Ty.' Tilda is beaming as she introduces us to her date, a tall, broad-shouldered man with blond slicked-back hair. 'My dispatcher guy. We're only staying for one drink and then we have dinner reservations.'

'Hi, Ty.' I hang my jacket on the coat stand beside the other coats and hats, and slide into the booth opposite them as Louis grunts in acknowledgement. Tilda turns her piercing blue eyes on me.

'What is that in your hair? Did you get Chinese food earlier?'

My hands go to my bun, and the chopsticks I threaded through to help keep it in place. It's something I did without thinking, grabbing them from a drawer in the apartment before I left this morning, just as I would have done in my own time. 'Um… no. Call it a fashion accessory? I have to keep my hair up somehow.'

Tilda raises an eyebrow before asking the question she really wants an answer to. 'Why did I have to hear from Louella that you had a gun turned on you last night? I knew I should have pressed Louella to let me stay.'

I glance at Ty, expecting some sort of reaction, but he just raises an eyebrow and sips his drink. All in a day's work for him, I guess. 'You were asleep when I got home,' I say pointedly, even though she wasn't. She wasn't home at all, she was out with Ty, but I'm not sure if Louis knows that. I explain what happened and then the events on the set today before filming restarted.

'Lily, you could have died,' Louis says, as I tell Tilda it really wasn't that much of a big deal. I've already forgotten the fear that gripped me by the throat as Camilla raised the gun and squeezed the trigger – I'm more concerned with keeping things on the straight and narrow so that Oskar doesn't pull the plug on the picture completely. 'Tilda, you have to be in agreement, all of this with Kitty has gone far enough.'

Tilda looks down at her napkin as she folds and refolds it. 'Lou, I know you're worried but I don't think you know Lily as well as you think, if you believe she's just going to leave Kitty to her fate.'

Louis glances at Ty, who is listening intently without saying a word, and changes the subject, knowing when he's beaten. 'Did you get anywhere with finding out any more about the investigation into the dead girls?'

Now Ty does perk up. 'I've been helping Tilda look into that, but whatever you do, don't tell anyone. I'll lose my job.'

'And we need him to keep that job right now.' Tilda winks. 'I've not uncovered much. The girl from Schwab's – Doris Gray – she moved out here from Alabama six months ago. She wanted to get into the movies, but no luck obviously. She apparently told a colleague that she had a screen test the week she died, but no one knows who with or what for.'

'And the other girl?'

Tilda sighs. 'Not much at all. Ty found an address on file for her. She was living in a boarding house with three other girls but none of them really want to talk, and none of them have any idea where she came from originally. She never mentioned any family. The only thing that was strange was one of the girls said the earrings she was wearing when she was found dead didn't belong to her. She apparently only arrived with a small bag and she didn't have anything worth any money on her.'

Excitement sparks in my veins. 'This could be a clue, Til.'

'How?'

'What if the killer gave her the earrings? Or left them as a calling card?' Fragments of hundreds of true crime podcasts and documentaries flitter through my mind. 'We need to find out if any of the other dead girls had some item of jewellery on them that didn't belong to them.'

Tilda whips out her notepad. 'You could be on to something here. Ty, you can help with this.'

'Still no confirmation that the girls are connected to Kitty though,' Louis says, one eyebrow raised.

'But we still know Kitty is going to disappear,' I snap back. 'Tilda, Ty, see what you can find out about the accessories the girls wore. I'm still going to keep digging around at the studio, and see what I can uncover. I'm still not sure about Jeremy – his behaviour just seems so *off* around Kitty. He's forever creeping around her hotel room, and I'm sure he's the one who's been following her. He knew Kitty and Art argued the night of the nominations party... and I can't figure out how. Camilla *hates* her. Things between them seem to be escalating... the episode with the gun just shows that when it comes to Kitty, Camilla gets so furious she can't seem to think rationally.'

We go back and forth for a while over drinks until Tilda and Ty head out for their dinner reservations, leaving Louis and me alone. Alone, for the first time since I told him I didn't think we could ever have a romantic relationship. The air feels charged between us, and I find that I can't think of anything to say, for the first time since I met him in the Polo Lounge at the Beverly Hills Hotel.

After a long pause, we both speak at the same time.

'Lily, I—'

'I wondered if—'

Louis grins, and the awkwardness between us dissipates. 'You go.'

Returning the grin, relief evident in my voice, I say, 'Let's get out of here and go back to my apartment. I'd rather eat microwave macaroni just the two of us, than here.'

'Micro...?'

Sliding out of the booth, I reach for our coats, knocking a hat and a floaty scarf to the floor as I do, and hold out a hand to Louis. 'Let's bust this joint.'

Back at the apartment I make us peanut butter and jelly sandwiches, because obviously microwave macaroni isn't a thing yet, and we settle on the couch.

'You're really set on this Kitty thing, huh?' Louis says with a mouth full of sandwich. I nod. 'I feel like I'm here for a reason, and maybe this is it.' I push away the notion that perhaps, once I've saved Kitty, there'll be nothing left for me to stay for and I'll be pinged back to my own time.

Louis finishes his snack and leans over to put his plate on the coffee table, keeping his eyes ahead. 'I'm glad we can still be friends,' he says quietly. 'What you were saying the other day... I do understand. Maybe we are just too different. But we still make a pretty awesome team.'

'Don't forget our third musketeer,' I say with a laugh that sounds forced. While I don't think I'll ever get over the fact that Louis and I can't be together (and that I can never really be honest with him about who I am), I am grateful that things between us haven't folded completely.

'As if we ever could.' Louis rolls his eyes. 'Listen, I'm going to get out of your hair before Tilda comes back and lectures me for keeping you up so late on a shooting night.'

I laugh, more genuinely this time, letting him wrap an arm around me in a hug, his hand lingering on my back for the briefest of moments before he pulls away and heads out into the night, leaving me confused about my own emotions once more. I wish things could be different – wish that I'd met Louis in my own time or that somehow we could make a life together here, but it's impossible. As I head for the bathroom to wash the smudged make-up from my face, there is a pang deep in my heart. The life

I have here in the 1950s is everything I ever wanted for myself. A great job (despite the drama that ensues on set), a nice apartment, good friends. *I don't ever want to leave*, I think, *but I don't know how I can stay indefinitely*. As I reach for a towel to dry my face, headlights sweep across the darkened sitting room, followed by the slamming of a car door and footsteps outside the building. I pause, waiting to see if Tilda thunders her way up the stairs, but there is nothing.

Maybe it's Louis, maybe he's forgotten something and he's come back. Smothering a smile, I hurry to the front door, not bothering to stop and put my shoes on. Running down the stairs and out the side door into the street, I look one way and then the other, a smile splitting my face.

'Lou?' My voice carries in the still night air, and I can smell honeysuckle from the neighbour's garden. There is no response. Whirling around, I see only shadows, stretching long fingers out towards the black van on the other side of the street.

That wasn't there before. When Louis and I came home, the street was empty apart from the old Ford that belongs to our neighbour. Senses tingling, the hairs on the back of my neck standing to attention, I glance over my shoulder again, but there is still no one there despite the unnerving sensation I feel that eyes are on me. My fingers itching to dial 911 on a mobile phone that doesn't exist yet, I walk carefully in my bare feet across the street to the van. It's only as I reach the rear doors that I hear it. The crunch of footsteps, breath heavy in my ear. There is a flash of something, a glint of gold caught by the moonlight, and then the rear doors of the van swing open. Hands shove me hard from behind and I tumble into the dark, the van doors clicking shut behind me.

Chapter Seventeen

Fuck. Blinking in an attempt to adjust my eyes to the dark, I stagger against the metal siding as the van takes off, cracking my head against the divider between the rear of the van and the front seats. Righting myself, I crouch on the floor, the crash of my pulse loud in my ears as the van takes a left, then a right.

They're heading towards the highway, I think, as I try to follow the route in my now pounding head. I've seen it before in a thousand documentaries – follow the route the vehicle takes in your mind; scrape your fingernails along the carpet to collect fibres, even better, scratch your abductor to get DNA under your nails; tug out strands of hair and leave them in the place you're taken to. Only, DNA testing doesn't exist yet. And I don't know the streets well enough in Los Angeles to figure out where they might be taking me.

Eyes finally adjusting to the inky blackness in the back of the van, I try to squash down the panic that claws its way up my chest, concentrating on trying to keep breathing. The air in the van smells musty, with a hint of something else that makes me think of Bonfire Night and my grandfather's house. I force myself to focus, running my hands over the sides and floor of the van, my fingers searching out anything that might lead me to the identity of my abductor. The metal siding is smooth and free of any snags or nails. The floor is clean too, a light dusting of what feels like sawdust or dried mud on my fingers the only hint that anyone else has been in here.

The van takes another sharp right, and I fall against the metal sheeting that divides the front seats from the rear of the van, the metal cold against my skin through my thin blouse as I rest my head back, fighting tears.

Will Tilda check on me when she gets back from her date? Will she even think anything of it if she does and I'm not home? She might just think I'm out with Louis, dancing the night away at the Palomino. I haven't told her yet that the two of us have knocked any romance on the head, and I'm sure if Louis had told her she would have been on my case already. The idea that no one might even notice I'm gone until the morning makes my throat constrict and I gasp, a thin, shallow breath as my vision dapples. *Keep it together, Lil. Try and think rationally.*

OK. I draw in a deep breath, hold it for five seconds and then slowly release it, just like Eric's mindfulness app taught me, repeating the motion until finally I feel calmer. I have no idea where the van could be now, any tracking I attempted long abandoned. I think perhaps we have left the highway, as the rush of other cars has disappeared and the road beneath the wheels feel distinctly less smooth, bumps and ruts juddering under my body.

Who did this? Is it connected to Kitty? Or am I about to become the West Hollywood serial killer's fourth victim? As I press my head against the divider, I realise I can hear the low murmur of voices, the musty scent growing slightly stronger as I turn and press my face against it.

'...idiot. She wasn't supposed to be...'
'...my fault... panicked... do with her?'

The voices are low, barely above whispering, but they sound male. They're discussing what they're going to do with me. Oh *shit*. Fear clatters through my veins, sharp and spiky, leaving me with shaking hands but a clear head. They'll have to pull over eventually, and then I need to be ready. The moment those back doors open I need to be ready to fight my way out of here, because I didn't leave twenty-first century Los Angeles to be murdered by some scumbag before I was even born. *I don't have a weapon, though. I don't even have any shoes on.* I run my hands over my outfit, searching for something – *anything* – I can use to defend myself, before my hands go to my hair. Or more specifically, to the chopsticks in my hair. Yanking them out, I grip one in each fist, and mime jabbing them, one, two, one, two. I'll have to be quick, and I'll have to be accurate if I have any chance of escape.

I am mid-thrust when there is the blare of a horn and the screeching of tyres. The van brakes sharply, but not sharply enough as there is an explosive bang and the crumpling of metal. I am thrown to the floor, narrowly missing gouging my own eyes out with the chopsticks, as I slide across the bottom of the van towards the rear doors.

Shouting fills the air and I get gingerly to my feet, my shoulder throbbing. Holding my chopsticks aloft I creep towards the van doors, and as they are thrown open, I leap forward with a strangled, '*Fuck you!*' – jabbing forward as hard as I can with my pathetic weapons.

Arms wrap around me and a voice I know so well whispers in my ear. 'Stop, Lil. Stop, it's me.'

Pulling back, I look into Louis's green eyes, adrenaline making my breath come short in my throat. 'Lou? What…?' Peering past Louis I see his pride and joy, the Cadillac, which now sports a slightly crumpled fender as the van beside it sports a matching dented bonnet, steam hissing from the engine. 'You ran them off the road?'

Louis nods, wincing slightly. He reaches out, intent on guiding me towards the car, but I step round him, moving towards the crumpled van. Through the cracked windshield, I can just make out two dark figures slumped against the dashboard.

'Lily...' Louis groans, as I tiptoe closer.

'I need to see who it is,' I say in an urgent whisper. 'They bundled me into the back of a van, Louis! It's OK, they're unconscious.' I reach the door of the van, and just as I am about to peer inside and catch a glimpse of my abductor, a loud moan comes from inside and a hand comes up to smack hard against the window. I let out a strangled yelp, and Louis's fingers come down hard on my bicep, yanking me towards the Cadillac. With my heart in my mouth I throw myself into the passenger seat and Louis floors it, peeling across the track with a stench of burning rubber. As the van recedes into the distance I turn back to watch out of the rear window, until it disappears from view completely.

—

'Ow.' I wince as Tilda dabs gently at my forehead with a cotton pad. 'That hurts.'

'You only have a small cut, but it's going to bruise,' she says. 'Hold still. You're going to need to cover that up tomorrow with panstick.'

'How did you know where I was?' Without moving my head I flick my eyes in Louis's direction as he lounges against the small table Tilda and I have wedged into our kitchenette.

'I came back,' he says sheepishly. 'After I left you, I don't know... I just had the strongest sensation that I needed to see you.'

'Why didn't you call the police? When you saw them shove her into the van?' Tilda asks as she carries on dabbing at my cut with rather less sympathy than I would like. 'Instead of haring off like a maniac like that. You're lucky you didn't kill the both of you.'

'There wasn't time,' Louis shrugs, his cheeks reddening. 'You guys don't have a telephone, and by the time I drove to the closest public payphone they would have been long gone. Anyway,' he turns back to me, 'I saw them bundle you into the back of the van and I just reacted. Jumped in the car and followed them. Once they left the highway and turned onto the road into the desert I knew I had to stop them somehow.'

'So you crashed your car,' Tilda says with a wry smile.

'Uh, yeah. I crashed the car. That was the only way I could think of to get them to stop.'

Tilda finishes her dabbing and inspects my face, lifting my chin and turning it one way and then the other. 'You're good. No stitches needed.' She holds my face still, gazing into my eyes. 'Who do you think it was, Lil? Who took you?'

I shake my head, wincing slightly. 'I don't know. I thought I could peep in the van and check but one of them banged on the window and I... well, I ran. Instinct, I guess. I thought if they were awake and able they might hurt both of us.'

'Anyone else would have done the same,' Tilda says.

I shrug, but now part of me wishes I'd been braver. At least then I might know who did this to me. 'Before it happened, I heard the door slam outside and when you didn't come in I thought maybe Louis had come back. I went down onto the street and I couldn't see anyone, but I could feel someone watching me. The same way I did on my way to the Chateau that time.' I pause, reliving the chaotic van journey. 'Hands shoved me inside... I could hear them talking, just words here and there discussing what they were going to do with me.' My hands go to my hair, to the spirals of curls that erupt from my scalp without the chopsticks to keep them in check. 'The van smelled odd, like... cinnamon? No. Something like that. Something aniseedy.'

'Liquorice?' Tilda raises her eyebrows. 'Lily, was it like liquorice?'

Suddenly nauseous, I swallow, my stomach churning. 'Yeah. It could have been liquorice, I guess.'

'Just like the guy who tried to grab Kitty on the red carpet!' Tilda yelps, jumping to her feet and reaching for her notepad. She flips the pages, pointing to a messy scrawl that apparently says that exact thing. 'She said he smelled like he'd just eaten liquorice or aniseed. Did he wear a ring?'

'I'm not sure.' Squeezing my eyes closed, I think about the moments before I was shoved in the van. The doors swinging open, the flash of gold in the moonlight. 'Maybe? I think maybe he was wearing a ring. It is all connected,' I say, slowly. 'In the back of the van I was wondering if this was something random, or if it was connected to Kitty.'

'Of course it is,' Louis says harshly. 'Lily, you can't go to the set tomorrow. You probably shouldn't go back there at all. Let's call Leonard in the morning and tell him what happened... Jeez, Lily, if I hadn't come back and seen them bundle you into that van we wouldn't even know you were gone.'

'No!' Tilda and I both exclaim in unison.

'No,' I say again, more gently this time. 'I have to go on set tomorrow, Lou. I have to behave as if everything is just peachy. Don't you see? This is proof that someone wants me out of the way, which means that this is all connected to Kitty. And someone is clearly worried that I know more than I should.'

—

Shouting fills the air as I hurry to the paddock where today's exterior scenes are being shot, a bundle of revised script pages in my hands. Bunny appears from the stables on the edge of the paddock and stoops to pick up the pages that have slipped from my hands, her brow creasing when she looks at me.

'Here you go, Lil. Ooh, what happened to your head? That looks nasty.'

I press a finger to the cut on my forehead, the one that Tilda assured me no one would notice through the thick layer of make-up she plastered onto it this morning. Clearly she hadn't reckoned with Bunny's eagle eyes.

'Walked into a door,' I say, taking the script pages from her and hoping they're not too muddled. 'What's going on here? Why all the yelling?'

Bunny sighs and gestures to where Kitty and Leonard stand toe to toe in the middle of the dusty paddock. A large chestnut horse tied to a ring on the fence nearby huffs softly and paws at the ground. 'The big scene today?' Bunny says. 'The one where Kitty chases after Art on a horse, and they fight? Kitty has decided she's doing the stunt herself.'

'What the...?' The scene is a big one. Kitty's character rides across an open plain, before jumping a fence and attempting to stop Art as he is escaping from the farm. There is a tussle, involving them both falling to the ground, and now I see why Leonard is going postal at Kitty. 'Why would she think this is a good idea? She must know that Leonard would never allow her to do it.'

Bunny shrugs. 'Her stunt double didn't show today. With all the rumours about Kitty going to hospital, and then the disastrous headlines about Camilla and what she did at the Academy Awards, I think she's hoping to spin some good press out of it. "Brave Kitty carries out own stunts", you know the kind of thing. To be fair, it'll get the crowds to the movie theatre if she can pull it off – everyone loves to see a movie star take their life in their hands for real.' Bunny gives a discreet nod in the direction of the outskirts of the paddock, where a journalist I vaguely recognise loiters. 'What better way to prove to Leonard that Kitty is a consummate professional than to bridge the gap and save the studio time and money on finding another stunt double? *And* bring in some good press to keep Oskar Goldstein happy.'

'This is a *horrible* plan. Maybe I can talk some sense into her.' I march across the paddock, dust rising to coat my shoes and the hem of my skirt. 'Kitty, do you really think this is a good idea?'

'Oh, not you as well, Lily,' Kitty huffs. 'What happened to your head?'

'Finally, someone else who thinks like me,' Leonard fumes. 'Kitty, this is a ridiculous idea. What if something happens to you? You're supposed to be the star of this movie.'

'And my stunt double didn't show. So, you want to waste time and money finding a new one?' Kitty snipes. 'You were so keen to save time and money that you let Camilla stay on even after she tried to kill me.' She gives me a sly look. 'And anyway, think of the publicity if I can pull this off... I'll be the daredevil star who will do anything to make sure a picture is a hit, and *you'll* be the forward-thinking director who makes it happen.'

Leonard flounders for a moment, his mouth opening and closing silently as Kitty waits, knowing she has him. 'If I am even going to *consider* this,' he says eventually, 'I need more information. What riding experience do you have?'

Kitty grins, her face lighting up. 'I rode every day as a child.'

'In New York?' I blurt out.

Kitty shoots me a look that makes it clear I'm not helping. 'As a *child* in upstate New York, before I moved to the city as a teenager to go on stage. I still keep a horse in stables out at Altadena, so, Leonard, you don't need to worry at all about my riding skills. I'm experienced enough to pull off this stunt – if anything, I'll do a better job than the stunt double.'

Leonard is silent for a long moment before he lets out a slow breath. 'Fine. We'll try one take, and if I think for a *second* that this isn't going to work, you're off the horse immediately. No arguments. And you'll need to sign a waiver. The studio is *not* going to be held responsible if this goes wrong.'

'Yes, sir.' Kitty gives him a sharp salute, before firing me a wicked grin.

An hour later, I can't shake off the sense of dread that creeps over me as Kitty approaches the horse. I know nothing about horses, but one thing I can tell is that the horse is fucking huge and Kitty looks like a tiny scrap of a thing beside it. She presses her hand to her belly for a brief second as if squashing down last-minute nerves and then swings one foot up into a stirrup. Moments later, Kitty is sat atop the horse, and I have to confess she looks as though she belongs there, as Art's stunt double – a man who, from the front, bears no resemblance to Art's handsome face at all, but is the spit of him from the back – rides into position at the far end of the paddock.

'Quiet on set.' Leonard holds up a hand. 'And... action!'

My nerves melt away as Kitty expertly steers the horse into position. Art's double spurs his steed and rides away, kicking up dust behind him, as Kitty waits for her cue before she gallops after him. I can't see her face but I can imagine the grin as she flies across the open plain, her hair streaming out behind her. Art's double clears the distance between the paddock and the fence with ease and as Kitty approaches, her legs spurring hard as she urges the horse ever faster, Bunny claps beside me.

'Go on, Kitty,' I whisper as she crosses the plain, headed towards the post-and-rail fence. All she has to do is clear it, and then catch up to Art's stunt double. She'll reach out and grab him, the horses coming to a stop as the two of them tussle, before Leonard will call cut and Art himself will jump up on the horse to finish the scene.

It's beautiful to watch. The dust flies, kicking up a storm behind the horses, the sun catching their silhouettes in just the right places. Art's character's horse sails over the fence like a winged Pegasus. It's going to look magnificent on screen, and I feel a swell of pride. Kitty was right to fight for this moment, until...

'Oh, no. No.' My heart crashes into my Converse sneakers as Kitty approaches the fence. Even from here I can see that she's misjudged the angle, and I watch in horror as the horse – that huge, hefty, muscled creature that probably weighs ten times as much as Kitty – pulls up short and stops dead at the fence, Kitty's slight frame flying up and out of the saddle to land in a crumpled heap on the dusty ground beside him.

Chapter Eighteen

Art freezes for a moment, seemingly glued to the spot before the spell breaks and he flies across the paddock, his feet barely touching the ground as he runs towards Kitty's still body.

'Fuck.' Leonard throws his clipboard to the ground and follows after him, yelling instructions to Bunny to call Doctor Astor, call the operator, get an ambulance. *I've never heard Leonard curse before*, I think detachedly before I run after him, shock making my legs weak and wobbly.

Art is leaning over Kitty as I reach them, his hands sliding under her neck and knees to lift her.

'Wait,' I gasp, my chest hitching. 'Should we move her? I don't think we're supposed to touch her... she might have...' *Broken her neck*. I can't say it out loud.

As I speak, Kitty's eyes open and she gives me the faintest grin. 'Turns out I'm a little rusty,' she wheezes, pressing a hand to her ribs.

'For fuck's sake, Kitty, you could have died!' My voice is shrill, pitchy with panic that doesn't subside as she reaches out and squeezes my hand.

Beside me, Bunny sucks in a sharp breath. 'Lily,' she hisses. 'You can't speak like that! Like a... a... *sailor*.'

'Lily's had a shock too,' Art says, his rich, deep voice like a soothing hot toddy. He scoops Kitty into his arms as if she weighs no more than a feather (which, in all fairness, is probably true. I'd hate for him to ever have to lift me like that). 'Let's get you to your trailer.'

As he walks away, I see his expression fall, the calm, placid look on his face replaced with the most fleeting glimpse of something that seems to be more than just worry. Poor Art. It was awful to watch Kitty come at the fence the wrong way, knowing she was going to take a tumble, and it must have been even worse for Art, loving her the way he does. For a moment I wonder if that's what it's like for Louis when I get myself into these situations, before I shake the thought away. I can't think about that right now.

By the time Bunny and I have gathered up the script pages that have fluttered from Leonard's clipboard, and I've stopped off at the catering truck to fetch Bunny a brandy to stop her hands from shaking, Doctor Astor is already in Kitty's trailer.

The doctor leans over Kitty as she lies on the sofa, Art and Leonard watching from opposing corners of the room. Art's face is full of concern as Kitty winces, Doctor Astor's fingers pressing against her ribcage.

'I think it's just some bruising.' The doctor straightens. 'Kitty is going to be in pain for a few days but I don't think anything is broken. You're a lucky girl.'

Kitty gives a wan smile. 'So I'm OK to go back out and reshoot the scene?'

Art casts a glance at Leonard, who shakes his head firmly. 'Are you mad, Kitty? Seriously, you're driving me to distraction. I can call Grace Kelly in to replace you, you know.'

Kitty smiles thinly. 'A joke, Len, that's all.' She lies back against the pillows with a soft huff. 'We could shoot a different scene. One where I don't have to fight.'

Doctor Astor shakes his head. 'You need to rest,' he says, as Leonard opens his mouth to argue. 'I know, you're concerned about delays, but Kitty will be in a lot of pain for the next couple of days at least. I'm serious, Leonard.' He glances down at Kitty, an almost fatherly expression on his face.

'She has to wear a corset in some scenes,' I say, as Leonard and Art both turn to look at me. 'I'm not sure we can lace her into it with bruised ribs.'

'We can shoot my scene with Camilla,' Art says. 'She's in her trailer rehearsing, so let's make the most of it. At least we're still shooting. Oskar can't complain if the cameras are still rolling.'

Leonard nods, as Kitty lies back on her pillows. She suddenly looks very pale, her forehead beaded with sweat.

'Are you OK?' I step forward, one hand raised to press against her forehead like my mother used to do with me as a child when I was sick.

Kitty nods. 'Tired.' Her voice is thick and drowsy in a way I recognise, and I turn to the doctor.

'Did you give her something?' I demand.

Astor waves me away. 'Just a small sleeping draught, that's all. Kitty needs to rest.'

'She can rest fine without you pumping sleeping pills into her.'

'It's all right, Lily,' Kitty says, her voice already being tugged under by sleep. 'I need them.'

'Lily.' Art rests a hand on my arm. 'You know Kitty, she won't rest. She'll be on her feet within the hour, trying to get on set to carry on filming.' He looks down at Kitty, running his eyes over her face. 'I could have lost you today, my love.' His eyes fill and he lifts his chin, blinking. 'How could you do something so reckless? I don't know what I would do without you. You're everything to me.'

In the doorway, Bunny sniffles and then holds out her glass of brandy to Art. He takes it, swallowing the remains in one gulp as Kitty's eyes flutter closed. The doctor reaches for his bag, tucking his stethoscope inside, and I catch a flash of red and purple on his wrist. Reaching out, I snag his hand in mine.

'You're hurt, Doctor.' There is a small gash on the thin skin of his wrist, the area around it dotted with purple bruising. 'Did you catch yourself when you went to Kitty in the paddock?' It looks as though he's been caught with a nail and I wonder if tetanus shots are a thing yet.

Doctor Astor pulls his sleeve down, a rueful smile on his face. 'A gardening incident, I fear. Nothing dramatic. It seems a rose bush got the better of me.'

Before I can respond there is a commotion outside, and then Jeremy forces his way inside the trailer. It's feeling distinctly cramped in here now, not helped by the way Art's face changes when he lays eyes on Jeremy, the atmosphere thickening.

'Is she OK? Someone told me Kitty was hurt.' Jeremy shoves his way past Art, barging him to one side, and kneels beside the sofa. 'Kitty? Can you hear me?'

'Of course she can't hear you,' Art snorts. 'She's sleeping. Can't you tell?'

Jeremy reaches out to stroke Kitty's cheek and Art's arm whips out like a cobra strike, knocking Jeremy's hand away.

'Don't you touch her,' he snarls.

Jeremy staggers slightly, before getting to his feet. 'Who are you to tell me what to do? You don't love Kitty

– she deserves so much better than you. Did you have something to do with this? Did you make her fall?'

Art pulls himself up to full height, towering a good two inches over Jeremy. 'I should be asking you the same question, pal. You're always loitering, always hovering over her, when Kitty has already told you she doesn't want anything to do with you. You're a creep, Jeremy.'

'Is that what you think?' Jeremy sneers, seemingly not intimidated by Art looming over him. 'You think you know Kitty inside out, but you know nothing about her. Nothing about what she really wants in life. What if she doesn't want this, doesn't want *you*? What if she wanted to go into nursing? Would you still want her then?'

Something about Jeremy's words chime with me, his intensity making my skin crawl, but before I can think about it in any depth Art swings a fist towards Jeremy's face. It glances off Jeremy's jaw, and Jeremy is rocked for just a second before he launches himself in Art's direction. Bunny squeals, and there is the sound of breaking glass as Art knocks the empty brandy tumbler to the floor, but before the fight can really get underway, Leonard wades in. He rips the two men apart and holds them at arm's length, both of them panting. Jeremy has the start of a faint bruise beginning under his jawline, and I catch Art smirk as he spots it.

'Get out, the pair of you,' Leonard barks. 'Be glad I'm not firing you both.'

—

Art and Jeremy both skulk away to their trailers, and Leonard tells me to meet him back at the office. Clearly, no filming will happen this morning at least, so he wants to use the time to go through yesterday's rushes and I nod, only too happy to try and keep the peace. As I make my way across the set, catching Bunny standing with Camilla at the vending machine – Bunny updating Camilla on this morning's events, no doubt – I double take at the flash of red hair that catches my eye outside the office.

'Tilda? What are you doing here?' Surely news doesn't travel that fast.

'I'm not checking up on you after last night,' Tilda says with a grin, 'although I might have arranged an "At Home With" interview with one Jean Langford today, and I might have told her that it would be good to get some photographs of her on set to go with the article.' She gestures to the chap standing in the corner, fiddling with a camera. 'And it might just have happened that I rearranged it for today, *just in case*.'

'How convenient.' I grin. 'Did you hear what happened with Kitty this morning?'

Tilda sobers now, reaching up and tightening her ponytail as she nods. 'I did. I've already put a call in to Louella. I only gave her brief details but she'd be furious if she knew I was here and I didn't tell her.' Tilda glances over her shoulder to where Art is throwing on a jacket, Camilla is sipping a Pepsi and Bunny hovers nearby, as if worried that if she leaves and does something related to her job she'll miss the drama. There is no sign of Jeremy. 'There are some things I found out that I didn't report to the newspaper.'

'Like what?'

'Follow me.'

Tilda takes me out to the stables on the edge of the paddock, where the horses are being kept for this movie. It's not too far from the set, but no matter how much I question her on the way, Tilda refuses to tell me what she's found until we arrive.

The horses are all stabled, safely cosied up with mounds of fresh hay, but even so I find nerves are fluttering in my belly. They're just so *big*, as they peer over the tops of their stable doors, snuffling and huffing, their huge hooves bashing against the door as they shift around.

'Did we really have to actually come out here for this?' The sweet smell of manure makes me wrinkle my nose. Growing up in London meant that, for me, horses were some kind of exotic creature that I only really saw when Chelsea were playing and the police blocked the road with their huge horses so the fans could leave quietly.

'Yes,' Tilda says firmly. 'You're going to want to see this.' She slips quietly past the stables, to a shed tacked onto the end. It's scrappy, almost falling down, but she pushes the door open and inside I see a small stove, a pot with water sitting on it, and two rickety chairs. 'This is where the stable boys have their breaks,' she says. 'I came out here when I heard what happened to Kitty because I knew there would be talk, and I wasn't disappointed.'

'What did you hear?'

Tilda sneaks past me and gently closes the door to the break shed before lowering her voice. 'It wasn't an accident, what happened to Kitty.'

'But... how? I watched it happen. She came at the fence from the wrong angle, the horse pulled up short. There was no way she wasn't going to fall.'

'But *why* did the horse pull up short? No offence, Lil, but you know nothing about horses.'

'And you do?'

Tilda looks affronted. 'I've at least ridden one, which is more than can be said for you. Anyway, I heard the stable boys talking, discussing how it could have happened. I think they were worried they would somehow be blamed for it.' Tilda pauses. 'The nails in the shoe of Kitty's horse were loose.'

'Um... OK?' This means nothing to me.

Tilda reaches out and plucks an old horseshoe from where it hangs on the wall. 'See these holes? That's where the farrier nails the shoe into place. If the nails are missing or loose, the shoe can slip, causing the horse to stumble or pull up. That on its own could just be down to a shoddy blacksmith and might mean nothing... but the stable boys said something else.'

A fist squeezes my chest, and the hairs on the back of my neck begin to lift. 'What?' I whisper, almost afraid to hear what Tilda is going to say.

'The stitching on Kitty's bridle had been unpicked. It snapped, Lily. The bridle snapped, and the horse's shoes were loose. Both of these things would lead to the horse spooking and Kitty taking a fall. It was deliberate, Lily. Someone sabotaged Kitty's horse. Someone deliberately tried to hurt her.'

Chapter Nineteen

It's as if the floor has given way beneath me and I press a hand against the rough, untreated wood of the shed to balance myself.

'It was deliberate?' This turns the whole morning on its head. I had thought the accident was a result of Kitty being overconfident in something she wasn't really qualified to do, but now... I press a hand to my mouth as nausea swirls in my belly. Someone really wants Kitty gone and it looks as if they'll go to any lengths.

'There's something else,' Tilda says. Her expression is serious, her eyes never leaving my face, and I want to groan aloud. 'I've noticed a pattern.'

'A pattern? What kind of pattern?'

Tilda reaches into her purse and pulls out her notepad, flipping through the pages until she finds the right one. 'Look,' she says, jabbing a finger at the yellow legal pad.

'With all due respect, Til, even if this wasn't in shorthand I wouldn't be able to read your writing.'

Tilda sighs, unable to hide her impatience. 'It might not even be relevant, but while I was looking into the murders of the other girls, I put some dates together. When you said you thought they might be connected to Kitty, I looked at the dates the girls were killed, and if anything had happened to Kitty around those times.'

'And?'

'There's a *pattern*,' she says again, thrusting the notepad towards me. 'Every time one of the girls was found dead, something happened to Kitty just before. Kitty is attacked on the red carpet – hours later a girl is found dead. Kitty almost dies of an overdose – another girl is found dead in an alley off Sunset the next day.'

'Jeez, Til.' I run my eyes over her notes, even though I can barely make out every other word. 'This is… huge. This is proof that the murders are connected to Kitty, just as I suspected.'

'Well,' Tilda winces, 'not proof, exactly, but there does seem to be some connection. Now Kitty has been in a riding accident – but survived – does that mean there's going to be another murder?'

I pause, my thoughts racing. *Does that mean the killer knows Kitty? Does that mean that I know the killer?* The thought of it makes my mouth go dry and my blood run cold. 'There's only one way to find out.'

Tilda raises her eyes to mine, unable to hide the twinkle there. There's nothing Tilda loves more than an adventure – even if it does lead to kidnappings, or worse.

'A stake-out.'

Tilda's mouth curves into a wide grin. 'This is a brilliant idea, Lil. I knew you weren't just a pretty face.'

'Thanks. I think.' I roll my eyes. 'So tonight we stake out Sunset. The girls have all been found in alleyways within a few streets of each other, so if we can position ourselves in a place where we can have eyes on at least two or three alley entrances, we might be able to spot something suspicious before anything bad happens.'

'I know just the spot,' Tilda nods, her face set. 'But you know nothing might happen, right? I've made this connection but it could just be a coincidence that these girls are being murdered right after something happens to Kitty.'

'Tilda, I trust your gut. It's never let me down yet.' It's got us into some sticky situations, but Tilda has never been wrong. 'We might be barking up the wrong tree... but if we're not, then this is our chance to figure out once and for all if these murders are connected to Kitty and her disappearance.' *And our chance to catch a killer in the act.* I try not to wobble at the thought. 'Just do me one favour?'

'What?'

'Can you be the one to tell Louis about our plan? Because I've a feeling that if I tell him about it, he'll murder me himself.'

I am blurry and distracted all afternoon, as Art and Camilla shoot their scene together, Kitty watching from the wings with one hand pressed to her belly.

'Do you need some painkillers?' I ask, as she takes a deep breath, wincing as she does so.

'Only for this horrible acting,' Kitty retorts, as Camilla swishes across the set to hit her mark. She winces again, this time as Art has to lean down and kiss Camilla full on the mouth. 'I hope he ate that sandwich I brought him for lunch.'

'Sandwich?' Kitty doesn't strike me as the domestic type, and anyway, she's supposed to be resting.

'It was delicious, I had it made especially for him.' Kitty turns to me, her eyes crinkling as her mouth turns up in a cat-like grin. 'Bologna, cheese, tomato and... raw garlic.'

'*Garlic?*'

Kitty shrugs, never taking her eyes from the set, where Camilla is now wiping her mouth and grimacing. 'Art has a cold coming, garlic is good for fighting germs. What can I say? It's hardly my fault Leonard rescheduled the scenes so Art had to kiss Camilla this afternoon.'

Ew. 'But… you'll have to kiss him later! Didn't you think about that?'

Kitty flaps a hand, that sly grin still wide on her face. 'Art loves to eat onions, so I regularly buy him fennel seeds to keep in his trailer. I'll get him to chew on some of them – he'll be fresh as a daisy.'

Camilla is now gulping from a glass of water and shooting daggers in poor Art's direction. 'Get him a mint,' she hisses at Bunny, who scurries away like a frightened field mouse.

Kitty presses a hand to her ribs as she stifles a laugh. 'Wonderful work, Art. You're brilliant.' She turns to me. 'I just hope those fennel seeds work before our date tonight.'

Even the drama on set – Camilla closes her eyes briefly now as Leonard calls for them to go again – isn't enough to distract me from the thought of the stake-out tonight, and by the time filming is over for the day, later than planned, my stomach is in knots.

Slipping out of the gates to the set, I squeeze through the crowds of fans who wait – even after dark – for Art, Kitty and the rest of the stars, to where Christine, Louis's beloved Cadillac, idles at the kerb. The dinged fender has been replaced and the car looks as good as new, with no sign at all of the dramatic car chase and subsequent crash. As he catches sight of me, Louis hops out and opens the passenger door, dropping a kiss on my cheek.

'A little bird told me this was all your idea tonight,' he says, as I slide into the passenger seat beside him.

'A little bird has a big mouth.' I turn around and shoot Tilda a look, as she shrugs her shoulders and grins.

'I'm not taking the rap for this one,' she says, and passes me a greasy paper bag. The smell from it is heavenly and my stomach gurgles.

'Fries from Googie's? You guys are heroes.' Opening the bag, I dive in and bite into a still-hot, crispy chip.

'It's going to be a long night,' Louis says, as he pulls away from the kerb and follows Tilda's directions. She's found a spot on Sunset, down an alley across the street from where the other girls were found. It's the perfect place to watch the street, with a view of three alley entrances. As long as the cops don't want to know why we're parked up, that is.

Sunset Boulevard is always busy, and tonight is no exception. People hurry along the pavements, some alone, some arm in arm. A woman in a silver frock, a shawl around her shoulders, laughs up at the man walking beside her, her face lit by the signs overhead. It still seems odd to me to see people walking along and actually engaging with each other, rather than hurrying with their heads down, AirPods in ear, or eyes glued to a smartphone in front of them.

In the seat behind me, Tilda stretches as I crumple the now empty paper bag that held the fries. 'I forgot how boring these things are.'

It's not the first stake-out we've done, but I'm hoping it will be the last. Tilda is right – hanging around waiting for something to happen *is* boring, but part of me is still hoping that nothing *does* happen, if it means another girl isn't hurt. We watch as the crowds on the street ebb and flow. Two men scuffle across the street, and Louis reaches for the handle of the car door before it transpires they are play fighting, and he sinks back against the seat with a sigh.

'OK,' I say, clapping my hands as Tilda stifles a yawn. 'Maybe we should run through what we know, who we feel suspicious about. We know Kitty is going to disappear and given what's been happening with the dead girls, my fear is she's going to come to a sticky end.'

Tilda nods, sitting up straighter in her seat. 'What does your gut tell you? You work with her every day, Lily, you're the one who knows her best.'

I think for a moment, running over the events of the past few weeks, both on and off set. 'There's something about Jeremy,' I say, with a frown. 'He's... intense. It's not that he's not nice, I mean, people seem to love him on screen, but when it comes to Kitty there's almost something obsessive about him. From what I can gather he's been hanging around her for years, ensuring that he's working on the same movies as her even though she broke things off with him ages ago.'

'You think he's still in love with her?' Louis asks, his eyes still combing the now quieter streets ahead of us.

I shrug. 'Maybe? I don't know. She's very charismatic, so I could see how men fall in love with her all over the place, but this feels even deeper than love. Like I said, it's obsession, almost.' A thought hits me, and I turn to face Tilda and Louis. 'He knows things.'

'Knows things? What things?' Tilda looks at me as if I'm mad.

I think about what Jeremy said to Art, when they were fighting in Kitty's trailer. 'He said to Art earlier, *what if she doesn't want this, doesn't want you? What if she wanted to go into nursing?*'

'And...?'

'Kitty told me that she always thought she would be a nurse, rather than a movie star. That it was her mother who pushed her towards acting.'

Louis frowns, the street light at the end of the alley casting an orange glow across his face. 'But Jeremy could have known that for years. They were friends at school, weren't they?'

I shake my head. 'Kitty told me she'd never told anybody that. So how could he know?'

'Maybe she forgot she told him? Maybe... maybe she was drunk and it spilled out? I don't know.' Even so, Tilda scribbles it down in her notepad, squinting in the poor light.

'There was another thing too,' I say, my stomach fizzing with the realisation. 'Kitty and Art argued before the premiere, in her bedroom. You remember, they arrived on the carpet separately.'

'The night Kitty was manhandled on the red carpet,' Louis says.

'Yeah. Jeremy knew they'd argued. Kitty asked him how he knew, and he came out with something about how she looked sad, or something, but she *didn't*. In fact, I thought how she didn't look sad at all. I think she'd taken something, an upper, to get her through the evening.'

'So, what are you thinking? That he's spying on Kitty?' Tilda's eyes widen.

'Maybe?' I don't know how though – could he have bugged her room? I didn't think that bugging devices were widely known about yet, unless you were in the FBI, but maybe Jeremy has a contact? That could explain how he knows things he shouldn't. If this was 2020 Jeremy would easily be able to spy on Kitty. He could have put a nanny cam in her trailer, hidden a listening device in her bedroom or set up motion cameras to record her every move, but now, in the 1950s? I just don't know how he could do it.

'What about Camilla?' Louis asks. 'She has every reason to want Kitty out of the picture. You saw how she reacted to Kitty winning the Oscar over her... I don't want to speak out of turn, but honestly... I think that lady is kinda crazy.'

'Amen to that,' Tilda agrees. 'Her showing up at the Oscars with a gun is a prime example of crazy.'

I watch a tall man in a raincoat hold the door open across the street for a woman in a feathered hat, as she ducks under his arm with a smile. 'The feud between Camilla and Kitty does seem to have taken a turn,' I say. In the beginning their rivalry had seemed pretty evenly matched, what with the heels being snapped off Camilla's shoes, and then Kitty's favourite make-up artist being lured away to work on Camilla instead, but now things feel darker. 'I don't think Camilla could be responsible for the deaths of those girls, but I could well believe she would sabotage Kitty's horse.'

'You're right,' Tilda says, 'it doesn't make sense for Camilla to murder those girls – there would be no benefit to her at all... and besides, it just... *feels* like the work of a man. But even so, I could see Camilla doing her darnedest to get Kitty out of the picture. Let's be honest, Kitty is her main rival, and there's no doubt that Camilla would be in line for an Oscar if there was no Kitty on the scene.'

Louis frowns. 'What about Art?' he says instead.

'Art Calloway?' Tilda shakes her head. 'He's too... lovely,' she declares as Louis swats at her arm.

'He is lovely,' I agree, 'but even lovely people can snap. Art does adore Kitty, and I think deep down she loves him, but the pressure gets to her. Art made a reference to the two of them being compared to Mary Pickford and Douglas Fairbanks, and that kind of pressure has to be hard on them both.'

'They are golden together,' Tilda sighs dreamily. As much as she can be a badass, she's a hopeless romantic really.

'On and off screen,' I say. 'Art loves Kitty for who she is, but I think he also loves the fact that all the time his star is hitched to hers they can't go wrong. I can't see him doing anything to jeopardise that. And anyway, he was with Kitty the night the last girl was killed.'

'There's the doctor too,' Louis says. 'What's his name? Astor?'

'Yeah, Doctor Astor,' I say, scratching at my chin. 'I don't know... I mean, he seems nice enough, and sometimes the way he treats her is almost fatherly. I think he's fond of her, but I don't like the way he feeds Kitty pills. When she fell off her horse she told me she "needs them" to sleep. What if he's got her hooked on them?'

'Then surely he'd want to keep her around?' Tilda says. 'Why get rid of her if she's an easy mark for selling drugs to?'

We fall silent, every theory we have somehow a little too square to fit our round hole. Louis stares moodily out of the windscreen, as Tilda stifles another yawn. The streets are much quieter now, the last of the bars closing and people making their way home. The odd car passes, and I feel my eyelids begin to droop.

'A crazed fan?' Tilda mutters from the back seat. 'That guy on the red carpet who grabbed her... he could be behind it all.'

'Kitty gets sacks of fan letters delivered to the studio every day. Bunny and I have spent hours sifting through them all, making sure she only gets the ones that say nice things. There's not been anything overtly threatening that I've come across, but it doesn't mean that someone out there doesn't wish her harm. After all, the red carpet guy did say to her, "You're next".'

'The problem is,' Tilda says wearily, 'that there are just too many people out there who could have a reason for wanting to get rid of Kitty once and for all.' She yawns again, loudly this time, and Louis reaches out to start the car.

'I'm calling it,' he says. 'Tilda's hanging by a thread back there. Lily, you have to be on set first thing and Leonard won't be happy if you're late.'

I am about to nod my agreement when movement across the street catches my eye. A dark figure walks hurriedly along Sunset, their head down, but there is something familiar about them.

'Wait,' I hiss, reaching for the door handle and sliding out of the car. 'That's... that's Bobby. The security guard.'

Louis and Tilda step out into the alleyway, and we watch as Bobby hurries past the entrance to the alley where the first dead girl was found.

'Maybe he lives around here,' Tilda says. 'Do we follow him?'

Stepping out onto the street, we walk quickly but quietly to the other side of the road and begin to follow the security guard.

'This feels weird,' Louis whispers. 'The poor guy is probably just walking home after a date.'

'Maybe,' I whisper back. Something feels a little off in the way he keeps glancing over his shoulder, but then maybe he senses he's being followed. 'Let's just see where he goes.' My heart clattering in my chest, we follow Bobby along Sunset, trying to hang back enough that we have time to step into the shadows if he turns back. He passes the second alley entrance, and then the third, pausing at a building on the corner. We stop, ducking into the alley along the street, as he fumbles in his pocket.

'This is where he lives?' Tilda presses her lips together. 'I guess being a security guard was never going to pay that well.'

The building is a hardware store, with apartments above it. The exterior is dingy, unloved, and I get the impression that if you stepped inside it would probably smell weird. Bobby pushes open the door, and his face is briefly illuminated with a pale yellow glow from the bulb in the hallway, before he steps inside and closes the door behind him. Moments later, a light goes on in the upstairs window and he appears, before the curtains are yanked closed.

'Come on.' I nudge Louis and step out onto the street, hurrying the last half-block towards the next alley and Bobby's building, my mouth dusty and dry. Slipping down the alley, I hold my breath. This is where the last girl was found, and I imagine I can smell the stink of death under the scent of urine and garbage. Two dumpsters line the walls, and a sturdy fire escape leads to the top floor. To Bobby's apartment.

'Did you see?' I say, as I squint up at the apartment. Every instinct is telling me to get the hell out of dodge, but my feet are rooted to the spot.

'Lil?' Louis reaches for my hand and I link my fingers with his, my nerves jangling as I look up at the darkened apartment, suddenly fearful Bobby will appear at the top of the fire escape.

'As Bobby pushed open the door, did you catch it? That glint on his left hand.' I turn to Louis, my eyes wide. 'Bobby was wearing a gold ring on the pinky of his left hand. Just like the man who tried to grab Kitty. Just like whoever it was who bundled me into the van.'

Chapter Twenty

Despite the late hour, I feel the urge to check on Kitty before we return to the apartment. Seeing the glint of the gold ring on Bobby's hand as he pushed the door open has left me unsettled, and as Louis pulls up outside the Chateau I slip out of the passenger seat.

'I'll be two minutes,' I swear, as the valet tries to direct Louis to the garage. I hurry up the driveway, into the lobby and up the stairs to Kitty's room, tapping lightly on her door. I know she was on a date with Art, and I hope she's come back to her own room just so I can put my mind at ease at least.

As I knock, the door moves under my fingers and I realise it isn't latched. Fear spikes in my veins, and I swallow hard, my mouth suddenly dry as I push the door open. The air feels recently disturbed, as though someone has not long stepped inside, and I pray it's just Kitty. There are no lights on, save for the soft glow of a lamp coming from the bedroom.

'Kitty?' I hiss, creeping inside the hallway. The kitchen is dark, the light from the hall illuminating an empty champagne bottle on the worktop, a pale puddle of over-spilled bubbles beside it. 'Kitty? Are you home?'

A muted murmuring comes from the bedroom, and I pause. *Oh God, have I walked in on Art and Kitty together?* While Kitty presents a good-girl image on set, I'm not stupid. I know Hollywood even in this age is rife with sex and scandal. I am about to leave when I hear a sob, and then what – weirdly – sounds like Camilla's voice. I creep along the corridor, not sure what I'm about to find, until I reach the almost closed bedroom door. I am ready to burst in and call Camilla out if she's even thinking about upsetting Kitty, but what I hear makes me pause.

'…same to me…' Camilla is saying in a hushed tone. 'I understand completely.'

There is a sniff, and I realise that Kitty might be crying. '…trusted… didn't listen… hurt…'

'I'm sorry. I'm so sorry.' Camilla's voice is low. 'You don't have to go through this on your own. But… best… as usual.' There is a rustling and I peep through the crack in the door to witness something I never thought I'd see in this lifetime: Camilla, leaning forward to put her arms around Kitty and pull her into a hug. Feeling as though I am intruding – and not sure of the reception I'll get if they notice me – I creep away, making sure to pull the door firmly closed behind me. I don't know what just happened but at least I know Kitty is safe. For now, anyway.

–

It's hard to believe that murders and abductions occur in a place as beautiful as Hollywood on an early morning when the sun is casting peach, gold and lilac rays over the horizon and the promise of another warm day is in the air, but they do. I arrive at the set early, just as the sun is peeking over the horizon, tiredness tugging at my bones.

I didn't sleep well at all, tossing and turning all night once I finally got to bed. Every time I closed my eyes I saw the glint of gold on Bobby's hand. Could it have been him who shoved me into the back of the van? Is Bobby the one who wants to see Kitty dead? It's difficult to reconcile the smiley, affable man on the gate who, while he may be a big fan of the women in cinema, doesn't seem capable of hurting a fly. On the surface, anyway. And what was that in Kitty's room with Camilla last night? Kitty seemed upset. Had she argued with Art again? Or was something else bothering her? Camilla is the last person I would have expected to find comforting her, making me wonder if Camilla might have an ulterior motive.

Nodding hello to the guard on the gate – who is not Bobby this morning, thank goodness – I sign in and ditch my jacket and purse in the corner of the tiny corridor outside Leonard's office, where I work. Someone has left new script pages on my desk, along with two phone messages to pass on to Leonard and a sheaf of studio memos. I scan them quickly. One is a memo about studio physical exams, and I think of Doctor Astor. It's unsettling, the way he has a pill for Kitty to pop at every turn, but that doesn't mean he's out to harm her – it almost seems normal, the blasé attitude that Hollywood has to medicating its stars. Then there's the fact that he's a doctor – he's signed an oath to save lives. Surely that goes against everything a murderer stands for? Sighing, I take the most important memos through to Leonard's desk and then slip out into the lot and make my way towards the stables.

After what Tilda told me yesterday about Kitty's bridle, I want to check out the stables for myself before everyone else arrives on set. They are on the other side of the studio and as I reach the gate through to the paddock, my head spins with déjà vu and I see Kitty fall all over again.

'Get a grip, Lil.' Pushing the gate open I head for the stable block. There are eight stalls in the long, barn-like structure, and the fresh scents of sawdust and manure reach my nose.

The stables are dark, but not in a threatening way. Early morning sunlight beams in strips through the slatted windows, and the huff of horses' breath is strangely calming. I was half expecting to have to deal with the stable boys, but it seems I am even too early for them. Breathing in, I peer into the first stall, to see a small brown horse settled on a bed of straw. She snorts as she looks at me, before tucking her feet under her and rising to a standing position, and I back away, my heart rate suddenly increasing. Maybe I'm not quite a country mouse just yet. The next stall along contains a huge grey horse that stamps its feet as I pass, not stopping to say hi. The third contains a sweet dusty-brown donkey and I pause, my mouth lifting. My mum used to take me for donkey rides on Weymouth Beach when I was a kid on our annual summer holiday, and I reach out a hand to pet his ears just as a scuffling comes from outside. *Shit.* Without stopping to think I unlatch the stable and slip inside, the donkey watching me curiously as I press myself up against the stable wall, crouching into a low ball amid the hay in the hopes that I won't be spotted. My palms are sweaty, and I lick my lips, as the donkey bumps up against me.

'Stop,' I hiss. There is definitely movement outside, but it doesn't sound like the bustle of stable boys coming to feed their charges. It's stealthier, as if someone doesn't want to call attention to the fact they are here. The donkey huffs, and beneath it I catch the sound of the latch on the stable block being lifted.

Footsteps creep across the concrete floor, and I clench my fists, trying to regulate my breathing. Fear builds, making my stomach roll and sweat prickle under my arms as the footsteps get closer. *What if it's Bobby? What if the person who bundled me into the van – the person who wants me out of the way so they can get to Kitty – saw me slip in here?* I wonder how much it would hurt to be trampled by, if not a horse, then a still incredibly solid-looking donkey.

The footsteps continue, quietly and slowly, pausing for a moment outside the donkey's stall. The furry traitor steps forward to have his ears rubbed and I stop breathing, pressing myself into the corner of the stable. The donkey brays, the sound cutting through me and making my heart almost explode, and then the footsteps move on.

There is a murmuring at the next stall, and a whicker of joy. Clearly, the horse – is it Kitty's? – recognises the mystery person. I stay in my crouched position as the intruder moves around, still murmuring in that low voice that is too quiet to make out.

'Come on,' I mutter under my breath, just as my calf picks that particular moment to cramp. 'Oh, *shit*.' The word is a hiss, and outside the stable door the rustle of movement ceases. Certain I am about to be discovered, I gingerly rise to standing, my hands gripping my calf as I try to massage the knotted muscle through gritted teeth, and then, to my relief, the feet turn and march back towards the stable doors. The latch lifts, and there is the sound of the door slamming closed and, finally, I feel as though I can breathe.

'Phew,' I say to the donkey, 'that was a close call.' The donkey lifts his tail in response.

–

In the few minutes it takes me to make my way to the back of the stable block, out the rear doors and around the tack room to the front, screaming has broken out. Hurrying around the corner, aware of the grassy stain of horseshit that coats the bottom of one sneaker, and the calf muscle that is now unknotted but sore, I pull up short to see Kitty and Camilla going at each other. This is a far more familiar sight than the one I witnessed last night.

Kitty stands with her hands on her hips, in red shorts and a white blouse, her face bare and her hair tied up in a hanky. 'You're mad, Camilla. Absolutely stark raving bonkers. I'm going to speak to Leonard, because honestly? I think you need to be committed.'

'Kitty? Camilla? What's going on?'

Camilla rounds on me, her nose wrinkling slightly. She too has a bare face, her red hair pulled into a low ponytail, and I deduce that both women must have just arrived at the lot. 'Kitty has accused *me* of sabotaging her horse yesterday. Me! Anyone who knows me knows I love horses, I would never do anything that could cause harm. Not to the horse, anyway.' She turns her gaze on Kitty, her lip curling.

'And yet here I find you, hanging around the stables, loitering outside with a carrot in hand.'

'What? How is that a crime? And you say *I'm* crazy!'

'You are!' Kitty yells back, and I catch a waft of alcohol on her breath, the sweet raisin-like scent of brandy. 'I never said a damn word about you and the horse! And if I did I would have told you to your plain-Jane face, not the newspapers.'

'The... newspapers?'

Camilla snatches up a newspaper from the rickety table outside the break shed. 'Look, Lily. It's all here in black and white – *Camilla Rey accused of pony sabotage. Kitty Fox takes a tumble!* It says right here that I am suspected of *somehow* causing Kitty's fall. I would never…' Her voice breaks and she dabs at her eyes. 'What will people think of me?'

Kitty snorts, her mouth opening wide in an exaggerated laugh. 'It's a bit late for that!' she says. 'You should have thought of that before you started waving a gun around at the Academy Awards.'

'I was *drunk*,' Camilla hisses, throwing the newspaper to the ground. 'You probably did this yourself, in another failed attempt to get me thrown off this movie. I won't let you win, Kitty Fox, I'll kill you before I let you ruin me.'

'Of course I never did it, you fool. Why on earth…' Kitty trails off as another figure rounds the corner and I let out a sigh of relief.

'I can hear you gals from the parking lot,' Art booms, wrapping an arm around Kitty. 'What in tarnation is going on?'

'Camilla has it in her head that I told the newspapers some old rubbish about her.' Kitty seems to stiffen for the briefest of seconds before she reaches up and plants a kiss on Art's lips, resting a hand on his cheek. 'Oh, darling. You've cut your face.'

Art strokes a hand over one cheek. 'Cut myself shaving this morning,' he tuts with a smug grin, as Kitty presses a kiss over the thin scratch.

'You poor darling.' Kitty flutters her eyelashes at him, and I frown. This is not a Kitty I have experienced before. Usually, she is not the one to instigate a PDA. Camilla presses her lips together and looks away, her face distinctly pale, and I see right through Kitty's behaviour. I had forgotten Camilla and Art used to be a thing before Kitty swooped in and snatched him from under Camilla's nose, but clearly Camilla hasn't.

'Just a silly misunderstanding,' I say breezily, as Camilla toes the dusty ground in front of her. 'How about I get Bunny to call the newspaper, Camilla? Get her to tell them to issue a retraction? They can't print these things without being certain they're true.'

Mollified, Camilla nods. 'I would never do something like this,' she says again, and I nod soothingly.

'Of course not. It was an accident, that's all.' No one else knows about the bridle or the loose shoe, it seems, and if I can keep it that way then I will. 'Bunny will be in the office by now – why don't you stop by on your way to your trailer? She'll get things sorted lickety-split.'

'Sounds like a good idea,' Art says, clearly enjoying the attention Kitty bestows on him. 'Nothing to get in a tizzy about, Cam.'

Camilla shoots Kitty a look, heavy with vitriol, before smiling at Art through gritted teeth. 'No, of course. We all know these things happen, and the truth always comes out in the end. I'll see you both on set.' With no hint of the fragile Camilla I glimpsed a moment ago, she stalks off with her head held high, as Kitty disentangles herself from Art.

'We'll be late,' she says, as Art reaches for her hand again. 'Lily, are you coming?'

'Err... yeah. You guys go on. I won't be a minute.' Waiting until the two of them reach the gate to the studio lot, I turn back and survey the stable block. The stable boys are starting to put in an appearance, and to one side of the building buckets of feed are being made up: molasses, oats and carrots being mixed with water. If I'm going to snoop, I'd better be quick about it.

Inside the stable block I rush past my donkey friend, and scan the remaining stalls until I spot Kitty's horse. The floors are freshly swept, the stable bed a new bundle of hay that looks weirdly inviting, and I cautiously reach out a hand to pet his silky-smooth nose. He whickers at my touch, and for just a moment I get why Kitty and Camilla are so into horses.

'Who did that to you, hey?' I soothe, the grassy scent of warm horse reaching my nose as I step forward. My foot hits something on the clean floor, and I stoop to see a blue button just outside the stable door. I pick it up, turning it over in my fingers as I lift it towards the shaft of sunlight cutting through the darkness. It's small – a shirt button, I think – in a distinctive shade of blue.

Camilla's? No. It was her I heard creeping into the stable to see the horses earlier, but she was wearing a pink sundress, without any buttons. This looks like the button from a man's shirt, and I can't shake the feeling that I've seen it somewhere before. The doors of the stable block open up and a cacophony of neighs and whinnies begins as the stable boys begin to make their early morning breakfast rounds. Tucking the button into my skirt pocket, I slip out the back doors, disappointment clawing at my insides. I wasn't sure what I was hoping to find in the stable block – something more concrete than a missing button, that's for sure.

The sun is higher in the sky now, the day beginning to heat up, and I realise I'm going to be late to the set if I don't get a wriggle on. The last thing I want to have to do is explain to Leonard where I've been, so with one last look over the stable buildings I move towards the gate. Only, there's one place I haven't scoped out.

The door to the old tack room is stiff, and at first I think it must be locked, but a hefty shove and a jiggle of the door handle springs the door free. The musty scent of pony and saddle oil hits me as I step inside, the room full of extra tack. Everything appears to be neatly organised in the front half of the storage room, bridles hung on nails in the wall and saddles racked up neatly, but the place is still cluttered, too small for all the equipment stored in here. I run my fingers over the bridles, over the stitching that I can now see was so sharply cut on Kitty's. Will anyone think to check the rest of them? I wander deeper into the small room, the door swinging closed behind me as I run my eyes over lead ropes, whips and bottles of horse shampoo. There is another, smaller door to the back of the tack room and when I step through, it leads me to a jumbled storage area. It's almost like a small shed has been added to the back of the tack room to make room for all the things that aren't used very often, and cobwebs tickle my nose as I step further inside. The smell towards the back of the tiny shed is stronger, and I wrinkle my nose. It's not just a horsey scent back here, it's something darker. More… *liquid* is the only way to describe it. This small storage shed is markedly less organised than the tack room, a jumble of rags and items that I don't recognise having never spent time at stables before, and I go to step back, towards the thin shaft of light that creeps between the door and the frame, towards the main tack room and fresher air. As I do, my foot catches on something hidden beneath a thin sheet and I fall to the dusty floor, my ankle snagging and dragging the sheet with me.

'Fuck.' Wrapping my fingers around my ankle, I press against the skin, hoping it isn't sprained, before reaching for the ledge above me, as I try to hoist myself to standing. My fingers close on the splintered wood of the ledge and my body freezes as I stare at the space where the sheet has slipped, revealing the unseeing eyes of a dead body.

Chapter Twenty-One

The scream lodges in my throat for what feels like hours before it strips free, echoing around the room as I scramble to my feet. The sheet wraps around my legs and I shake it off, revealing more of the dead body as I stagger back towards the crowded tack room and out into the sunshine. Bending at the waist I draw in a breath, my throat on fire as the stable boys run towards me.

'In there. Right at the back, in the add-on.' I gesture towards the open door of the tack room. 'No, wait.' I snatch at the sleeve of one of the boys as he moves towards it. 'Don't go in there. Get Leonard. Call the police. Oh, Jesus.' I bend over again, pressing a hand to my mouth.

'Lily, what is it?' Jeremy is there, seemingly out of nowhere, his hands steadying me. 'What's happened?'

'In the add-on to the tack room,' I gasp. 'There's a... a girl. At the back. She's...' I swallow. 'She's dead. I think she's dead.' I choke back a sob as I see Art and Kitty round the corner, Kitty breaking into a sprint that coats her pumps in dust as she sees me.

'Lily, are you all right?' She pulls me into a hug and tears begin to leak out, running down my cheeks and onto her shoulder.

'You're right, Lily.' Jeremy appears from the tack room door, his face grave. 'She's dead.'

'Who?' Kitty lets go of me and whirls on Jeremy. 'Who's dead? Where?'

I reach out to her as Art goes to the door, his expression unreadable as he peers into the darkness beyond. 'I don't know her name,' I say. 'I should do, I should know who she is, but I don't, I'm sorry. All I know is... she was your stunt double.'

'*Oh.*' Kitty makes a noise somewhere between a gasp and a sob as her knees buckle, and Jeremy steps neatly forward to catch her, guiding her towards a stool that the stable boys have dragged out from somewhere. 'Sally,' she sobs. 'Her name was Sally.'

Art hurries over, a reassuring sense of calm surrounding him. 'Leonard is on his way over from the studio office, and the stable boys have called the operator to get the police out here.' He crouches beside a distraught Kitty, taking her hands in his and rubbing them gently. 'Kitty, darling. I'm so sorry. I know you liked Sally.' He leans in to kiss the top of her head, and I catch a whiff of fennel on his breath.

'She was incredible,' Kitty sobs. 'So brave. Nothing was ever too difficult for her. Her riding...' She trails off, her mouth dropping in horror. 'Lily, she didn't show up yesterday. Has she been here all this time?'

I shake my head. 'I don't know. Kitty, please try not to think about that. The police will be here soon. They'll be able to give you some answers.'

'This is horrifying,' Jeremy mutters, as he paces back and forth in front of the tack room door that thankfully is now closed, giving Sally some privacy. 'Kitty, here, take one of these.' He pulls a paper bag of candy from his pocket. 'You need some sugar, you've had a terrible shock and you're awfully pale.'

Kitty shakes her head, but Jeremy insists, shaking the bag under her nose.

'No, Jeremy. Thank you,' I say. 'Kitty doesn't want one. Why don't you head to the front gate, and wait for the police? It'll be quicker if you show them exactly where to come.'

With a long look at Kitty, Jeremy stuffs the bag back in his pocket, nodding, and I watch him walk away towards the gate, trying not to let the butterflies in my stomach take flight as I think of how quickly Jeremy stepped inside the shed. *Was it because he wanted to make sure that Sally really was dead?*

—

The police arrive quickly, and Kitty manages to pull on a professional face as they briskly shake Art's hand and he leads them towards the shed.

'I can't watch,' Kitty says, her hand shaking as she presses a hanky to her eyes. There is still the faintest smell of brandy around her and I wonder if it's from last night, or if she took a drink this morning before she arrived on set. 'Lily, how has this happened? I just saw her, not two days ago.'

The police officers move in and out of the shed, murmuring to each other. Art and Jeremy seem to have called a temporary truce, the pair of them standing quietly to one side. Leonard arrived with the police and he paces back and forth now, his face sombre. I hate to wonder what he's thinking, about the implications that this will have for the film and for Kitty's mental health. To realise the dead girl is someone she knows, someone she's grown close to, must be heartbreaking.

There is a flurry of activity as a private ambulance arrives, and two ambulancemen step out of the back, carrying a stretcher. Kitty presses a hand to her mouth, her eyes filling again.

'Tell me when it's over,' she says, before heading into the stables to seek comfort from her horse. The air is still, and a respectful hush descends over the paddock as, a short while later, the stretcher emerges with Sally laid peacefully on it.

Leonard crosses himself as they pass, and I force myself to look. Sally's face is waxy and pale, her eyes closed now as a string of bruises rings her throat like a necklace. Nausea lurches in my stomach and I take a deep breath. Her hair is still curled in the style favoured by Kitty, even though it is a little mussed, and she wears the same riding coat that Kitty sported for her scene yesterday, with one exception. There is a glint of gold on the lapel, and I take a small step forward to get a better look. Kitty's coat was unadorned, but this one has a tiny brooch, with small pearls inlaid into the gold setting, and I frown. Brooch aside, this could be Kitty laid out the stretcher, being loaded into the back of an ambulance to be taken to the morgue, and immediately my head spins, black spots dancing at the edges of my vision.

'Thanks, gentlemen.' Leonard shakes the police officers' hands, one after the other, as the doors slam closed on the ambulance and it heads out to the back entrance of the studio, away from the crowds that loiter at the opposite end. 'Let me know if I can be of any assistance.'

'We'll be in touch,' the officer says in a sombre tone. 'Please don't make any announcements until you hear from us. We'll be contacting her next of kin when we get back to the station.'

At least one of the dead girls is being taken seriously, it seems. 'Don't you want to talk to us?' I say, before the officer can head back to his car. 'I mean, I found her and you haven't asked me anything. Nor Kitty, and she was Kitty's stunt double. Surely you'll want to interview all of us?'

The police officer looks amused. 'Why would I need to do that?'

I blink. 'Because she was murdered, wasn't she? Like the other girls? I saw the bruising around her neck as she was brought out.'

'Other girls?' Leonard frowns.

'Murdered?' The police officer looks as though he wants to laugh, but restrains himself, given the fact that a dead body has just been carted off the property. 'Who told you that, sweetie?'

The *sweetie* rankles and I have to fight to keep my expression neutral. 'No one. I mean, I just assumed—'

'Never assume, honey.' The police officer gives me a patronising smile and I'm pretty sure I feel Leonard wince beside me. 'She wasn't murdered.'

'But her neck... the bruising...'

'A horrible accident.'

Art appears beside me, his expression serious. 'Is that right, officer?'

'Yes, Mr Calloway. A terrible, tragic accident. It appears that Miss Moss – Sally – went into the storage room for whatever reason yesterday morning, and tripped in the dark. You may not have noticed but the lightbulb was out, and if the door slammed closed behind her she would have been disorientated.'

She tripped? Exactly the way I did when I came across her body.

'A lead rope was tight around her throat. It was still attached to a bridle on the wall, and as she slipped it must have caught around her neck. In her panic, and in the dark, the more she struggled to get free, the more twisted the rope became, and so it tightened on her neck until she must have passed out. A simple accident,' he gives a hard stare to Leonard, 'but one that could be avoided if this place was tidied properly.'

'Of course.' Leonard gives a sharp nod. 'I'll get the stable boys on this straight away. Lily, perhaps you could arrange for some flowers to be sent to Sally's family.'

'Yes, no problem.' Leonard walks away with the police officer, as Art lets out a long breath, his voice oddly shaky when he speaks.

'A terrible accident, Lily. Utterly devastating. Keep people from Kitty's trailer, won't you? She wants to be alone.'

I nod. I'm sure she does want to be alone. *A terrible accident.* That's what the police, and the studio, and presumably the newspapers, are calling it, and if I didn't know about the other girls then maybe I would believe it. But the deaths of the other girls – all of whom bore a resemblance to Kitty, none more so than poor Sally Moss – and the fact that Sally was wearing a piece of jewellery that I'm pretty sure I recognise, means I don't believe there was anything accidental about this death at all.

Chapter Twenty-Two

The atmosphere on the lot is thick with tension, as Leonard disappears into his office, and the rest of the cast and crew head off to their respective trailers and the catering truck to try and wrap their heads around the events of this morning, before we are all called back on set to continue shooting. Not even the death of one of our own is enough of a reason for the schedule to slide, not to the studio anyway.

Bunny is pale and tear-stained, a hanky pressed to her nose, and I breathe a sigh of relief when she eventually agrees to go and see if the caterers hold a bottle of whisky she can have a snifter from to calm her nerves. I want to see Kitty, to make sure she's all right and to surreptitiously see if I can still smell alcohol on her, so I head towards her trailer.

Art crosses the lot ahead of me as I walk towards Kitty's trailer, so I speed up and hurriedly tap on the door, wanting to speak with Kitty privately. There is no answer, but when I press my ear to the door there is the rustle of movement from inside.

'Kitty?' I tap again, glancing over my shoulder in case Art is on his way back, but there is no sign of him. 'Kitty? It's me. Lily.' Without waiting, I gently open the door, my jaw dropping at the sight in front of me.

Jeremy Knox stands in Kitty's empty trailer, his hands deep in the small mahogany jewellery box she keeps on her dressing table. As I enter he looks up, his face flushed with guilt before he straightens up and irons out his expression. 'Lily. What do you want?'

I glance over his shoulder, hoping to see Kitty lounging on the sofa behind him, but the trailer is definitely empty. 'I could ask you the same question.' I smile, softening my words.

'I was looking for Kitty,' he says, his hands falling to his sides.

'In her jewellery box?' The smile stays on my face, but my heart is racing as if I've just run a marathon.

Jeremy's hands sneak into his pockets. 'Well, anyway, she's not here,' he says with a shrug. 'Point her in my direction if you see her. I've got some exciting news for her.'

'Are you sure she'll want to hear it?' Whatever Jeremy has to tell Kitty, it doesn't warrant him rummaging through her things, and I'm pretty sure Kitty is going to be too cut up over Sally to hear what he has to say.

'I'd say she's going to want to hear that Joseph L. Mankiewicz has a project for the two of us to work on together as soon as we wrap on this picture.' Jeremy can't contain the grin that marches across his face despite the horror we just witnessed at the stables.

'Joseph L. Mankiewicz?' I swallow. This is a *huge* deal. Mankiewicz is the biggest director in Hollywood – even bigger than Leonard – since he just won an Academy Award for Best Director, and for him to request Kitty to work on his movie means she's more than hit the big time. She *is* the big time, and Jeremy too by the sounds of it. Lord knows how Art will take this news.

'The man himself. He was so impressed by our work on *The Last Station* – I mean, the fact that we both scooped an Oscar speaks for itself, doesn't it? – that he wants us both for his next picture.' With his hands still in his pockets, Jeremy slips past me and out onto the lot, leaving me feeling conflicted. While this is wonderful news for Kitty, it still doesn't explain why Jeremy was lurking alone in her trailer, his hands rifling through her jewellery, almost as though he was looking for something. The hairs rise on the back of my neck, and I shake the sensation away, moving to the dressing table to peer into the jewellery box. Kitty only keeps the costume jewellery she might use on set in here, the rest of it – her personal collection – is kept in a separate box in the safe at the hotel. I am ninety-nine per cent sure that the brooch pinned to Sally's coat was one I've seen Kitty wear before in a previous scene. I paw through the costume jewellery, trying to figure out if anything is missing, but I couldn't say for definite. I turn to leave and, as I do, something on the floor catches my eye, a slip of paper that has floated to the ground to rest right where Jeremy was standing. Curiosity burning, I stoop to snag it between my fingers, my heart lurching when I see what it is. A clipping, from a newspaper. A brief article about the discovery of the dead girl Tilda saw being taken out of the alley off Sunset. The girl who wore the expensive emerald earrings. My eyes go to the jewellery box on the dressing table, and that flicker of fear flutters even more brightly in my stomach.

−

Leonard catches me a little while later as I am headed to the catering truck, hoping to find something that I can persuade Kitty to eat, and my heart sinks.

'This way,' he says, guiding me towards his office. 'We need to talk.' His tone is grave and his face is solemn, and I realise why once we reach his office and he closes the door behind us.

Oskar Goldstein sits at Leonard's desk, his fingers steepled under his chin, as Jeremy Knox stands beside him. There is a messy sheaf of newspapers on the desk, as if someone has been urgently leafing through them. My hand goes to my pocket, to the clipping I found in Kitty's trailer.

'Lily.' Oskar's voice is like ice. 'How nice of you to join us.'

I say nothing, glancing from Oskar to Jeremy, who stares back at me impassively. 'I'm not really sure why I'm here.'

Oskar picks up a newspaper and throws it back down on the desk, making me flinch. '*This*. This is why you're here. Do you remember when I told you I wanted only good publicity for this movie?'

I nod, and Leonard shifts in his seat as if he wants to say something. 'I remember.'

'Then *what* in the name of God is this?' He jabs a finger at the front page, at the article accusing Camilla of sabotaging Kitty's horse. 'This isn't what I call "good publicity" – look here, they're insinuating that this picture is cursed! After the events at the Oscars, now this, it doesn't look good.' Oskar's eyes glitter with fury. 'I should fire the lot of you.'

'Oskar, you asked us to leak the news that Camilla would win Best Actress. None of us knew she would react that way,' Leonard says, his voice firm and even.

'Jesus H. Christ.' Oskar rubs his hand over his eyes. 'I didn't ask you to leak everything that happens on set! Do you know how this looks? First Camilla tries to shoot the main star and then Kitty falls from her horse, doing her own stunt? It looks as though we have no control over this entire operation! The gossip columns are talking – saying the picture is cursed, that the studio is losing money hand over fist. Leonard, you're making us look bad, and that won't do. That won't do at all.'

Jeremy leans forward, placing his hand on the article as he stares directly at me. 'I think we need to know where the leak is coming from. It shouldn't be too difficult.'

My cheeks burn, even though I know none of this has come from me. I look down at his hand on the pile of newspapers. At the gold ring on his pinky finger. *A gold ring*. My stomach clenches and I think for a moment I might be sick.

'Lily?' Leonard's voice infiltrates my thoughts as I try to make sense of things. 'Can you explain how these things have been leaked to the press?'

'Me? I don't... I don't know. It could have come from anywhere.' Camilla herself. Any of the extras that hang around the gates every day until they get their moment. Bobby, on the gate.

'I think it's more than likely it's come from someone who has direct access to the newspapers. Don't you?' Jeremy's eyes are hard as he glances at Oskar to make sure he grasps exactly what he's saying. 'After all, Lily, isn't your room-mate Tilda Jardine? The girl who works for Louella Parsons? Oskar, I really think you should reconsider Lily's role on this movie.'

My stomach lurches and the hot prick of tears stings my eyes. I can't lose this job. I've given up everything – and I mean *everything* – to stay here and, besides, I need to find out how Kitty is going to disappear. I can't do that without access to the set.

Leonard bangs a hand down on the table, making me jump. 'Jeremy, are you seriously suggesting that Lily has been leaking private information about this picture to her room-mate?'

Jeremy lifts his chin. 'It is the most obvious explanation.'

'Well, clearly you don't know Lily like I do.' Leonard shakes his head, a muted fury burning through his voice, and I really do want to cry now. 'She absolutely knows the importance of keeping things under wraps. The leak must have come from somewhere else, and rest assured I will get to the bottom of this, but Lily is not being removed from this picture. Thank you for your time, Oskar.'

Oskar glares at Leonard. 'This really is the final warning.'

With a sharp nod Leonard gets to his feet, gesturing for me to follow him. Once outside, he turns to me, his face grave. 'It wasn't you, was it?'

'No, sir.' I blink back the tears that still threaten. 'I would never do anything to jeopardise this movie, you know that.'

Leonard nods again, the lines on his face etched deeper than ever, and then strides away towards the set, ready to call everyone back to filming. I follow behind, keen to put space between myself and Jeremy. Clearly he was the one who went to Oskar, telling him I was behind the leak to the press, but why? I think of the way he follows Kitty, of how I found him rummaging through her things. Was Jeremy the one who broke into my apartment? Who shoved me into the back of the van? Because it seems as though Jeremy wants shot of me just as much as someone wants shot of Kitty.

Chapter Twenty-Three

Shooting is subdued all afternoon, with everyone trying and failing to give their best on screen in one shot. I am distracted by thoughts of Jeremy and worry for Kitty, who turns up late with no explanation of where she might have been. She is quiet between scenes, standing on her own, even avoiding Art. When Leonard calls cut, Kitty doesn't even wait for Art to walk her out, she just heads straight for her car.

By the time I leave the studio, shooting has overrun by an hour and a half and I am drained and exhausted. I decide to head to the Beverly Hills Hotel where Louis is on shift, in the hopes of grabbing a drink and a debrief about the events of the day. As I turn onto the hedge-lined path, the sight of that beautiful pink building perks me up no end, and I almost run up the red carpet through the main entrance, towards the Polo Lounge.

'Hey, Lily,' Louis grins as he sees me, and slides a cocktail glass towards me. 'You look like you could use a drink. Rough day?'

'Jeremy tried to get me fired, and I found the missing stunt double,' I say, gratefully accepting the pink liquor. 'Dead. In a storage room behind the stables.'

'Jeez, Lil.' Louis cuts his eyes to the man sitting on the bar stool beside me, and leans in. 'What in the heck?'

'Long story, but yeah. She's dead. The cops are calling it a "tragic accident", as is everyone else at the studio, but it's not. She was murdered. I know she was.' I sip the drink. 'What is this?' It tastes familiar.

'I call it the London Queen,' Louis says. 'I named it for you. It's just a little vodka, triple sec, some cranberry juice, shaken together with the tiniest dash of lime.'

'Wow. Thanks. I never had a cocktail named after me before.' I don't want to tell Louis that I think he's just invented the most basic bitch of all cocktails, the Cosmopolitan.

'So, back to the stunt double?'

I sigh, the bridge of my nose fizzing at the memory of poor Sally, slumped under that sheet. 'She was murdered, Lou. Things aren't adding up and I really believe the clock is ticking on Kitty. I think we need to tell her.'

'Sure.' That's the thing I love about Louis. Sometimes he tries to push back, to turn me into the kind of woman he's used to, one who listens to him and takes his advice like a good girl. But when it matters, he knows to just run with things. 'Tilda's over in a booth hashing out some bits with Louella, but she's not going to be long. I knock off in ten.'

For the first time ever, I feel a stutter in my chest at the thought of discussing things with Tilda before I shake it away. She's my friend – my *best* friend. If I can't trust her, then I can't trust anyone. Jeremy might think I'm the source of the leak, but I believe Tilda would never repeat anything I've told her, not without my permission. *At least, I hope not.* I remember her, standing outside the office the day she came to set to interview Jean. *Could she have heard the rumours circulating the set herself?* But I know

Tilda, I remind myself. She would never leak secrets from the studio. Not even for Louella.

Half an hour later we arrive at Chateau Marmont, Louis handing his car keys to a valet as I finish updating Tilda on the day's events, and the three of us make our way upstairs to Kitty's suite. There is a very different vibe here to the Beverly Hills Hotel. At the Beverly Hills everything is vibrant and loud, a place to be seen. The Chateau, on the other hand, is soft lighting and empty stairwells, a place to go about your business without being seen or heard. A ripple runs down my spine at that thought, and I tap lightly on Kitty's door.

'Lily. I wasn't expecting you.' Kitty is in a robe, her face free of make-up and her curls brushed flat, a glass of brandy in her hand.

'I'm sorry to interrupt, I know you've had a hell of a day. You know Louis and Tilda, right?'

Kitty nods and steps aside to let us in. 'What are you doing here?'

'Are you alone?' I peep into the kitchen area, then the bathroom, but it's all clear. 'We need to talk to you. It's serious, and you're probably going to tell me it's all rubbish, but…'

Kitty raises her glass in my direction. 'Can I get you one of these? You seem a little… off, Lily.'

'I'll take one.' Tilda throws herself down in an armchair. 'But Lily's already had a cocktail and trust me when I say this girl can't hold her liquor.'

Kitty gives a tired smile and pours Tilda a hefty shot of brandy. 'What is it that has you three knocking on my door this late?'

I sink into the armchair beside Tilda's, Louis perching on the arm. 'I'm going to cut to the chase. Kitty, you're in danger.'

'Danger?' Kitty blinks as she looks down at the three of us. 'What are you talking about?'

'You're in danger,' I repeat. 'Tilda, show her.'

Tilda reaches into her purse and pulls out the three tiny news clippings relating to the girls found dead in the alleyways. It makes my heart hurt to see that a couple of inches in the back of the newspaper are all they're worth. 'These girls were all found dead along Sunset in the last few weeks.'

'And? What does that have to do with me?'

'They all look like you, Kitty,' I say softly. 'Every one of them bears a resemblance to you, and every time one of them is found, something has happened to you a day or two previously. The assault on the red carpet at the premiere. The overdose.'

'That doesn't mean anything.' Kitty frowns. 'I rather think you're clutching at straws, Lily. Do you know how many girls come here to make it and disappear somehow or other? Hollywood is a seedy little town, surely you must know that.'

'There's a real bad guy in town, Miss Fox,' Louis says. 'And he's targeting girls who look like you. Murdering them. I would say that puts you in great danger.'

'But, I...' Kitty flounders, the rosy spots in her cheeks from the brandy paling to a sickly cream. 'This is ridiculous. No one is going to kill me – people can't get near me half the time, they have to go through Art. I can't even eat what I want without Doctor Astor looming over me.'

'There's something else,' I say. 'I think Sally is a victim of the same killer. She was wearing a brooch, tiny pearls inlaid in gold. I've seen one before in your costume jewellery on set. I think it was yours, and I think it was a sign, if you like, from the killer.'

'Well, it probably was mine,' Kitty stammers. 'Sally would have been wearing it, if she was supposed to shoot a scene.'

'The first girl found dead was wearing a red scarf,' I interrupt. 'The same colour and style as the scarf your character wore in *The Last Station*.'

Tilda turns to me, her eyes wide. 'Oh, well spotted, Lil.'

'And are you missing anything else?' I go on. 'I couldn't tell if anything apart from the brooch was missing from your costume jewellery on set today. What about your personal jewellery? Can we call down and get the box brought up from the safe?'

Kitty nods, and then moves to the phone and calls down to the lobby. Moments later, the jewellery box is delivered and we wait in thick silence as Kitty goes to the dressing table and rifles through it.

'Nothing's missing,' she says as she runs her fingers through the trinkets inside. 'Oh, wait! No. There is something.'

'A pair of emerald studs?' Tilda guesses, her eyes never leaving my face.

'How did you know?' Kitty whirls round, her hair flying around her head as she gapes at us. 'That's the only thing missing.'

'The second girl,' I say. 'She was found wearing them. It's all connected to you, Kitty. I think someone is going to try and make you disappear.'

Kitty sits abruptly down on the end of the bed, pressing her hands to her temples. 'No, this is impossible. Who…'

'There are a few people,' I say gently, not wanting to make things sound as though everyone on set hates her. 'I've wondered about Bobby on the gate – he wears a pinky ring like the man who grabbed you – although Doctor Astor also wears one, Camilla… even…' I tail off. 'I found Jeremy looking through your costume jewellery in your trailer today.'

Louis steps forward to sit on the bed beside Kitty. 'We think Jeremy might be involved.'

'What?' Kitty drops her hands to her lap and shakes her head fiercely. 'No. There's no way Jeremy could ever do something like this. He's… he's loyal to a fault, he could never see someone hurt me. He'd protect me to the ends of the earth.'

'That's what we're worried about,' Tilda says, dryly. 'What if he thinks the only way to protect you is to kill you?'

'You're crazy, the lot of you,' Kitty whispers. 'Jeremy isn't like that.'

'He's stalking you, Kitty,' I say gently. 'He turns up on every movie you work on. He knows things he shouldn't have any way of knowing. He's going through your things behind your back. He's convinced that Art isn't good enough for you – and I don't think he'd ever think anyone could be good enough for you.'

'I can't believe it. I won't believe it.' Kitty is adamant.

Frustrated, I get to my feet and pace the bedroom carpet. 'I'm trying to help you, Kitty. I want to stop this person before it's too late and something really awful happens to you. I don't know why you're so convinced it couldn't be Jeremy.' Stopping, I reach into my pocket and pull out the shirt button. 'Do you recognise this?'

Kitty peers at it, squinting slightly. 'Is that... a button from the shirt Jeremy wears in the wedding scene?'

I knew it. 'Yes. I found it outside your horse's stall this morning. You might think Jeremy could never harm you, but at the very least I think it's entirely possible that he sabotaged your horse yesterday.'

Kitty's fist closes around the button, a huff of disbelieving laughter escaping her lips. 'What?'

'I know it's hard to think that someone you thought was a friend could do something so awful,' I say gently, 'but do you see why we're concerned? Your bridle was damaged and the horse's shoes were loose. These things were done deliberately. He could have killed you, Kitty.'

'I know the bridle was damaged!' Kitty yells suddenly, tossing the button in my direction, her eyes meeting mine. 'I know exactly who sabotaged my horse.'

Chapter Twenty-Four

Tilda, Louis and I exchange a brief look, as things start to fall into place. 'Kitty? What did you do?'

Kitty's chest hitches as she covers her face with her hands, her sobs filling the room. Tilda slides stealthily over to the silver tray that carries the brandy decanter and discreetly refills Kitty's glass. She taps Kitty on the arm and hands it to her. 'Tell us what happened,' Tilda says in a soft voice. 'Whatever it is, we want to help you.'

Kitty takes a mouthful of brandy, wincing at the burn as she swallows. 'I have a confession to make.' She raises her eyes to mine, the lids swollen and pink with tears. 'I know it wasn't Jeremy who sabotaged my horse, because I was the one to damage the bridle and take the nails out of his shoes. I sabotaged my own horse.'

'But... why?' Louis asks. 'Why would you put yourself – and your horse – in danger like that? It doesn't make any sense.'

I think of the way Kitty cradled her belly as she watched Art and Camilla film their scene hours after the fall. I had thought that she was sore, tender and bruised from the way she hit the deck, but now I understand it's something completely different. 'You're pregnant.'

Kitty closes her eyes as the words hit her, and my eyes go to the brandy glass. 'You probably shouldn't be drinking that.' I reach for it, but Tilda stops me.

'Let the girl have something,' she says. 'A little drop of brandy never hurt a baby before.'

I beg to differ, but I drop my hand and remind myself that hundreds of babies were probably born just fine before any advice came in about pregnancy and booze.

'Yes, I'm pregnant,' Kitty sighs, another tear sliding down one cheek. 'And it's quite possibly the worst thing that could have happened.'

'Should I…?' Louis gestures towards the hall, his cheeks an endearing shade of pink. 'I mean, I probably need to…'

'Yes,' Tilda says, ushering him out into the hall. 'Maybe go over to Schwab's and fetch Kitty a milkshake and something to eat? We'll catch up with you later.' Louis beats a hasty retreat and I come to sit beside Kitty on the bed.

'Is it Art's? He is the father, isn't he?'

'Of course it's Art's! What do you take me for, Lily?'

Tilda chimes in. 'Then is it really the worst thing? Accidents do happen, but if you and Art marry quickly, no one even has to know. We can say the baby came early, and people can speculate all they like but no one will know the truth.'

'I don't want a baby,' Kitty says, flatly. 'That's why I tampered with the tack. I've ridden for years, Lily, I knew exactly how to sabotage things so that the horse would pull up, and when he did I knew exactly how to fall so that I wouldn't break my own neck. I thought if I fell, I could somehow…' She swallows, her chin trembling. 'Somehow stop the pregnancy. Get rid of it.' Her hand goes to her still-flat stomach. 'But it didn't work. I've had no bleeding, no pain, no nothing. The stubborn little thing is still clinging on for dear life.'

'Oh, Kitty.' I press my hand into hers, squeezing tightly.

'I was desperate, Lily.' Kitty's voice is barely above a whisper. 'I can't have a baby, I'm not ready. Maybe if things were different… If I wasn't stuck in this endless cycle of learning lines, filming, premieres and events, if I didn't have a camera on every aspect of my life, then perhaps…' She shakes her head. 'I don't even know if I want to spend the rest of my life with Art – I certainly don't want to be forced into it, just because we weren't careful enough.'

I had a pregnancy scare once, with my last boyfriend. Rex Crawford was a cheating, lying shithead, so panic was the first emotion that flooded my veins when I realised my period was late. There was nothing that terrified me more in that moment than the thought of the rest of my life spent knee-deep in nappies with a man I didn't love enough to marry, and I understand exactly how Kitty feels right now. 'You don't have to have a baby, Kitty. There are ways for us to stop this from happening without you hurling yourself off a galloping horse.'

'Lily, can I have a word?' Tilda hisses, pulling me to my feet and tugging me towards the bathroom, away from Kitty's ears. 'What are you doing? She can't have an… *abortion*. It's illegal! She could go to prison!' She glances over my shoulder at a weeping Kitty. 'We all could! My parents would kill me.'

'She can't have the baby,' I hiss back. 'Look at the state of her! What if being forced to have the baby is what tips her over the edge? Imagine the reason Kitty disappears is because she has a baby she doesn't want, and she ends up doing something silly.' I push past her, rage and fear ripping through me at the idea that Kitty has no control over her own body. The studio deciding what she eats to the point that she's been driven to an eating disorder is bad enough; I can't let her deal with this alone. 'Kitty, I'll help you. We'll figure this out, I promise.'

'I'm sorry, Lily, I just can't do it. In an ideal world this would be an opportunity, perhaps.' Kitty sniffs. 'A chance to evaluate what I really want. But now... if it means tying myself to Art, I don't think I can. I'm just not sure enough about us.'

Tilda takes a seat on the other side of Kitty, and squeezes her hand. 'It's a bum rap, Kitty, but it doesn't have to be. You could go away somewhere? Have the baby and give it up for adoption. Girls do that all the time.'

Kitty shakes her head. 'Jeremy told me Joseph Mankiewicz wants to sign us both for his next project the minute we wrap on this one.' She looks less enthralled by the idea than I thought she would. 'How could I disguise it? I'd have to be gone for months, and anyway, I don't know that I could carry a child for all that time, only to give it away at the end.'

'What about going to the studio?' Tilda's brow crumples as she thinks. 'They must be able to do something – delay filming, or... I don't know.'

'No,' Kitty almost yelps. 'I don't want the studio to know anything, not if I can help it. I need to deal with this by myself.'

'Maybe the studio can help,' I say. 'But the more we can keep this under wraps the better, especially from Jeremy and Art, even Doctor Astor.' Kitty might trust Doctor Astor, but I sure as hell don't. I haven't forgotten the cut on his wrist, or the fact that he's slipping Kitty drugs.

Tilda gets to her feet, pacing. 'Kitty, you're not the first actress this has happened to, and you won't be the last, and I'm betting that the studio would rather help you out than lose you. I can speak to Louella – discreetly, of course – I've heard rumours before about girls who have been caught, and the studio have helped them to cover it up.'

'Of course they have,' I say. 'Tallulah Bankhead, Jean Harlow, Bette Davis… all of them have been in your situation, Kitty, and they came out unscathed.'

Kitty gapes at me, Tilda's face matching her incredulous expression. 'Lily Jones, are you after my job?' Tilda quips.

'Don't quote me,' I say, unsure of which darkened area of the internet I was reading may have revealed these rumours. 'Trust me, Kitty, you aren't going to have to go through this alone.'

Kitty begins to cry again, and Tilda hands her the brandy glass. I guess if Kitty's pregnancy is going to be dealt with, she can drink a shot of brandy.

'Thank you,' Kitty slurs a little later as we tuck her into bed. She's pale and drawn, her eyes ringed with dark circles, and she yawns the moment her head hits the pillow. 'You girls are so lucky… I'm so lucky to have found you. I've never had friends like you before.' She snakes out a hand from under the blankets. 'Pass me the phone, would you, Lil?'

Reluctantly I pass her the phone, not sure it's a good idea for her to call anyone in the state she's in, half drunk and upset, before stepping out into the hall, pausing to make sure she's not calling someone she'll regret speaking to in the morning.

'Mom?' Kitty's voice trembles a few seconds later. 'It's me. I'm OK.' There's a muffled sob and then she says, 'Well, I'm not really. Mom, I'm just not sure…'

I pull the door closed, giving Kitty her privacy, and let out a long breath. Things just got even more complicated.

'Fucking hell,' I breathe as Tilda and I step out into the hallway outside Kitty's room. Louis has left a shake and bag containing a burger and fries outside the door, but seeing as Kitty's calling her mother – and the studio wouldn't let her eat it anyway – Tilda is scoffing the cold burger as she hands me the milkshake. 'What a mess.'

'Potty mouth, Lil. Kitty threw herself off a horse.' Tilda shakes her head, her cheeks bulging with food like a hamster. 'She must really be desperate.'

'How can we help without getting the studio involved? Oskar Goldstein is going to have kittens if he finds out, and I don't know about you, but Doctor Astor is not someone I think we can trust to have Kitty's best interests at heart.' If the doctor – and the studio – are controlling things, even down to what Kitty eats, what else could they take control over?

'It's a criminal offence, Lily,' Tilda sighs. 'I want to help her, but at the same time we have to tread carefully. There's a girl I know, she works at a bar on Hollywood Boulevard. She had a… situation like this and I'm sure she got it taken care of. It might mean that Kitty has to have "appendicitis" or an "ear infection" for a couple of weeks, but if it means we can save her…'

I want to cry. Kitty is right – I am so lucky to have found Tilda, to have found someone who would go to the ends of the earth (or maybe even jail) to help me, and there is a tugging in my chest at the thought that we are the closest thing Kitty has to real friends. 'There's one thing we can agree on,' I say. 'The longer we can keep this from the studio the better. If Camilla finds out, she'll make sure Kitty's reputation is mud. Jeremy will kill Kitty if he hears she's pregnant, and if Art finds out—'

'He'll be down on one knee with a big, fat diamond.' Tilda wrinkles her nose. 'And that's the last thing Kitty wants.'

'This could be the thing that gets her killed,' I say, my mouth filling with a sour taste that the milkshake can't wash away. 'Even though Kitty is convinced Jeremy doesn't have anything to do with the murders, I still can't shake the feeling that something about him isn't right, and finding him going through her things has only made me feel more uncertain. He had a clipping about the dead girl, Til. He was looking through Kitty's jewellery.' Making the connection between the two the way we have intensifies that sour taste in my mouth.

Tilda stops dead at the top of the staircase down to the lobby. 'Maybe I've been looking at things all wrong the whole time, Lil. Maybe I shouldn't have been digging into the girls' backgrounds after all. Maybe…' Her eyes light up. 'Maybe I should be digging into Jeremy's past. You say he's been hanging around Kitty for years, right?'

I nod, the milkshake not the only reason there is ice in my stomach. 'Yes, since they were kids. He's filmed on location all over the States with her.'

'Then if Jeremy is connected to this, it won't be the first time he's acted out on other women. Leave it with me. If Jeremy has done this before, then I'm going to find it, and then, Lil… then we've got him.'

Chapter Twenty-Five

Leonard and Jean are seated on the small patio at the edge of the Chateau gardens, an open bottle of white wine on the table between them as Tilda and I walk out the rear doors of the hotel. Bunny perches on a seat beside them, her face glowing in the warm lights that are strung between the trees, but her eyes are still puffy, and even Jean looks peaky.

'Lily, there you are.' Leonard pushes a smile onto his face, but I can still hear the strain in his voice. 'How is our star performer?'

'She'll be all right. She's on the phone to her mother, but I think she'll sleep well tonight.'

'Brandy,' Tilda says, with a wide smile. 'For the shock. Just brandy, that's all. That's why she's tired.'

'Right. Of course.' Leonard looks at Bunny. 'Run along and get some more glasses from somewhere, would you?'

Bunny scurries away and I feel a pang of sympathy for her. The Chateau doesn't have a restaurant or bar, so everything has to be brought in from the outside. It was originally built as an apartment block, so there is no fancy lobby, no place for people to walk in off the streets and mingle with the celebrity guests, and I wonder if this is why Kitty has chosen to stay here, despite it being inconvenient in some ways – for Bunny, at least.

'It's going to be a tough few weeks ahead,' Leonard says, as Tilda and I take a seat and he plucks a cigar from his pocket. 'Oskar is already clamouring for us to finish the movie on time despite the delays, so we'll have no option but to work longer hours on set. I dread to think how Art and Camilla are going to react to this.'

The days are already long on set, with start times often before the sun is even up, and most evenings after Leonard has called cut, he and a few of the others in the production team spend the night going over the rushes. While I don't mind the long hours, Kitty is going to be exhausted and Camilla, for one, is a big fan of her free time, using most of it to be seen out and about on the arms of various actors in order to boost her own profile. I can see her being *very* disappointed at the idea of working until late.

'Surely it's better than the studio pulling the picture?' I say. 'I can handle Camilla, don't worry.' I'll figure it out somehow.

Leonard sucks on the cigar, the end glowing a fiery red before he breathes out a puff of smoke and Jean wrinkles her nose. 'I'll get this picture finished if it kills me,' he says. 'So Kitty had better be back on set first thing tomorrow morning, or I'll kill her myself.'

'Len, darling.' Jean reaches out and places her hand on his knee. 'Let's not forget that a girl really has died. Poor Sally. Her family must be devastated.'

Leonard's cheeks colour slightly in the dim light. 'Of course, I'm sorry. It's just they're on my back about the budget, and…' He blows out a long breath. 'I'll call the family in the morning. I'll pay for the funeral myself.'

'Kitty will be on set tomorrow,' I reassure him, crossing my fingers that I'm right. 'I promise. And Leonard? Sally's death wasn't your fault.' Feeling my nose give the familiar itch that means tears are on the way, I get to my feet. 'Excuse me for one moment.'

I hurry inside, my chest aching with unshed tears as I run into the bathroom that Kitty was locked in the night of the nominations party, and slam the door shut. Resting my hands on the sink, I stare into the tarnished mirror over it. *This is all too much*. Blinking, tears slide down my cheeks, and I battle to draw in a breath. So much has happened over the past few weeks that I feel as if I have barely had time to process it, and all I need now is a long soak in a hot bath, with a flannel over my face to suck up the tears, just like I did for months after my mother's death. In lieu of that, a bawl in the ladies' toilets will have to do. I let myself think of Kitty, of her desperation at the idea of having a baby she doesn't want; of Sally, who just turned up at the lot to do her job; of the girls found dead in the alleyways off Sunset. All of them just going about their business until someone (*Jeremy?*) decided their time was up.

'Hello? Is someone in there?' A knock comes at the bathroom door, and I hurriedly splash my face with water, washing away the black dregs of mascara that ring my eyes.

'Just a minute!' Patting my cheeks dry, I force a smile in the mirror, smooth my hair down and open the door.

'Oh! It's you!'

My heart sinks, and I plaster on the fakest of smiles. 'Evelyn! How lovely to see you. What are you doing here?' Louis's ex-girlfriend – and the woman who got us into a hell of a mess in Las Vegas – is the last person I was expecting to see.

Evelyn runs her eyes from the top of my head to my shoes, in that way she has. 'Oh, we just dropped by to see a friend. A movie star, actually. I don't know if you've heard of him? Darling Marlon is a friend of my husband's.'

'Uh, yeah. I know Marlon. We've met before.' I frown. 'Husband? Congratulations.'

'Thanks.' Evelyn preens, flashing a rock of a diamond on her ring finger. 'Paulie and I are very happy.' *Oh, she really did marry Paulie Brooker after all.* 'And I probably shouldn't tell you, but I'm so excited, I just can't keep it in! We're going to have a baby!'

'Oh… wow.'

Evelyn smooths her hand over her concave belly, a satisfied look eating up her face. 'Just six… er… seven and a half months, and I'll be a mommy! I'm thinking of naming her after you, if it's a girl, as a thank you for all you did for me with the whole… *Vegas thing*.' She whispers the last part.

'*Wow*,' I repeat, not sure how to respond.

'Iris is a beautiful name for a girl, don't you think?' Evelyn grins and flashes her ring again as she pushes her hair away from her face. In the beginning I thought that perhaps Evelyn got my name wrong by mistake, but by now I know better. Evelyn gets a cheap thrill about pretending I am too far beneath her for her to remember my name. 'Oh, Lily, don't look like that. I'm sure you and Louis will be next to get married and have a baby!' She sashays past me into the ladies' bathroom, while I feel her words like a punch to my gut.

I'm not jealous of Evelyn, despite her being convinced that I am, but her words about me and Louis being next have made my sense of being out of place ever stronger. I know I don't belong here, that I should be back in the 2020s, cooking up ramen in my shitty apartment and waiting for Eric and Saffron to invite me to their wedding (presumably), all the while still waiting for my Mr Right to come in and sweep me off my feet. But there is a part of me that never wants to leave the past. I have the best friends, my dream job – despite dealing with Oskar Goldstein and his fiery temper – but deep down I know I can never settle here. I will never really fit, not properly.

There's also the fact that if you stay here, your life will never really be your own, a little voice whispers at the back of my mind, and it's true. I've grown up in a world where women might not be equal, but things are a damn sight fairer than they are here, in the 1950s. I can't help but compare Evelyn and Jean's reactions to being pregnant with Kitty's, and tonight Evelyn's excitement is dampened for me by Kitty's fear and anxiety. Pushing all thoughts of marriage and babies from my mind – let's be honest, I have enough to be dealing with here already – I push open the doors to the garden and head back to the table.

'You OK, Lil?' Tilda rakes her eyes over me and I nod, even though I know she can tell I've been crying.

'Yeah, I just saw—' Before I can finish my sentence, there is a scuffling from the opposite end of the garden, by the small gate that leads out to the road behind.

'You're a deadbeat! No wonder she doesn't want anything to do with you!' Raised voices reach us, and Leonard and I both have our chairs back and are on our feet within seconds.

'What about you?' another voice yells. 'I know what you are! So does Kitty!'

Oh yikes. As I run across the grass, Louis appears at the rear gate, his eyes wide, just as I make out the figures of Art and Jeremy tussling on the lawn. Jeremy swings for Art, his fist narrowly clipping his ear as Art spins away.

'Chicken-hearted, that's what you are,' Art jeers. 'No wonder Kitty left you. She wanted a real man.'

Jeremy laughs at this, his face twisting into something ugly and vicious. 'And you think that's *you*?' He bends with an *oof* as Art thrusts a fist into his stomach, winding him.

'What in the name of God is going on here?' Leonard roars, as he marches across the grass towards the squabbling actors.

Art pauses, his arm around Jeremy's neck, as Jeremy twists awkwardly, his hands scrabbling for Art's balls, presumably to land a hefty punch. 'This… pathetic *milksop* is trying to tell me that Kitty doesn't love me. Apparently she doesn't want to be with me at all anymore…'

Jeremy gets free and immediately grabs Art by the collar, pushing his face right into his, blond hair falling over one eye. 'Better a milksop than a goddamn scoundrel,' he hisses, tightening his grip until Art's face turns an alarming shade of puce. 'I'm not lying, Art. I'll ruin you, and Kitty will never want to see your face ever again. You make her skin crawl.'

With a roar, Art yanks himself away, as Jeremy pulls back a fist and lands a punch Anthony Joshua would be proud of on Art's nose. Blood splatters the front of his shirt, and then Louis and Leonard wade in, each of them grabbing an actor and pulling them apart.

'You're like goddamn children,' Leonard snarls, as he shoves a bleeding Art towards the bushes. 'You,' he points at Louis, who grips a furious Jeremy by the bicep, 'get him out of here. Now.'

Art stares Jeremy down, dabbing at his bleeding nose as Louis deftly manhandles Jeremy towards the back gate, none of us speaking until Jeremy is safely out of sight.

'I should get you a tissue for that nose,' I say eventually, just as Kitty appears, still in her white nightgown.

'What's going on? Art, your nose is bleeding.' Kitty looks frantically from me, to Art, to Leonard, shivering slightly in her thin nightwear. 'Bunny came and woke me, she said there was a fight?'

'Just a misunderstanding,' Art says, his voice thick as Bunny hands him her hanky and he presses it to his face.

'Lily? Leonard?' Kitty turns her attention to us.

Leonard shakes his head. 'I've had enough of the lot of you,' he growls. 'All of you on set at seven o'clock sharp tomorrow. I don't want any excuses, and I don't want any more of this.' He gestures to Art. 'I should fire you all,' he mutters, before marching across the lawn to where Jean waits, her handbag already over one arm.

'What the hell, Art?' I whisper, as Kitty shivers beside him. 'Fighting with Jeremy, in front of Leonard too? I swear you guys are going to kill me off.'

'He deserved it,' Art snaps. 'Saying Kitty didn't want to be with me. He said she doesn't even want to act anymore! Where does that dunderhead get off? Someone needed to put him in his place.'

'Yeah, but maybe not with your fist,' I say. 'Bunny, go and clean Art up, will you? That shirt is going to need soaking in cold salt water.'

'Honey, don't be upset.' Art leans over to kiss Kitty, who I notice doesn't have any shoes on, her knees knocking with the cold. 'I'm OK. You head on up to bed and I'll be there in a minute.'

Kitty shoots me a look that the others miss, before she gives a slow nod. 'OK, Art. Lily, come up with me?'

'Sure.' I turn to Louis. 'Meet you in reception in ten?' I check over my shoulder as Tilda guides Kitty towards the warmth of the hotel, and Art leans on Bunny as she marches him to the bathroom.

—

'How did he know?' Kitty wails the moment the door to her suite is closed. 'Lily, I did say those things about Art! I said those things to my mother on the telephone, but she would never have repeated it and certainly not to Jeremy. I've never said anything like that to anyone else… I wouldn't. And never to anyone on set – imagine the drama it would cause if Leonard thought I wanted to give up acting! How could Jeremy possibly have known? I can't have Art come here tonight, knowing I said all those things.'

'Honestly, Kitty,' Tilda says as Kitty begins to pace the floor of her suite, 'I think he was just trying to get a rise out of Art.'

'That's true,' I say. 'Art loves you, and the easiest way to rile him is to get all up in his grill over you.'

'Up in his…?' Kitty frowns. 'So you think it could just be a coincidence?'

'Sure,' Tilda says, guiding Kitty back towards the bedroom. 'You're freezing, sweetie. Maybe we should get you back into bed.'

Maybe it is a coincidence, but my gut says not. Jeremy has mentioned things he has no business knowing before, and now I'm left to wonder what else he might have somehow overheard. I can't ponder it too long as there is a knock at the door, and then Doctor Astor pokes his head in.

'Knock knock,' he says cautiously. 'I heard there was a slight altercation in the garden this evening. I've just been to put a cold compress on Mr Calloway's nose.'

'Is he OK?' Kitty's voice floats from the bedroom and I gesture for Doctor Astor to head inside.

'I'm rather more concerned about you,' the doctor says. 'Bunny said you were shaking and shivering like a leaf in fall, and we can't have you catching cold.' He bustles around Kitty as she sits up in bed, listening to her chest and taking her blood pressure. 'Nothing a little brandy won't cure.' Doctor Astor moves to the silver tray holding the brandy and Kitty presses her hand to her mouth, her face pale.

'Are you sure you're all right?' I whisper to her as she nods frantically.

'Just nauseous,' she whispers back. 'I caught a whiff of his aftershave and it made me feel all funny. Art's toothpaste made me feel sick this morning too.'

'I'll bring you some ginger tomorrow,' I say quietly. 'It'll help the nausea until you can... you know.'

Doctor Astor hands Kitty a glass of brandy. 'This should do the trick. Let me know if you have any flu symptoms though. It won't do, you catching a cold during filming.' He reaches out and takes her free hand, giving it a brisk rub to warm her up.

'Yes, Doctor.'

Tilda walks him to the door and, as he reaches it, he whips off his trademark boater and holds it to his chest in a gallant gesture, one that makes my blood run cold. 'Good evening, ladies.'

Rushing to Tilda's side, I smile and nod on autopilot until the doctor reaches the staircase, when I slam the door closed and whirl on Tilda. 'He took his hat off.'

'Yeah? And?' Tilda walks into the bedroom, where Kitty has already fallen asleep, her hands tucked under her cheek and the blankets pulled up to her chin.

I dig in my purse, fumbling past receipts, hair grips and a pencil before I pull out the now battered photograph I stole from Kitty's drawers. 'Look.' I jab a finger at the photo as Tilda tidies the glasses from Kitty's bedside table. 'See here? That's Kitty on the stage on Broadway, but look at this. The back row of the audience is in shot... see this guy?' I point to a bald guy in the far corner, finally realising what it was that was bugging me every time I looked at the photo.

'It's him.' Tilda squints, drawing the photo close to her nose. 'That's Doctor Astor.'

'Right!' I crow, as Tilda shushes me. 'I didn't recognise him without his hat,' I say as we sneak out of Kitty's suite and head for the stairs. 'Let's show Louis and see what he says, but I think this is looking more and more like the doctor has known Kitty for far longer than we thought.' At the foot of the stairs I pause, as Tilda bumps into me from behind.

'Yeah, he's...' She blinks slowly, her tongue slipping out to run over her lips as if her mouth is dry. 'He's... he'shhh...' Her voice slides away, thick and unintelligible.

'Tilda? Til?'

Tilda stares at me blankly for a moment, her eyes heavy, and then I watch, horrified, as she crumples into a heap at the bottom of the stairs.

Chapter Twenty-Six

'Tilda? Wake up!' Dropping to my knees, I pat at her cheeks, softly at first and then harder when she doesn't respond.

'Lily? What happened?' Louis is beside me, his face frantic as he tugs at Tilda's hands, trying to pull her into a sitting position. 'Tilda? Can you hear me?'

'Don't…' I ease his hands away, Tilda flopping like a rag doll back to the floor. 'We need to put her in the recovery position…'

'What?' Louis shakes his head, his hair flopping over one eye. 'No, Lily, we need to get her to a hospital! What the heck happened?'

'She just kind of slurred her words and then she went down, like a light went out.' I tap Tilda's face again. 'Til? Wake up, come on.' My fingers are icy as something burns in my chest, dread and fear making me clumsy. What if she's had a stroke? Or worse? Louis's right, we have to get her to a hospital.

I am about to instruct Louis to grab Tilda under her arms when she rolls over of her own accord, onto her left side, and lets out an almighty snore.

'She's… not dying?' Louis steps back, his brow furrowed.

'She's asleep,' I say, a bubble of hysterical laughter threatening to burst out of my throat in relief. *Tilda isn't dying*. But still, we need to get her out of the hotel lobby before someone sees her. She'll be furious if someone clocks her passed out with her skirt above her knees. 'Lou, can you grab her shoulder? I'll take the other side, and we'll manoeuvre her out to the car.'

With one of Tilda's arms thrown over Louis's shoulder, the other over mine, we walk her out to the car the best we can, and it's a relief to tuck her into the back seat. She might be tiny, but a dead weight is still a dead weight. The valet stops us as we pull out of the garage.

'Everything OK there?' He peers in through the window at Tilda sprawled across the bench seat.

'A little too much sauce.' Louis mimes drinking with his thumb and little finger. 'You know how it is, right? They only eat a salad at dinner, but then they think they can drink cocktails all night.'

The valet laughs, Louis joining in as I force a smile. 'Right! You have a pleasant evening, sir.'

As we drive away, I don't know whether to be relieved that the valet stopped us, given that Tilda was unconscious on the back seat, or furious at the way he so blithely believed Louis's story, especially as there seems to be a serial killer hanging around the streets of Hollywood. Back at the apartment, Louis carries Tilda up the stairs and lays her gently on the sofa.

'Phew,' he huffs. 'She really is out for the count.' Tilda lets out another snore and I carefully tuck a blanket over her legs.

'It's as if she's been drugged. You don't think...?' I pause, my mind racing as I sink into the armchair beside the sofa. The shock of Tilda keeling over is wearing off, and now I fight off a throat-stretching yawn. 'What if she drank some of Kitty's brandy? That's all I can think. And if she did that…'

'Then Kitty's drink must have been spiked,' Louis finishes as he perches beside me. 'Who spiked it though?'

I shrug. 'Tilda poured it from the decanter in Kitty's suite. I guess anyone who has access to Kitty's room could have done it.'

'Or…' Louis pauses, his face thoughtful, as a thought hits me and I have to swallow hard.

'The doctor,' we say together.

'What if,' I go on, 'Doctor Astor put something in Kitty's drink? I know she takes pills to keep her pepped up at times – especially when there are events she doesn't really want to attend – but I'm pretty sure he's sedating her at night. She said something about needing the pills when he gave her something to help her sleep before… Whether she realises it or not, I think he's got her hooked on them. It's not the first time I've seen him give her something… and Oskar Goldstein is adamant that Kitty be kept in line until this movie is done. Maybe the doctor's giving her other pills we don't know about and he's keeping her under control that way? The pill bottle in the bathroom had her name on it when I found her unconscious in the tub, and she swore blind she wasn't prescribed anything.' I feel nauseous, my stomach rolling. 'There's something else.' I pull out the photograph of Kitty on Broadway and hand it to Louis, pointing out the younger version of Doctor Astor. 'He was at Kitty's show years ago. Has he been watching her for all this time?'

Louis scours the picture, his mouth twisting. 'That's just… weird.' He hands the photo back to me. 'So you think Doctor Astor has known Jeremy all this time too?

Does this make Doctor Astor our main suspect now? And where does Bobby come into it?'

I rest my head in my hands. 'I have no idea. All of them wear a gold ring just like the guy who shoved me into the van and who grabbed Kitty on the red carpet. None of this makes any sense – I mean, why would Doctor Astor or Bobby want to harm Kitty? I know Bobby is a huge fan and he's very insistent that he wants a signed photo of her for his wall, but would he kill her over it?'

'He might do it for Camilla.'

'What?' The photo slides to the floor as I stare incredulously at Louis.

'Bobby is a bigger fan of Camilla than he is of Kitty,' Louis says. 'If Camilla asked him to do something to get rid of Kitty, maybe he would do it, even if it meant bundling you into a van to scare you off. Camilla would have access to Kitty's trailer too.'

'But Jeremy is obsessed with Kitty… Jeremy not only has access to her trailer, but he's been in her suite. He could have taken those earrings and the scarf and left them on the dead girls. I still think Jeremy is connected to all this.'

I just need to figure out how to prove it.

—

Tilda wakes up shortly before I leave for work in the morning, stretching and yawning on the sofa as I dab rouge onto my cheeks in the tiny sitting-room mirror. 'I slept like a log,' she beams, before her smile drops and she frowns, taking in her surroundings. 'Why am I on the sofa? And how did I get home?' She presses a hand to her mouth. 'Did I drink gimlets again, Lil? You know I'm never good on gimlets.'

'I wish it was gimlets,' I say, grimly. 'Did you drink anything in Kitty's suite last night?'

Tilda frowns. 'Maybe? Yes, I did! That's right, there was a fight and we took Kitty to her room. I drank her brandy, she fell asleep before she could finish it. *Oh*. But that doesn't explain how I got home.'

I tell Tilda how she passed out on the stairs and Louis and I brought her home, her cheeks growing paler with every sentence. By the time I remind her of the photograph, and tell her how it seems that not only Jeremy but Doctor Astor too have known Kitty for far longer than we realised, her face is like chalk.

'Where are you going now?' she asks in a small voice.

'To the set,' I say, tying a silk scarf around my wild curls and snatching up my purse. 'I might just have a word with Bobby on the way in.'

—

Bobby gives me a grin as I approach the gate, and I can't help but glance at his hand as he reaches for a pen so I can sign in.

'Morning, Miss Lily. How are we today?'

'Just swell, Bobby.' I smile back, feeling my teeth grit. 'Say, that's a pretty ring. I've never noticed you wear it before. It mean something to you?' A small gold signet ring winks at me from his pinky finger. The same style of ring I spotted on Doctor Astor's hand. The centre has a V etched into it, with what looks like a compass engraved over it.

If I'm expecting Bobby to react, I'm mistaken, as he just grins his usual grin, his Brooklyn accent thickening. 'Sure does, miss. It means I'm a Freemason. It's sort of a secret club. Just for men. No ladies allowed.'

'Oh, sure. I've heard of it.'

'You have to be real lucky to be part of it,' he says proudly, and it's on the tip of my tongue to ask about initiation rites and whether they involve bundling young women into vans, or indeed murdering them down dark alleys, when he says, 'But I'm only in the lower tiers, I'm nobody important.' He leans in, peering over my shoulder to make sure he's not overheard. 'You know who is real important though? The good Doctor Astor himself. He gets to host meetings and everything.'

'He does? Where?'

Bobby rears back, as if I've blasphemed in his face. 'Oh, I don't know if I should say. I'm not really meant to talk about it at all. You won't say anything, will ya?'

I give him my best smile, the one that got me free boba tea for a week in twenty-first century LA. 'Come on, Bobby. We're good friends, aren't we? I reckon I could get you that signed photo of Kitty today, you know.'

He pauses a moment, nodding hello as one of stable boys passes by before lowering his voice. 'OK. But you'll get me the photo of Kitty tonight?'

I nod.

'The meetings are at his apartment, but you can only go if you're invited. I went the other night for the first time.'

'You did?' Something spicy flares in my veins, and my hands grip my purse to hide the telltale shake of an adrenaline rush. 'Where?'

'On Sunset. Doctor A. has an apartment above a hardware store. Lily? Lily, I—'

'Thanks, Bobby!' I call over my shoulder as I hurry towards the set, not waiting to hear what else Bobby has to say. 'I'll get you that photo, I swear!' *An apartment above a hardware store.* That's *Doctor Astor's* apartment? I had envisioned him living somewhere far swankier, maybe over in Beverly Hills, but perhaps a dingy apartment that leads on to a seedy back alley is the kind of place that suits him better. I am almost certain now that Doctor Astor is involved with the dead girls, and potentially Kitty's disappearance. I think of his wrist, the slight cut and bruising that he told me he got from doing battle with a rose bush, and then of the dingy alley behind the apartment building, with the smell of the dumpsters filling the air, and my feet slow. How could he possibly have been cut pruning a rose bush, when he doesn't even have a garden?

Chapter Twenty-Seven

My head is so full of Bobby and the ring on his pinky finger, and Doctor Astor and his bruised wrist, and Jeremy's obsession with Kitty, that I don't even hear Art calling my name until he reaches out and grabs me by the arm.

'You're in a world of your own today, Lily.' Art smiles, but there is a flatness to his tone that tells me he's annoyed at being ignored.

'Sorry, Art, I only just arrived—'

'Listen, Lily, I need to talk to you. It's about Kitty.'

'Where is she?'

'I don't know, I haven't seen her yet.'

I frown. It's not like Kitty to be late, at least it wasn't when we first started filming, but now she seems to be arriving later and later every day. Before I can comment on it, Art pulls me to one side, almost pushing me into a rail of costumes that is waiting to be wheeled back to the wardrobe department. 'I was thinking, I need to make things official with her.'

'Official?' I press my hand to my forehead, as if warding off a migraine. He's not going to say what I think he is, is he? Before he can go on, Camilla strides past, pausing and doubling back when she sees us.

'Oh, Art, let the poor girl go,' she says, an undertone of something I can't quite read in her voice. 'Lily, you look like you're getting a terrible headache – it must be all Art's bellyaching.' She laughs and rolls her eyes when Art stares at her, stony-faced. 'Oh, lighten up, Calloway. There must be something in the air this morning. Kitty already screamed at me to get out of the bathroom, she was throwing up her breakfast again.'

I cast a quick glance in Art's direction and change the subject. 'I think they're calling for you, Camilla. I'm sure Leonard was shouting your name just now.'

'Oh, shoot.' Before she leaves, Camilla reaches up and turns Art's face this way and that. 'Oh dear, Art, there's some bruising under your eyes. Some right hook Jeremy has, eh? I hope Kitty was worth it.' And she sashays away, leaving Art with balled fists and a clenched jaw.

'Let's get you to make-up, shall we?' I say, brightly. 'They'll hide that bruising in no time. To be honest, it's barely there...'

'No, Lily, wait. I need your advice.'

Oh, shit. He is going to say what I think he is, isn't he? Plastering on a smile, I turn back to face Art. 'Sure. No problem.'

Art fidgets with his cufflinks, adjusting them just so as he speaks. 'I was thinking... I was thinking that I'd like to ask Kitty to marry me.'

'Oh. Wow.' *Shit.* 'Why... er, why now?' *Does he know about the baby?* I'm pretty sure Kitty wouldn't have told him, but what if Jeremy has said something? It's entirely possible that Jeremy could have found out somehow, after all, he seems to know other things he shouldn't.

'Why not, Lily?' Art looks at me sharply. 'Kitty and I are in love, surely this is the next logical step? I mean, look at us! We're a Hollywood power couple... or at least we could be once we're married. We'd easily knock Vivien and Laurence off their perch as Hollywood's golden couple. I have a project lined up for the two of us once we finish shooting here, and if we combine that with a wedding…'

'A project for you and Kitty to work on together? But what about…' I break off abruptly. Clearly Kitty hasn't mentioned the movie Jeremy has been offered for the two of them by Joe Mankiewicz.

Art frowns for a moment before ploughing on. 'I want to make things official with her, Lily, she's the love of my life.' His tone darkens. 'And if we're married then maybe Jeremy Knox will keep his nose out of our business.'

'Is that the real reason?'

Art hesitates for a fraction of a second. 'Of course it isn't. Kitty and I are meant to be, anyone can see that. Just think what the public will say when we announce our engagement!' He gazes into the distance, suitably misty-eyed. 'The wedding will be wonderful, I can picture it now.'

'When are you thinking of proposing?' I ask, internally wincing at the thought of Kitty's reaction to Art getting down on one knee.

'Well, soon. This week? Tonight? It depends on how special you can make this for her, Lily. I want you to set everything up, and I want it to be spectacular.'

'Tonight? Bloody hell, Art. Wouldn't it be better to wait until filming has wrapped?' Hopefully I can get Kitty in a private hospital for her 'appendicitis' long before then. 'And have you even sounded Kitty out about whether she wants to get married?'

Art lets out a long hoot of laughter. 'Oh, Lily, of course she does! There isn't a woman alive who doesn't want to be married to Art Calloway!'

To be fair, there are *a lot* of women who would jump at the chance to be married to Art.

'And anyway,' Art goes on, insistent, 'I want to get things wrapped up sooner rather than later. The more time that passes before Kitty agrees to marry me, the more time Jeremy has to drip his poison in her ear.' Art's eyes search my face, as his voice thickens. 'I can't lose her, Lily. I know Jeremy won't rest until he turns Kitty against me, but I won't let him. I can't bear the thought of losing her, not now. I'm worried about what he'll do.'

'You are?'

'The things he's saying about Kitty and me, the things he's saying she's said. I know Kitty would never speak about me that way. I'm worried he's going to take things further – too far, if you like.'

I know that Kitty *has* said these things, but I wonder again how Jeremy knows. Clearly, Art is concerned about Jeremy and Kitty, and it's on the tip of my tongue to ask Art about Doctor Astor and how he feels about him, but then that could be opening a whole other can of worms.

'...why, when he's got an apartment in Beverly Hills?' Art is saying.

'Sorry, Art, what was that?'

Art tuts impatiently, pushing a lock of luscious dark hair off his forehead. '*I said*, I don't know why Jeremy insists on hanging around at Chateau Marmont every night, when he's got a perfectly good apartment to go back to in Beverly Hills. It's clearly so he can torture me by mooning over Kitty.'

The Chateau. Could Jeremy be sneaking into Kitty's room somehow? I bounce on my toes, suddenly itching to get back to the hotel and snoop around while Kitty is on set. 'Probably,' I say without thinking. 'Sorry, Art, I have to dash, but if Leonard asks, will you tell him I've gone to pick up his dry-cleaning?'

Art looks puzzled as I flash him a grin and turn on my heel. His voice floats after me as I hurry towards the exit. 'So, you'll set it up for me, Lily? Excellent.'

—

Chateau Marmont has a different feel to it in the daylight hours. Usually when I visit Kitty in the evenings, it's quiet, an almost respectful hush over the building, unlike the buzzy vibe of the Beverly Hills Hotel. Now a maid hurries up the stairs as I enter the lobby, and I can see the gardener pruning the bushes out in the garden, as a man who looks suspiciously like writer-director Nicholas Ray strolls towards the bungalows, a cigarette in one hand, pencil in the other.

I head for the stairs, Kitty's room key tucked into my purse. Hopefully I'll be in and out, and have it back in her trailer before she finishes shooting her scenes today. Pausing outside, I knock on the door of her suite even though I know it's empty, and then slip inside, hanging the *Do Not Disturb* sign on the handle as I do so.

It's a tip, but as far as I can tell, the mess is all Kitty's and not the work of some rubbish burglar. When I worked with Honey Black, she still had that sweet small-town girl attitude about her, which meant room turndown or not, Honey made her own bed and hung her own clothes up every day. Kitty, on the other hand, is the complete opposite. The counter in the small kitchenette is littered with empty glasses, all ringed with the dregs of unknown liquid in the bottom, and I lift one to my nose and sniff. *Brandy*. I place it back down, resisting the urge to lick my lip where it touched the glass, just in case.

Moving to the bathroom, I run my eyes over the uncapped bottles and tubes of make-up sprawled above the sink and along the edge of the bath. The scent of Kitty's perfume lies heavy in the air, as if she spritzed just as she ran out the door, and there is a smear of red lipstick on the mirror, as though she kissed her reflection.

The cosy sitting room is neater, with just some script pages, the edges curled and the front page ringed with a water stain, and a small pile of letters from fans, that I recognise as having been sent over from the studio. There is nothing out of place, no sign that Jeremy has been here. Scratching my head, I move into Kitty's bedroom. The pillows are on the floor, the blankets rumpled, and I have to resist the urge to start tidying.

'Your chambermaid days are over, Lil,' I mutter to myself. The telephone sits on the bedside table and I lift it to my ear. Could Jeremy somehow have tapped Kitty's phone conversations? I run my hands under the bed, under the table and over the curtain poles, sure I won't find any bugging device, but trying anyway. There is nothing. I have no idea how on earth Jeremy is listening in on Kitty's conversations. Kitty swears blind she hasn't spoken to him about how she feels about Art, and she has no reason to lie.

'Fuck, shit, bollocks, *wanker.*' It feels good to let out a stream of expletives, given that if I did this in public Louis would likely die of a heart attack at the language, and in my frustration I kick out at a jumble of clothes – probably very expensive designer dresses, knowing Kitty – that is thrown against the skirting board. 'What the…?'

Kicking at the clothes has unearthed a small, ornate air vent tucked into the bottom of the wall. Shoving the rest of the clothes to one side, I lie down on my stomach and inspect it closely. It's beautiful, if such a thing can be beautiful. The gap in the wall is covered with an iron grate, the metal twisted into neat, identical bars that curl across each other, and when I peer into it I can see there is a void that runs beneath the floor. A thin beam of daylight wisps up through a gap in the floor below, and a spurt of excitement thunders through my veins like lava. *Is this how Jeremy has been listening in?* Wriggling closer, I can feel the faintest breeze on my face, and a whirring that could be coming from a ceiling fan. *The vent is over another room in the hotel – and daylight is coming through a tiny hole in the ceiling below.* This is the room where Kitty sits in bed and talks to her mother on the phone, telling her how she really feels about life on set... and it's where we've had our conversations about Art previously. *Jeremy, I've got you now.*

–

Tugging my ponytail tighter, I smile my best and widest grin at the lady on the reception desk in the dimly lit lobby. 'Hiii,' I say, sweet as a California raisin. 'I'm working on a movie and I think one of my actors left something in his room. He's sent me back to check. I need the key to room four, please.' The room directly below Kitty's.

'Yeah?' She raises an eyebrow at me. 'Sorry, sweetie, we don't give out room keys to just anybody. You tell your guy to come back and check for himself.' Her hand goes to the drawer under the desk unconsciously. The drawer where the keys are kept, which I've seen pulled out multiple times for Kitty.

'Oh shoot, I guess I didn't think of that.' I slap my own forehead and grin, the very definition of a ditz. 'Here, let me show you my identification, maybe that...' I open my purse and then immediately drop it, sending lipsticks, a spare pair of stockings, tissues and a miniature perfume among other things rolling across the floor. 'Oh gosh, I'm so sorry.' The receptionist bends to pick up my things and I lean over the desk and swipe the key to room four while she isn't looking.

'Thank you so much,' I say as she hands me my sanitary belt (this is one thing I do not love about the 1950s). 'Gosh, I'm just *mortified*.'

'Don't be, sweetie.' She bestows a motherly grin, and I don't have to fake the blush that burns my cheeks as I move away towards the rear doors, the key hot against my thigh through the fabric of my skirt pocket.

When she turns away to answer the phone, I almost sprint to room four and slide the key into the lock, stepping inside with a quick glance over my shoulder. Jeremy's room — of course Art was right to be suspicious, when Jeremy has a place nearby in Beverly Hills — is immaculate. Almost *too* immaculate. There is a single toothbrush in the bathroom, the bed is neatly made. In fact, there is no sign that Jeremy has even been here at all, and for a moment I feel a twinge of doubt. Even so, I peer up at the ceiling, in the general direction of the grate in Kitty's room above, my breath catching when I see it. *I wasn't wishing things into existence.* Right there, right below where the air grate is in Kitty's room, there's a tiny hole in the ceiling, and a chair has been placed beneath it.

'You dog,' I whisper, as I step up onto the chair. The hole is small enough to miss if you don't know it is there, but when I stand on the chair and lift my face, I can see the daylight streaming in through the grate above. It must be like having a bugging device in Kitty's room, her voice wafting through the gap in the ceiling straight into Jeremy's ear.

There has to be something here to prove it is Jeremy who has been using the room. I can't ask the woman in the lobby – for all I know she's noticed the missing key and is on her way up here right now. The toothbrush in the bathroom isn't exactly evidence either; it's a generic toothbrush used by thousands of people all over America. Opening the wardrobe, I find it empty, as are the drawers, and the desk is clear. Even the trash can is empty. Aware of time ticking away, I look around one more time, before dropping to my knees and peering under the bed, and that's when I know I have him.

Tucked away, loitering with the dust bunnies, is a single sweet wrapper. Reaching in, I pull it out, the dust tickling my nose, and open it flat in the palm of my hand. *A Fireball wrapper*. Jeremy's favourite sweet. I lift it to my nose and sniff, the scent of cinnamon and aniseed dragging me back to the rear of the van, and the strange smell that I couldn't put my finger on. It really was Jeremy all along, and now I have the proof.

Chapter Twenty-Eight

The moment Leonard calls cut I slip away, detouring out of the rear gates to the lot that isn't manned by Bobby, before Kitty, Art or anyone else can collar me. It's been a difficult afternoon since I stealthily dropped the key to room four by the lobby desk on my way out. Although Kitty and Camilla managed to shoot an entire scene without killing each other, Kitty seems distracted and unengaged, and I don't think it's just down to her secret pregnancy. I've found myself slinking behind curtains and burying my face in memos and script pages to avoid catching Art's eye. That last thing I want to talk about is his planned proposal. Jeremy didn't have any scenes today, but even so he appeared on the edge of the set as Kitty told Camilla that she was dying (or, at least, her character was. The whole scene gave me the shivers), and when he pulled out his little bag of sweets and nonchalantly offered me a Fireball it was all I could do not to hiss in his face that I knew what he had done.

By the time I arrive at Villa Nova and slide into one of the rear booths I am desperate for something containing hard liquor, and I order an old-fashioned, sighing as the whisky burns its way to my stomach.

'You're starting early.' Louis winks as he slides into the booth opposite me, followed by Tilda.

'Long day,' I say.

Both of them order a drink and then Tilda turns to me. 'You look like you have stuff to say,' she says. 'Do you want to go first? Because I also have news.'

'OK, sure.' I take another gulp of my drink. 'So, Jeremy is definitely spying on Kitty. I found evidence in the room below hers that he's been listening through the air grate in the wall.' I pull out the Fireball wrapper. 'I found this under the bed. Jeremy has a terrible sweet tooth and he's always munching candy on set, Fireballs being his favourite. The smell of them is very similar to the odour in the van.' While it pulled me back there, it still doesn't smell exactly right, the aniseed diminished by the faint scent of exhaust fumes, perhaps.

'Jeez,' Louis breathes. 'What a... a *creep*. So all the time Kitty has been in her suite, thinking she was in a place where she could talk freely, Jeremy was listening in the entire time?'

'It seems like it.'

Louis's mouth twists in distaste. While a lot of men in 1950s Hollywood wouldn't see much of a problem with this, Louis is clearly uncomfortable. 'The man is a jerk. Just wait until I see him. He's cruising for a bruising, taking advantage of a lady's privacy like that.'

'Chill, Lou.' Tilda's voice is sharp. 'It's definitely weird, but it doesn't mean he's a murderer.'

'I think he's in league with Doctor Astor,' I whisper, as the door to the restaurant opens and I spot Camilla's bright hair.

'You mean that Doctor Astor, who just walked in with Camilla?' Tilda nods in their general direction, her face stretching into the fakest smile I've ever seen. 'They're coming over,' she says through gritted teeth.

'Lily!' Camilla squeals, leaning down to kiss my cheek and almost suffocating me in a cloud of Chanel No. 5. 'This is where you're hiding, is it? Art's been looking all over for you. Something about a big surprise you're planning for Kitty this evening?'

'I thought he'd forgotten about that,' I say faintly. 'You got me, Camilla! What are you two doing here?'

'Dinner, of course,' Doctor Astor says, his hand moving to rest on the small of Camilla's back. My stomach churns and I have to force myself to meet his eye. 'I promised Camilla cocktails and a good steak.'

'Great.' I stop myself from glancing down at his hands. His big, strong hands that could easily wrap around Camilla's throat and choke the life out of her in seconds. The hand that wears a gold ring on the pinky, a ring to match Bobby's. 'We should let you guys get on. See you tomorrow, Camilla.'

They head to their table and Tilda waits until they're seated before she speaks. 'You're as white as a sheet, Lily. What were you saying about the doctor before he walked in?'

'Do you think he and Jeremy could be working together? Jeremy is obsessed with Kitty and now we know he's been spying on her for sure. The dead girls all look like Kitty, so this all has to be connected, right? Whoever threw me into the back of the van wore a gold ring… just like Bobby. I saw it today, and when I asked him he told me it's a Freemasons' ring. Doctor Astor was wearing the same ring just now, and Bobby told me that he's high up in the organisation – when we saw Bobby the other night it was the doctor's apartment he was visiting. The dead girl was found in the alley behind Astor's apartment building… Astor and Jeremy were both in the photograph of Kitty on Broadway, taken years ago. Astor and Jeremy could easily have killed the girls in his apartment and moved them to the alleys nearby.'

'Why is Art looking for you?' Tilda says, her brow furrowed.

'Huh? What does that have to do with all of this? Don't you see, I don't think Jeremy would be able to harm the girls by himself. Yes, of course women would follow him, he's a movie star, but seeing as how Doctor Astor is keeping Kitty sedated at night, what if he drugs the girls for Jeremy—'

'Lily! Why is Art looking for you?' Tilda asks again, her face deadly serious as she reaches out and grabs my hand. 'It's important.'

'Uh, he wants me to organise a big proposal for Kitty,' I say. 'He's going to ask her to marry him. I've tried to put him off, but he's insistent. If Jeremy finds out then this could be the thing that pushes him over the edge into getting rid of Kitty for good. An "if I can't have her, no one can" kind of thing.'

Tilda shakes her head and lets go of my hands. 'Remember I told you I had some things to say too? Wait until you hear what I found out.'

Tilda pulls out her notepad and neatly folded scraps of newspaper from her purse and fixes her eyes on me. 'You wanna order another drink before I start? You're going to need one.'

Once the waitress brings over another round of old-fashioneds, Louis urges Tilda to get on with it, as my legs jiggle under the table and I run a finger under my collar, the temperature in the restaurant seeming to rise by a degree or two along with my anxiety.

'I was looking into Jeremy,' Tilda begins, flipping through her pages. 'And to be honest, Lil? There's nothing much there at all. He attended the same high school as Kitty, which we already knew, and while it's clear he's followed Kitty from job to job, I couldn't find anything nefarious on him. No complaints from women, no harassment cases, nothing. If anything, he's a perfect gentleman, even if he is a little intense.'

'So... maybe he's just covered his tracks really well?'

Tilda shakes her head. 'If there was something to find I would have found it. I even got Ty involved, and when he checked the police files, there was nothing on Jeremy at all. So I started digging into the other people around Kitty.'

'And?' Louis leans forward, and I find myself mimicking his position, my knees no longer jiggling under the table. In fact, my entire body seems to be frozen as I wait for Tilda to speak.

'Art,' Tilda croaks, before clearing her throat. 'There are two cases of women turning up dead in places where Art has lived.'

'Art?' I let out a snort. 'Art Calloway? You are joking, aren't you? He's the epitome of the perfect man. He's the golden boy of the studio.' There is a moment of silence. 'You're not. You think Art is going to be the one to hurt Kitty.' It's on the tip of my tongue to say, *But he loves her*, even though it doesn't matter. Just because you love someone doesn't mean you won't hurt them. 'Oh my God, Tilda, what did you find?'

She rifles through the old newspaper articles she's clipped. 'The first one was a girl from his school. She and

Art dated for a short while, and then broke up before the end of their senior year. She went to prom with another guy, Art went with another girl. Early the next morning, the girl's body was found in a field that backed on to the high school. She'd been strangled.'

'Like the other girls,' Louis murmurs.

'Right.' Tilda nods, glancing down at her notes. 'The kids at the prom were questioned – even Art – but no one saw anything, and when a vagrant was found at the other end of the field a couple of days later, drowned in the creek and stinking of whisky, it was assumed that he was the one who killed her. Art reported to the police that the girl had told him a few weeks before that she thought she was being followed, and she thought someone had been in her bedroom, so it all seemed to make sense.'

She was being followed. Was it Art who followed me that night on my way to the Chateau? Was it him following Kitty? Was it *Art* who broke into my apartment? My lips feel numb, my hands ice-cold as I try and process what Tilda is saying.

'What about the other girl?' Louis asks. 'You said there were two.'

'Right. After he left school Art moved to New York to study acting at the Dramatic Workshop.'

'Wow.' I'm impressed. The school has produced stars like Tennessee Williams, Harry Belafonte and dear old Marlon. 'Was that where Kitty studied?'

Tilda shakes her head. 'She was at the Neighborhood Playhouse School of the Theatre.' Tilda shuffles through until she finds the right clipping, unfolding it and smoothing it neatly over the table. It's dated 1940, and there is a photograph in the centre of the article. 'This is Lissa McCaid. She was an actress, but you won't know her, she died before she made it big. She was a student at the Dramatic Workshop the same time Art attended... I didn't find anything to show they were close, but they certainly moved in the same circles. They were in the same class, and had mutual friends.' Tilda pauses, making sure Louis and I are still following along. 'Lissa was supposed to play the lead in a play on Broadway back in 1940. Look at her, Lil. Does she seem familiar?'

I pull the article towards me and squint at the photo. 'She looks like Kitty. Not madly, but there is a resemblance.'

'Exactly. She was the lead in *Beverly Hills* on Broadway, but when she died, her understudy took over. It was Kitty, Lil. Kitty was the understudy.'

'How did she die?' Louis taps the dead girl's picture. 'Strangled?'

Tilda shakes her head. 'No. She was found dead in her bathtub, a bottle of whisky and a tub of pills beside her. It was ruled a suicide.'

'Just like Kitty would have been.' I go hot, then cold, nausea leaving a sour taste in my mouth. 'And you think Art was behind it?' Could Art have also known Kitty all this time? Or has he become so enamoured with Kitty because she reminds him of the girls from his past?

'Who else?'

'Doctor Astor,' I say faintly, pulling the photo of Kitty on Broadway from my purse. 'He was there, remember? At that show. He's known Kitty all this time... what if he's sourcing the girls for Art? For all we know Astor knew the first girl too.'

'Art doesn't need anyone to source girls for him,' Louis says quietly. The colour has drained away from his face, and his fingers shake as he points at the photograph. 'Any woman would follow Art if he asked her to, you said so yourself, Lily, he's the golden boy of Hollywood. Astor might be drugging Kitty to keep her under the studio's control, but Art can control these other women just with his charisma.'

'I can't believe this.' I press a hand to my mouth. 'I liked Art. I trusted him, and I genuinely believed him when he said he loved Kitty.' I look up, fixing the other two with my gaze. 'We know she's going to disappear, and if this is anything to go by, then we know Art is going to be responsible. We have to warn her.'

'How?' Louis says. 'You saw how she reacted at the thought of Jeremy doing harm to her – she'll never believe you if you tell her Art is going to try and kill her.'

A surge of anger runs through my veins, fierce and spiky, and I draw in a deep breath. 'You're right. She won't believe me. That's why I'm going to get proof.'

Chapter Twenty-Nine

I notice that Tilda has picked all the polish off her fingernails, and Louis has looked over his shoulder four times in the time it's taken us to walk over from Villa Nova to Chateau Marmont. My own nerves scratch just below the surface, my pulse jittering as we step into the empty lobby.

'Which room is Art's?' Louis whispers out of the side of his mouth, like he's in a bad gangster movie.

'He's in one of the new bungalows,' I say. It never occurred to me that it would be odd for Art to stay here when he also has a house nearby; I just assumed that because Kitty was staying here, he would too, but perhaps Jeremy isn't the only one who wants to keep an eye on her. 'We don't have a key though.' There's no way I can go through my circus act of throwing the contents of my purse all over the floor again and get away with it, and prior experience tells me I'm not the quickest or most skilled at picking locks.

'What are you doing here?' A voice in my ear makes me jump out of my skin, my heart leaping into my throat and almost strangling me.

'Jesus Christ, Bunny. What the fuck?'

Bunny rears back, her eyes wide. 'Lily! There's no need for *that*.' She presses a hand to her chest. 'I was merely wondering what you were doing here. I thought you'd gone home for the night. No one even saw you leave set.'

'I… err, I had some stuff to do. Just…'

'Checking in on Kitty,' Tilda says, with a sweet smile. 'What on earth are you doing here, Bunny? Surely you should be off the clock by now.'

Bunny preens. 'Well, I'm doing some work for Art, he asked for me specially. Actually, I should run along, he's out in the gardens so he's probably waiting for me.'

'Oh, really?' Tilda's brow creases for a fraction of a second. 'Yeah, you should probably go. But, Bunny… just be careful.'

'Huh?' Bunny looks confused and I dig an elbow into Tilda's side. No one else knows what we know about Art Calloway just yet.

'It's dark out, you know?' Tilda fudges. 'Just take care getting home later.' Tilda turns to me with a grim smile as Bunny hurries out through the rear doors. 'So, we know Art isn't in his room. Let's go.'

Tracing Bunny's steps, we slip into the garden, walking the concrete path along the edges of the lawn towards the bungalows. I am hyperaware that Bunny said Art was waiting for her in the garden, and every shadow that shifts slightly makes my breath catch in my throat until finally we reach Art's bungalow.

'Bungalow three. Huh. Nice. Looks like Art's going all out.' Louis approaches the sturdy red door, a number *3* in gold on the front. Bungalow three is where John Belushi will die of an overdose in March of 1982, and I suppress a shiver. Reaching out, I try the door, but of course it's locked.

'You know how to pick a lock like this?' I say to Louis, as Tilda's voice wafts around the corner.

'Guys? Come here.' At the rear of the bungalow Tilda peers in through the wide patio doors, hoping to catch a glimpse inside between the gap in the curtains. 'I knocked but no answer. We are in luck though.' She puts out a hand, tugging at the handle of the patio door, and it slides open soundlessly.

'I guess Art isn't that bothered about security,' I say with a shrug.

Tilda pulls back the curtains and we step inside, closing them firmly behind us. Tilda flicks the lock closed with a snap and turns to me. 'Lil, you take the sitting room and kitchen, I'll take the bathroom, and Lou? You take the bedroom.'

We split up, the other two disappearing off down the hall while I survey the sitting room. A tall lamp has been left on in one corner, and I hope I don't cast shadows as I begin to search. There are two couches arranged in an L shape, with a small coffee table in the middle. A couple of magazines are stacked neatly on it, alongside a pile of opened fan letters. There's another bigger table behind the second couch, in the small area between the sitting room and kitchen that also has papers on it. After sliding my hands under the sofa cushions and checking around, I rifle through the magazines and letters on the coffee table, before moving towards the kitchen table and reaching out to pluck a paper from the pile there. It's a glossy black-and-white photograph of Art's face and, as I sift through, I see there is an entire stack of them, half of them signed with Art's sprawling hand. I can picture him, sitting here of an evening signing one after another, doggedly scrawling his signature even after his hand cramps to keep his fans happy, and then I think of the dead girls and I drop the photo, swiping my hand over my skirt.

'Lily?' Tilda calls from the bathroom, her voice drifting towards me as I wander down the hall. The bathroom is clad in pristine white tiles, with a long bath running along one wall. It's deep and square, and I know if I laid in it my feet would never reach the end. On the other wall are his and hers sinks, and this is where Tilda stands now. 'Look at this.' Tilda lifts a delicate gold chain from where it lies puddled beside the sink. 'This belongs to a woman. Do you recognise it?' The thin gold chain has a tiny heart at the end of it in a hammered metal and I run my fingers over it.

'I think it's Kitty's,' I say eventually. I'm sure I've seen her wear this before. 'Do you think Art stole it from her? What if...' I swallow, my mouth dry. 'What if he's taken it for the next girl he's going to...'

'He could have.' Tilda holds it up to the light, the heart spinning on the end of its chain. 'Or Kitty might have left it here. There's no way to know.'

She's right. At the moment, we have no definitive proof that Art has harmed anyone, or has any intention at all of hurting Kitty. All we have are two other dead girls – one strangled in Art's home town, the other dead in her bathtub on Broadway.

'There's nothing in the sitting room either. Just a pile of glossy photos with Art's face on. I'm going to help Louis in the bedroom.'

The bedroom is not as luxurious as I was expecting. In fact, no part of the bungalow feels anywhere near as special as the suites at the Beverly Hills Hotel. It's quite sparsely decorated with a double bed in the middle, a small lamp on the bedside table beside it. A battered paperback copy of Raymond Chandler's *The Lady in the Lake* rests on the nightstand, next to a half-empty glass of water. On Art's pillow is a nightshirt with a tennis ball sewn into the back of it.

'What the...' I gingerly lift the edge of the nightshirt with one finger. 'Is this some kind of weird fetish thing?'

Tilda looks up and grins. 'Jeez, Lil, it's an anti-snoring device! If Art rolls onto his back the ball will dig into him and he'll roll back onto his side, stopping him from snoring. Seems Art Calloway really is human after all.'

A human monster, maybe. 'Anything, Lou?' I ask as I move to the wardrobe. Louis shakes his head and gets on his knees to peer under the bed. Shoving my hands into the clothes hanging in the wardrobe, I begin to shuffle through the hangers, not sure what I'm looking for but knowing that I'll know when I see it. It doesn't take long. 'Tilda? Louis? Look at this.' I pull out a blue shirt with a missing button. A distinctive missing button.

'What is it?' Tilda appears in the doorway, her hair wisping out of her ponytail at her hairline.

'This shirt. The button that's missing. It's the same as the button I found in the stables, the day I found Sally's body in the storage area behind the tack room.' Cold fingers inch their way down my spine at the memory. 'I thought it was Jeremy's and so did Kitty, but look.' I shove the shirt in Tilda's direction. 'Art has the same shirt... and the button is missing. That day, the day I found poor Sally, Art had a cut on his face. He said it was a shaving nick.'

'And you think it was really from Sally?' Tilda says, turning the shirt over in her hands, her fingers plucking at the thread where the button was attached.

'She could have caught him with her fingernails if she fought back.' The very idea makes me queasy, imagining the fear Sally must have felt as she realised Art wasn't just flirting with her, or making conversation.

'Lily!' My name is a holler from the other side of the bedroom, where Louis is currently kneeling beside the bed and waving a small square at me. 'You've got to see this.'

Dropping the shirt, Tilda and I move around the bed and Louis hands me a black-and-white photograph.

'This was under the bed,' he says. 'You recognise her?'

Studying the picture, I narrow my eyes, taking in the curled blonde hair, the pouting lips and the arms crossed over a naked bosom. 'That's Doris Gray,' I say quietly. 'The girl who worked at Schwab's. She was the second girl they found in the alley.'

'Didn't she say she had an audition with someone the day before she disappeared?' Tilda frowns, trying to recall what we know. 'What's that around her shoulders? A scarf?'

'It could be red.' I blink, my eyes suddenly stinging with tears. 'That could be the scarf she was found with.'

'It's still not proof enough though,' Tilda says, her lips pressing tightly together. 'All this means is that Art met Doris, and yes, it looks as though she posed for him with... well, with no clothes on. Maybe that's his thing? Getting young, unknown actresses to pose for him in the nude. But it isn't proof that he killed them, even though we know he must be behind it. Put him on the stand and any defence lawyer would rip this to shreds as evidence.'

She's right. All this proves is that Art knew Doris Gray.

'They couldn't rip this to shreds though.' While Tilda and I have been discussing the photograph of Doris, Louis has flipped up the mattress to reveal a slit, sewn back together with rough stitches. He pulls at the thread, widening the gap in the fabric, and a bundle of slick photographs tumbles out.

'Jesus Christ.' This is the first time I have ever heard Tilda curse, as she stoops to pick up one of the fallen photos. 'Lily, look at this.' The picture, black-and-white, the surface matt with fingerprints where it's been handled over and over, shows a girl smiling at the camera in a close-up shot, her blonde hair curled just like Kitty's. Around her neck she wears a heavy costume jewellery necklace, a square-cut gem in the centre of it.

'That's Lissa McCaid,' Tilda says, the words strangled as she chokes them out. 'And that necklace... I've seen it before.'

'Kitty wore it to the premiere the night that guy tried to grab her,' I say, ice trickling through my veins. 'What if Art took it from Lissa when he killed her, and then gifted it to Kitty?'

'There are more.' Louis looks as if he's going to be sick.

I pick up another photo from the floor, holding it by the edges with just my fingertips. 'This girl... it's the other girl they found.' She's in a similar pose to Doris and Lissa, her smile more uncertain, only this time there is a hand in the frame, a man's hand reaching out to lift her chin so she stares right at the camera. 'I think that's Art's hand,' I say, queasily. 'That's his watch. I'd recognise it anywhere.'

'She's wearing the earrings,' Tilda says. 'Look – the earrings that were missing from Kitty's jewellery box. The ones the girl was wearing when she died.'

I'm not sure if this is proof enough to show that Art killed these girls, but it feels like too much of a coincidence – his having photographs of all these girls, wearing Kitty's things, the same things they were found wearing when they died. I run my eyes over the photo again, forcing myself to drink in every detail of what might be the last photograph taken of this girl before she died. 'Look at the background.' With an audible intake of breath

Louis glances at the photo. 'It wasn't taken here. It's somewhere else.'

'Where was it taken though?' Tilda peers over my shoulder, her breath hot in my ear.

I go to shrug, when I notice something in the background. 'There, look.' I point at the corner of the couch, where a shadow can be seen. 'See that? That looks like a bag. A big bag. The kind of bag a doctor carries.' It is, I'm sure of it. It's the worn brown leather holdall Doctor Astor uses as a medical bag.

'This was taken in Doctor Astor's apartment,' Tilda breathes. 'This is it, Lil. This is the evidence we need to put both of them in jail and save Kitty.'

'Louis, pick the rest of the photos up, but try not to touch them, I—' I freeze, the photograph of the first dead girl still in my hands as there is the sound of footsteps outside and then the front door to the bungalow swings open.

Chapter Thirty

I'm having a heart attack. That's the thought grabbing me by the throat as fear constricts my chest to the point that I can barely breathe. Footsteps echo along the hall, as Tilda, Louis and I look at each other in panic. It's too late to run, too late to hide the mess we've made in Art's bedroom before he reaches us. We have no choice, we just have to front it out. Tilda's arm snakes out and she grabs the small lamp from the nightstand, hefting it from hand to hand as if weighing it up as a weapon.

I snatch up the photographs of the dead women, stuffing them into my pockets and inside my blouse, tucking them into my bra. If I can get out of here alive, I'm taking as much evidence with me as I can. The door creaks open, and terror blitzes through me so hard that for a moment I think I might pass out.

'*You*,' Tilda breathes, as the bedroom door swings wide open and a head peers around the door jamb. 'What are you doing here?'

'I could ask you the same question,' Jeremy says, as he steps into the bedroom, his eyes running over the crumpled shirt on the floor and the upturned mattress, stuffing leaking out of the hole cut into the bottom. 'What the hell happened in here?' He looks at me, and I see my own fear reflected back at me. 'Does Art know you're in here?'

'Does it look as though he does?' Tilda sasses back, gesturing to the bomb site we've created. It's as if a hurricane has torn through the bedroom.

Panic freezes my brain as I think for a moment that I got it all wrong. It was Jeremy. It was Jeremy and Art working together. It was Jeremy, Art *and* the doctor, a triumvirate of murdering bastards. And then I remember Jeremy picking through Kitty's jewellery as if looking for something. The article on the dead girl found on Sunset on the floor of the trailer right where he stood, as if it had slipped from his pocket. I meet his eyes again, seeing that fear still reflected back at me, and something clicks, putting things together in a very different way.

'You think he did it too, don't you?' I say quietly, as I watch Jeremy's gaze fall to the remaining photos on the floor, his brow wrinkling. He looks up, his Adam's apple moving as he swallows.

'What do you mean?'

'Art,' I say, stepping closer to him, the faint scent of aniseed reaching my nose. 'You think he murdered those girls. You think he's going to hurt Kitty.'

'Murder...' Jeremy says faintly, as he stoops to pick up a glossy picture. He closes his eyes, pressing his thumb and forefinger to the bridge of his nose at the image of Sally, grinning into the camera, the tack room in the background and Kitty's brooch glinting on her lapel.

'The dead girls that have been found off Sunset,' Tilda steps in. 'There's a... what did you call it, Lil?'

'A serial killer,' I say. 'Three girls have been found dead – and then there was Sally too – and all of them bear a resemblance to Kitty.'

Jeremy rubs his hands over his face, letting Sally float gently to the floor. 'I thought it was only me... thought maybe I was going mad, that I hated Art so much that I'd try and pin anything on him but... I knew he wasn't right for Kitty,' Jeremy says, gazing past me as if running over things in his mind. 'And I knew it, I *knew* that she wasn't safe around him.' He turns to me, giving me that heavy stare that he has. 'I know you think I'm obsessed with Kitty, Lily. I wouldn't be surprised if you thought I might have been the one to kill those girls.'

I say nothing but I can feel the blush burning to the roots of my hair.

'Kitty is so naive,' Jeremy goes on. 'She's good and kind, and she can't see that anyone else could possibly be any different to her. But Art... I've known he was a dark one from the moment I met him.'

'You can hardly blame us for thinking you might be the one who wanted to hurt Kitty,' Tilda says blithely. 'I mean, you do act as if you're obsessed with her, and everyone knows you hate Art. You know things you shouldn't know, so of course people are going to think you're a bit of an oddball.'

'Tilda!' Louis hisses, but I hold up a hand.

'She's got a point, Jeremy.'

Jeremy shakes his head, suppressing a smile. 'I'm not in love with Kitty. Gosh, I haven't been for years, not since we were teenagers. But I am her friend and I do care about her. Since Art got his claws into her, she's changed. She's not the Kitty I used to know – that Kitty is loud, vivacious, with a zest for life. That Kitty would never have turned down a party or an event. That Kitty loved to act, but now she has to force herself to turn up on set. She's quieter, more timid, and I knew he was the reason for it, as though she's making herself smaller for him. Yes, I'll be honest with you, I have been spying on Kitty.'

'From the room below hers?' I say.

Jeremy looks at me askance. 'How do you know that?'

I pull out the Fireball wrapper I found under the bed. 'You're not the only one around here who can play detective, you know.'

'The only reason I was spying on Kitty was to protect her,' Jeremy goes on. 'I knew she was unhappy, but I also know that Art will never let her go. When those girls started turning up dead every time something happened to Kitty, I knew Art had to be behind it somehow, so I started listening in on Kitty's conversations, trying to gauge when something would happen.' Jeremy blinks, his face sombre. 'Clearly I didn't realise Sally would get caught up in it all.'

'You could have told us,' Louis says now. 'I wish you had. Maybe we could have stopped him before now.'

Jeremy lets out a sad huff of laughter. 'How could I confide in you? Lily, you made it perfectly clear you thought I was odd, and I heard you telling Kitty I was stalking her, that night you were talking in her bedroom.' He pauses. 'I thought you might be in league with Art. That's why I told Oskar I thought you were leaking things to the press in the hopes that he might fire you.'

Guilt makes my armpits prickle. 'I'm sorry, Jeremy. If I'd known…'

'But we didn't,' Tilda says briskly, 'and now I think we'd better get out of here before Art comes back and murders all of us.'

'Have you told anyone else what you suspect?' I ask Jeremy, as he steps forward to help Louis flip the mattress back into the right position.

Jeremy shakes his head. 'No, but I think Camilla might be starting to get concerned.'

'Camilla?' I frown. 'I wouldn't have thought Camilla would be concerned about anyone except herself.'

'You've got her all wrong,' Jeremy says. 'She's actually a wonderful person. Very bright and funny.' His cheeks redden and I realise dear old Jez has a huge crush on Camilla. I was so busy focusing on Kitty that I never even noticed it. 'I heard her and Kitty talking in Kitty's room earlier this evening.'

'Really?'

'Of course. They get along rather well. Honestly, Lily. You must have noticed the feud between them seems to have died down on set.'

I think back now to the evening I overheard Kitty and Camilla talking in her room. With everything else going on, and the fact that Camilla had seemed her usual acerbic self the following day, I'd not given it much of a second thought, but now I realise that while Camilla still has an acid tongue, there don't seem to have been any malicious incidents on set since the row outside the stables.

'Why has it died down?' Tilda straightens the bedcovers as Louis slips the last of the photos into his back pocket. Now, when Art comes back, it'll be as if we were never here.

With one last glance around the room, Jeremy guides me towards the front door, as he speaks. 'Their rivalry was genuine in the beginning, but things changed after Camilla came back from a night out to find Kitty was quite upset. It transpires that Art had got a little heavy-handed with Kitty on their date, refusing to take no for an answer, and Camilla revealed he'd done the same to her when she went out with him. It seems to have dampened the fury they had towards each other and given them somewhat of a bond.'

That must have been the night Camilla went to Kitty's room. Part of me wishes now that I had made my presence known because I wouldn't have hesitated to report Art's behaviour to Leonard. None of that Harvey Weinstein shit on my watch, thank you very much. But if I had, perhaps I would have put Kitty directly in danger's way.

'I heard what Kitty said to you,' Jeremy says, close to my ear as we walk along the path towards the gardens. 'About giving it all up?'

'Oh.'

'She should,' Jeremy says. 'If that's really what she wants. Kitty deserves to be happy. She's been living a life that she was never really certain she wanted for the last fifteen years. Surely it's time for her to live one that she does?'

'I don't know,' I say honestly. 'I don't think even Kitty knows what she wants. She's so loyal to the studio that she even lets them tell her what she can and can't eat.'

Jeremy stops on the path, so suddenly that Tilda walks into him. 'She doesn't want to marry Art.'

'Jeremy—'

'She doesn't, Lily.' Jeremy reaches out and grips my upper arms, holding me in place so I'll listen.

'Hey, buddy. Back off.' Louis steps around to stand beside me and I shake my head. 'It's OK, Lou.' I shake myself free and we carry on walking the path, reaching the edge of the gardens.

'Kitty told Camilla this evening that she doesn't want to be with Art anymore. I don't know what's happened to make her change her mind, but she's going to tell Art tonight that it's all over.'

'Uh, Lily...' Tilda nudges me, just as Bunny hurries across the grass with an empty champagne bucket, almost tripping over her own feet as she dashes towards the Chateau.

'Tonight, Jeremy? She said she's going to tell Art tonight?' *Shit. I can't let that happen...* I follow Bunny into the lobby. 'Bunny! Bunny, wait!'

She turns, her plump face flushed as her blonde curls bounce around her head, the ice bucket balanced awkwardly in her arms. 'Oh, Lily! You're still here! You could have left, I was here to help Art. I'm just going to fetch a fresh bottle.' She peers past me. 'Oh, and Jeremy is here too. How... wonderful.'

'Who's the champagne for?' Louis asks, gesturing towards the empty ice bucket. 'Are you celebrating something?'

'Why, it's for Art, of course.' Bunny beams, showing perfect white teeth. 'Oh, Lily, it's so exciting. This is why I've worked late this evening, to help set everything up. Kitty is in the garden with Art right now. He's going to propose to her!'

Fuck. With a panic-stricken glance at the others, and leaving a confused Bunny staring after me, I whirl around to head back out to the gardens. We have to get to Kitty before Art proposes. If she turns him down, it might be the last thing she ever does.

My feet slide in my sandals as I hurry over the damp grass towards the rear of the gardens, Louis, Tilda and Jeremy following in my wake. Bunny wasn't lying about the proposal – the garden has been dressed for the occasion, as rose petals line the path towards the trees and tiny lights have been strung to light the way. A

Japanese-style privacy screen has been erected at the far end of the garden and tea lights sit along the edge of it, giving off a soft, warm glow in the darkness. There is something oddly sacrificial about it, and I can hear my pulse hammering in my ears, not just from my dash across the grass. Faint strains of violin music reach my ears, and my feet slow. If this wasn't the last thing Kitty wanted it would have been hella romantic, but as it is, something turns in my stomach, a twisted knot of apprehension and anxiety that slows my footsteps as though I'm wading through treacle.

'Lily? Why have you stopped?' Tilda's breath is hot in my ear as I pause, drawing in long, deep breaths to calm my racing pulse.

I hold up a hand. 'Hang on,' I whisper. Expecting to hear arguing, Art's deep voice raised in anger, or Kitty's high-pitched screams, I strain my ears to hear over the music, which has given way to something tinkly played on a piano. There's nothing. All I can hear is this irritating music more suited to an elevator than a proposal, and the privacy screen is doing exactly what it's supposed to do. Blocking out any sign of movement behind it.

Shadows move in the corner of my vision, and then Jeremy pushes his way past me. I reach out and snatch at his sleeve.

'Wait,' I hiss. 'Let me go first.' Fully expecting to see Art on bended knee, I run through the best excuses to drag Kitty away – a phone call from her mother citing a family emergency? A meeting with Leonard that simply cannot be missed? – and squeeze my way past Jeremy to the screen, peering cautiously around the edge in the hopes of catching Kitty's eye. Instead, what I see behind the screen is the last thing I am expecting, and the breath leaves my body as if I have been sucker-punched, a scream pressing against my teeth, desperate to rip through the cool night air.

Chapter Thirty-One

'Hey!' Far from the blood-curdling screech I feel inside, the word is a strangled yelp, as I rush forward on legs that don't seem to get the memo, my ankles rolling and my knees weak. Kitty lies on the grass, her skirt hitched up almost to her waist, her blonde curls spread around her head. Her eyes are closed, and one shoe has slipped from her foot, a single rose petal clinging to her bare sole as Art looms over her, his back to me. 'What are you doing? Art? Get off her!'

I want to step forward, to shove him hard, to pummel him in the back, the chest, the head until he loosens his grip on Kitty, but it's as if my blood has turned to ice and I can't move.

'Lily! Oh thank God, you have to help me!' Suddenly Art is crawling off Kitty's limp body, his hands raised as Jeremy rushes past me and grabs Art by the throat.

'You bastard,' Jeremy hisses, as his hands squeeze tighter and tighter, Art's face turning pink, then red, then purple. 'I'll fucking kill you myself.'

'Help,' Art wheezes, his hands flailing as he struggles for air. 'Help me.'

Louis strides forward and in a single motion reminiscent of Bruce Willis in *Die Hard* (and one that I will probably replay in my head over and over until I die), yanks Jeremy off Art as Tilda crouches beside Kitty. Art massages his throat, shooting Jeremy a look steaming with venom before turning to me.

'Is she breathing, Lily?' he rasps, swallowing dramatically. 'Lily, is Kitty still alive? Please, you have to help me. Help *her*.'

Joining Tilda on the grass beside Kitty, I press my fingers against the side of her neck. Mottled bruising is already starting to bloom over her porcelain-white skin, and I wince as I hold my fingers tighter in search of a pulse. 'She's still alive,' I say weakly, as the faint thud of Kitty's heartbeat presses against my hand and her chest rises shallowly.

'You were trying to kill her.' Jeremy's voice is like a shard of glass, sharp and deadly as he glares at Art. 'I've known all the time that you…' He pauses as Louis whispers something in his ear, before turning his back on Art and staring down at Kitty. 'Kitty,' Jeremy says quietly, 'can you hear me?'

Tilda moves to one side as Jeremy gently brushes Kitty's hair away from her face. 'Kitty, it's me, Jeremy. Please, please wake up.' He shakes her by the shoulder, gently at first and then a little harder, and I am about to step in when her eyelids flutter and she gasps.

'Oh, thank goodness,' Tilda breathes. Art moves as if to step towards Kitty, and Louis bars his way.

'Not so fast, buddy.'

I am expecting Art to argue, but he just looks down at Kitty, one hand still massaging his throat where Jeremy grabbed him. Frowning, I try to put the pieces together. I thought Art was strangling Kitty, and given the photographs of the women we found hidden inside his mattress clearly taken only a short while before they died, I wouldn't have been out of order in believing that, but then he started calling to us for help... *Was I wrong about Art? Have I been wrong about all of this the entire time?*

'He's a goddamn maniac,' Art is saying, as Tilda and Jeremy help a groaning Kitty into a sitting position, Tilda tucking her sweater around Kitty's shoulders.

'Who is?' I say sharply.

'Astor, who else?' Art's own tone is sharp as he side-eyes me. 'He's a goddamn maniac and a murderer. I came out here to meet Kitty and there he was with his hands around her throat, all over my sweet girl.'

Doctor Astor. With his medical knowledge, and his big gold ring that I caught a flash of as I was shoved into a van. It's been him all along.

'But...' *How were the photographs in Art's room?*

'He's trying to frame me,' Art is saying as he begins to pace back and forth in front of Kitty, who sits with her eyes closed, her head pressed against Jeremy's shoulder. 'I've been suspicious of him for weeks now, and tonight just proved everything.' Art reaches out and grabs my hands in his, squeezing my fingers so tightly I have to stifle a gasp. 'You must believe me, Lily. I was trying to save Kitty. I love her, she's my everything. You know that, you know how much I love her.' He gestures to the rose petals, the lights, the privacy screen. 'I was going to propose to her, just like I planned. You knew I was going to do it, and when I couldn't find you, Bunny agreed to help.'

'And did you ask Kitty to marry you?'

There is a flash of emotion on Art's face, there one minute and gone the next, as he glances down at Kitty. 'I never got the chance. Astor was already attacking her when I arrived. He ran off the moment he saw me.'

'And you didn't try to stop him?' Louis's eyes search Art's face, as if looking for that brief hint of emotion, but there is only sadness in his expression as Art shakes his head.

'Kitty was my priority.' Art punches himself in the thigh. 'I should have gone after the little creep, should have busted his jaw for this.'

'Art, this isn't your fault—' My words are cut off as a blonde head appears around the privacy screen with a gasp.

'Oh! Oh, what's happened?' Bunny slips around the screen, one hand pressed to her mouth. 'Is Kitty all right?' The ice bucket containing a fresh bottle of champagne drops to the grass with a clang, bubbles fizzing out of the open neck and over Kitty's lost shoe. If Art had only just arrived as Astor was strangling Kitty, Bunny might have seen him in the lobby when she went to fetch the champagne.

'Bunny, did you see Doctor Astor anywhere just now?'

Bunny frowns, biting down on her lip so that lipstick grazes her teeth. 'Yes. He was hurrying out of the Chateau ahead of me as I went across the street for the champagne. I did call out to him, but he didn't seem in the mood to talk. He never even turned around. Honestly?' she says. 'He was like a scalded cat. I've never seen him move so fast.'

Everything Art is saying seems to add up, but I still can't shake the unease that cloaks my shoulders. Maybe it's concern for Kitty, who is now struggling to her feet, clutching tightly to Tilda's arm.

'Maybe you should stay here,' Tilda says, with a desperate glance at me. 'We should call the doctor, get you checked over.' But Kitty is already shaking her head.

'No, I just want to go to bed,' she says, her voice a raspy whisper. 'I'm OK, just shaken up.' Her fingers tremble as she pushes her hair out of her eyes, and Jeremy wraps an arm around her, helping her to her feet as Tilda leans down and snatches up Kitty's sodden shoe.

'Let's get her into the lobby at least,' I murmur to Louis.

'I'll come too,' Art announces, his voice still gravelly, but Louis catches the slight shake of my head and takes his arm.

'Art, what do you say you and I grab a brandy across the street? You've had a terrible shock, and I think you might need to take a load off for a bit. A stiff drink, and then maybe a lie-down will sort you out.' Without giving Art the opportunity to refuse, Louis guides him towards the gate at the back of the garden, as Tilda, Jeremy and I take Kitty towards the lobby, Bunny following behind with the ice bucket in one hand.

Kitty limps on her one bare foot into the lobby, her head lolling on her shoulders until Tilda sets her down on the battered sofa in the corner of the lobby.

'Kitty,' I say, 'are you sure you don't want to see a doctor?'

A fleeting look of panic washes over Kitty's face and she shakes her head, pressing one hand against her bruised throat. 'No. Definitely not.'

'What do we have here?' A voice trills from the entrance to the Chateau. 'A mothers' meeting? And of course, I wasn't invited.' Camilla strides into the lobby looking every inch the movie star in a gold gown that hugs every curve, a fur stole thrown around her shoulders. Her steps falter as she takes in Kitty's bruises, and the way Tilda, Jeremy and I have formed a protective circle around her. 'What... what's happened? Kitty, are you hurt?' Camilla drops to one knee, and gently lifts Kitty's face to the light. 'Oh,' she breathes, her voice catching as a tear glints at the corner of her eye. 'What bastard did this to you? Was it Art?'

Jeremy was right after all. Camilla and Kitty have buried the hatchet, and not in each other.

'I think Art knows about the baby,' Kitty says quietly, and a hot spurt of fear injects itself into my gut. 'I can't do this anymore, Lily.'

Sliding onto the sofa beside her, I take her hand. 'Kitty, what happened tonight? Was it really Doctor Astor who did this?' There is a double intake of breath beside me as both Camilla and Bunny gasp.

'Baby?' Camilla says.

Kitty frowns. 'Everything is so foggy. Bunny called up to my room and told me that Art was waiting for me in the garden. She said he had something very important that he wanted to talk to me about.'

Bunny moans softly, and I shush her.

'I got dressed – I'd just had a bath – and went down to the garden, but Art wasn't there yet. Doctor Astor was there, and he handed me a glass of champagne, then the next thing I knew I was on the grass and everyone was yelling and my throat was on fire.'

Astor gave Kitty a drink. 'You don't remember if Astor attacked you?'

'It had to have been him,' Camilla says grimly. 'He gave Kitty the champagne. It must have been drugged.'

Kitty drags her gaze to meet Camilla's. 'I think it was,' she says, pressing a hand to her head. 'I feel foggy and my mouth is dry. My head is pounding. The same way I've felt so many times after Doctor Astor has given me pills. I haven't been taking them, Lily,' she says earnestly. 'You were so shocked that I just took them without asking what they were, and then once I found out about the baby…

I've been pretending to take them, flushing them away when no one is looking, and I feel so much better. I feel like my old self again, the real Kitty, not the studio Kitty.'

'*Baby?*' Camilla says again.

'I'm pregnant, Cam. And Art must know about the baby,' Kitty goes on, 'why else would he want to talk to me? Honestly, Lily, I've thought about things and I can't do this anymore. It's not what I want.' Her hand goes to rest gently on her belly in a gesture I've seen countless mothers-to-be do before. 'I don't want to live a life where I'm controlled by everyone around me, where the studio, and Art, and everyone except me, it seems, has a say in my life. I just want to vanish into thin air and leave all of it behind.'

Tilda meets my gaze, her eyes wide at Kitty's words.

'Art wanted to talk to you because he was going to propose,' I say. 'As far as I know he doesn't know about the baby, but there's a possibility that Doctor Astor has figured it out. I think I got it wrong, Kitty. It's Astor who's obsessed with you, ever since your stint on Broadway a decade ago. Maybe that's why he attacked you tonight.'

Kitty closes her eyes, a single tear tracking its way down her cheek. 'I can't marry Art, Lily. I can't.'

Camilla looks from me to Kitty, her mouth agape. 'Forget about *Art*,' she hisses. 'What about Astor? If he's attacked Kitty this evening then we need to call Leonard, we need to call the police and get him locked up! I knew there was something fishy about him, about the way he skulks about, letting himself into our trailers—'

'We can't yet,' I say. 'I promise we will, we'll shop him to the cops and get him banged up for life, but we need to get Kitty to safety first.' I turn to Kitty, my eyes never leaving her face. 'How serious are you about leaving all of this behind for good? If you give it up, there's a chance you can never come back to it.'

'Deadly,' Kitty says, sitting up straight as Jeremy watches her every move. He might not be in love with her, but there's no doubt at all that he *loves* her.

'In that case then,' I say, 'I've got an idea.'

Chapter Thirty-Two

'I'm going to make you disappear.'

'What?' Kitty leans forward, resting her elbows on her knees, her perfect brows knitting together with confusion.

'Trust Lily,' Tilda says. 'She knows what she's doing.'

As much as I appreciate Tilda's blind faith, I can't help the butterflies that swarm in my stomach. I have to pull this off to ensure Kitty is safe.

'But... what about the movie?' Kitty asks, her blue eyes wide. 'We still have a month of shooting left. And Leonard... he's already in trouble with the studio.'

'The dang movie is going to be pulled anyway,' Jeremy says in a gruff voice. 'Once the newspapers get wind of that murdering scoundrel Astor, all of us will be picked to pieces, and Oskar will call time on the movie before anyone can even ask "Where's Kitty?" We're already over budget and behind schedule – this will be the final straw.'

Jeremy's right. I already know that this movie won't get made, because Kitty disappears. The studio does pull the plug on it, and Leonard does have a brief battle with the studio, but he's too talented to not come out the other side. He'll win not one but two Oscars for Best Director, in 1955 and again in 1958. Leonard will be just fine.

'I'm going to make you disappear,' I say again. 'No one will know where you are – it'll be a mystery that will be talked about for decades. If you stay here there's a high chance that you'll disappear anyway, only it'll be because Doctor Astor has got to you. This way, you'll be safe. But it means leaving everything you know behind, and having no contact with anyone you know. A bit like being in witness protection.'

'I have no idea what that is but it sounds... serious,' Camilla muses. 'Are you sure this is the only way to keep Kitty safe? Why can't we just call the police?'

I shake my head, my heart heavy. 'And risk Astor weaselling his way out of things? What if the police let him go and he comes after Kitty again?' Everything I know about solving crimes I've learnt from Jessica Fletcher, but even I know that the slim evidence we have against Astor might not be enough to get him put behind bars.

'But where will I go?' Kitty bites her lower lip, suddenly not so sure about her decision to give everything up. 'Can I speak to my mother? Do I really have to leave everyone behind?'

'For a while at least,' Tilda says gently. 'Right now you're in great danger from the doctor. He tried to kill you tonight, Kitty, and you're not the only girl he's hurt. He's killed before. He's a... a... serial killer.'

Kitty's eyes widen, and I can't shake the feeling that something still doesn't feel right about Tilda's words, but I push it away. Getting Kitty to safety is the most important thing right now.

'Where will I go?' Kitty says again, more quietly this time.

I pace the lobby, thinking hard. Leonard probably has somewhere to hide Kitty, but then that would mean telling him what's going on. I can't risk word getting out to Doctor Astor before I can spirit Kitty away.

'My mom has some connections in New York,' Tilda says. 'My aunt still lives in Brooklyn. What if we sent Kitty there?'

Jeremy shakes his head. 'Too crowded, and besides, Kitty is from New York. That's the first place anyone would look. It needs to be somewhere more remote – Kitty's face has been on screen for years. It'll be hard to find anywhere where people won't recognise her.'

'Mexico?' Bunny asks, her mouth twisting even as she suggests it. I'm guessing Mexico wouldn't be Bunny's first choice for herself. 'Although it is terribly hot there. And the food can be a little spicy. A bit like the men.'

'No.' I shake my head. 'Spicy food – and men – aside, Kitty would have to use a passport and the last thing we want to do is have a record of her movements. I have no idea how to go about getting a fake passport either.'

'Fake passport?' Bunny gasps. 'Lily, that's illegal.'

Camilla rolls her eyes, and then turns to me with a cat-like smile. 'I might know somewhere.'

'Where?'

'My aunt runs a ranch in Wyoming. It's just her and the ranch hands, who change most years… my uncle died five years ago. She's always looking for help, especially around the house now she's getting older. Kitty could go there. It's out in the middle of nowhere, surrounded by mountains. Kitty could hide out there quite easily, and no one would ever think to look for Oscar-winning star of the silver screen Kitty Fox out in the acres of ranch land in Wyoming.' Camilla pauses, her eyes going to Kitty's hands, which are folded neatly across her still-flat belly. 'My aunt is good friends with a woman in town there… she has some herbs that could help with your *problem*. If you wanted her to.' Camilla's own hands drift unconsciously to her belly, and I realise that perhaps Camilla has used her aunt's friend's help before.

'Kitty? What do you think?'

Kitty lifts her head to meet my eyes, a glimmer of excitement in her own. 'I think that sounds just about perfect.'

—

The sun is barely above the horizon the next morning as, with gritty eyes and aching bones, I tiptoe through the Chateau to Kitty's room after a sleepless night. Tilda yawns beside me, as the door to Kitty's suite swings open and Camilla greets us, her eyes sporting matching dark rings under them.

'She's ready,' she whispers. 'Is the car downstairs?'

I nod. 'Louis is parked down a side road so no one will see us leave. What time do you need to be on set?'

Camilla glances down at the elegant watch on her slim wrist. 'Not for another hour or two yet. I'll make sure to cause a scene when Kitty doesn't show on time. That should stall people wanting to search for her immediately, and Bunny has already said she'll offer to come back to the Chateau to look for Kitty so she can take her sweet time about it.'

'And everything has been left as we agreed? Kitty's purse is on the desk, her bed unmade, all her things left in the closet?' Tilda asks, shifting on the balls of her feet. I know how she feels, the electricity buzzing through my veins won't settle until Kitty is safely on that train to Wyoming. 'It has to look as though she just vanished, no sign at all that she left of her own accord.'

Camilla nods. 'All as we agreed. Oh, Kitty! Are you ready?'

Kitty appears in the bedroom doorway, looking like a stranger. A dark brown wig sits on her head (thank you, Camilla, for never returning your props to the prop department), and she wears a dull olive-green skirt suit with flat black pumps. Her face is bare of make-up, and small round-framed glasses sit on her nose. She looks like a governess, or a missionary on her way to do God's work. There is no hint of the smoking siren that has graced our screens for fifteen years. She takes a deep breath and smiles at me.

'How do I look?'

'Like my great-aunt Gertrude.' I grin back. 'Are you ready?'

Kitty nods. 'Yes. I'm ready. More than ready, actually.' She turns to Camilla. 'Thank you. I know we didn't always see eye to eye but I'll never forget what you've done for me.'

'Oh.' Camilla flaps a hand, but I catch a gleam of a tear in her eye. 'More room for me now you're out of the way,' she says with a wobbly smile, her voice catching before she pulls Kitty in for a hug. 'I know you can't contact me, but know I'll always be thinking about you.'

Kitty presses her hand gently to Camilla's cheek, and then stoops to pick up the small bag I've allowed her to pack with the bare essentials. 'This is it. No more Kitty Fox – I can go back to being me. Plain old Sarah Brown.' She takes a deep breath and turns to me. 'Lily, let's go. Before I chicken out.'

With one last look around the hotel room, Kitty steps out into the corridor, but as we hit the staircase, she stops.

'Wait! What about Art? He's going to be distraught when he finds out I'm gone. What if he tries to track me down? Hires a private investigator? He loves all that kind of thing, I wouldn't put anything past him.'

Camilla shakes her head. 'I'll handle Art, don't worry. If he starts making noises about looking for you I'll find a way to stop him. Go, Kitty. Before it's too late.'

Without another word, we hurry out of Chateau Marmont and along Sunset to the side road where Louis is parked. My pulse is racing as I slide into the passenger seat, Kitty slipping into the back with Tilda where she slouches down, out of sight. I don't think anyone saw us, the streets are empty at this time of the morning, but even so I don't feel like I breathe until we are standing on the station platform, the train that will carry Kitty to Cheyenne, Wyoming, puffing its way into the station. It'll take several days for the train to reach Kitty's end destination, and she's promised to send word via Camilla's aunt that she's arrived safely.

'Thank you, Lily,' Kitty says, opening her arms for me to step into. 'You don't know what you've done for me. There's a whole other life waiting for me in Wyoming, one that I never thought I'd have. Things are going to be difficult for you over the coming weeks... people might accuse you of things you haven't done, and I know there'll be speculation over what has really happened to me.'

There will be, I think, *but not for long*. I can't tell Kitty that in seventy years' time no one but the most hardcore of movie buffs will remember who she is, that her disappearance will be something that sits only vaguely on the radar of cinematic history.

'Don't worry about us, everything will be fine. Go and live your life, Kitty.' I kiss her cheek, and then she thanks Tilda and Louis, scoops up her bag and boards the train without a backward glance. My eyes prickle and my chest is tight as I battle the emotion that swells in my ribcage. Despite everything, I have become fond of Kitty, and it stings a little to think that I'll never see her again. But then I remember that if I hadn't made Kitty disappear, it's likely Doctor Astor would have. Maybe I didn't fully change history this time, but at least I tweaked it enough to keep Kitty safe.

We wait on the platform until the train has pulled far into the distance, and then I turn to the others.

'We did it. She's safe. Now let's go and take that fucker Astor down.'

—

I get Louis to drop me at the studio, in the interests of appearing business as usual, and I don't have to fake my surprise at the chaos that reigns on set after I sign in with Bobby.

'Lily! Where the hell have you been?' Leonard roars as I sidle onto the set, my palms sweaty. 'Where the hell is Kitty? She's not in her trailer and no one has seen her this morning, and now Art and Camilla have disappeared too.'

'I...' I swallow, my mouth ashy. 'I don't know. Isn't she here?' I catch Bunny's panicked glance as she hurries past. 'I had a... doctor's appointment this morning, sorry, I didn't realise I would be this late.'

'Doctor?' Leonard frowns. 'Why didn't you just get Doctor Astor to check you over? Jesus, Lily, we're running behind already, you know that! Go and find Kitty, and tell her if she doesn't get her ass on set in the next five minutes I don't give a damn what the studio says, she's out.'

'Yes. Of course.' Hell would freeze over before I let that pervert anywhere near me, even if I had needed to see a doctor. I am heading over to Camilla's trailer when Bunny hurries over and snags my sleeve between her fingers.

'She's not there,' Bunny says in a hushed whisper. 'When Art found out Kitty wasn't here he stormed back to the Chateau to find her. He seemed agitated. Camilla followed him.' She pauses. 'Did everything…?'

'Like clockwork,' I say, distractedly. 'I'm going back to the Chateau to find Camilla and Art. If I'm not back in half an hour then come and find me, and bring Leonard too.' I don't know why but I have a very bad feeling about this.

Chapter Thirty-Three

A short while later I am hurrying past the valet, through the lobby of the Chateau and up to Camilla's hotel room. I don't know if it's women's intuition, but something doesn't quite sit right with the idea that Doctor Astor is solely responsible for the murders. The photographs hidden inside Art's mattress play on my mind, and although he said Astor is trying to frame him, there's something else that keeps niggling at me, I just can't put my finger on it.

Camilla's door is closed tight and I knock lightly, but there is no answer. Reaching out, I test the handle, surprised when it springs open.

'Camilla? Are you in here?' The heavy scent of Camilla's perfume stains the air, and I step over discarded heels and a fur jacket as I approach her bedroom. 'Camilla?'

There is a strangled cry from behind the closed bedroom door, and my heart leaps into my throat, adrenaline screaming a hot trail through my body. Without thinking I shove the door open and burst into the room to be greeted by a familiar sight.

Art Calloway, straddling a woman lying on the floor, and this time I can see his hands are wrapped tightly around her throat as he throttles Camilla.

'You!' I gasp, casting around for something to use as a weapon as Art throws an unconscious Camilla to the ground and turns his murderous gaze on me.

'Little Lily Jones,' he snarls, his face twisting into something unrecognisable. The affable, handsome man who holds everyone on set in the palm of his hand is gone. 'You don't know how long I've dreamed about getting my hands on you.' Art runs his gaze over my body, licking his lips lasciviously. 'And now it's your turn, you interfering, meddling little bitch.'

I turn, ready to flee, but Art is quick, his hands reaching out to grab my blouse. The flimsy fabric tears as he yanks me towards him and reaches for my hair, tugging it back so sharply that my head tilts to expose my neck and my eyes sting with tears.

'It *was* you.' The words are a breathy gasp. 'I should have known. The photographs...'

Art's eyes narrow and he yanks my hair harder, as a tear leaks its way down my cheek. 'What?'

'We found them inside your mattress and you said Astor was trying to frame you...' I gulp back a sob, as the thing that was niggling at me finally shows itself in full technicolour. 'But you... you're the one with the camera. You took the photos, not Astor. It was all you.'

Art lets out a laugh, grating and rusty. 'Just because Astor didn't take the photographs doesn't mean he wasn't involved. Who do you think shoved nosy little Lily Jones into the back of a van?'

I think back to the flash of a gold ring, the scent of aniseed in the air. The way something about him felt familiar.

'You weren't supposed to be there, Lily. You were supposed to be out on a date with your boyfriend, but you came home early. We just wanted to have a look through your apartment again, that's all.' He smirks. 'There had to be something in there that I could use to get you thrown off the set, get you away from meddling in Kitty's business.'

'You were there. In the van.'

'Of course I was there,' Art goes on. 'Astor can't drive, and some things can't be trusted to be outsourced. Your friend was excellent, by the way, cutting us off like that. He could be a stunt driver, you know.'

'All of it was you,' I say, a hot spurt of fury making me reckless. 'That guy on the red carpet who grabbed Kitty – that was you too, wasn't it? You wanted to scare her. Why? Was she too powerful for you? Too famous?' I bite my tongue, stopping a flow of acid from spilling over the man who is most probably going to kill me in a minute.

Art tightens his grip, making me gasp. 'It was supposed to be me who swooped in and saved the day on the red carpet. The guy was some fella from Astor's lodge, who Astor had dirt on. I even fed the guy a Fireball so Kitty would think Jeremy was behind it, but the timings were wrong and I wasn't even there, thanks to Camilla waylaying me. Kitty was pulling away from me, Lily. I was trying to get her to realise that she couldn't live without me.' He loosens his grip, but before I can pull away his hands are around my throat.

Is that why he was so insistent on Camilla staying on set? Because he knew about the feud, knew that Camilla upset Kitty and thought that she would run into his arms? The thought makes me feel ill, the idea that Art has been manipulating things around Kitty all along. Another thought strikes me, one that makes my skin shrivel into gooseflesh.

'Is that why you killed the other women?' Art's hands are not tight enough to choke me yet, but are too tight for me to pull away. I have to know, before he finishes me off, why he did it.

'They had it coming,' he snaps. 'Kitty pushed me away, so I found other women who looked like her to fill the gap... to ease the pain. They all wanted to know Art Calloway. To be with him – the movie star, not the real me. And then they all wanted to know about *her*. What she was like. Could they meet her? They were no better than Kitty, so they had to go.'

'And that's why you killed them every time Kitty had the tiniest hint of success. You couldn't bear to accept that Kitty was the brightest star. You were just riding her coat-tails and she didn't even want you there. She didn't even want the fame that you've sought so desperately.' His hands start to squeeze and my pulse roars. 'Where does Astor come into things?'

Art pauses.

'Come on,' I jeer, my knees giving away the fact that I feel like I might pass out from fear. I'm hoping that Camilla is playing dead rather than is *actually* dead, and if Art is going to kill me she might at least be able to tell the full story. 'I know the women were killed in his apartment – I saw the photographs. Was he the brains behind it all? Are you just following his orders? Lord knows he's a creep, keeping Kitty dependent on booze and pills.'

Art's hands tighten and I gasp, the crook of his thumb pressing against my windpipe. 'It started back in my home town after my girlfriend refused to go to the prom with me. She thought she was better than me, so I had to teach her a lesson.'

'You stalked her. Broke into her room, just like you did mine. You're the maniac, not Astor.'

Art closes his eyes briefly. 'I wanted to scare her, that's all. I never meant it to go so far, but then I got away with it and I've never felt so... *powerful* in my life. I moved to New York, which is when I met Peter Astor and came across Kitty, though of course she never looked twice at me then. She was just an understudy on Broadway but I knew she could be so much more, and she could take me with her.'

'So you murdered Lissa McCaid and staged it to look like a suicide.' My words are hushed, my hands coming up to grasp at Art's wrists as he tightens his grip.

'Lissa was in my class at college, and I went to see her on Broadway, only she was sick and Kitty performed in her place. Lissa was nowhere near as good as Kitty, I had to get her out of the way. I used the drugs Astor had prescribed Lissa to knock her out, giving her too much to make sure she didn't wake up again. Astor walked in on me with Lissa's body. I told him it was his fault, that she'd overdosed because he gave her the wrong dosage and then I... well, I staged a suicide and made Astor help. Astor was freaking out, of course, but I had him in my pocket then. All I had to do was threaten to expose him, and it turns out blackmail is one of my strengths. His family emigrated here with nothing in the Twenties – he worked so hard to become a doctor and was supporting his parents and siblings. He had no choice. He had to do as I said, or I'd tell the police everything, planting him squarely in the frame. Who would believe I was responsible for the deaths of these women over him?' Art squeezes now, his fingers tightening as I struggle to breathe.

I'm sorry, I think, as dark spots dance at the edge of my vision, my heart thundering in my chest as I gasp and struggle. *I'm sorry I never figured things out before I could save*

Doris Gray and Sally Moss, the stunt double. I'm sorry it's going to end this way. I'm sorry I don't get to live the rest of my life with you, Louis. If I'd known I never would have turned you down, I would have relished every kiss, every single moment together. Everything goes dark, my tongue bursting from my mouth as I feel the fight inside me begin to ebb away, and then there is an almighty crash and I can breathe again.

I fall to the floor, gasping, my breath seeming to trickle into my lungs as Art hits the deck beside me, a stream of blood gushing from his temple. Hands appear before me, tanned and familiar, and I look up to see Louis standing over me.

'Lily! Are you all right? Can you breathe? The cops are on their way.'

'Louis, I...' I swallow, wincing. Everything hurts. 'He was going to kill me.' Tears, hot and salty, spring to my eyes and run over my cheeks. 'What happened? How did you know...'

Tilda appears in my line of vision, a small Tiffany lamp in one hand. The shape of it exactly matches the shape of the dent in Art's bleeding head. 'Well, Bunny raised the alarm when you didn't return, and as we were dashing over here, Louis had a lightbulb moment.'

A flush creeps over Louis's cheeks, as he crouches beside me and pulls me into his arms. 'Not a lightbulb exactly, but nothing about the way Art blamed Astor seemed to sit right with me. When I took Art back to his bungalow last night, I used his bathroom and it was his toothpaste that tipped me off, only I didn't realise until now.'

'His toothpaste?'

'Fennel. He uses fennel toothpaste. That's what you could smell in the van – you said it smelled similar to the aniseed Kitty smelled on the guy who grabbed her but not quite right. Fennel does smell kinda like aniseed... I realised it must have been Art who was behind you being abducted in the van.'

'It was. He told me everything.' I begin to cry properly now. 'He killed those women, Lou, and he blackmailed Astor into keeping his secrets. He killed them because he was frustrated with Kitty's success. They died because he was a small, tiny, insecure man and he deserves to rot in hell for what he's done.'

There is the scream of sirens from outside and Louis helps me to my feet, as Tilda lifts a conscious but groggy Camilla onto the bed, and then moments later three police officers run into the room and bind Art's hands behind his back as he comes to, immediately shouting his innocence.

I watch as they lead him away, and my emotions must be written all over my face as Tilda hands me a hanky from her purse.

'You did it, Lil.' Tilda gives me a watery smile. 'You made Kitty Fox disappear.'

I did it. Somehow, I changed history without changing history.

Epilogue

The movie is cancelled, of course. None of us is particularly shocked when Leonard wearily announces the news, but given that the main star has disappeared into thin air and the other is currently behind bars awaiting trial for the murders of several women, there wasn't really a movie to be made.

Even Camilla doesn't seem too upset by the cancellation of the movie. Apparently the girl tipped to star in the new Henry Hathaway movie has pulled out and Camilla has been approached to test for her role. I don't tell her that she's not going to get it – that Grace Kelly will star in the role meant for her – but that she will instead make a movie with Spencer Tracy and Katharine Hepburn that will win her an Oscar.

'How are you feeling now, Lily?' Bunny brings me a chamomile tea, as I perch on the chair at the desk in the corridor outside Leonard's office.

'Not bad. My throat is just a little sore, that's all.' I adjust the scarf that I've taken to wearing knotted around my neck while the bruising fades. 'I've got some script submissions that I need help reading, if you don't mind?'

'Of course.' Bunny beams. She's been helping out with paperwork while Leonard is in talks with the studio regarding his next movie. It never stops in Hollywood, even after multiple murders. 'Have you er... heard anything?' She hisses in an urgent whisper.

I shake my head. 'Not since the first telegram.' Camilla received a telegram from her aunt the week after Kitty left, simply stating:

GOODS RECEIVED

There's been no word since, as agreed, and the press and public have gone wild with speculation as to what really happened to Kitty Fox. General consensus is, Art did away with her the night before he tried to kill me and Camilla, and drove her body out to the desert. To defend him would mean telling the truth, so we've all just kept quiet. Kitty would have had a life sentence if she'd married him, so it makes a strange sort of sense that Art should carry one for her. What's one more when you're a serial killer anyway?

Picking up my bag and smoothing down my curls, I smile at Bunny. 'I'm done for today. See you tomorrow?' Movement in the doorway makes me jump as Louis pokes his head around the door with a grin.

'Ready to go? Tilda's in the car. She's got something to show us.' He winks at Bunny, purely to make her blush, and I swat him on the arm before following him out to the car and a waiting Tilda.

In the twenty-first century I'm pretty sure Tilda would have been a true crime podcaster, or at least have been approached by one of the big five publishers to write a book on Art, whom the press are referring to as the Hollywood Hatchet. However, she's more than happy with the new gossip column she's been gifted by Louella in the *Hollywood Post*. A tiny paper, mostly only read by those in the business, but she's on the road to great things. Her own words, obviously.

'Now I'm intrigued,' I say, as I waggle my fingers in Bunny's direction and allow Louis to guide me out to where Christine sits at the kerb, his hand warm on the small of my back. I can only hope that whatever it is Tilda wants to show me, I'll still be around to see it. I'm still wondering every morning where I'll be when I open my eyes, half of me expecting to wake up in my own bed back in the twenty-first century, in my grotty WeHo apartment, Eric banging on the door because I've overslept. Every morning that I've woken up in my tiny single bed, listening to Tilda squawk along to the wireless on the other side of the wall, I've wondered why I'm still here. Does the very fact that I haven't been catapulted back to my own time mean that someone here still needs my help?

Tilda is leaning forward, hanging onto the passenger seat, her eyes bright with excitement as I jump into the car and turn to face her.

'Hey,' I say, 'Louis said you've got something to show me. What's happened?'

Tilda reaches across the back seat of the car and picks up a copy of the newspaper, jabbing a finger at the front page. 'Look,' she says, reading from the article. 'Max Hayden, star of multiple comedy movies, has been found drowned in the swimming pool at the Garden of Allah Hotel.'

'Blimey,' I breathe, 'that's awful. Poor guy. Did he drink too much?'

Tilda shrugs. 'I don't know, but we're going to find out.'

'Huh?' I have no idea what she means. All I want to do is maybe go to Googie's for fries and then see if Louis will come back to the apartment and rub my aching feet.

'We're going to investigate this and find out what really happened to Max Hayden.'

'And why would we do that?' Louis sighs. 'First of all, the police will be dealing with it; second of all, it looks like a tragic accident; and third of all, haven't we just had a really exhausting time with Kitty? Lily nearly died, for gosh sakes. I'm ready to live a quiet life.'

He has a point.

'Because,' Tilda says with a grin, 'I got a note hand-delivered to my desk at the column – addressed to me personally, I should add – a week ago, telling me that Max Hayden was going to die in an accident.'

Damn. It looks like the question I've been asking myself every morning has just been answered.

Article in the Los Angeles Times, dated 24th October 2024

DECADES-OLD MYSTERY SOLVED AT LAST

It appears a years-old mystery that has baffled Hollywood for decades may have been resolved this week. In 1951 Oscar-winning actress Kitty Fox disappeared from her Chateau Marmont hotel room and was never seen again. The following day, her on- and off-screen lover Art Calloway was exposed as a serial killer stalking the streets of Hollywood on a murderous rampage that saw the deaths of multiple women, including Fox's own stunt double. It was widely believed at the time that Mr Calloway was also responsible for Ms Fox's murder, although he maintained his innocence for years until his death in 1995.

Now though, it appears the mystery of Kitty Fox's disappearance might have been solved. A nurse in Buffalo, Wyoming, was clearing her mother's house after her mother passed away and found evidence that suggests she was the elusive actress.

'I found articles and clippings about Kitty's disappearance hidden away in her things, along with a pair of sapphire earrings that Kitty Fox wore in her last movie and a photograph of my mother, standing with another girl in what looks like a hotel room, although the other girl's features are blurred. The back of the photograph says "Kitty and Lily, 1951",' says Shona Scott. 'I always believed that my mother grew up on the ranch I was born on, until she also became a nurse later on in her life, but these items lead to her being Kitty Fox.'

Photographs of Mrs Scott's mother, who went by the name Sarah Brown, in her later life are now being scrutinised by experts, who will compare them to photographs of the missing actress. While not yet confirmed, it seems as though the truth about the disappearance of Kitty Fox may be about to be revealed.

A Letter from Lisa

Dear Reader,

Another Hollywood book! I am so thrilled to have written another adventure for Lily and the gang. As always, I've tried to keep things authentic, but sometimes you have to play with poetic licence to make things work.

The feud between Kitty and Camilla (as I am sure fans of Old Hollywood will have guessed) is loosely based on the feud between Bette Davis and Joan Crawford. Early on, Joan announced her divorce from Douglas Fairbanks Jr. on the day Bette's first lead role movie was released, overshadowing Bette's big moment. Then, Joan married Franchot Tone, whom Bette was in love with, and Bette openly accused her of stealing him. Later on, when Joan was married to the CEO of Pepsi, Bette had the Pepsi bottles on set switched out for Coca-Cola. There were many other incidents between the two women, but in short, their feud was probably one of the most exciting and long-lasting feuds in Hollywood history...

The film being made by Henry Hathaway, which would star Grace Kelly, was of course *Fourteen Hours*. This film was already released when the Academy Awards took place in 1951, but I couldn't resist threatening Camilla with someone as incredible and talented as Princess Grace. Let's pretend they didn't start shooting until a year later!

Bungalow #3 wasn't built at Chateau Marmont until 1956, but I took the liberty of having it built earlier, so that Art could stay somewhere significant. The Chateau itself has a long and rich history, some of which I have referenced – Desi Arnaz really did throw his money out of the window – but there are many, many other stories hidden in those walls. If you'd like to read more about the Chateau, I highly recommend *The Castle on Sunset* by Shawn Levy.

Nothing as exciting as shots being fired has ever happened at the Oscars as far as I know, although plenty of other stuff has – Will Smith slapping Chris Rock, Marlon Brando refusing his award, and a streaker hitting the stage in 1974 just before Elizabeth Taylor went on. Apparently David Niven was the only one who found that last one amusing.

Thank you once again, dear reader, for coming on this adventure with me. If you've enjoyed *The Strange Disappearance of Kitty Fox* please do leave a review – it helps authors more than you can ever know.

Love,
Lisa x

You can contact Lisa at:
Instagram: @lisahallauthor
X: @lisahallauthor
Facebook: https://www.facebook.com/lisahallauthor

Acknowledgements

I find acknowledgements are always the hardest part of writing the book. Writing is like raising a child, it takes a village and I am always terrified I will forget someone… If your name doesn't appear on this page, it doesn't mean I am not thankful for you. It means I have probably panicked a little bit…

First, thank you to my amazing agent, Lisa Moylett. It is because of you that this series is even a thing – I thought I'd written a one-off novel that might sit in a drawer for the next hundred years, but you had a vision and a plan, and I am so grateful. This book is dedicated to you (about time, after all these books eh?!).

Thank you to my editor, Jennie Ayres. It is so rare to find an editor who knows exactly what to say and when to say it! Your notes are always incredible, and this book is a hundred times better thanks to your insight (and your first-rate knowledge of Old Hollywood!).

The entire team at Hera/Canelo. You all rock. I've never had covers so beautiful.

Darren O'Sullivan, Annabel Kantaria, Steve Kedie and Diane Jeffrey. Writing is a lonely old game, but having you guys on the end of the phone (or indeed, in Dishoom over orange wine) makes things infinitely more fun.

To my book club girls, who never fail to make me laugh my socks off, but especially to Caz Redpath for bringing out the absolute worst in all of us...

The readers and bloggers who have taken Lily, Louis and Tilda into their hearts. I am so thrilled and grateful for the response to this series, more than you'll ever know.

Nick, Geo, Miss and Mo. I am always grateful for you guys.

And lastly, the stars of Old Hollywood. Thank you for behaving so badly that I don't think I'll ever run out of adventures for Lily Jones.